Praise for

Monica Burns

"Burns doesn't disappoint!"
— **RTBOOKreviews**

Monica Burns writes with sensitivity and panache.
— **Sabrina Jeffries, NYT bestselling author**

"powerfully done...the scenes between Tobias and Jane mesmerized me. I loved it."
— **Joey W. Hill**

"No one sets fire to the page like Monica Burns."
— **eCataromance**

"Definitely recommended reading."

— **The Romance Studio**

"Ms. Burns is masterful at escalating the sexual tension and suspense with her characters."
— **Coffeetime Romance**

Redemption

by

Monica Burns

Copyright ©2012 by Kathi B. Scearce
ISBN 978-0-9971592-8-8
Cover Design: Viviana Izzo, Enchantress Design & Promo
Copyeditor: Debbie Sansom-Fitts

Kathi B. Scearce DBA Monica Burns - Maroli SP Imprints
P.O. Box 75072
Richmond, VA 23236

Publishing History
Print 1.0 edition / November 2016
Print 2.0 edition / August 2019 New Cover
Print 2.1.1 edition / July 2021 -Updates& New Cover

Contents

Acknowledgements

Special thanks to Viviana Izzo, Enchantress Design and Promo for an extraordinary cover. Viv, thank you for being such an awesome friend and for the wonderful covers you do for me. You take my abstract vision and just do magic! And the fact that you listen to me whine ad nauseum makes you a saint!

To the wonderful Debbie Sansom-Fitts. Thank you! You are an exceptional cheerleader, and no matter how many times I think I've caught all the typos to make your life easier, you're able to find ones I've missed. I can't thank you enough for all you do for me. I'm blessed to know you.

A special shout out to Kathryn Tesh, who came up with the title for Percy's and Rhea's book. She pulled it out of thin air for me, and I love it. It so fits the theme of the book. Thank you Kathryn.

Last, but never least, to all my readers. The fact that you love my stories is humbling. I am doing what I love to do, and I'm so grateful that with your help, I'm able to continue doing so

Prologue

June 1898

"*D*amn it to hell*," Percy Rockwood muttered under his breath as he emerged from the well-lit New Library into the near darkness of the British Museum's main reading room. In the shadows, he made out the night watchman sprawled on the floor a short distance away.

Afraid for the man's safety, Percy crossed the carpeted floor of the large room and knelt beside the man. Fingers pressed into the side of the police officer's neck, Percy breathed a sigh of relief. Alive, but out cold. A small sound in the distance echoed in the large, oval-shaped room museum patrons used daily.

It was the same noise he'd heard while reading the latest Coptic scrolls Wallis Budge had brought back from Egypt. Although how he'd not heard Smythe crash to the floor was surprising. The officer was a burly man, and he could only surmise that the guard's assailants had eased him to the floor after subduing the guard.

Once more, the sound whispered through the air. Percy cocked his head to one side and determined the noise was coming from the Egyptian wing. Without thinking twice, he pulled a small pistol out of his coat pocket. He'd taken to carrying the weapon since he'd had his vision two weeks ago. The vivid imagery of his body lying prone in a dark place wasn't the type of omen a Rockwood who possessed the *an dara sealladh* ignored.

Over the years, he'd learned to accept the fact that he'd inherited a small amount of the family's gift of sight. But the *an dara sealladh* seldom offered up as much detailed graphic information as his latest vision had. The woman's face had haunted him for the past two weeks. Her features had been hazy at best., but it had been impossible to forget her eyes. They'd been the dark color of wild violets that grew in the meadows around Melton Park.

He had no idea what the vision meant. Even now, he wondered what the connection was between the woman and the image of him lying on a dark floor. But it was the hopelessness Percy had seen in her beautiful eyes he couldn't forget. She was in trouble. He was certain of it. His tread quiet and cautious, Percy approached the wide archway leading into the Egyptian section of the museum. His back hugging the cold stone of the ceiling-high columns marked with hieroglyphics, Percy peered around the edge of the cylindrical architecture.

At the far end of the north wing, he saw a light where the pendant of Nephthys was displayed. The jeweled necklace that was said to have once been worn by Nefertiti had been put on display for only a short time. Other than a glass-enclosed display case and the police who guarded the museum night and day, there was no other protection for the precious artifact.

Anger made his jaw hardened. He'd warned Budge this might happen, and the director had agreed. Percy didn't enjoy being right, but he would love to be a fly on the wall when Budge lambasted the board for their resistance to reinforce security. As Director of the Egyptian and Assyrian Antiquities, Budge would not withhold one iota of his contempt for the men who'd brushed aside his concerns about the lack of security during the night hours. They'd dismissed the director's recent appeal for more police officers to safeguard the treasures added to the Egyptian collection only a few months ago. Aside from Smythe, there was only one other officer on duty tonight as the third one had taken sick and gone home for the night.

A sharp crack followed by the brittle sound of splintering glass confirmed his worst fears. Someone was stealing the pendant. Slowly, he made his way past one of the mummy displays as he headed toward the end of the exhibition hall. The low murmur of voices floated toward him, but it was impossible to hear what was being said.

Percy crept forward, sidestepping the narrow stream of moonlight that had found its way past the clouds and through the glass ceiling of the large exhibition chamber. Ahead of him, he saw a small movement in the shadowy recesses of the exhibition hall.

"Whoever you are, come out now before I shoot," he said quietly.

The sudden loud click of a pistol being cocked made Percy draw in a sharp hiss of air between his teeth. Whoever they were, they'd just called his bluff as nicely as if they were playing a cutthroat game of brag.

"Then you and I are at an impasse, sir. There are *three* of us, and just one of you. I believe the odds are considerably more in my favor than in yours."

The disembodied voice sounded different from what one might expect a thief to sound like. Perplexed, he frowned at the cultured inflections in the voice. They were intonations one might expect to hear from someone of noble birth.

A shadow emerged from the pitch dark into the area just on the edge of the patch of moonlight. Percy narrowed his gaze at the dark figure. The fellow stood just a foot shorter than him and seemed more round than angular. A youngster, no doubt, but Percy knew better than to discount his opponent. Age had nothing to do with felons and their street savvy. The youth would do what he had to in order to survive.

"If you're willing to leave the necklace you've taken, I'll not prevent you from escaping."

"Unfortunately, that's not possible." The shadow's soft voice reverberated in the darkness with a distinct note of regret. Percy scowled in the direction of the voice.

"You'll find it incredibly difficult to sell the pendant."

"Perhaps, but that's my employer's dilemma. Not mine." Despite the casual note in the thief's statement, Percy could have sworn there was a significant amount of regret as well.

Muscles taut with tension, Percy watched the dark figure take two steps toward him. Overhead, the clouds parted farther, and the narrow stream of moonlight widened its path across the museum floor. Almost as if he knew it was dangerous to stand in the moonlight, the other man hesitated. The increased amount of light outlined Percy's opponent more clearly.

A black mask covered half the man's face, and although he was in process of committing a crime, there was a politeness to his manner that said he regretted his actions. In fact, the thief projected an image of respectable gentility, despite the patches covering his coat and pants.

In his swift appraisal of the man, Percy realized the distance between them was smaller than he thought. The moment he took a step forward, the other man leveled his gun at him. The light from the moon danced off the barrel of the pistol pointed in his direction.

"Do not mistake me for a fool, sir." The sharp words made Percy stiffen. A woman—a well-bred woman. The familiarity he'd recognized in her voice earlier was rooted in his knowledge of the female sex. He'd heard the soft, womanly cadence and pitch of her voice, but had unconsciously dismissed them. He took a step closer.

"Stop." Was that a hint of fear in her command?

"I'm afraid I can't do that," he murmured with growing

irritation. "I can't allow the pendant to leave the museum."

"Then you're a fool. Your life is far more valuable than a trinket, no matter how old." Her sharp words made him frown. She sounded almost worried for his safety.

"Nevertheless, I have no intention of allowing anyone to leave the museum with the pendant." Percy's mouth tightened with a grim sense of foreboding.

The instant the premonition sailed through him, he uttered a soft oath beneath his breath. Someone was approaching him from behind. In a swift move, Percy sprang forward. Behind him, a loud pistol shot cracked the air. The bullet was more of a sting than anything else as it entered his back. The impact of the bullet made him stumble, and his gun flew out of his hand. He sank to his knees, and she was there to catch him.

"You are a reckless fool," she chastised him in a voice filled with agonized regret.

"It's a family trait," he rasped as pain seeped its way across his back. He raised his head to look into her eyes and went rigid.

"*Bloody hell, it's you.*" The tension in her body pulsed its way into his. He understood her fear. Murder, or even just accessory to the crime, carried a stiff penalty.

"How do you know me," she whispered as her violet eyes widened with horror.

The dark purple hue of her eyes was even more beautiful than in his vision. His thoughts suddenly became cluttered with all manner of images. The fire at Westbrook Farms, his grieving family at the cemetery at Caleb's and Devin's funerals. Sebastian glaring at him, and Aunt Matilda with dismay darkening her warm gaze. One by one, the faces of his family drifted past his eyes. They'd been through so much in the last four months. Now another Rockwood would be dead soon. The thought surprised him somehow. He was dying. It had never occurred to him that his vision would have such a negative outcome. Percy had expected to be knocked unconscious, not shot. A violet gaze met his. Her eyes shimmered with unshed tears.

"I'm so sorry. This wasn't supposed to happen." The sorrow in her voice equaled the pain in her eyes.

"I don't understand…my vision…" he mumbled as the pain intensified and continued its way across his back. He tried to move, but only managed to increase the searing pain slashing through him. Unable to help himself, he closed his eyes and slumped deeper into her arms.

"Leave him."

The harsh, uncultured voice penetrated the cloud of pain pulling Percy under. Desperately, he fought to remain conscious. If he lived, he needed to remember the man's voice and everything he could about this miserable incident.

"Why did you shoot him?" The woman's question reverberated with fierce anger. "You could have knocked him out like you did the guard."

"Don't matter none now, does it? The bloke is dead."

"You're a bastard, Ruckley."

"So you keep saying, my poppet," the man said in a salacious manner. It made Percy long to get up and pummel the son of a bitch until the man begged for mercy. The thought evaporated as pain tugged him closer to the abyss.

"I'm not your poppet or anything else."

"Go easy now, dearie. We both know I have a soft spot for you, but unless you want the little 'uns to suffer, ye'll let me call ye whatever I please."

"One day, I *will* kill you, Ruckley."

The anger and hopelessness in her voice was the last thing Percy heard as a yawning hole opened up. He struggled not to fall off the cliff into the darkness below. But it was the touch of a warm hand on his cheek that told him he had to live. She needed his help. It was the last thought sinking its way into his head before the black engulfed him.

Chapter 1

Melton Park
June 1899

You look lovely, Rhea. I'm glad I insisted we take an extra day to visit Madame Solange before we returned to Green Hill House two months ago," her aunt said with a smile as their carriage rolled up the long drive to Melton Park Manor.

"It was an unnecessary extravagance." Rhea softened her reply with a smile. "But thank you. At least I have an opportunity to wear it."

"It was nothing of the sort. It makes me happy to see you looking so beautiful. When I think about the day Mr. Ashford brought you and Arianna to Fremont Place…" The moment her aunt's voice faded into nothing, Rhea reached across the space between them to touch her aunt's arm in a reassuring gesture.

"It's in the past, Aunt Beatrice. All of it," she said in a firm voice as she smiled at her aunt. The older woman nodded as she squeezed Rhea's hand.

"Agreed," Beatrice Fremont said with quiet determination. "With Arianna firmly settled in her role as Viscountess Sherrington, I think it's time we concern ourselves with your prospects."

Rhea ignored the comment and turned her head away to look out the carriage window. A small lake shimmered beneath the moon, while the rolling landscape made her believe daylight would reveal magnificent green pastures with wildflowers adding splashes of color.

Arianna had been fortunate to find a man willing to love her in spite of the horrific years they'd spent under Ruckley's thumb. Rhea had done her best to protect her sister while Ruckley had controlled their lives, but their past was grim enough to prevent even a commoner from marrying her sister, let alone the viscount. Despite all the odds, Arianna had found happiness, and that was all that mattered. She, on the other hand, had no intention of surrendering to a man ever again.

"You might wish to ignore me, Rhea, but I don't believe your heart is made of ice. It can't be when I see you with the children." Her aunt's words made Rhea turn her head to eye her relative with annoyance.

"I thought we'd settled this. I will *never* marry," she replied coolly.

"No matter how terrible the past, denying yourself happiness is wrong, Rhea."

"I'm quite happy with my life the way it is now," she bit out between clenched teeth before she looked back out the window and into the darkness.

Obviously, it would take a great deal of time to convince Aunt Beatrice that marriage was out of the question. Nothing would change Rhea's mind when it came to the subject. The thought of her every move being controlled again made her skin grow cold. She refused to ever go back to that type of servitude.

Marriage would be no better than what she'd experienced at Ruckley's hand. It didn't matter how many times she'd stood up to the man. Ruckley had found a way to torment and control her. His threats to Arianna and the children had always made her yield to whichever of his dictates she'd failed to circumvent.

She'd seen how married women in the East End were

treated by their husbands as well. They'd been little more than chattel with bruises and marks to prove it. A small voice reminded her that there had been two or three men she'd seen who'd clearly loved their wives despite the hardships they experienced. The past charged out to engulf her, and Rhea closed her eyes in an effort to stop the vivid memories.

The image of Ruckley taking coin from a man who had paid to bed her made Rhea's stomach lurch as a familiar queasiness swept over her. Fingers curled into tight fists in her lap, she fought back the nausea that always came when thinking about the past.

The soft summer night air filled her lungs as she drew in a deep breath. That life was behind her now. She and Arianna had escaped. She'd even made progress in beginning to bring several of the children with them to Green Hill House. They were out of Ruckley's reach. A voice in the back of her head told her none of them would be safe until Ruckley was dead.

Even when she saved all the ones she'd cared for while in Ruckley's grasp, there would always be more she couldn't help. She didn't have the means to save every child, no matter how much she wanted to, and it made her heart break every time she had to accept the reality of the situation. Timothy's terror-stricken expression flashed before her eyes, and her stomach lurched as remorse and guilt spread through her veins. Determined not to let her emotions control her, Rhea pushed the memories deep to avoid crying. She'd not cried since that terrible night, and she wasn't about to start now.

"Rhea, I cannot begin to imagine what you and Arianna had to...what you endured all those years," Beatrice Fremont said in a voice filled with pained regret. "But you cannot let the past keep you from finding happiness."

"Taking care of the children and watching them grow will be enough to make me happy," she said as she looked at her aunt once more.

"Don't you want children of your own, Rhea?" her aunt

pleaded.

"Vincent, Lucy, Rufus, and the others are just as much my children as any I could give birth to." Rhea stressed her reply in a voice designed to end her aunt's protests as their carriage rolled to a stop in front of the Earl and Countess of Melton's country manor.

Aunt Beatrice nodded, but in the shadowy confines of the small carriage, Rhea could see her reply had not dismissed the older woman's dark misgivings. The door to the carriage was opened by a footman, and Rhea waited as her aunt descended from the carriage. Light streamed out from every window of the manor, presenting a welcoming, cheerful atmosphere. As they entered the large house, the sound of music drifted out into the main foyer.

It was a Scottish reel, and despite herself, Rhea found herself tapping her foot on the marble floor as they waited in the receiving line. When she was a child, she'd always loved dancing with her mother. Thomas Bennett had disapproved of dancing, so her mother had waited for those moments when Rhea's father wasn't in the house to whirl her and Arianna around the parlor. In the receiving line in front of her, Beatrice Fremont offered the Countess of Melton a small curtsey.

"Thank you for coming, Mrs. Fremont," the countess said with a warm smile. "I understand you enjoyed a family reunion just recently. I think it wonderful you have found each other again."

"Yes, finding my nieces has brought me immense joy. Although, Arianna was only with me for a short time before she married this past March." At her aunt's remark, the countess reached out to take Beatrice's hand. A wistful look transformed the younger woman's face, and her green eyes shimmered with a bittersweet sadness.

"I know what it is like to be reunited with a loved one after so long a time. I'm certain nothing will prevent you and your nieces from making up for time lost," she said as she turned toward Rhea. "Welcome, Miss Bennett. I'm so pleased you could join us."

"Thank you for your kind invitation, my lady," Rhea said as she curtseyed. The countess nodded at her as she gestured toward the man at her side. "Have either of you met my husband, Lord Melton?"

As her aunt greeted the earl, fear spread an icy layer over her skin. Rhea barely heard her aunt introduce her as she met the earl's gaze. Dear God, was it possible the earl was the man Ruckley had shot last year in the museum? Lord Melton's welcoming smile faded as puzzled amusement made him arch an eyebrow at her.

"Good evening, Miss Bennett."

The moment he spoke, she knew he wasn't the stranger she'd left to die in the museum. Aware she'd been staring, Rhea's cheeks grew hot.

"Good evening, Lord Melton. Please accept my best wishes for a happy birthday."

"Thank you," he replied with a congenial grin.

With a forced smile, she turned away from the earl and followed her aunt deeper into the ballroom. "What's wrong, dearest?" Beatrice asked as she opened lace fan with an expert snap of her hand and waved it to create a soft breeze. "You look as though you've seen a ghost."

"It's nothing. Just a bad memory." Her reply caused a pained look to cross her aunt's features. Rhea caught Beatrice's hand in hers and shook her head with a gesture of reassurance. "The past can't find me here—not this far away from London."

"Would you prefer we go home? We can plead the sudden onset of a headache." Beatrice frowned, as if contemplating what reason they could use to excuse themselves.

"Absolutely not," Rhea exclaimed as she rejected her

aunt's suggestion. A small smile curved her lips as she eyed the older woman with affectionate amusement. "You seldom ventured out while we were in London, and I'm not about to deny you the chance to renew old acquaintances, especially of the male persuasion. I'm of the opinion that *you're* in need of a husband more than me."

The blush darkening her aunt's cheeks made Rhea laugh. Although her aunt had been a widow for several years, Beatrice was still young and quite lovely. A smile curving her lips, Rhea turned away to survey the large room. From the books lining the far wall, it appeared the library had been called into service for the evening's festivities. Despite its imposing, opulent appearance, the room radiated a warmth that said it had seen many happy occasions. Behind her was a row of doors that opened onto a long terrace. They stood open in an attempt to ease the already warm temperature of the room. Something told her that a number of guests would take advantage of the patio's cooler temperatures as the night wore on.

Across the room, Rhea caught sight of a man with a small amount of silver at his temples who was looking in their direction. She was certain the man was studying her aunt, and Rhea turned her head toward Beatrice.

"Do you know the man standing across from us?"

"Where?" Beatrice asked with a curious look of puzzlement.

"It appears he's headed our way," Rhea murmured as she saw the man begin to mauver his way through the throng to head in their direction.

"*Oh dear God,*" her aunt gasped, with a distinct note of panic filling her voice. Concerned, Rhea jerked her gaze in her aunt's direction. The apprehension on Beatrice's pale features made Rhea touched the older woman on the arm.

"Are you all right, Aunt Beatrice?"

"I…yes. I'm…I'm quite all right."

The agitated response made Rhea frown. Before she could probe for a more definitive explanation, the gentleman in question was standing in front of them. He offered a smile to Rhea before bowing in her aunt's direction.

"Good evening, ladies. Beatrice, you're as lovely as I remember."

When her aunt didn't extend her arm, the gentleman reached out to capture Beatrice's hand and carried it to his lips. His mouth lingered on Beatrice's fingers for a fraction longer than was respectable, and her aunt breathed in a sharp breath as she tugged free of his grasp.

"Lionel...I hadn't heard you'd returned from the continent." Her aunt's breathy response made Rhea glance at the woman. The pink in her aunt's cheeks had returned, and Rhea bit back a smile.

"And this must be your daughter. The likeness is uncanny." A hard glint flashed in the man's dark eyes as he smiled at Rhea, then pinned his gaze on Beatrice again. Startled by the gentleman's observation, she glanced at her aunt. All the color was gone from Beatrice's face as she met Rhea's gaze, then turned her attention back to the handsome man in front of her. With a slight shake of her head, Beatrice exhaled a soft sigh.

"No, this is my niece, Rhea Bennett. Alfred and I didn't have any children." Regret echoed in her aunt's voice, but another emotion ran beneath the obvious disappointment. Rhea found it impossible to define what it was. The gentleman's eyes narrowed as he pinned his gaze on Beatrice, causing pink color to flare in her cheeks.

"Rhea, may I present Lionel Nesfield."

"A pleasure, Miss Bennett. And it's Viscount Foxworth now," he murmured as he kissed Rhea's hand before his attention returned to Beatrice, who eyed him with compassionate sorrow.

"I *am* sorry, Lionel. I hadn't heard that your father was

gone."

"Just a few months ago. I had a great deal of estate business to attend to before I could renew old acquaintances." Something in the way the man looked at her aunt said Lord Foxworth was referring to Beatrice in particular. Her aunt paled beneath his steady gaze, and Rhea decided to help ease the tension between the older couple.

"Do you live nearby, Lord Foxworth?"

"Yes," he said with a smile as he looked at her. "It's less than a half-hour ride from Green Hill House as the crow flies. Do you ride, Miss Bennett?"

"I used to before…when I was a child." She forced a smile as Lord Foxworth's gaze narrowed at her.

"Then I'd like to offer you one of the horses from my stables. I have far more than I could ride with any sort of regularity."

"That's exceedingly generous of you, my lord, but I couldn't accept such an extravagant offer," she said with surprise as her aunt gasped.

"Lionel, you cannot—"

"I'm a wealthy man now, Beatrice. I can afford to be generous."

There was almost a note of anger in the viscount's voice as he eyed her aunt with an arched look that was difficult to read. The tone of the conversation had become a silent exchange of something altogether different from the words being spoken out loud. Lord Foxworth looked back at Rhea and smiled.

"Well, Miss Bennett? Will you give me the pleasure of presenting you with a mount suitable for riding?" There was a gleam in his dark-brown eyes that said he was determined to have his way. Rhea understood the unshakeable resolve in his gaze. She possessed a similar trait.

"Perhaps a compromise," she said with a smile. "I shall accept the *loan* of one of your horses."

"Excellent," Lord Foxworth said with satisfaction. He looked at her aunt again. "Naturally, I expect you to accept one of my animals as well, Beatrice. I know how much you always enjoyed our afternoon rides."

"But I...it's—"

"I no longer accept no as an answer when it comes to something I want, Beatrice," he said with a quiet authority that even Rhea would have felt compelled to obey.

The older couple stared at one another in a silent battle of wills. Despite her stubborn look, Beatrice Fremont appeared to give way beneath the viscount's inflexible gaze. With a soft sound of irritation and a sharp nod of defiance, Rhea's aunt agreed to his demand. Beatrice's blatant display of resistance didn't appear to trouble Lord Foxworth as a look of triumph lit up his distinguished features. A wicked smile tilted his mouth as he extended his hand to Beatrice in a commanding gesture.

"I believe you still owe me a dance from the last time we saw each other," the viscount murmured. Her aunt looked in her direction in a silent plea for assistance. With a smile of amusement, Rhea shook her head.

"Go, I'll be quite all right on my own." Her encouragement earned her a scowl from her aunt and a chuckle from Lord Foxworth.

"It appears you're outnumbered, my...dear Beatrice."

The viscount's slight stumble over his words made Rhea think the man had been about to express a more fervent endearment. His earlier mention of afternoon rides only reinforced Rhea's suspicions that her aunt and Lord Foxworth were more than old friends. Now, as she watched the couple's silent battle of wills, she saw something more than determination in the man's gaze as he studied her aunt. Lord Foxworth's fingers flicked in a commanding gesture for Beatrice to accept his hand. Rhea almost laughed at the flush of color filling her aunt's cheeks as she scowled at the man. At her obstinate glare, viscount arched his eyebrows then narrowed his gaze as he waited for Beatrice to place her hand in his. With obvious reluctance, her aunt accepted Lord Foxworth's hand and allowed him to lead her out onto the dance floor.

Rhea watched the jovial throng of guests dancing and mingling in the room. When she and Arianna had been reunited with their aunt less than a year ago, it had taken Rhea time to feel comfortable at the few soirees her aunt insisted they attend. She still found social occasions somewhat off-putting.

In the little more than three months since arriving at Green Hill House, the vicar and his wife had been their only callers. It was an arrangement Rhea was quite content with, but she'd seen how much her aunt had enjoyed visiting with the older couple. The soiree at Melton Park had presented the perfect opportunity for her aunt to enjoy the company of people other than Rhea.

It was for that reason Rhea had agreed to attend the party at Melton Park. She'd witnessed how much the invitation had excited Beatrice, and she'd not protested attending for fear her aunt would not go at all. But there was something different about tonight's soiree. She couldn't tell if it was the party's relaxed atmosphere or the fact that she wasn't in town.

In London, she was always on her guard for some wayward encounter that would reveal her past. But tonight, the past seemed far behind her. One or two men had glanced her way, and each time she averted her gaze. Even in this relaxed atmosphere, she was unwilling to engage in small talk. She also had no interest in fending off unwanted attentions.

In one corner of the room, she saw two men flanking a woman of medium height. Rhea eyed the trio with curiosity. It was obvious they were standing guard over the woman, but she couldn't discern why. Like Lord Melton, both men were dressed in formal Prince Charlie jackets and kilts. Tonight was the first time she'd ever seen any man wearing formal Scottish dress, and it was impressive.

Aunt Beatrice had mentioned the other day that the earl's family was descended from the Stewart line of Highlanders. The woman standing between the two men wore a pale yellow gown with a dark red tartan sash attached to her left shoulder. The two men exuded a commanding, protective nature as they greeted several guests who'd approach the trio. As the man closest to the woman turned his head to speak with someone, Rhea sucked in a sharp breath of horror and froze. Dear Lord, it was him.

A relief, unlike anything she'd ever known, spiraled through her. He was alive. In the next breath, she dismissed the notion. She'd already thought the earl was the man in the museum. She was far too given to fancy tonight. London was more than two hours away by train. The man Ruckley had shot was dead. She bore as much responsibility, if not more, for the man's death because he might have survived if she'd stood up to Ruckley.

It was a deed she would regret for the rest of her life. But she was allowing an over-active imagination to get the better of her. The likelihood the man across the room was the man Ruckley had shot in the museum a year ago was an outrageous thought. Almost as outrageous as when she'd thought the Earl of Melton was the man she'd left to die. She dragged in a deep gulp of air as she tried to dismiss the notion, but with each subsequent breath, she found herself questioning her rejection of the idea. The more she studied the man, the more convinced she became he was the man she'd left to die on the British Museum floor.

Rhea remembered her arrival and how she'd found herself staring at the Earl of Melton. The resemblance between the two men was uncanny, and she was certain they were related. But it wasn't just this man's face that was so familiar. It was the way he moved. Everything about him reflected a fluid power she'd observed in him a year ago in the museum's dark hall.

As it had that night, every bit of his tall, well-built frame resonated with raw, masculine strength. It made her realize how easily he could have subdued her if he'd not had a gun pointed at him. A tremor rocked its way through her body. Even when he'd been rendered helpless by a bullet, there had been something strong and powerful about the man. The memory of him falling into her arms made her mouth go dry.

His body had been hard and solid against hers, and she'd been stunned by the connection she'd felt with him. She had been no more capable of explaining the sensation then than she could now. As she studied him, she was amazed the bullet from Ruckley's pistol hadn't killed the man, let alone allowed him to walk. She'd seen what a bullet wound in the back could do to a man. Almost as if he were aware he was under scrutiny, the man swung his gaze across the room. He reminded her of a dangerous predator ready to strike in a blur of motion that would leave its prey incapacitated.

The moment their eyes met, an arrogant amusement curved his firm lips as he studied her with blatant curiosity. His manner declared he was accustomed to women falling at his feet. She tried to look away from him, but there was something hypnotic in his gaze. It had become difficult to breathe, and as his eyes narrowed, panic lashed out at her.

Dear Lord, had he recognized her? No. That wasn't possible. She'd been wearing a mask that night in the museum. In the back of her head, a small voice reminded her of that heart-stopping moment when he'd looked into her eyes. The haunting memory of his exclamation and the way he'd stared at her in recognition still had the ability to make her tremble. She had to have misunderstood him. He'd just been shot. It was reasonable to believe he'd been in great pain. The man had been dying, and she knew how easy it was for a dying person to mistake someone for a loved one.

It was the only explanation she'd ever been able to rationalize and accept. There wasn't any other way he could have recognized her that night or now. Fear crashed through her as she dragged her gaze away from the stranger. What was she going to do?

In a single heartbeat, her panic was gone, and a calm serenity wrapped around her like a warm cloak. It was the same collected composure she'd learned to maintain while she'd been at Ruckley's beck and call. It subdued her fear and panic. She'd never removed her mask during those few short moments in the museum. There was no reason this stranger might connect a street criminal with Miss Rhea Bennett, let alone think they were the same person.

With a furtive glance in his direction, she saw him speaking with an older woman, and a sigh of relief escaped her. She'd been allowing her imagination to run amok. Rhea retreated into a corner where it was possible to watch the guests while going unnoticed. Although her foot continued to tap in time with the music, she was content to watch Lord Foxworth spin her aunt around the dance floor for a second dance.

The couple would argue, then dance in silence before having words again. Rhea could tell from her aunt's face that Lord Foxworth was winning whatever argument they were having. Voices nearby caught her ear, and she turned her head to see Lady Melton moving in her direction. The woman's mischievous smile made Rhea respond in kind, but a second later, it died as she saw the man behind the countess. Unable to move, she tried to maintain her composure and quell the urge to run.

"Miss Bennett, my brother-in-law has asked me for an introduction." Lady Melton glanced over her shoulder with a smile before looking at Rhea again. "He noticed you weren't dancing and insisted on rectifying that problem. Miss Bennett, allow me to introduce Mr. Percy Rockwood. Percy, Miss Rhea

Bennett."

"A pleasure, Miss Bennett."

Amusement made Percy Rockwood arch his eyebrow upward in a manner reminiscent of his brother as he offered a small bow in her direction. No longer shadowed by the darkness of the British Museum, Percy Rockwood was even more handsome than she remembered. Perhaps devastatingly so if she were any other woman.

Rhea tried to swallow the knot swelling her throat shut, making it difficult to breathe. Determined to regain her composure, she reminded herself that he couldn't possibly connect her to the British Museum robbery. She forced a smile to her lips and nodded her head in a polite greeting.

"Mr. Rockwood," she murmured. The countess's curious gaze flitted from her brother-in-law to Rhea, then back to Percy.

"I promised my husband this next dance, Miss Bennett, but I leave you in good hands. Percy is an excellent dancer."

With an affectionate peck on her brother-in-law's cheek and a smile at Rhea, the countess walked away. Silence filled the air in Lady Melton's wake, and when Percy didn't speak, Rhea's mind screamed at her to flee. Worse, she wasn't sure why she had referred to him by his first name in her head. After a long moment, he stretched out his hand to her.

"Shall we?" Rhea jumped as she stared down at his strong hand. Terrified to be any closer to the man, she dismissed his offer with a hard shake of her head.

"I think it best you find another partner, Mr. Rockwood. I'll only step on your toes." For all that she loved to dance, she knew it was far too dangerous to remain in this man's company.

"I insist," he said with a firmness that made her heart skitter out of control.

In the space of a second, he'd gone from charming rogue to a man unwilling to accept her refusal. Percy's hand wrapped around her wrist, and he led her toward the dance floor. Caught off guard, Rhea gasped at his autocratic action, but it was the electric charge streaking up her arm that prevented her from freeing herself. When they reached the dance floor, Percy pulled her into his arms. A waltz was playing, and with a skillful move, he swung her into the crowd of dancers.

Despite her trepidation, it was impossible to ignore the way her body reacted to being so close to him. It was as if every inch of her was on fire. The sensation sent tension streaking through her body. A subtle woodsy aroma mixed with frankincense and another spice created an exotic, almost hedonistic, scent in her nose. It was a warm smell that coaxed her to breathe him deep into her senses.

Everything about him was raw, potent male. It was a sharp, tactile sensation. The large hand braced against her back emphasized the sinewy strength of the arm that pressed into her as they circled the floor. Chiseled features further accentuated the hard strength of him. Even his beautiful mouth emphasized a resolve that declared him a man of purpose. He was a man capable of bending a woman to his will in the manner that said she wouldn't know what was happening until it was too late.

Suddenly, she realized her response to him was blinding her as to who he was. The knowledge sent a tremor through her. Percy executed a polish move that carried them past another couple. Chestnut-colored eyes met hers with a look that sent another shiver sliding through her.

Alarmed by her response to him, she averted her gaze to stare over his shoulder. The minute she was free, she intended to seek out her aunt and plead a headache. If she was lucky, Lord Foxworth would see her aunt home, and Rhea would have the carriage to herself.

"I wonder what nefarious plot is being hatched in that pretty head of yours, Miss Bennett."

Startled, Rhea jerked her attention back to him. He'd

narrowed his gaze as he studied her. Something unreadable glinted in his eyes, and her heart skipped a beat while an icy layer of fear coated her skin. Refusing to show she was afraid, she called upon the steely calm she'd learned on the streets of the East End.

"I'm not in the habit of nefarious plotting or anything else so wicked, Mr. Rockwood."

Rhea arched her eyebrows in disdainful bewilderment as she struggled to control her breathing, which was far too rapid for her liking. Anger flashed in his brown gaze as he pulled her deeper into his embrace. Heat engulfed her skin the moment he tightened his arms around her. Rhea wasn't sure whether it was his fierce gaze or the way she was pressed into him that made the room feel so warm. She concluded it was both.

"Your eyes are quite lovely, Miss Bennett," he murmured. "In fact, they are quite unforgettable."

Rhea's heart sank as a wave of nausea rolled through her. He knew. Somehow he'd recognized her from across the room. She didn't know how, but he knew she'd been in the British Museum a year ago. Rhea stumbled only to have a steely arm lift her off her feet for a brief moment before setting her down once more to continue their dance.

"Have I said something to upset you, Miss Bennett?"

"Not at all. I did warn you that I have a tendency to step on toes." The breathless reply only emphasized how difficult she was finding it to maintain her composure.

"Yes, you did," he said wryly with what she was certain was sardonic amusement. It said he knew she was lying. "Tell me, Miss Bennett, have you ever been to the British Museum?"

Panic sliced through her with all the force of a sword cutting its way through her flesh. Her throat closed as she stared up at him. Percy's features darkened when she remained silent.

"It would appear the cat has got your tongue, Rhea."

There was a dark, sensual vibration to the way her name rolled off his lips. The sound made her mouth go dry as she averted her gaze from his and another shiver streaked down her back. The music rose to a final crescendo bringing the waltz to an end. The moment the last note was played, Percy whirled her across the floor to stop in front of the doors leading out to the terrace. As she freed herself from his arms, he caught her by the elbow and ushered her out into the warm summer night.

It happened so fast, Rhea didn't have time to protest. Several couples were already on the patio, and Percy guided her past them without a break in his stride. In silence, they walked down a small stairway onto a gravel path at a fast pace. Torches lined the walkway, but Percy didn't stay on the well-lit footpath. Instead, he made a sharp right turn, half dragging Rhea after him. Although something inside her said he wouldn't harm her, she'd learned years ago never to trust a man when it came to her safety.

"Would you care to explain what you're doing, Mr. Rockwood?" she demanded in an imperious tone as he dragged her to a halt inside a small gazebo. The moon illuminated one side of the structure, but Rhea made a concerted effort to remain in the shadows.

"I'm attempting to solve a mystery, and I believe you can help me."

The dark drawl in his voice was as silky now as it had been that night in the museum. It made her heart skip a beat. In the next breath, she chided herself for being distracted by his voice and everything else about him.

"I doubt I can be of any assistance to you. My deduction skills are nonexistent," Rhea said with a calm that belied her current state of mind.

Panic was driving a need to run as fast and far away as possible. But to leave now would only confirm she had something to hide. Tension held her rigid as she eyed him with a wary look.

"You intend to make this difficult, don't you," he growled.

"I am *not* being difficult. I simply cannot help you. Now, I would like to leave." Rhea took a step toward the open archway of the gazebo, but in a flash of movement he blocked her path.

"You underestimate yourself, Rhea. You're quite capable of helping me solve this particular mystery," he murmured seductively. Trapped in a web of tension that left her frozen where she stood, she tried to steady her breathing.

As he closed the small distance between them, his slow walk possessed the same raw power she remembered. His stride was reminiscent of a tiger's lazy gait that belied a deadly strength beneath the relaxed prowl. It was as disturbing as it was beautiful. Her throat closed and threatened to stop the flow of air to her lungs.

What in heaven's name was she thinking? The man had the power to destroy her. Worst of all, it would take little to deliver a crushing blow to Arianna's happy marriage. Rhea would go to hell and back to keep that from happening. Determined to protect her sister at all costs, she straightened her shoulders as she mustered every ounce of disdain she could find inside her.

"You've either had too much to drink this evening, Mr. Rockwood, or you're delusional. I cannot help you," she said in an icy voice. She was resigned to the fact that her bluff would be a futile effort, but she would do whatever necessary to protect those she loved.

"You didn't answer me before, Rhea," his voice was a low growl that heightened the image of him as a predator. "Have you ever been to the British Museum?"

"Yes," she said and arched her eyebrows at him. "Most Londoners have at one time or another."

"Have you ever visited the museum at night?" The anger in his voice scraped across her senses.

"As I recall, the museum closes well before nightfall."

"Then allow me to refresh your memory," he snarled. "How did you put it? Oh, yes—'I'm so sorry. This wasn't supposed to happen.'"

Although she'd accepted the fact that he'd guess the truth, hearing her words flung at her made her flinch. In an attempt to hide the way her hands were shaking, Rhea clasped them in front of her. Years ago, she'd learned that silence was the best weapon she possessed when it came to escaping a desperate situation unscathed. This was one of those moments. Warily, she met Percy Rockwood's hard gaze. When she didn't answer him, he released a loud noise of disgust and anger.

"Sit down, Rhea." He gestured toward the bench that curved its way around the gazebo's interior.

"I prefer to stand," she said with quiet defiance.

"I *said* sit down." His command said she would pay a price for disobedience. Instincts honed on the streets made Rhea sink down onto the wooden seat as her heart skidded out of control with fear. Her steady gaze met his as he glared at her.

"I don't appreciate being held hostage, Mr. Rockwood. I would like to leave. *Now.*"

"And I don't appreciate being shot," he ground out with a harsh anger that echoed like thunder between them.

The accusation in his voice sent an icy blast of cold air across Rhea's skin. Frozen in place, she offered up a silent prayer of gratitude for her ability to remain unflinching despite his fury. Percy folded his arms across his chest and pinned her beneath his gaze as if she were a butterfly he intended to place under glass. Even his stance declared he expected an explanation or, at the very least, a response from her.

"I've never shot anyone," she choked out.

Although she'd never shot or killed anyone, until tonight she'd believed herself responsible for Percy's death because she'd left him lying on the museum floor. She'd not even been able to kill Ruckley when she'd had the chance. The thought of killing was abhorrent to her, which was why she'd been so tormented ever since that terrible night in the museum.

She hadn't wanted to leave him on the museum floor to die alone. Even if all she could have done was to hold him until he took his last breath, she would never have left him if it hadn't been for Ruckley. It had been a horrible choice to make when Ruckley had forced her hand.

"But you *did* leave me on the floor of the British Museum to die." The brutal contempt in his voice made her jump. She shook her head vehemently.

"No, it wasn't like that."

Her sharp denial made Rhea suck in a sharp breath as she saw the triumphant gleam in his eyes. Horrified, she struggled with the folly of her error. She'd just confessed to a crime. One of the first lessons Ruckley had taught her was to never admit guilt. Rhea stared at her accuser in terror as her heart slammed into her chest. The moment his gaze narrowed on her, the sensation of being pinned to a lepidopterist's board of butterflies sped through her again.

"Then explain your actions," he bit out in angry frustration. "Explain why you would leave me lying on the museum floor in a pool of blood."

The bitterness in his voice made her close her eyes. How could she make Percy Rockwood understand what had driven her to ignore every universal law of compassion and kindness? She met his gaze for a long moment then looked away.

"I thought you were already dead. If I had protested any more than I did, Ruckley would have shot me too."

"Your desire to live is something I understand all too well," he said with a sardonic twist of his lips. At the suggestion that her life was all that mattered Rhea directed a cold look at him.

"My life wasn't mine to give away. There were others to consider."

"And yet, here you are, at my brother's estate, dressed like a woman of means without any encumbrances." The sarcasm in his words was stressed all the more by his scowl of contempt, and Rhea flinch as if he'd slapped her. She didn't understand why, but she didn't want him to think ill of her.

"Leaving you on that gallery floor that night has haunted me ever since," she said in a hoarse voice.

"How touching. But the fact is you *did* leave me, didn't you, Rhea?" The harsh condemnation made her tremble. She'd wronged him terribly. She knew that, but he didn't know her reasons, and any explanation would reveal her shame. It would also open up Arianna to a scandal.

"I'm sorry for what I did. I shall have to live with that sin until my dying day," Rhea said with pained regret. "I'm simply grateful I was wrong in thinking you dead."

"Of that I'm certain." Each word of the icy statement pierced her like a knife. "Accessory to murder isn't quite as serious a crime."

Rhea could feel the blood draining from her cheeks, and her body was as cold as if she'd fallen into an ice-covered pond. If she'd been standing she knew her legs would have given way beneath her. Rhea's stomach churned and braced herself with one hand against the bench not to slide to the floor. Accessory to murder. Yes, that's what she was—an accessory.

She'd done nothing to stop Ruckley, and she'd done nothing to save Percy Rockwood. A surreal calm washed over her as she met his angry gaze. She would accept her punishment, and she would see to it that Arianna and the children wouldn't be implicated. She would lie if necessary to ensure that.

"I understand," she whispered.

"Understand what?" Percy's words cracked through the air with viciousness of a bullwhip.

Unable to help herself, she flinched. Ruckley had never used the whip on her or Arianna. He'd not wanted to damage valuable merchandise. But the bastard had not hesitated to use the lash on any of the boys. She'd often thought it deliberate on Ruckley's part because he'd know how much it horrified and sickened her.

Her stomach roiled as she tried to accept the fact that Percy Rockwood was going to ensure she was punished. She would no doubt go to prison. She might even be hung. The thought made her light-headed. Rhea swayed again where she was sitting and felt her head loll backward as she fought to remain conscious.

"Bloody hell."

In seconds, Percy was seated beside her with his arm around her waist. The warmth of him enveloped her as she sank into his side, and he pulled her close. There was great strength in the shoulder that supported her head. A sudden rush of awareness spiraled through her, and she found herself wanting to sink deeper into his embrace.

The knowledge stunned her. Ruckley had made a fair profit off her as she'd serviced the needs of men who'd paid to use her body for their satisfaction. It had made her numb to all sensation where men were concerned.

At least that's what she had believed. Now, to experience attraction for a man was a startling revelation. But of all the men she might ever have been drawn to, she would never have expected it to be Percy Rockwood. A man she'd left to die in a dark museum.

She stared up into a pair of dark-brown eyes still bright with fury, but there was concern reflected in Percy's gaze as well. Why would he be worried about a woman he intended to hand over to the police? Rhea gulped back her fear, drew in a deep breath, and released it as she tried to pull away from him. She failed and sagged with resignation.

"When you summon the police, if you would have them remove me as discreetly as possible I would be grateful. I have no wish to embarrass my aunt." The serenity Rhea heard in her request pleased her. At least she was still capable of hiding her emotions.

"*Damnation*, I have no intention of sending for the village constable or the metropolitan police in London," he ground out almost as if he were angry she'd even suggested such a thing. "However, you *are* going to tell me how you came to be at Melton Park and where this Ruckley fellow is."

The mention of Ruckley sent a shudder sailing through Rhea. How in God's name had she failed to keep the name of her onetime master a secret? The less information she provided, the safer all her loved ones would be. With renewed strength, she freed herself from the solid strength of Percy Rockwood's embrace. He didn't stop her as she slid across the bench to put distance between them. Almost immediately she found herself wishing she could return to his side. There was something about the man that made her think he'd keep her safe from harm. She dismissed the thought with silent disgust. He knew nothing about Ruckley or how the bastard thought. Percy couldn't keep her or anyone else she loved safe. The only person she could trust to do that was herself.

Chapter 2

The moment Rhea slid away from him, Percy missed her soft warmth. His jaw clenched with irritation at the thought. What the hell was wrong with him? The woman hadn't hesitated to leave him for dead a year ago. In the back of his mind a voice protested his harsh judgement.

She'd not done so willingly. In fact, the regret and horror in Rhea's voice had revealed an anguished that was hard to dismiss. He was a fool to believe her remorse as genuine. It was sheer fantasy to think otherwise.

Rhea Bennett was a thief. She'd picked more pockets than he'd bedded women. He ignored the voice in his head that objected to the way he'd categorized her. Percy waited for her to look at him with a mixture of anger and confusion. When she did, the horrified look in her eyes was the same now as it had been in the Egyptian exhibit hall a year ago. It eased much of his anger.

For whatever reason, he had no choice but the accept that her regret at having left him for dead was sincere. But he couldn't forget why she'd been in the museum in the first place. What had she done with the pendant? There had been no clue as to the fate of the necklace since the burglary.

Budge had been resigned to its loss for good and had suggested it had been added to a private collection. Percy studied Rhea's profile for a long moment. Her features had been obscured by her mask that night more than a year ago. But something had registered with him the moment their eyes had met across the ballroom floor.

His initial reaction when he'd caught her watching him had been amusement. Whether it was a mother seeking a husband for their offspring, the wide-eyed admiration of an ingénue, or the sultry widow interested in a dalliance, he was well acquainted with the female sex and their behaviors.

It was only as he had continued to study her from across the expanse of the ballroom, that he'd sensed Rhea feared him. The realization had startled him. It had been an instinctive knowing that had puzzled him for the briefest of moments before he'd made the connection to the woman in the museum a year ago.

It had been the strongest clairvoyant sensation he'd had since the night he was shot. It had been even stronger than the ghosts that had assaulted his senses during his hospital stay. Despite the faint touch of the *an dara sealladh*, he'd not trusted what his gift was telling him until he'd looked into the deep violet of her eyes the moment Helen had introduced them. Percy gritted his teeth. One thing was for certain, the woman was distracting him from his purpose. The color of her eyes was irrelevant to the matter at hand.

"I asked you where I can find this Ruckley fellow."

"I don't know where he is," she replied without emotion as she turned her head and met his gaze steadily. There wasn't a trace of deception in those violet depths, but something else flickered there before it was extinguished.

"And if you did know his whereabouts?" His question hung in the air between them for a long moment. With a shake of her head, Rhea looked away.

"I wouldn't tell you." The flat response made Percy blow out a breath of exasperation.

Again, he wondered what prevented him from not handing her over to Scotland Yard. Percy couldn't attribute his decision to being blinded by her beauty. Rhea was lovely, but she didn't resemble the women he usually favored when it came to liaisons. Still, there was something unforgettable about her expressive countenance. Wisps of dark-brown hair had freed themselves from her up swept hair and framed her face in a way that made her look vulnerable. But it was her mouth that captured his imagination. Her full lips were an enticing dark pink. It was a mouth made for kissing. Percy frowned at his fantasizing as her gaze returned to his.

Apprehension shimmered in her eyes, and her fear made his muscles harden at the terror he saw in her gaze. That it troubled him to see Rhea afraid of him startled Percy. Surprised and annoyed by the realization, he clenched his jaw. The woman had left him for dead. Yet in true Rockwood fashion, he'd acted on impulse and declared he wouldn't hand her over to the police.

He didn't know what to make of his decision. Nor did he understand his need to protect her or convince her that she had nothing to fear from him. Tension flooded Percy's body. What the devil was wrong with him? All he cared about was finding the bastard who'd shot him. The thought almost made him snort out loud in self-disgust.

It wasn't just this Ruckley fellow he was interested in. He wanted to know more about Rhea. Despite his instinct telling him she was innocent of any crime where he was concerned, it was still difficult not to eye her with suspicion. A low grunt escaped him.

"Tell me how you came to be at Melton Park. Are you and your aunt planning to steal something from my brother's house?" He immediately regretted the question.

"*No*," she exclaimed with fierce vehemence. Anger reminiscent of a mother protecting her young darkened her violet eyes. "My aunt bears no responsibility for my actions or anyone else's. If not for Aunt Beatrice…"

She wasn't just afraid. She was in trouble. He knew it with the same certainty he'd known it that night in the museum. The knowledge became a deep rooted conviction as the *an dara sealladh* crashed through him like a raging river. The image of a beefy man with pock-marked skin and a bulbous nose filled Percy's head.

Ruckley. He didn't question how he knew who the man in his vision was. He simply accepted it as fact. The flashes of insight flooding his head were chaotic. Images tumbled over each other as if they were pieces of debris tossed about in dangerous, churning waters.

He saw Rhea riding across a meadow with tears streaming down her cheeks. The image vanished to become a vivid picture of Rhea dressed in a gown a decade older than current fashions. While another woman distracted a well-dressed gentleman, Rhea picked the man's pocket.

With amazing speed, another image filled his head of Rhea arguing with Ruckley. A child clung to her skirts as she argued with the man. He couldn't hear their words, and while she was stoic, her posture was filled with defiance, anger, loathing, and fear. Ruckley's salacious smile said the man could read her emotions as well.

In another flash of changing imagery, he saw Rhea comforting a small child. She turned her head toward someone in the shadows and her poignant air of hopelessness deepened his unexplained need to protect her. As quickly as the images of his vision came to him they were gone. Most of what he'd seen made little sense, but that was typical of the *an dara sealladh*. He knew things would sort themselves out in time. But what Percy's vision had shown him was convincing enough to know Rhea's theft of the pendant was not by choice.

More importantly, his vision had shown him that Rhea wasn't the person his eyes and personal experience suggested she was. Sorrow and pain were lodged deep inside of her. From the little he'd seen in his visions, her past had taught her to hide her emotions well. The cool, serene expression she'd worn since Helen had introduced them had barely faltered.

Yet despite her ability to hide behind that polite mask, it was her eyes that betrayed her.

"Does your aunt know about your past?" His question made Rhea grow still. Her eyes met his for a brief moment before she turned her head away. Her profile was soft and feminine, but revealed nothing of what she was thinking.

"Yes, she knows."

"But she doesn't know everything."

The statement was a stab in the dark. Percy was certain Rhea had done more than pick pockets. When she jerked and looked at him again, he knew he'd struck a nerve. Her violet eyes were as wide now as they had been the night he'd been shot. The moon cast its light on her pale features. The vulnerability he'd seen earlier flitted across her face before it vanished, and her expression became devoid of emotion.

"No, she doesn't know everything. If Aunt Beatrice knew the whole truth, it would break her heart. We couldn't do that to her."

Shoulders rigid, Rhea stared down at the gazebo floor. His gaze followed hers, and he noted the uneven boards, which were due to the inexperience of its builders. He and Caleb had built the small structure when they were younger. The memory was a bittersweet one. He missed his older brother. Percy pushed the thought of Caleb's death aside as he realized Rhea's response had been in the plural.

"*We?*" The single word question made her flinch. Rhea glanced in his direction before her gaze focused back on the lopsided flooring. She hesitated for a moment before her shoulders slumped in defeat.

"My sister, Arianna." Resignation vibrated through her response. It was obvious she'd not meant to reveal she had a sister. When she didn't expand on her statement, Percy shook his head with exasperation.

"And where is your sister this evening?"

"She's at home." The response was clipped and matter-of-fact. Frustration tugged a sigh of irritation from him.

"So she lives at Green Hill House with you and your aunt."

"She lives in London."

"*Alone?*" Percy raised his eyebrows as he stared at her in amazement.

"*No*," Rhea exclaimed. "I would *never* have left her alone if she and Blake hadn't married this past March."

"*Blake?*" Percy frowned for a moment. It wasn't an uncommon name, but it triggered something in his head the moment she mentioned marriage and the date. Percy frowned as he searched his memory for the elusive thought Rhea's words had sparked. The instant the riddle was solved, he stared at Rhea in disbelief. "*Blake?* As in Blake Hawkstone, Viscount Sherrington? Your sister is Lady Sherrington?"

Rhea jerked in horror and slid further away from him until she was completely out of reach. She didn't answer, but he knew he was right. He'd gone to school with Blake, and the two of them had become stalwart friends and saw each other quite often at the club, but he'd not seen his friend since his marriage. Only a handful of guests had been invited to Blake's wedding, and his friend had asked Percy to attend.

Any other time, he wouldn't have missed the occasion, but he'd been at Callendar Abby to celebrate his nephew Braxton's sixth birthday. Ever since losing Devin and Caleb in the fire at Westbrook Farms, he and his siblings put family above all other things. However, the significance of Rhea's sister being married to a friend of his was not lost on Percy.

Coincidences in the Rockwood clan were viewed as signs the universe had placed them in a certain place and time for a reason. When Rhea didn't respond, he decided to change the direction of their conversation.

"*How much* does your aunt know?"

"She knows Ariana and I were pickpockets."

The finality in her voice said she wasn't about to expand

on her statement with him anymore than she intended to discuss her sister. But it was enough to convince him that their association with Ruckley had involved more than pickpocketing. The memory of Ruckley's image was more than enough for Percy to come up with any number of things the man had forced Rhea to do.

The most unsavory one made Percy's gut knot with revulsion. As much as he didn't want to believe it, he would be a fool to think Ruckley hadn't had his way with Rhea. Anger swept through him. The thought of Ruckley or any other man touching her made his muscles harden with a rage he didn't understand. Hell, he didn't know *what* to make of this entire situation.

"How did you come to be in Ruckley's employ?"

The question was barely past his lips before Rhea was off the bench in a flash of movement. She stood in the moonlight with contempt darkening her eyes, and Percy frowned. He'd made a mistake to presume her connection to Ruckley had been by choice. It only emphasized the fact that if he wanted to know all of Rhea's secrets, he needed to earn her trust. He wouldn't gain her confidence by bullying her into telling him the truth. Her posture stiff and unyielding, she stared at him with an icy scorn that would have chilled even his unflappable brother, Sebastian.

"*First*, you drag me into the dark against my will, Mr. Rockwood. Then you have the audacity to *assume* my aunt intends to steal from your brother. *Now* you insist on asking questions that have nothing to do with that fateful night at the museum. Questions you have *no right* to ask."

She glared at him with an outrage he realized was driven by fear. Percy could read it in the deep purple of her eyes.

"The minute you stepped across the threshold of Melton Park, you made it my business," he replied as he kept his voice quiet and soothing.

"I would never have done so if I'd realized you would to

be here," she snapped. "I'll not answer any more of your questions. Even if you change your mind and turn me over to Scotland Yard, I'll not answer their questions either."

"Perhaps Lady Sherrington will be more forthcoming," he snapped.

The moment his words of frustration split the air, Percy bit back a groan of disgust at having made threat he had no intention of carrying out. Rhea's head snapped back as if he'd slapped her. Abject horror widened her eyes and twisted her mouth into a silent gasp of obvious fear. She became so pale her skin looked as if it were the hue of white marble. Her entire demeanor was almost deathlike, and for a brief moment he thought she might faint.

Pale as the moonlight pooling at her feet, she remained frozen in place. The threat had been a cold, unfeeling remark his family would have objected to with harsh disapproval. His sisters in particular would have subjected him to vehement condemnation. Regret and self-disgust lashed out at him. For not the first time in his life, he was reminded he was a member of the reckless Rockwoods.

Percy rose to his feet, and Rhea immediately took a step backward. It seemed out of character for her to do so. He was certain she wasn't the kind of woman to retreat. Despite the short amount of time he'd spent in her company, Percy had already surmised she possessed the strength of a seasoned soldier. It was an apt description. She'd survived what he was certain had been a horrific life under Ruckley's thumb. It was impossible not to admire her for having lived through such a nightmare without losing her ability to remain loyal to others. Percy cleared his throat.

"My threat was an empty one, Rhea. I said I would not turn you over to law enforcement, and I honor my promises. I've no intention of denouncing you or your loved ones."

His statement seemed to have no impact on Rhea as she remained still and nonresponsive. Silence spread a tenuous and uncomfortable web between them for several long moments. Percy was about to speak when she relaxed slightly. She eyed him with icy disdain.

"An apology, Mr. Rockwood?" The derision in her voice made Percy grit his teeth. Apologizing didn't come easily to him, and as much as he deserved her scorn for threatening her, he didn't enjoy the way it made him feel.

"A concession that as a member of the Rockwood family, I possess the familial trait of reckless conduct."

"It's a behavior that can get you killed," she snapped. "You should be grateful you *don't* know where Ruckley is. The man would make sport of you before he killed you."

"Did Ruckley make sport of you or your sister, Rhea?" he asked quietly.

The moment the question echoed between them, he realized how much he wanted to ease the pain he knew Ruckley had caused her. Percy was accustomed to being protective of his family. But Rhea was the first person outside of the Rockwood clan he'd ever wanted to keep safe from harm. Not even Nellie had aroused such strong protective instincts inside him. But he was certain Nellie hadn't experienced the horror he was certain Rhea had endured.

When he'd found Nellie, she'd been a street urchin in need of care. A skinny girl of ten, she hadn't trusted him at first. It had taken him several days to convince her that all he wanted was to help her. Nellie had finally agreed to go with Percy to the family orphanage, and there he'd put her under Mrs. Hughes's tutelage.

Over the years he'd taken an interest in Nellie's education and taken her for the occasional outing whenever she achieved a certain waypoint of success. Sebastian had once warned him that Nellie might take his interest and friendship to mean something deeper, but he'd brushed off the words of the head of the Rockwood brood. He'd been certain Nellie viewed him as a dear friend, just as he did her. Percy's muscles knotted with disgust as he shoved his memories of Nellie into the far reaches of his mind. His gaze met Rhea's, and her stoicism didn't surprise him. If he'd lived through the kind of existence she had, he would be just as unwilling to speak of the past as she was.

"I believe I've indulged your curiosity quite enough, Mr. Rockwood. I would like to return to the ballroom." Bitterness threaded through her words as her contemptuous gaze swept over him.

Percy frowned. From the tension holding her rigid he had to believe he'd pushed her to the edge of an abyss. There was more to her story, but he was certain she'd shared far more with him than she had with anyone else. Unfortunately, what little information she'd revealed to him had been given under duress. It would never make her trust him, and oddly enough Percy wanted her to feel safe with him—to believe he wouldn't do anything to harm her. Tomorrow he'd call on her at Green Hill House. He'd find a way to convince her that she needed his help, just as much as he needed hers.

"I'll see you back to the house," he said as he gestured for her to take his arm.

Rhea appeared ready to protest until he narrowed his gaze and dared her to object. With an abrupt bob of her head, she took a quick step forward. Percy never had the chance to warn her about the uneven section of the gazebo flooring in front of her. A split-second later, Rhea uttered a low cry of alarm and tumbled downward. Percy lunged forward and caught her before she hit the floor.

As he pulled her close, the warm scent of her filled his nostrils. She smelled like a honey blossom—sweet, but with a tantalizing note of beguiling heat. The intoxicating essence of her stirred his senses in the way he'd not experienced in a long time. Although fear still shimmered in her violet gaze, there was an awareness darkening her eyes that gave her a sultry look. It made his body responded to her natural sensuality.

Every inch of him tightened and hardened in the space of seconds. The tip of her tongue flicked out to dampen her upper lip. There was no artifice in the action, and it ignited an acute need to taste her sweetly shaped mouth. Without thinking, Percy bent his head to caressed her mouth with his in a brief, light kiss. A small gasp of surprise escaped her, but she made no attempt to reject him. Unable to stop himself he deepened the kiss as he pulled her closer. She didn't resist.

Instead, her fingers splayed across his chest as she leaned into him. It sent a rush of desire coursing through his blood. With a gentle nip on her lower lip, he startled her into parting her mouth beneath his. She stiffened against him for a brief moment before her body became soft against his, and he tightened his embrace.

As his tongue swept in to the heat of her mouth, a tremor vibrated out of her before she responded by tentatively mating her tongue with his. With each stroke of his tongue against hers, an unexpected hunger pounded its way into every inch of him. He couldn't remember the last time he'd tasted a woman so fresh and sweet.

In the back of his head, a bell clanged a loud warning. He ignored the sound as he continued to enjoy the tangy sweetness of Rhea's mouth. The alarm clanged even louder until it broke through the desire gripping his body and alerted him to the sound of voices close by. With a jerk, he released her and put a respectable distance between them.

As the voices grew louder with each passing second, Rhea's demeanor was one of calm serenity. The only sign she'd just been in a passionate embrace was the soft luminescent glow on her face and a plump mouth darkened by his kiss. The fact that she appeared unmoved by what had just transpired between them irritated him.

Most women he kissed still had the look of a lover wanting more when he released them from his embrace. Rhea Bennett looked as though she'd just exchanged a perfunctory kiss with him. In fact, the casual observer would never even contemplate the possibility that she'd just been kissed passionately. And the fact that she'd stirred such a raw desire in him without her experiencing the same emotion pricked his pride.

It had been a long time since he'd allowed himself to become so enthralled with a woman as to lose his head as he had just a moment ago with Rhea. The voices grew louder and dismay caused Rhea to gasp softly and press her hand to the base of her throat. Percy frowned and turned his head toward the gazebo's archway.

"If possible, you're even more autocratic than you were *before* you left England, Lord Foxworth."

"And you've grown more stubborn," Foxworth snapped. "Time might have altered us somewhat Beatrice, but you cannot deny you still desire me."

Percy raised his eyebrows in amusement as he glanced at Rhea. It appeared Foxworth had renewed an old love affair. Percy's amusement changed to puzzlement at Rhea's consternation. It took a second for her dismay to trigger the sluggish part of his brain. Beatrice. Rhea's aunt was the woman with Foxworth. Clearing his throat in as loud a manner as he could, Percy looked at Rhea and jerked his head toward the gazebo doorway.

"If you are recovered from the heat of the ballroom, Miss Bennett, I suggest we return." The strength of his voice rang out through the air in such a way that there was no doubt the approaching lovers would know he and Rhea were in the gazebo. A look of relief and gratitude softened Rhea's expression as she matched the volume of his voice.

"Yes, thank you, Mr. Rockwood. I'm feeling much better now." The moment she took a step toward the gazebo's archway, Percy caught her arm and brought her to a halt.

"Careful, this floor is quite uneven. I wouldn't want you to take a spill." His words caused her cheeks to darken with color, and he bit back a grin. Rhea Bennett might present the façade of a woman unmoved by his kiss, but she'd just betrayed herself. She'd not been quite as unaffected as he'd thought.

"Why on earth don't you have this floor repaired," she bit out in a low voice.

"Because my brother and I built it when we were younger. The somewhat perilous footing has been a family joke for years."

"Has it never occurred to the two of you to correct the problem?"

"That's no longer possible. Caleb died last year," Percy said with an almost crippling sense of sorrow he'd not felt in months. Her hand touched his arm in a consoling gesture.

"Oh, *I am* sorry, Percy." The gentle way she said his name was pleasing to his ear. "I would never have…"

"You didn't know. How could you?" he said with a small shrug not wishing to stir up old memories at the moment. "Come, I'll see you back to the house."

Together they walked toward the arched opening of the gazebo. In the moonlight he saw Foxworth and Beatrice Fremont walking toward them.

"Rhea, dear, what on earth are you doing out here." There was a somewhat breathless note in Beatrice Fremont's voice as she looked at the two of them, but there was disapproval in her voice as well.

"I have a small headache and felt a bit faint in the ballroom." Rhea replied as she looked at Percy with a plea in her gaze. "Mr. Rockwood was quite accommodating in finding me a place to sit down away from the heat and noise. I'm surprised to see you as well. I know how much you love to dance."

"I convinced your aunt to take a walk with me in the gardens," Lord Foxworth said.

"Ordered is more like it," Beatrice Fremont said beneath

her breath with fierce displeasure.

Beside him, Rhea made a small sound Percy thought might be laughter. It made him want to hear what her real laugh sounded like. Beatrice frowned as her gaze flitted from Rhea to Foxworth back to Rhea. A second later, the older woman hid whatever she'd been thinking behind a small frown of concern. In the space of a split-second, Beatrice Fremont masked her emotions with the same skill Rhea had displayed. It convinced him it was a family trait.

"If you're feeling unwell, dearest, perhaps we should go home."

Beatrice Fremont's suggestion made Lord Foxworth frown with irritation. The sudden thought of not being able to hold Rhea again, if only on the dance floor, sent disappointment shooting through Percy. He didn't care for the sensation. It meant something he didn't want to acknowledge.

"And ruin your evening?" Rhea shook her head. "No, I'll manage."

"Might I offer a solution," Foxworth said silkily as he cast his gaze on Mrs. Fremont. "I'll escort your aunt home later, which will allow you to leave without worrying that you've interrupted Beatrice's enjoyment of the evening."

"I couldn't possibly stay knowing Rhea is ill." It was obvious the viscount's recommendation appalled the woman as Beatrice Fremont had the panicked look of someone attempting to avoid a punishment.

"I think it's a perfect solution, Aunt Beatrice," Rhea said as the merest hint of a smile touched her lips. "It would make me unhappy to know I was taking you away from the party."

"But I—"

"It's settled then," Lord Foxworth said with satisfaction. "If it makes you feel better Beatrice, we can see your niece to the carriage."

"No," Rhea said as she winced with what appeared to be

actual pain. It made Percy wonder if her headache wasn't a fabrication after all. "I can fend for myself."

"I'm happy to see your niece to her carriage, Mrs. Fremont." At his offer, Beatrice Fremont narrowed her gaze at him. She studied him for a moment before she nodded.

"Very well." Beatrice turned toward Rhea and stretched out her hands. "Are you certain you wouldn't like me to go home with you?"

"No," Rhea said as she clutched the older woman's hands and kissed her cheek. "I'll feel better in the morning, and I would feel guilty if I made you leave the ball when I know how much you enjoy dancing."

With a sigh, Beatrice Fremont nodded then locked arms with her niece and urged her down the path leading back to the house. Left behind to follow the women, Foxworth muttered something beneath his breath. The man was exhibiting the same frustration Percy had experienced with Rhea. A wry smile twisted Foxworth's lips as he met Percy's gaze. The viscount shook his head and grimaced with exasperation.

"Beatrice is far more stubborn than I remember. Does Miss Bennett possess the same trait?"

"Although I'm unacquainted with Mrs. Fremont, I would be willing to stake money that Rhea's tenacious manner is the same as her aunt's." His reply made Foxworth nod thoughtfully as if contemplating a puzzle.

"It's not just their temperaments that seem quite similar. They look a great deal alike," the man murmured. Percy arched an eyebrow in contemplation.

"Now that you mention it, I would have to agree," Percy said as he studied the women in front of him. "They could almost be mistaken for mother and daughter. However, it's not unusual for aunts and nieces to be so similar in looks and temperament."

"Yes, and I understand her sister, Olivia, looked

remarkably like Beatrice," Foxworth said with an odd note echoing in his voice as if he'd stumbled onto a new piece of information.

Although Percy didn't question the man, his curiosity was aroused as he watched Rhea and her aunt step onto the torch-lit path leading to the house. Rhea's head was bent toward her aunt, who had wrapped her arm around her niece's waist. It was a clear sign Rhea was feeling unwell. Guilt nudged at Percy. He was certain the inquisition he'd subjected her to was the cause of her distress. It couldn't have been easy for her to be interrogated the way he'd questioned her.

"It would appear you find Miss Bennett quite interesting." The man's quiet observation made Percy glance at the viscount who was studying him with a narrowed gaze. Puzzled by the man's stern tone of voice, Percy acknowledged his interest with a brief nod.

"I'll not deny that she intrigues me."

"Intrigue where a woman is concerned can be a dangerous path, Rockwood," the viscount said in a voice that made Percy think the man was issuing a warning. Puzzled he frowned as he saw a calculating gleam in Foxworth's eyes.

"I think any path where Rhea is concerned could be treacherous in more ways than one."

"All the same, I urge you to tread with care. While I've only been back in England for a few months, I've heard you have a particular reputation for breaking hearts," Foxworth said. This time Percy was certain the man was issuing a warning to take care with Rhea's feelings.

"My intentions are quite honorable where Rhea is concerned," Percy said in a stilted voice.

It irritated him that Foxworth was cautioning him to take care where Rhea's feelings were concerned. He'd been more than considerate of her emotions tonight. A voice in the back of his head decried that conviction with a sneer of contempt. He shoved the thought into a dark corner of his mind. If anything, he was Rhea's best chance at redemption.

She might not realize it yet, but he knew he could help her break free of the hold Ruckley had over her. Rhea might think that being out of Ruckley's reach meant freedom, but it wasn't. That kind of freedom would only be achieved when she no longer feared Ruckley, which meant one of two things had to happen, either the man ended up incarcerated or dead. Somehow he didn't think either option would undo the harm the bastard had done. Beside him, Foxworth cleared his throat.

"Forgive me for being blunt, Rockwood. I have feelings for Beatrice. Therefore, I am protective of her *and* anyone she cares about even if Beatrice hasn't granted me that right as yet."

"I understand completely," Percy accepted the viscount's apology with a nod.

It was clear the man was determined to make Beatrice Fremont his, but also obvious that the woman was balking at the man's effort to succeed. Whatever the history between the two, Foxworth seemed determined not to let it stand in the way of obtaining the woman's surrender. As they reached the top of the steps to the terrace, Percy hurried forward to stop Rhea from returning to the ballroom.

The moment his hand caught her elbow it sent a charge of current surging through him. Startled by the sensation, his astonishment disappeared as she turned her head toward him. Self-reproach tightened his muscles at her wan appearance. It was obvious she was ill, and he despised himself because he was certain he was responsible for her suffering. Fear was a draining emotion, and he'd dredged up her past in all its ugly glory during his interrogation.

"Why don't you say your goodbyes here. I can take you through my brother's study to the front hall. It will save you from the noise and heat of the ballroom." At his offer, relief swept across Rhea's pale features.

"Thank you."

When Rhea and her aunt had kissed each other's cheek in farewell, Foxworth bid Rhea good night as well. The man's remark as to a horse he was loaning her made Percy tuck the odd fact away in his brain. A few short moments later, he guided Rhea through Sebastian's study and into the main entryway. Here the music was still loud, but not as clamorous as in the ballroom. Percy ordered Rhea's carriage brought to the front of the house then turned toward her. Wan and forlorn-looking, she sank down onto one of the Queen Anne chairs situated against the entryway's wall. Frowning, he moved to her side.

"Are you feeling faint again?"

"I'm fine," she said a hint of annoyance. "I don't faint."

"Perhaps," he acknowledged with a bob of his head. "But you came close to doing so earlier."

Rhea's only response was a sniff of exasperation. The wait for her carriage was a short one. When the footman informed them her vehicle was ready, Percy escorted Rhea out the front door to the vehicle. As he opened the carriage door, her hand touched his arm. Once more a shock of electricity raced up his arm to barrel its way through his body.

"Is it really your intention to find Ruckley?" There was a small note of panic running beneath her question.

"Can you blame me?" Percy said with suppressed anger at Ruckley's callous, cowardly act. "The man shot me in the back. That's not something I'm willing to walk away from."

"I understand your desire for justice, but you'll not find it. Not where Ruckley is concerned." There was a conviction in her voice that infuriated him. He wasn't about to let Ruckley escape responsibility for any of his crimes, and he found it damned frustrating that Rhea was unwilling to help bring the man to justice.

"I don't understand why you're so hell-bent on protecting a man who clearly forced you to do things against your will."

"I am *not* protecting Ruckley." Her sharp reply held the sting of a whip cracking through the air between them. "I'm trying to save lives."

"Elaborate." The sharp demand made her go rigid, and she narrowed her gaze on him.

"I don't deny the terrible crime Ruckley inflicted on you, but you were one of the lucky ones. He's done far worse to other than you can even imagine," she said with a ferocity that was emphasized by the horror flickering in her gaze. "There are lives at stake. Lives that are precious to me, and I'll not help you if it means jeopardizing their safety."

With a sharp gesture, Rhea asked for his assistance to enter the carriage. The moment her hand slid into his, an intense need to keep her with him crashed through him. There was a possessiveness to the sensation that troubled him. It was a desire to protect her that paled in comparison to what he'd felt when he'd sought to keep Nellie safe from harm. This was primal and territorial at the basest of levels and it made him uneasy.

As he helped her into the carriage, Percy glimpsed a feminine ankle and calf. A knot formed in his throat at the way his hand twitched to slide his hand over her leg as he kissed her. He rolled his head to alleviate the pressure his collar was applying to his throat. Every inch of him was taut with tension, and he suddenly realized his fingers were wrapped tightly around the side of the carriage door. Vaguely, he noted his knuckles were white before he met Rhea's violet gaze.

The challenging tilt of mouth had softened to one of resignation. As they stared at each other, color rose in her cheeks. Once more the need to pull her from the carriage and keep her with him barreled through him like a wild bull. Rhea leaned forward slightly to touch his hand that still gripped the vehicle's door frame.

"Finding Ruckley isn't the problem, Percy. It's what will

happen when you do." A note of horror echoed in her soft words, and her look of concern said she was apprehensive for his safety. "Ruckley is not to be underestimated. He won't hesitate to shoot you a second time, and this time he *will* kill you."

"Your concern for my safety is appreciated, but unwarranted," he said as he heard the fear in her voice. It pleased him that she was worried about him.

Percy released his grip on the carriage door to capture her hand in his. With his gaze locked with hers, Percy carried her hand to his mouth. He caressed her fingertips with his lips before he turned her hand over. As his thumb brushed over her skin, then pressed down to feel her pulse, Rhea inhaled a sharp breath.

The sound stirred the devil in him and he pressed his lips to the inside of her wrist. A tremor reverberated out of her and into his hand. He looked up at her and saw her mouth was parted in a way that said she'd enjoyed the caress. The moment her gaze locked with his, she tugged against his grasp, and he released her with great reluctance.

"I shall remind you of your concern for my welfare the next time we meet." Percy stepped back and closed the door of the carriage.

"There *will not* be a next time, Mr. Rockwood," she snapped.

"Oh, you can count on it, Miss Bennett," he said mockingly before he ordered the driver to move along. The carriage rocked forward, and he saw her look of dismay as the vehicle disappeared into the dark. Rhea Bennett would be seeing a great deal more of him than she realized. The cheerful thought made him grin as he returned to the house. He was looking forward to paying a call at Green Hill House tomorrow.

Chapter 3

hea pressed her fingertips against her temples as the hackney cab rolled toward Arianna's London townhouse. The headache she'd developed last night after her confrontation with Percy still throbbed, although lack of breakfast was no doubt contributing to the pain. Rhea knew Aunt Beatrice would find her early departure without saying goodbye as odd, but her aunt wouldn't question Rhea's change in travel plans. Beatrice knew Rhea had intended to leave London in three days' time.

At least her aunt knew her primary reason for traveling to London was to meet with Ashford. The private detective had made arrangements for Peter's escape from Ruckley's street gang, and she insisted on shepherding her charges back to the country. They'd been taught to trust no one. They would be skittish enough with Ashford if she wasn't there to reassure them.

She could only hope the note she'd left for her aunt would make the older woman believe she'd wanted to visit with Arianna for a couple of days. But if Percy Rockwood held true to his word appeared at their front door, her aunt was certain to believe otherwise.

Instinctively, she knew the man had no intention of leaving the issues between them unresolved, which meant he would call at Green Hill House. The last thing she wanted was to be there when he paid a visit. She needed time to collect her wits.

Last night he'd been an unstoppable force that had buffeted her senses on every front. He'd been a mixture of anger, kindness, and seduction. It had been easy to shield herself from his anger. Seven years of bearing the brunt of Ruckley's foul temper had taught her to remain silent until the storm had passed.

She'd even managed to block herself off from Percy's kindness, although that had been far more difficult. What had been the most alarming of all was her reaction to the man. Ruckley had sold her body many times, but Rhea had never allowed the men who bought her to kiss her. It had allowed her to distance herself from the horror of being used for a man's pleasure. The handful of men who objected, had found a knee pressed threateningly between their legs or her fingers pressed into their jugular. Their protests had died quickly.

But last night Percy had broken through that barrier. When he'd kissed her, she'd experienced no repugnance. For those few moments in the Melton Park gazebo, she'd believed herself capable of giving herself to a man without hesitation— freely offering herself in a mutual exchange of pleasure. The realization had haunted her through the night. She'd slept fitfully with Percy intruding her dreams in such a way that it frightened her.

This morning, the memory of that seductive kiss to her wrist when they'd said goodbye had only reinforced her need to flee. While Percy frightened her for what he knew about her, it was the feelings he aroused in her that were even more terrifying. She liked the way his touch warmed her. Something about his strength made her feel safe, and that made him dangerous. She couldn't afford to believe someone else could keep her safe. Not even Percy Rockwood.

While the man hadn't said he would protect her from Ruckley, she knew he would attempt to do so. Rhea wasn't sure how she knew that. She'd certainly done nothing to deserve his protection. Yet, instinct told her he had decided to take on the role of her champion. Why else would he forgive her for leaving him to die in that dark museum? But Percy couldn't protect her from Ruckley any more than she'd been able to keep Timothy safe from the sadistic brute. The thought of the boy made her throat close with tears. She'd failed him, and she could never forgive herself for it.

After a brief second, she suppressed the urge to cry and swallowed her emotions. Percy Rockwood was a problem she'd have to deal with soon, but she needed time to think before she faced him again. It was imperative she warn Arianna, especially since she had a strong suspicion Percy knew her brother-in-law quite well. The hackney rolled to a halt with a jerk, and Rhea winced as her head protested the abrupt stop.

In minutes she was standing inside Sherrington House with her small collection of luggage. Arianna emerged from the morning room and hurried across the foyer to greet Rhea with a smile of surprise and pleasure.

"Rhea." Arianna kissed her cheek warmly then stepped back to study her affection. "I wasn't expecting you until Wednesday."

"I needed to speak with you about a matter that couldn't wait."

"All right, why don't you freshen—"

"No. I need to speak with you now."

Arianna raised her eyebrows in concern, but nodded her head in understanding. Her sister instructed the footman to take Rhea's things upstairs, then Arianna guided Rhea into the morning room and closed the door behind them. A tray with tea and scones rested on a table in front of a dark blue couch. Arms entwined, Arianna pulled Rhea toward the sofa.

"Come. Have a cup of tea. I'm certain you're parched. When did you last eat?"

"I don't want tea."

"Well, you'll drink a cup all the same. You look as though

you've not slept in days. I'll not have Aunt Beatrice chide me if you fall ill." The stern reprimand in her sister's voice made Rhea stare at Arianna in startled amazement. "Don't look so surprised, Rhea. You're not the only one capable of giving orders or taking care of those we love."

"I'm just unaccustomed to seeing you so strong-willed," Rhea said with a sense of bewilderment. Almost overnight, it seemed her sister had gained a large measure of confidence, and she found it surprising. Arianna urged Rhea to sit down.

"That's because you're older than me, and you believed you had to be the strong one."

Satisfied Rhea wasn't about to leave her seat, Arianna turned and lifted the teapot to pour a cup of tea. Her sister added a delicately made scone to the saucer of the tea cup she handed to Rhea. As she took a sip of the hot brew, Rhea was glad her sister had insisted she eat something. The scone melted in her mouth, and without thinking, Rhea reached out to pick up another one of the treats as she sipped the hot beverage in her cup. Arianna sat opposite her in silence, only moving to refresh Rhea's tea. Two more scones disappeared from the serving platter before Rhea picked up her fifth scone. She stared at it in surprise for a moment before putting it down on her tea cup's saucer.

"I didn't realize how hungry I was," she murmured as she set her tea down on the table in front of her. The fragile china was reflected in the soft, polished sheen of the furniture.

"I think it comes from going hungry for almost seven years," Arianna said in a somber voice. "I often find myself stuffing bite after bite into my mouth whenever I eat. It troubles Blake although he understands why I do so."

"How much have you told him about Ruckley? Does he know…"

Rhea's words trailed off into thin air as her sister paled and a look of intense pain swept across her beautiful face.

"That I was a whore?" Arianna choked out. "Yes, he

knows. I would not have married him without telling him the truth."

"And Lucy? Have you told him about her?"

"No." She shook her head in an imperceptible movement. "I don't know how, and I'm afraid of what he'd say."

"He loves you, Arianna. He'll understand."

"I lied to him. I told him I had no more secrets."

"Why would you do such a thing?" Rhea said with a shake of her head.

"I didn't want to lose him, Rhea. I was afraid he…it's one thing for him to accept that I was far from chaste. But to forgive my bearing a child without knowing who her father is…that was too much to ask of him."

"I think you misjudge Blake's love for you, Arianna." She leaned forward to touch her sister's hand. "I've seen the way he looks at you. If you asked him to give you the world, he would move heaven and earth to do so."

"I wouldn't be asking for the world. I'd be asking him to take my bastard daughter into his house. Love or not, what man would be willing to do that?" Arianna closed her eyes for a brief moment before looking at Rhea again. "Even if he agreed to Lucy being here, how would we explain her presence?"

"I don't know, but he deserves to know the truth, Arianna. She's not even one yet, but she already looks like you. We both know he will realize the truth one day soon. What will you do then?"

"I shall cross that bridge when I come to it," Arianna bit out as her mouth thinned into a thin line of irritation. The look warned Rhea not to press further on the topic. "Now then, why don't you tell me what was so important that you had to arrive three days ahead of your scheduled arrival?"

Her sister's abrupt change in subject made Rhea flinch as she remembered why she'd come to London earlier than planned.

"He's alive."

"What?" Arianna looked at Rhea in puzzlement. "Who's alive?"

"The man from the museum." An image of Percy popped into her head. As frightened as she'd been last night, it relieved her greatly to know he hadn't died. "The man Ruckley shot is alive."

"Dear God." The color left Arianna's cheeks at Rhea's news. Relief followed her first reaction then pained dismay. "Did he recognize you?"

"Yes." The instant Rhea saw her sister's hand clutch at her throat, Rhea rushed to kneel at her side. Arianna's knuckles were white as she gripped the wood arm of her chair, and Rhea gently wrapped her hand over her sister's.

"It will be all right, dearest. Percy said—"

"*You know him by name*," Arianna exclaimed in horror.

"It seems rather absurd to call a man I left for dead by his last name." Rhea omitted the fact that he'd kissed her as well.

Arianna leapt from her chair to pace the floor. Her sister's panic was the same emotion Rhea had experienced last night. But her fear had dissolved into something else when she'd been in Percy's company. For all his arrogant, demanding questions she'd never sensed anything from him other than a desire to help and his determination to find Ruckley. It was obvious he wanted to bring the criminal to justice. And she trusted him not to reveal her part in the museum incident. In truth, everything about him encouraged her to trust him.

The sudden realization stunned her. She'd learned never to trust a man, but for some unfathomable reason, she believed she could confide in Percy Rockwood without risk of betrayal. However, his insistence on finding Ruckley was troubling.

The man didn't understand the danger in doing so. Worse, any effort he made to find Ruckley posed a great risk to the children she'd rescued and the ones she intended to save as soon as Mr. Ashford arranged it. Last night when she'd told Percy she didn't know where Ruckley was, it had been a small lie.

While Rhea didn't know where Ruckley was, Ashford did. Their aunt had hired the private investigator to find Arianna and Rhea after their father had died almost two years ago. A bitter taste filled her mouth at the thought of her father. The loathing and hate that welled up inside her threatened to overwhelm her senses, but she managed to bury the emotions beneath the rubble of pain and anger in the recesses of her mind.

When Ashford had found her and Arianna, they'd been picking pockets with Vincent. With Lucy in her arms, Arianna had been the distraction, while Vincent and Rhea worked their mark. Ashford had not wanted to bring Vincent with them, but Rhea's stubborn refusal to leave the boy behind forced the private investigator to reluctantly agree.

After being reunited with their aunt, Rhea had approached the man to ask his help in her rescue efforts. Ashford had agreed more readily than she'd expected. Her decision to ask the investigator's help had been a good one. The man exercised great caution in his efforts to rescue the children she'd cared for the entire time she was at Ruckley's mercy. His methods had proven successful more than a month ago when Jack had raced into her arms with tears of gratitude on his cheeks. Luke Ashford hadn't said why he was so eager to assist her, but the man clearly had a big heart, and she was grateful for his help.

Perhaps she should have explained to Percy what she was doing. Somehow she was certain he would approve of her actions. The moment the thought flitted through her head she brushed it aside. If she'd told Percy about her efforts to rescue the rest of the children, it could easily jeopardize her efforts to rescue the remaining children. She understood Percy's desire to see Ruckley punished. No one, with the exception of perhaps Arianna, wanted to see Ruckley swinging from a gibbet as much as she did. She wanted to see the bastard held accountable for all the crimes she'd seen him commit. Achieving that end wasn't a simple matter to resolve. The man's power in the London underworld was far greater than Percy knew. Ruckley was second only to Thomas Gray when it came to power. Trying to bring Ruckley to justice would be like trying to enter Buckingham Palace uninvited.

It was difficult and dangerous enough just spiriting the children out of the man's clutches without revealing she was behind the scenes giving the orders. One of the conditions Aunt Beatrice and Arianna had demanded of her was that Ruckley would not be able to trace the rescue of the children back to her. That had been an easy promise to make.

Rhea had no intention of letting the bastard learn she was working to rescue the children. It was just one more reason it was imperative to prevent Percy from finding Ruckley. She couldn't risk Ruckley doing something to the children. The crime lord wouldn't hesitate to harm them simply because he knew how much it would hurt her. He'd proven that time and time again.

But none of those thoughts confused or troubled her as much as the emotions Percy had aroused in her with his touch. The memory of his kiss sent a wave of heat washing over her skin. Unsettled at the vivid recollection, Rhea pulled herself back into the present as she watched her sister pace the floor. Slowly she rose to her feet.

"Arianna, it will be all right. You must believe me," Rhea pleaded softly. "Percy made it very clear he'll not report me to the Metropolitan Police. He gave me his word, and I believe him."

"Won't report you?" Arianna snapped fiercely. "Why

would the man agree to such a thing?"

"I... I don't know," Rhea said hesitantly as she contemplated her sister's question. Why had Percy said he wouldn't go to the police?

"And what will we do if he goes back on his word?" Arianna stood tall and rigid with tension.

"He won't do that," Rhea said with a conviction that surprised her.

"You seem remarkably certain of a man we left to die on that museum floor," her sister snapped viciously

"I'm the only one he knows was there. You know I would never betray you or Vincent."

"I'm not suggesting you would, but what if the man decides to go after that bastard? If this Percy of yours goes after Ruckley, we both know what will happen. Ruckley will do whatever it takes to save himself. He won't hesitate to name us as the guilty party when it comes to that night in the museum."

"It won't come to that," Rhea said firmly, despite her fear of Percy's determination to find the crime lord. "I'll do whatever it takes to prevent Percy Rockwood from finding Ruckley."

The minute the words were out of her mouth, Rhea knew what would be called for when it came to distracting Percy from his search. It startled her that the idea of seducing Percy Rockwood didn't appall her. Not because she was incapable of doing so. Over the years, and simply out of self-preservation, she'd learned how to control the men who'd paid to use her body. The idea of entering Percy Rockwood's bed wasn't a frightening one. It was that she *wanted* to seduce him that made her heart skitter wildly in her chest. Rhea didn't want to feel anything for any man. Yet Percy Rockwood *did* make her feel things. Sensations she'd never felt before. Arianna met her gaze with a look of horror.

"*Never*. You're never to do such a thing again, Rhea

Bennett," her sister spat out with a vehemence that would have alarmed someone who'd not known what they'd been through. "Do you hear me? *Never.* Not even if you think it will save me or someone else."

"Whatever choices I make are mine, but your concern is unwarranted," Rhea said . "I trust Percy not to break his word. I don't know why. I just do."

The anger on her sister's features slowly disappeared before she nodded with a reluctant understanding. Fingertips pressed into her forehead, Arianna grimaced. Rhea immediately closed the distance between them. She wanted to avoid distressing her sister any further, but she knew that was impossible. Rhea swallowed the knot in her throat.

"There's something else." She hesitated slightly as her sister's already pale cheeks became almost deathly in pallor. Arianna shook her head and waved her hands in a gesture of defeat.

"I doubt it can be much worse than what you've already shared with me."

"Have you told Blake about that night in the museum?"

"No, I've already told you that he only knows a small bit about my past. I've never even mentioned Ruckley's name, simply out of selfishness. I know Blake would hunt the bastard down. I've lost too much in my life to Ruckley already."

"Well, you may have little choice but to tell him now."

"I don't understand," Arianna said with confusion.

"Percy knows Blake." The words seemed to have little impact on her sister as Arianna stared at her in confusion before shaking her head.

"A great many people know who Blake is simply because of his work in Parliament."

"No, I think he knows Blake better than that. In fact, I think he knows Blake quite well." Rhea's stomach lurch slightly as she remembered Percy's reaction to her brother-in-law's name. Something about his astonishment had made

Rhea believe he was friends with the Viscount. "I could be mistaken, but I don't think I am. I had the distinct impression he and Blake are good friends."

Arianna pulled free of Rhea's grasp and moved to stand at the window. There was an air of defeated resignation about her that made Rhea's heart ache. When Arianna had married the viscount, Rhea had been certain the past would never touch her sister again. Arianna's vanquished look served as a reminder as to how fragile the wall was between their past and the lives they led now. She had hoped never to see her sister look so overwhelmed with fear again. Suddenly, Arianna swayed like a drunken sailor and grabbed at the window drapery to steady herself. Alarmed, Rhea hurried to her side.

"You're unwell."

"No, I'm fine." The quiet response made Rhea frowned. "Are you certain?"

"I'm perfectly fine, Rhea," Arianna snapped. "It's just a slight headache brought on by all this talk of Ruckley."

Taken aback by her sister's abrupt reply, Rhea stared at her in surprise. Her sister winced, but before she could speak, the door to the morning room opened. They both turned to see the Viscount Sherrington entering the room. The moment she saw her husband, the troubled expression vanished from Arianna's face. In its place was a look of intense relief and happiness as Arianna hurried forward to greet her husband.

"Blake, I thought you would be gone until late this afternoon," Arianna said as she kissed him then drew back to look up at him with amusement.

"I finished my business much earlier than I expected." Blake gently caressed his wife's cheek then looked over her shoulder to smile at Rhea. "Good morning, Rhea. This is an unexpected, but pleasant, surprise. Arianna said you wouldn't be here until Thursday."

"I thought I'd come early so Arianna could take me shopping." The moment she saw Blake raise his eyebrows in amazement, Rhea realized her mistake. Her brother-in-law was well aware of her aversion for dressmakers. She winced and shrugged.

"Actually, Aunt Beatrice threatened to order something made without my being present." Rhea grasped at the first thing she could think of to hide her real reason for arriving at Sherrington house so early. "I decided to circumvent her efforts."

"I think you made a sound decision," Blake chuckled. "I've witnessed your aunt's undaunted perseverance when it comes to achieving a goal. It's a trait I've witnessed in other members of your family as well."

"We've not even been married six months, and you're already taking me to task for one of my idiosyncrasies," Arianna said with a sniff of false anger at the teasing note in her husband's voice.

"It is those very idiosyncrasies that make me love you all the more, my darling."

As Rhea observed the couple's playful banter, she noted Arianna's fear had completely disappeared. In its place was a happiness that Rhea envied. The moment the emotion swept through her, Rhea viciously destroyed it. Arianna was lucky, and she was content to be happy for her sister without feeling the need for a similar happiness.

The stairs and lobby of the Lyceum Theatre were crowded as Rhea followed Blake and Arianna out onto the sidewalk. With a confident gesture, Blake pointed toward their carriage, which was a short distance away. Cheerfully, he urged his wife and Rhea along the sidewalk toward the vehicle. As the three of them made their way toward the carriage, Rhea found herself falling behind.

The crowd continued to grow as attendees of the evening's performance exited the theatre, making it difficult to stay with the couple. While trying to stay close behind her sister and her brother-in-law, a man shoved her out of his way as he moved past her. Thrown off balance, Rhea stumbled backward into a solid object and a strong arm wrapped around her waist to steady her.

"Careful now, we don't want you to end up on the sidewalk," the stranger said cheerfully as he helped Rhea regain her balance. As she brushed aside a wisp of hair that had fallen into her eyes, Rhea turned toward her good Samaritan.

"Thank you," she replied as she regained her composure. "I'm afraid I wasn't paying attention."

"I think you're being too kind to the boor who pushed his way past you a moment ago." The man said with disapproval as he watched the offender disappear before he looked back at her and grinned. "However, I shall be eternally grateful for his rude behavior as it presented me with the opportunity to introduce myself. Colonel Dewhurst, at your service—miss?"

"Rhea Bennett," she said with a restrained smile at his jovial temperament. He repeated her name as if testing the sound of it on his tongue. He directed another broad grin at her as a pretty woman appeared at his side.

"Really, George, must you accost every young woman you meet?" The words were uttered with affectionate exasperation. Dewhurst turned his head toward the woman before looking back at Rhea.

"You must forgive my sister. She thinks I am too forward." Dewhurst waggled his eyebrows at her as he turned his head toward his sister. "Matilda, this is Miss Bennett, who I saved from falling."

"How do you do, Miss Bennett. I take it you are unharmed." Matilda Dewhurst nodded in Rhea's direction and the woman's mouth twitched with sisterly surprise at her brother's gallantry.

"Thanks to the colonel's quick action I am quite free of injury." Rhea smiled at the woman before casting a glance in Dewhurst's direction. "I am quite grateful for his assistance."

The sound of someone calling her name made Rhea look over her shoulder. Blake was pushing through a stream of theatergoers in his effort to reach her. She waved to her brother-in-law then returned her attention back to her new acquaintances.

"I must be going. Thank you again for your help, Colonel Dewhurst. I am truly grateful." Rhea extended her hand, and the gentleman brushed his lips over her fingertips.

"It was my pleasure." His grip firm, he refused to let go of her hand. "Would you allow me to call on you tomorrow?"

"I'm not certain —"

"The day after then, unless of course the gentleman approaching will object."

"Blake?" Rhea looked at the colonel with puzzlement before she laughed. With another glance over her shoulder, Rhea shook her head. "No, the viscount is my brother-in-law."

"Then say you will allow me to call on you."

"I really don't think —"

"Surely you'll not deny your rescuer the chance to ensure you are fully recovered from your harrowing experience." The playful plea made her laugh again.

"Very well, tomorrow morning Sherrington House." Rhea pulled her hand free of Colonel Dewhurst's grasp, and he bowed slightly.

"I shall count the hours," he quipped. Rhea laughed at his roguish manner. Still smiling, she said goodbye and turned to make her way through the crowd. A few seconds later, she reached her brother-in-law.

"We were worried about you." Blake's voice held the

slightest note of rebuke, and Rhea touched his arm in an apologetic gesture.

"I'm sorry, Blake. The crowd was so thick, and I almost fell. Colonel Dewhurst saved me." At her explanation, she looked over her shoulder in the direction of the colonel who was already guiding his sister in the opposite direction. As Blake's gaze followed hers, the viscount nodded with rueful regret.

"Forgive me for chastising you, Rhea. It was simply that Arianna was frantic when we reached the carriage and you were no longer with us."

"I'm sorry I worried you both."

"All is well," he said as relief eased his frown into a pleasant smile.

In moments they reached the carriage, and with Blake's assistance, Rhea climbed into the coach to see Arianna's cheeks were wet with tears. Appalled she'd upset her sister, Rhea sat opposite her and caught Arianna's hands in hers.

"I'm sorry I made you worry so, dearest."

"What happened to you? One minute you were with us and the next…"

"I almost took a tumble," she said with a frown as she saw how pale and drawn her sister was. It was unlike Arianna to exhibit such distraught behavior. "A Colonel Dewhurst rescued me from harm."

"Colonel Dewhurst?" Arianna turned to her husband as Blake closed the carriage door and tapped on the ceiling of the vehicle to notify the driver to head home. "Do you know him, Blake?"

"Not that I recall," her brother-in-law shrugged as he met his wife's panicked gaze. The Viscount wrapped his arm around Arianna and pulled her close. "What's wrong, sweetheart? This is not like you at all."

Arianna didn't answer him, and simply buried her face in her husband's chest. Over his wife's head, Blake stared helplessly at Rhea. With a shake of her head, she indicated she had no explanation for his wife's behavior. Her brother-in-law turned his attention back to his wife, his voice inaudible as he sought to comfort Arianna. Rhea stared at the couple for a long moment before she looked out the carriage window.

No doubt she was to blame for her sister's anguish. If she'd not gone to Melton Park last night, she wouldn't have needed to tell Arianna about Percy. Arianna hadn't said it out loud, but Rhea knew her sister well enough to know she was worried Percy Rockwood would lead Ruckley right to them. Rhea closed her eyes for a moment. She would have done anything to spare her sister pain. This morning when she'd shared her news, Rhea had expected Arianna to be upset. But her sister's reaction was far more extreme than she'd expected, and it worried Rhea.

Arianna had been in such a state of sheer panic this morning she'd nearly fainted. Rhea could recall only one other time when her sister had been so irrational and emotional. Tension streaked through her body at the thought. Pregnant—Arianna was pregnant. It was the only explanation for her sister's excitable state and wan appearance.

It was apparent she'd not told Blake yet, and the fact troubled Rhea. Why hadn't her sister told her husband she was with child? As the carriage rolled to a halt, Arianna straightened upright and accepted Blake's handkerchief to dry her tears. Moments later, they were inside the house. In silence, Rhea watched her brother-in-law help Arianna up the stairs. At the earliest opportunity, Rhea intended to ask her sister to explain why she'd not told Blake she was carrying his child.

Chapter 4

The next morning, the quiet murmur of conversation reached Rhea as she walked down the hallway and halted just outside the dining room. Arianna and Blake sat at the table, their heads together in a moment of tender affection. Feeling like an intruder, Rhea was about to retreat when Blake saw her standing in the doorway.

"*Good morning,*" Blake exclaimed with an air of excitement and a happy laugh. "Congratulate me, Rhea. Your sister has informed me that I am to be a father."

Relief swept through Rhea as she took in the viscount's jubilation. He grinned broadly as she quickly circled the table to hug her sister and kiss her brother-in-law's cheek. Delighted for them both, Rhea couldn't stop smiling as she took a seat across the table from her sister. The flush of excitement and joy on Arianna's face warmed Rhea's heart. She loved seeing her sister so happy. It was as if the news she'd brought yesterday and their painful past had never touched Arianna.

"I had planned on telling Blake sooner," Arianna said. "But I never found an opportunity to do so until last night."

"It explains her overwrought behavior last night at the theater." Blake smiled at his wife with such adoration that it made Rhea want to kiss the man again for caring so deeply for her sister. Arianna took her husband's hand in hers as Blake shook his head in happy bemusement. "I should have guessed her condition sooner. She's been quite irritable and prone to tears of late."

"And I should have recognized the signs more than a month ago. It's not as if—"

Arianna flinched as her voice broke off in mid-sentence. Rhea saw the flash of fear and panic in her sister's gaze. As Blake eyed his wife in puzzlement, Rhea quickly filled the breach to allow Arianna time to regain her composure.

"I'm surprised I didn't recognize the signs myself when I arrived yesterday," she said with a smile. "We shall have to watch you closely to ensure you don't overtax yourself."

"Agreed," Blake nodded his head in concurrence. "I'll have Marston send for the doctor immediately."

"Is that really necessary?" Panic flitted across Arianna's features again.

"I must insist, my darling," Blake said with a slight frown.

Fear darkened Arianna's blue eyes as her gaze locked with Rhea's. Her sister's obvious trepidation made Rhea stiffen. Arianna was afraid a doctor would know she'd already borne a child, and might tell Blake. Rhea leaned forward slightly in a silent effort to comfort and calm her sister's fears.

"Will it make you feel less anxious if I'm present during the doctor's visit?"

At Rhea's offer, relief flashed in Arianna's eyes as she nodded. They both knew Rhea would ensure the doctor would not report any evidence of Arianna's previous pregnancy. Although relief lightened her countenance, Arianna still clung to her desire to avoid the doctor paying a house call. Her mouth stubbornly set, Arianna shook her head as she directed a look of pleading at her husband.

"What can a doctor do other than to tell me what we already know?"

"He'll offer advice as to what you should or shouldn't do to ensure you and the babe come to no harm." Arianna opened her mouth to argue, her husband eyed her sternly. "This is one battle you will not win, my love. I indulge you far too much as it is."

Something silent passed between the two, and Arianna blushed. When her sister didn't speak or protest, the viscount looked at Rhea with a wicked glint of mischief in his eyes. The man clearly knew he'd won the argument. Arianna blew out a breath of aggravation to which Blake simply raised an eyebrow. Frustrated, Arianna glared at her husband. Her reaction made both Rhea and the viscount laugh at his wife's disgruntled frown. With a small sound of disgust, Arianna reached for a piece of toast and buttered it as she cast looks of exasperation at her husband and sister.

The remainder of the meal was filled with laughter as Arianna's rebellious manner quickly evaporated, and the discussion focused on preparations for the baby. Blake mentioned his desire to see his old nurse come to care for the baby, and a haunted look darkened her sister's eyes. Arianna had hesitated at Blake's suggestion, but when she'd seen her husband's disappointment at her initial refusal, she quickly ended her protest. But when Arianna had made it clear she intended to be deeply involved in their child's upbringing, Blake had agreed. Despite his reassurance, it didn't extinguish the soft shimmer of pain in Arianna's eyes. Rhea knew her sister's anguish was because Arianna's daughter, Lucy, was growing up without her mother.

Breakfast finished, Blake left them to attend to several business matters, while Arianna and Rhea moved to the morning room. With her sister occupied with responding to daily correspondence, Rhea wrote a quick letter to their aunt then retrieved a book from the small library across the hall. Engrossed in her book, Rhea jumped as Arianna touched her arm more than an hour later.

"You have company." At her sister's words, Rhea's heart skipped a beat.

Percy. Anticipation spiraled through her and her mouth went dry. A second later, when Arianna said Colonel Dewhurst's name, the disappointment Rhea experienced made her stiffen. She knew it was inevitable Percy would arrive on her sister's doorstep, but she didn't like the fact that she found the prospect a pleasurable one. The man posed a danger to her loved ones, but an even greater danger to her sensibilities. As she met Arianna's gaze, she nodded her understanding and rose to her feet to greet her caller.

Colonel Dewhurst proved to be an entertaining visitor with the stories of his military service in Egypt. Rhea and Arianna were laughing heartily more than an hour later when Marston entered the room to announce Percy's arrival. Until she heard his name, Rhea hadn't realized how on edge she'd been anticipating his arrival. Every part of her grew rigid, and she wasn't sure if it was from alarm or anticipation. She refused to answer her own question as a mixture of emotions swept through her.

The delight she'd experienced earlier at the sound of his name had returned. It was a reckless emotion. Even her heart was pounding as if she'd run a long distance, and she berated herself for it. Percy Rockwood had come here to continue a conversation she had no intention of finishing. She'd said all she had to say on the subject of Ruckley and her past. But if there was one thing she'd already learned about Percy, it was his determination to have his own way.

Beside her on the sofa, Arianna grew still, and without thinking Rhea reached out to touch her sister's hand. Across from them, Colonel Dewhurst noted Arianna's consternation and Rhea's protective gesture. The man's eyebrows arched upward as he eyed her with curiosity and concern. Rhea forced a smile to her lips as her sister instructed Marston to show Percy into the room.

"As you can tell, my sister is a bit unsettled by Mr. Rockwood's arrival. The last time they saw each other there were unpleasantries exchanged." Rhea looked at Arianna as she squeezed her sister's hand again. "I've told her that Percy bears neither of us ill will."

"As if anyone could be unforgiving of you or the viscountess," Dewhurst said with a sympathetic smile.

Before she could reply, fire danced across her skin. She didn't need anyone to tell her that Percy had entered the room. Tension pulsated through her, and her heartbeat quickened to a frantic pace. It was disconcerting how easily his presence could throw her into a state of confusion simply by entering the room. A shiver skimmed down Rhea's spine as she rose to her feet and faced him.

Arianna made a small sound, and Rhea touched her sister's shoulder in a gesture of reassurance. Satisfied Arianna's composure was intact, she moved toward Percy with her hands outstretched in an effort to ensure Colonel Dewhurst's curiosity didn't deepen. She didn't know the colonel well enough to know whether he was prone to talking out of hand. While it was unlikely any gossip about her or Arianna would reach Ruckley's ears, she wasn't willing to risk the possibility.

"Percy, how lovely to see you." Her enthused greeting made him arch his eyebrows slightly before his sensual mouth quirked upward slightly.

"When your aunt told me where you were, I decided I'd have to call on you as soon as I arrived in town." His words made Rhea's heart skip a beat. She'd been right to think he would call at Green Hill House after the Melton Park affair.

In the light of day, he seemed even taller than she remembered. A knot formed in her throat the instant her gaze focused on his mouth. The memory of his kiss sent her heart skittering out of control. Almost as if he could read her mind, an unreadable emotion darkened his brown eyes. His gaze narrowed as he studied her with an intensity that only heightened the unexpected excitement suddenly streaking through her.

Amusement curved Percy's mouth upward slightly, and she swallowed hard as his smile broadened. It was obvious he was a man accustomed to convincing others to do his bidding before they realized what had happened. She refused to be one of those people. But Rhea was forced to admit that she could easily succumb to his persuasive manner if she didn't take care. With his height and penetrating gaze, the man projected a powerful strength that was as comforting as it was intimidating.

The instant Rhea placed her hands in his, an electric shock of awareness made every inch of her tingle. Shaken by her reaction, she drew in a sharp breath. Rhea tried to draw her hands free from his, but Percy tightened his grip. He bent his head to kiss her cheek as one might an old friend, and she barely managed to suppress the tremor threatening to sail through her.

"I can easily forgive your efforts to avoid me, when your sweet lips utter such a warm welcome," he murmured for her ears alone.

The sinfully husky note in his voice caused a vibration of something hot and enticing to slide across her skin. As he drew back from her, heat flushed her cheeks at the laughter she saw dancing in his eyes. It reminded her of the warmth and comfort of his embrace when he'd reassured her that he had no intention of turning her over to Scotland Yard. Flustered and fighting to control the sensations engulfing her, Rhea choked out a laugh.

"I'm glad you came. I'm having difficulty convincing Arianna that you're no longer put out with either of us. You must reassure her."

She bit down on her bottom lip as she heard how breathless she sounded. Percy studied her for a moment longer then slowly released her hands. His strong fingers gently gripping her elbow, he escorted her across the room to where Arianna stood. With a smile, he nodded at Rhea's sister as Arianna offered her hand to him.

"What Rhea says is true, my lady," he said quietly and kissed Arianna's hand. "I'm happy to say that all is well between us."

"I'm happy and relieved to hear you say so, Mr. Rockwood. I'm very pleased that we can put the past behind us." At Arianna's soft greeting, Percy smiled reassuringly at her sister, and Rhea saw her sister's anxiety ease slightly.

"As am I, my lady. My friendship with your husband would be in jeopardy if I allowed any discord to continue between us."

"Have you met Colonel Dewhurst?" Arianna gestured toward the other man in the room.

"I have. Dewhurst and I met at a museum benefit several months ago." Percy turned toward the man and nodded a polite greeting. Although his tone was pleasant, something about his manner made Rhea think he was far from happy to see the colonel. "His contributions to the Egyptian wing had just been put on display."

"After a rather lengthy and arduous authentication process," the colonel said with restrained acrimony as he rose from his seat and shook hands with Percy.

"I'm sorry to hear that," Percy murmured politely, but his manner indicated he was far from sympathetic.

"As was I," Dewhurst said with a distinct note of pique. "It seems there were questions as to the validity of my ownership."

"Whatever the questions, the artifacts are now on display for others to enjoy," Percy said with a small smile.

An awkward silence filled the air for a brief moment. In an effort to ease the tension that had taken root in the morning room, Arianna encouraged the two men to sit down.

Rhea returned to her seat next to her sister, and she darted a look in Percy's direction. He was watching her intently, and it was impossible to read the emotion she saw glittering in his eyes. In his chair a few feet away, Colonel Dewhurst cleared his throat.

"And how do you know these lovely ladies, Rockwood?"

Dewhurst smiled warmly at Arianna and Rhea.

"Lady Sherrington's husband and I have been friends since our days at Radley." Percy turned his head toward the colonel, his tone nonchalant. "Rhea and I have known each other slightly longer than my acquaintance with Lady Sherrington."

Percy leaned back in his chair in a relaxed manner, projecting the image of a man completely at ease. But Rhea could see the tension in his body. She was certain he wasn't happy to find the colonel here. Almost as if sensing her gaze on him, Percy turned to look at her with a wicked gleam in his eyes, while out of the corner of her eye, Rhea saw Dewhurst watching them with curiosity and assessment.

"Then you're more fortunate a man than I," the colonel said with a warm smile in Rhea's direction.

"*Quite* fortunate, I can assure you."

Percy's response implied his relationship with her was something far more personal than the troubled history they shared. Percy's gaze swung to her, and the wicked glint in his eyes slowly darkened. Immediately, her mouth went dry at the seductive gleam in his dark brown eyes. A taut web of tension hovered between them as everything in the room faded away and only Percy filled her senses. It was an unsettling sensation, and when the corners of his mouth tipped upward slightly, a slow fire rose to heat the skin beneath her cheeks. Her gaze flitted back to Colonel Dewhurst to see him watching her and Percy with suspicion. Her cheeks still burning, Rhea darted a glance at her sister who was staring at her with barely disguised horror.

"You mustn't let Percy mislead you. I'm certain he's found me to be little more than a thorn in his side for most of our...friendship." Rhea prayed the breathless note in her voice would go unnoticed, but one look at Percy said it had been quite noticeable.

"Despite Rhea's somewhat obstinate nature, Colonel,"

Percy said as he held her gaze. "I can say without a doubt that our friendship, as *she* refers to it, has been a delight."

Flustered by Percy's words, she jerked her gaze back to the colonel who was clearly disappointed at the implications Percy had made. Eager to end the awkward moment, Rhea smiled at the man and immediately sensed Percy's displeasure. The fact that she knew he was unhappy about her conciliatory manner with the colonel startled her. Even more surprising was the small part of her that took pleasure in knowing he didn't like her attention being focused on Dewhurst. At the man's almost hopeful look, she took pity on him.

"Colonel Dewhurst saved me from injury last night, Percy. If not for him, I would have fallen and quite possibly been trampled by the theater crowd. He was quite gallant in coming to my rescue." She smiled warmly at the colonel.

"Then I am in his debt for rescuing you," Percy said with a condescending smile in the colonel's direction. "Not only for his efforts in keeping you safe from harm, but for ensuring that our afternoon plans to visit the orphanage and have lunch with my sister need not be postponed."

"I don't—"

"Patience will no doubt be grateful for the colonel's efforts to keep you safe. She will also be delighted to see you in spite of your mishap."

The autocratic interruption made Rhea glare at him, but the moment their gazes locked, the air in her lungs disappeared. Something in his expression made her realize things had changed between them. The sudden memory of his reference to visiting her aunt made her grow cold. Had Aunt Beatrice told him about her efforts to rescue the children?

Dear God, had he met Vincent and Jack? Ginny? Worse, had he seen Lucy? Would he think her niece was her child? That she had even considered the possibility of such a question made her stomach lurch. Percy Rockwood had become a dominating figure in her affairs in less than forty-eight hours. Even more troubling was her desire that he not think ill of her because of her past. The sudden need for his approval horrified her. Fear closed her throat until she was struggling to breathe. When she remained silent, Percy leaned forward to pin his gaze on her. The look caused her heart to pound violently in her chest.

"As I've already promised, I will keep Patience's sisterly interrogations in check," he drawled with amusement, which belied the hard light of determination in his eyes.

Suddenly, Rhea realized it was a two-prong attack to get rid of the colonel. The mention of his sister suggested to Colonel Dewhurst that her relationship with Percy was far more serious than she'd initially indicated. It was a clean warning shot across the colonel's bow to ensure the man understood Rhea was otherwise engaged. Perhaps most disconcerting of all was the silent confirmation that Percy had no intention of letting her escape him or his questions. With one simple statement, Percy had eliminated the colonel as competition, while silently confirming he wouldn't let her escape him or his questions.

"You must forgive Percy, Colonel Dewhurst. His penchant for arrogance is only outweighed by his sometimes reckless behavior."

"Indeed," the colonel said with a smug smile as he looked at Percy. "Doesn't the Set refer to your family as the *reckless* Rockwoods?"

"They do. But there are few who dare to say it to me publicly." Percy said in a cool voice that once again took the wind out of Dewhurst's sails. The man blanched beneath Percy's cold look of censure, then cleared his throat.

"Forgive me, Rockwood. I meant no insult to you or your family." The man's apology sounded sincere but Rhea heard something else she couldn't decipher running beneath the colonel's words. Percy studied Dewhurst for a long moment before breaking the tense silence with a sharp nod.

The moment he put the colonel out of his misery, Percy turned to Arianna.

"The colonel's reference to my family reminds me that my sister-in-law, the Countess of Melton, sends her greetings." Percy's charming smile coaxed Arianna into returning his.

"That's most gracious of her ladyship."

"She also encouraged me to invite you, Blake, and Rhea to supper Friday night before the Earl of Hardwick's ball."

"That's very thoughtful of her—" Arianna was unable to complete her sentence as Percy interrupted her, his sensual mouth curving in a persuasive, determined smile.

"Then I'll be happy to tell her you're coming? Helen will be delighted," Percy said with quiet confidence. "She was quite taken with Rhea and your aunt at Melton Park the other night. She's eager to meet you as well."

Clearly surprised by the unexpected invitation, Arianna glanced in Rhea's direction. With a shake of her head, Rhea immediately rejected the idea. Ashford intended to bring the children to her aunt's small Mayfair townhouse Friday night. Their plans had been in place for more than a week. She refused to be attending a dinner when the children would need her reassuring presence.

"That's very kind of the countess," Rhea said. "But I'll be returning to the country Saturday morning and shall retire early."

Percy's mouth tightened, but he didn't argue with her. His gaze shifted to Arianna, and he arched his eyebrow imperiously. It was a look that dared her sister to refuse the invitation. The man hadn't even flinched when she'd refused his invitation on the behalf of this brother- and sister-in-law. He was up to something.

"Blake and I would be delighted to join the Earl and Countess for dinner on Friday," her sister said with a small smile.

"Excellent," Percy said with immense satisfaction. "We

dine at six."

"*Six*," Rhea exclaimed softly. At her surprise, a shadow darkened Percy's features. It was a look of deep sorrow, and she experienced the urge to reach out and comfort him. As his gaze met hers, Percy's expression became shuttered.

"Since losing my brother, and brother-in-law, more than a year ago, the family makes every effort to dine with the children whenever we can," Percy replied without emotion. "We have learned how fleeting life is, and we no longer take things for granted. It's actually the reason I was unable to attend your wedding, Lady Sherrington. The family was in Scotland for my nephew's birthday celebration."

"I understand completely, Mr. Rockwood. Family *is* everything." Sympathy softened her sister's features as she nodded in agreement and touched Rhea's hand in a gentle gesture of affection. As if suddenly aware the colonel had been shut out of the conversation for far longer than was polite, Arianna looked at the man. "Would you not agree, Colonel Dewhurst?"

"I do indeed, Lady Sherrington. My sister means the world to me. She's the only family I have."

The colonel bobbed his head in agreement, and Percy's gaze settled on the man as he studied him with narrowed eyes. His dislike of the colonel puzzled Rhea. With a sudden movement, Percy reached into his breast pocket and produced a pocket watch. He flipped open the lid to check the time then snapped the timepiece closed and looked at Rhea.

"It's almost noon, shall we?" The nonchalant arrogance in his voice made Rhea frown, but she reluctantly nodded her head in acquiescence. At her silent agreement, Colonel Dewhurst rose to his feet.

"I believe I've out-stayed my welcome, Lady Sherrington, Miss Bennett. Thank you for an enjoyable morning's conversation."

"It was kind of you to call, Colonel Dewhurst," Arianna

said as she rose to her feet. Rhea stood up as the colonel kissed her sister's hand.

"Let me walk you out," Rhea said with a smile.

The instant she spoke, she saw Percy scowl. His frown darkened as the colonel directed a smug look in Percy's direction. She didn't know whether to be amused or dismayed at Percy's obvious displeasure. With a smile at Dewhurst, she walked the man out of the morning room into the hallway. As Marston offered the colonel his hat, Rhea smiled.

"Thank you for calling on us this morning, Colonel. And thank you again for your kindness last night."

"It was my pleasure," he said with a cheerful look that faded into one of rueful contemplation. "I would ask if you would take a ride with me tomorrow afternoon, but it's obvious you are otherwise engaged."

For a brief second, Rhea stared at the man in puzzlement before she realized he was referring to Percy. She grimaced. Percy's earlier insinuations had been high-handed and unwelcome. But at the moment she was grateful for an excuse to avoid any entanglements. As much as she found the colonel's company quite pleasant, she had no wish to encourage him.

It would be unfair to do so considering she had no desire to pursue a romantic relationship with any man. A small voice in the back of her head scoffed at her. She silenced the intrusive thought with calculated precision. The question now was how to explain Percy's blatant suggestions that she was unavailable without backing herself into a corner and confirming his remarks. With the sigh, she shook her head.

"Mr. Rockwood and I have a...complex relationship."

It was a truthful statement. She knew full well she was on a slippery slope with Percy. Even if she'd had the inclination to do so, a relationship with Colonel Dewhurst would shift the balance of her precarious connection to Percy. For some unfathomable reason, she knew Percy wouldn't break his word, but another small part of her questioned why she had placed her trust in him. Colonel Dewhurst met her gaze with a fatalistic one then bobbed his head in comprehension.

"I understand. However, should the *complexities* of your current situation become more...*simplified*...I hope you will consider me a friend you can rely on." The sincerity in his voice made Rhea step forward to take his hand and squeeze it in gratitude.

"That is a generous offer, and I will not forget it if I should have need of a friend."

With a wistful contemplation in his gaze, Dewhurst kissed her hand and walked out of the house. Rhea closed the front door behind him and pressed her brow against the warm wood. When had her plan to rescue the children and retire to the country changed so dramatically? The sound of voices echoed into the main entryway, and she turned to see Percy and Arianna emerge from the morning room. Although her sister's demeanor still held a trace amount of trepidation, Percy had managed to make her laugh. It was a sound that made Rhea feel indebted to him. Percy had obviously recognized Arianna's wariness where he was concerned. As a result, it appeared he'd made a concerted effort to ease her sister's fears and succeeded. As the two of them stopped in front of her, Percy met Rhea's gaze.

"Your sister tells me you enjoy riding, Rhea." Assessment and curiosity crossed his handsome features, and she bit down on her bottom lip. She needed to warn Arianna that she would have to be less forthcoming with the man. Percy Rockwood clearly had a talent for making people reveal their secrets. She'd already fallen into that trap herself.

"I did as a child," she said crisply.

"Then it's time you did so again. Why not join me tomorrow morning for a ride in the park. If Blake doesn't have a suitable mount, then I'll arrange for one to be at the doorstep."

A stark memory of Bluebell galloping hard across the fields with her clinging to the small mare as tears streamed down her face filled her head. It had been the last time she'd ridden. A day later Bluebell had been sold. Rhea was certain her father had deliberately sold the horse. There had been a number of horses in the stables at the time, but her father had chosen Bluebell. The painful memory made her flinch. As her gaze met Percy's penetrating one, Rhea didn't avert her eyes and forced herself to maintain a serene countenance.

"Thank you, but I must decline. I haven't ridden in a very long time, and I doubt my skills will allow me to ride even tolerably well."

"You underestimate yourself, Rhea. If I recall, you also said you weren't a very good dancer, and we both know that's not the case."

The gentle note in his voice made Rhea stiffen. What was it about this man that made her feel as though she could go to him with a problem, and he'd find a way to solve it for her? She quickly cast the thought aside. She might trust him not to betray her, but it was a narrow ledge she was on when it came to relying on Percy Rockwood.

With a shake of her head, she silently refused his invitation. It was bad enough he'd coerced her into the luncheon appointment with his sister. Heaven knew why he would feel the need for her to meet the woman. She could only assume Percy's obvious antipathy for Colonel Dewhurst had been the driving force behind his subterfuge.

"I believe you indicated earlier that we have an appointment?"

At the accusatorial note in her voice he nodded without any sign of remorse for his coercive methods. The smile curving his lips made her grit her teeth. Confidence was the one thing Percy Rockwood possessed in abundance.

"I did. If you're ready?"

"I simply need to retrieve my hat," she bit out crisply.

His smile became a charming grin, which made some of her irritation disappear. On the verge of smiling back, Rhea quickly turned away and hurried upstairs to fetch her hat. She'd known from the moment she'd seen Percy in the ballroom at Melton Park that he would be trouble. She'd been right. But the question now was exactly what *kind* of trouble. The answer that flitted through her mind wasn't one she wanted to consider.

Chapter 5

"Percy Rockwood, where have you been? You were supposed to have been here almost an hour ago." Patience's voice stressed her irritation as she walked into the small entryway of the orphanage.

Her head bent over the sleeve of her gown, his sister didn't bother to look up as she scolded him. The fingers of Patience's scarred hand fumbled as she worked to adjust the cuff of her sleeve. As Percy took in his sister's efforts to straighten the material around her wrist, he clenched his jaw.

He was taking a huge risk bringing Rhea here without warning Patience or for that matter without Rhea knowing about his sister's terrible scars. But he was counting on the fact that his sister was stronger than she believed. He was also placing a great deal of faith in the *an dara sealladh*. In his visions, Rhea had exhibited a kind, generous, and protective nature.

There was also his visit to Green Hill House that reinforced his impression of Rhea's good heart. He'd been greeted at the door by two boys whom Mrs. Fremont had stated Rhea had taken in as her own after finding them on the streets. Although Beatrice Fremont had made it sound as if Rhea had simply stumbled across the boys' plight, Percy had no doubt the children were refugees from Ruckley's gang of pickpockets.

But it was the more recent information he'd gleaned from Beatrice Fremont that had sealed his belief in Rhea's compassionate nature. The risks Rhea was taking to free children from Ruckley's gang made him admire her, while at the same time wanting to issue a severe admonishment for the fool-hardiness of her venture. He'd considered questioning her on the ride to the orphanage, but had decided against it given the chilly atmosphere in the carriage. All of it made him willing to wager Rhea would not be repulsed by Patience's scars. The moment his sister looked up, she came to an abrupt halt. Panic flashed in her soft brown eyes as her mouth formed an O of alarmed surprise. Cold anger quickly replaced his sister's look of horror as she held his gaze for a long moment.

Tension hung thick and heavy in the silence that filled the entryway. Damnation, he should have thought twice about his spur-of-the-moment decision. The entire family had been gently encouraging Patience to go out in public more, but she still balked at most outings. He'd been far more persistent than the rest of the family in his efforts to make his sister meet the world head on. The lot of them wouldn't be happy with him for pushing the issue as he was doing at this moment. Even Julian had not been quite as unrelenting as he had at insisting Patience confront her fears.

Patience's decision to spend time in White Willow House whenever she and Julian were in London had been viewed by the family as a major step forward. Her willingness to work in the family-sponsored orphanage had made the Rockwood clan optimistic that she was finally beginning to overcome her fear of being seen in public. Now as he met her gaze, he realized he might have made a monumental mistake. Julian was going to have his head for upsetting his wife. Percy cleared his throat to swallow the knot of shame pressing against his Adam's apple as he stared at his outraged sister who was skillfully hiding her aversion to meeting a stranger.

"I was delayed as it was necessary for me to stop and collect Miss Bennett." His quiet words made his sister's gaze flit to Rhea standing beside him. "Rhea, this is my sister, Lady Patience. Patience, may I present Miss Rhea Bennett."

"Miss Bennett," Patience said in a polite, stilted voice.

His sister nodded sharply in Rhea's direction while turning her head so her scarred profile was covered by the shadows of the dimly lit hallway. Her anger had disappeared beneath the frozen, shuttered mask she wore whenever she was in the company of strangers.

"Lady Patience," Rhea nodded her head in greeting then scowled up at him. "It's obvious my presence is unexpected. Clearly, your brother is in the habit of making decisions *and* appointments without consulting the affected parties. I apologize for any inconvenience my presence may cause."

The censure in Rhea's clipped statement made Percy start with surprise. He'd expected Patience to be furious with him, but Rhea's voice held a far healthier note of scorn. He looked down to meet her look of contempt and winced. He should have known from the icy silence in the carriage ride to the orphanage that charming his way into Rhea's good graces wouldn't be easy. But something about Rhea's demeanor suggested she was angry at having been party to upsetting his sister. He bit down on the inside of his cheek. Percy's gaze shifted to Patience, and he saw a look of surprise on her unmarred profile.

"Recklessness is a family trait, but my brother appears to have inherited a *larger* portion than the rest of us."

His sister's sharp words of chastisement were bad enough, but it was the look she directed at him that stung. It was clear Patience believed his actions were a form of betrayal. Not since he was a boy of six when Sebastian had caught him dumping a bucket of water on Constance had Percy felt so remorseful. The last thing in the world he would ever think to do was cause injury to any of his family. But Patience had always held a special place in his heart. She'd always looked up to him, and it was the first time he could remember ever having disappointing her with his behavior. He cleared his throat and swallowed the shame that was a knot lodged in his throat.

"I should have sent word that I was bringing a guest, Patience. I ask your forgiveness."

Percy's quiet apology made his sister narrow her gaze at him. Despite the anger tightening her mouth into a frown of displeasure, Patience's brown eyes softened slightly at his visible remorse. She nodded sharply.

"Forgiven." Patience's gaze moved back to Rhea, and he saw his sister's throat bob with what he knew was trepidation. "Since you were late, I ordered Mrs. Hughes to set our meal aside as the children have already eaten. It's a simple meal, Miss Bennett. I hope you don't mind."

"I prefer simplicity," Rhea said.

With a nod, Patience gestured for the two of them to follow her down the hallway. Rhea didn't look up at Percy, and he released a small noise of disgust. He'd bungled things badly with both women. Especially Rhea. Patience would not remain put out with him for long as she was family and loved him. Rhea, on the other hand, didn't take well to coercion, and yet he'd done just that. The original intent of his visit to Sherrington House had been to gain Rhea's trust. He knew her help was critical when it came to finding Ruckley. But he had to convince her that he would see to it that the man wouldn't harm her.

The worst of it was he'd forced Rhea's hand not because of his desire to find Ruckley, but because of Dewhurst. He didn't like the man. The colonel was a womanizer and a social climber. Even more troubling was that his dislike of the man couldn't account for the fury he'd experienced the moment he'd walked into the viscountess's salon. The sensation that had swept over him had been territorial in nature. It had dug into him with the ferocity of an eagle's talons the minute he'd seen Dewhurst. Rhea's warm greeting had only strengthened the possessive sensation. In that split second, he'd realized he didn't want Dewhurst anywhere near Rhea.

Percy gritted his teeth as he looked down and met her scornful gaze. His desire to convince Rhea he could be trusted had been made all the harder simply because he'd allowed Dewhurst to get under his skin. A mocking laugh filled his head as he was forced to admit his reaction would have been the same no matter who the man was. In silence, Percy gestured for them to follow Patience, and his fingers cupped her bare elbow. Her skin was soft against his fingers, and he wondered if the rest of her was as warm and silky. The tactile sensation made him want to find out for certain.

The thought tightened his muscles with anticipation, and his heart slammed into his chest with the strength of a sledge hammer as desire surged through his blood. Quickly jerking his hand away from her. Christ Jesus, what the hell was wrong with him? He was acting like a school boy blinded by the smell of a woman. And she smelled delicious. Her scent was that of honey and lemons. Without thinking, he turned his head slightly to breathe in the soft fragrance of Rhea's hair.

The sweet aroma had barely grazed his nostrils when the *an dara sealladh* overwhelmed his senses. He stumbled sideways and managed to brace himself against the wall. The strength of the vision dragged him downward into a whirlpool of darkness. When the light appeared it blinded him for a moment before he was able to see a small group of children surrounding Rhea. Several appeared to be the same age as his nephew, Charlie, who would be six in a few months.

The images shifted quickly to Rhea retching into a small basin. Another picture flashed in front of him. It was Rhea struggling with the same pock-marked man he'd seen before. The images blinked into oblivion as quickly as they'd come. As if coming up out of dark waters with no air left in his lungs, Percy dragged in a deep breath. Sweet Jesus. He would kill Ruckley for touching Rhea. He sucked in another harsh breath as the images from his vision played over again in his head. Slowly his breathing became less desperate as the *an dara sealladh* released its grip on him. Almost as if she'd sensed his distress, Patience glanced over her shoulder, and her eyes widened with alarm.

"*Percy.*" The moment his sister cried out his name, Rhea whirled around. Violet eyes reflecting her dismay, Rhea was at his side in two quick steps. Patience was only a short distance behind her.

"You're ill," Rhea exclaimed softly. "You look like death warmed over."

"It's a headache. I'm fine," he said as his head began to pound. It wasn't often that his visions caused him a headache, but when they did, they were severe. Fortunately, they never lasted long.

"Liar," she muttered as Patience reached them.

"Miss Bennett, if you would, please help me get him into the dining room. He gets these unexpected headaches from time to time."

"Leave me be. *Both* of you," he growled in frustration at their mothering behavior. "It's just a headache."

"A bad one from the looks of you," Rhea snapped. "You need to sit down before you fall down. So *stop* arguing and let us help you."

"I agree with Miss Bennett, Percy," his sister's voice echoed with exasperation. "We need to get you to a chair."

"I can manage to find my way to the dining room on my own power," he muttered as the sound of their voices intensified the pounding in his head. With a wave of his hand, he directed both women to move forward.

Despite her worried look, Patience slowly nodded. As his sister turned away and continued down the hall, beside him, Rhea made a sound of annoyance. When she didn't move, he glared down at her and saw a dark frown of aggravation furrowing her lovely brow.

"How do you propose we lift you up off the floor if you faint?" The glare she directed at him made his lips twist in a slight smile.

"I imagine you'll have to leave me where I drop," he grunted. One hand still braced against the corridor's wall, he slowly began to make his way to the dining room.

"Stubborn man."

He barely heard her retort, but it tugged another pained smile to his lips. Upon entering the dining room, the table with its two place settings was a reminder that his sister had been expecting only him for the meal. He grimaced as Patience disappeared into the kitchen. Despite the throbbing in his head, he pulled out a chair at the table and politely gestured for Rhea to take a seat. She released a sound of disgust and nodded at the chair.

"Oh, *do* sit down before you collapse, Percy." Despite the harsh sounding words, there was a soft note of concern in her voice. Her full lips thinned with exasperation, she moved to the opposite side of the table. She sat down and scowled at him. The headache had drained him of energy, and he sank into the chair he'd pulled out for Rhea. The tension of her mouth eased slightly, and relief swept across her face. The fact that she'd been worried about him sent an unusually large amount of pleasure sailing through him. Violet eyes narrowed, Rhea studied him for a moment.

"Why did you bring me here if you were feeling unwell?"

"I was feeling perfectly fine. I have these headaches unexpectedly from time to time."

"And you have no warning at all when you're about to have one?"

"No." It was the truth. He never had any idea when the *an dara sealladh* would rear its head, or whether it would leave a painful reminder of its presence.

"And you accuse *me* of brevity."

The mockery in her voice made him grit his teeth. The consequence was another jolt of pain. A frown furrowed her forehead, but anything she was about to say was preempted by Patience.

"Mrs. Hughes will bring our meal in momentarily." His sister set a plate and flatware in front of him and eyed him carefully. The curiosity in her brown eyes said she knew the *an dara sealladh* was the reason for his sudden headache. "You still look a bit pale, Percy."

"I'm fine," he bit out. "The pain is already beginning to dissipate."

"As Miss Bennett has already pointed out—*liar.*"

Clearly annoyed with him, Patience's sympathy for his discomfort vanished as she sat down at the head of the table. Seated between him and Rhea, his sister's scarred profile was fully exposed to him, while Rhea only had glimpses of Patience's burnt flesh. With a clarity that startled him, Percy realized Rhea had deliberately refused his chair to save his sister any emotional distress. He wasn't sure if his conclusion was based on what the *an dara sealladh* had shown him or his growing understanding of the woman Rhea was. The only thing that mattered was her kindness. It warmed his heart that she would be so thoughtful where Patience was concerned.

"I hope you like mutton stew, Miss Bennett."

"I do," Rhea replied with a smile that vanished almost before it tilted her lips. It was like watching the sun suddenly blotted out behind a dark cloud. "I've not had it since... my mother died."

Although he was certain she'd been about to say something else, the pain in her voice twisted his gut. It made him want to leap to his feet, charge around the table, and scoop her up into his arms. It was a primal urge, and for not the first time, he found it impossible to understand his reaction. In a gesture of sympathy, Patience reached out to touch the back of Rhea's hand.

"It's obvious you miss her a great deal." Patience's voice was soothing as she shook her head with understanding.

"Yes, very much," Rhea said softly.

"I think you are most fortunate. I don't remember my mother."

Whether it was their mutual loss of a mother or Rhea's lack of curiosity about Patience's scars, his sister seemed to warm to Rhea. They exchanged a few more pleasantries before their conversation was forestalled by Mrs. Hughes entering the dining room. The cook carried a steaming bowl of stew, while behind her was a boy Percy hadn't seen in the orphanage before. Tall and lanky, he carried a basket of bread and a crock of butter. As Mrs. Hughes walked around the table, the boy came into Rhea's line of sight. The instant Rhea saw him, she stiffened, but other than a flash of emotion in her violet gaze, there was no sign she recognized the boy.

"Don't just stand there, Edgar, set the bread in front of Mr. Rockwood, and get back to the kitchen. You have potatoes to scrub for supper," Mrs. Hughes scolded. The cook made a clucking noise with her tongue as she looked at the boy.

Edgar quickly obeyed the cook's order and placed the basket of warm bread in front of Percy. A quick glance in the boy's direction revealed the lad was staring at Rhea with cold calculation. Rhea reached for a piece of bread and began to butter it as if she were completely unaware of the boy. Percy met her gaze across the table, and she arched an eyebrow at him in a quizzical fashion. He frowned in puzzlement as she dropped her gaze to stare at the plate Mrs. Hughes had filled with hot stew. Edgar hadn't moved since setting the bread on the table, and as Percy glanced at the boy, he saw Edgar still studying Rhea. Percy coughed softly.

"That will be all, Edgar."

At the quiet dismissal, the boy jerked his head toward Percy. There was something insolent in the lad's expression, and Percy narrowed his eyes as he met the boy's defiant gaze. Immediately, Edgar's impertinent look changed to a sulky one. Eyes glittering with rebellion, the boy looked at Rhea one last time and left the room. Mrs. Hughes filled Percy's plate with a healthy portion of stew then set the bowl on the table.

"Edgar is a new stray," Percy murmured as he carefully watched Rhea, but she didn't react to his statement.

"He came to us two weeks ago," his sister said with a weary sigh. "I don't think he's taking well to the rules we have here in White Willow House. Wouldn't you agree, Mrs. Hughes?"

"I'm afraid you're right, Lady Patience. The lad is one for mischief. However, he is extremely good with the younger boys. He already has a number of them following him around like lost puppies." At Mrs. Hughes' words, Rhea coughed, and he could have sworn it was to cover a small cry. As if she'd read his thoughts, she lifted her head, but quickly averted her gaze.

"How did he come to the orphanage?" Percy asked as he looked at his sister.

"He simply showed up at the back door asking for something to eat," Patience said with a small shrug. "Mrs. Hughes fed him, and we offered him a place to stay with the understanding he needed to work if he wished to remain."

"Which is something I should see the boy is doing," the cook muttered as she turned to leave the dining room. Prompted by an inexplicable sense of foreboding, Percy acted on his instincts.

"If you don't mind, Mrs. Hughes, I'd like to speak with Edgar after lunch. I have need of a messenger from time to time. He might be of use to me. That is if you don't mind me stealing the lad out from under your nose." Percy smiled and winked at the older woman whose cheeks flushed with sudden color.

"Of course not, Mr. Rockwood. I'll send Edgar in when you've finished your meal."

"Thank you, Mrs. Hughes, that's most kind of you. I can see why Lady Melton and my sisters speak so highly of you."

"I'm happy to help," the cook said as her blush became even more visible, and she scurried from the room. Patience laid down her spoon to study him with astonishment.

"Since when do you have need of an errand boy?" his sister asked with a skeptical frown.

"I often have need of one when I'm working with Budge at the museum," he lied unwilling to explain he simply needed to reassure himself the boy had no connection with Rhea or Ruckley

Percy ignored his sister's snort of disbelief and took a bite of his stew. His headache was little more than a slight twinge now, and he was pleased he could eat his meal without his stomach threatening to rebel. Surreptitiously, he watched Rhea as she conversed politely with Patience. When she looked at him a second later, his muscles knotted and hardened with tension. Until now, he'd never seen such an exceptional performance of emotional control.

Even Sebastian would have been hard pressed to match the way Rhea had veiled her horror. Despite her outward appearance of calm serenity, the dark emotions shimmering in her eyes indicated she was in a state of panic. Her fear only strengthened his belief that Rhea was acquainted with Edgar. With a grimace, he realized he'd made the right decision to meet with the boy. Instinctively he knew Rhea had done everything she could to keep Ruckley from finding her.

Whatever he did, he needed to ensure the boy didn't tell anyone he'd seen Rhea in the orphanage. Somehow, he thought convincing Edgar to remain silent would be easier said than done. Edgar's attitude had been one of insolence for authority, which meant it would be difficult to ensure the boy didn't betray Rhea's whereabouts for the sake of a few coins. Percy had barely finished his second spoonful of the beef dish when Mrs. Hughes reentered the room.

"I'm terribly sorry, Mr. Rockwood, but Edgar is gone."

"*Gone*," Patience exclaimed in surprise.

"Yes, my lady. Robbie told me the boy ran out to the mews and didn't come back."

"How odd," his sister said with a frown as she contemplated the boy's behavior. Percy quickly directed his attention to Rhea, and the look of sheer terror that slipped through her serene expression made him bite back the dark curse that almost passed his lips.

"You did say he was having trouble adjusting to life in the orphanage," Percy said quietly.

"Yes, but I didn't think it was quite that bad." Patience nodded as her frown deepened and she sighed. "Hopefully he'll return. I hate to think of him on the streets, but there's little we can do unless he comes back. Thank you, Mrs. Hughes."

The cook nodded and retreated to the kitchen. Still frowning, Patience released a soft sigh of resignation before turning her head toward Rhea. It didn't escape his notice that Patience turned her head only just enough to avoid exposing her scarred features to Rhea. Even though the two women appeared to be comfortable in each other's company, Patience still exhibited her reticence to trust people she didn't know. He clenched his jaw. The fire at Westbrook farms had taken more than two well-loved members of their family.

In some ways they'd lost Patience as well. His sister had possessed a cheerful, outgoing nature before the fire, but her physical and emotional scars still plagued her more than a year later. And all of it because of a log that rolled out of the fireplace, crashed through the fire screen, and set the main parlor's carpet on fire. It had been a terrible, unfortunate accident that had left all of them struggling with grief.

"I'm sorry we didn't meet the other night at Melton Park, Miss Bennett," Patience said with a small smile. "I understand you became ill and left early."

"Yes... I... I'm not fond of large social affairs."

"I quite understand." Patience nodded as she shot a

glance in his direction. "I avoid them as well, *particularly* when I'm in London."

Percy frowned at his sister's comment. It was a subtle reminder of Patience's refusal to attend Sebastian fortieth birthday celebration in little more than a week. The birthday party the other night at Melton Park had been for friends and neighbors in the country. It had been an enormous feat to convince Patience to attend that social event. Her acquiescence had only been because the guests were people she knew from childhood.

The upcoming party was for friends and acquaintances who resided in town. If bringing Rhea to the orphanage resulted in Patience digging in her heels even more than she already had when it came to attending the upcoming celebration, he was doomed. It wouldn't just be Julian who would have his head. He would be severely censured by the rest of the family. Even Helen would be upset with him, and his sister-in-law's gentle spirit rarely saw her angry. The thought wasn't a pleasant one. Out of the corner of his eye, he saw Patience look at Rhea before she turned her head to meet his gaze.

"So tell me, how did the two of you meet?" There was a gleam of curiosity in his sister's eyes Percy recognized all too well. Patience sensed a mystery to solve, which meant he needed to quickly put an end to her prying.

"Rhea's sister is Viscountess Sherrington."

"Blake's new bride?" Patience looked at him with surprise then focused her attention on Rhea. With a sudden smile, his sister shook her head. "Why that almost makes you *part of the family*. Blake always came home with Percy on holiday while the two of them were at Radley. It was as if I had one more big brother to hound me."

"My sister is exceedingly fortunate to have found a husband…who loves her as much as Blake does."

As she stumbled over her words, Percy knew she'd been

on the verge of saying Blake had overlooked Lady Sherrington's history. Once more he reminded himself that Ruckley had a great deal to pay for. Unable to help himself, Percy wondered how much Blake knew about his wife's past. He watched Rhea take another bite of food before she looked at his sister.

"This mutton stew is quite delicious. Do you think Mrs. Hughes could be persuaded to part with her recipe?"

"Of course, I'm certain I can convince her to reveal her secret," Patience replied with a warmth that surprised Percy.

The remainder of the meal was spent in polite conversation, and while Rhea maintained her serene appearance, he could tell she found it an effort to do so. When they'd finished their meal, Percy managed to quickly arrange for his and Rhea's departure. To his surprise, Patience walked them to the front door of the orphanage.

"Despite Percy's failure to tell me you would be accompanying him for lunch, Miss Bennett, I'm delighted to have met you."

"Thank you. It was a pleasure to meet you as well," Rhea said with a reticent smile that the Sebastian of his youth would have approved of wholeheartedly.

Patience, her brow furrowed in puzzlement, sent him a curious look. Percy grimaced and bit back a groan. Despite his efforts, the gleam of determination in his sister's brown eyes, said there was an inquisition in his future.

"It's obvious my brother thinks highly of you," Patience said as she reached out to touch Percy's arm in a gesture of affection. Rhea's cheeks fired with pink color under his sister's approving smile. "I would like very much to further our acquaintance. You must come to dinner Saturday night at Melton House."

"I doubt you'll be able to convince her to do so," Percy murmured with irritation as he recalled his lack of success in convincing Rhea to dine at the family's London seat Friday night.

Surprise widened Patience's gaze as she looked up at him. He suppressed another groan. He'd spoken too hastily. Now his sister would be certain to think his interest in Rhea was something other than his effort to bring Ruckley to justice. In the deep recesses of his mind derisive laughter mocked him. He ignored the sound.

"Is this true, Miss Bennett? Has Percy finally met a woman he can't bend to his will?"

"I do seem to frustrate him on a consistent basis." A touch of amusement curved Rhea's lips. It eased the tension of her mouth and softened it.

"Then I *insist* you come to dinner."

Patience smiled with a glee he'd not seen in more than a year. That he was the cause of her amusement rankled slightly, but it was a price he was happy to pay to see his sister cast off her frozen shell with someone she barely knew. Beside him Rhea appeared ready to decline Patience's invitation. A streak of devilment passed through him.

"You're wasting your time, Patience. She's already turned down Helen's invitation for dinner this Friday," he murmured. Satisfaction made him bite back a grin as anger sparked in Rhea's beautiful eyes. She shook her head.

"As I've already explained, I am leaving for the country early Saturday morning," Rhea said emphatically.

"Then if you won't come this weekend, you must come to Melton House this evening." Patience's dogged determination was a familiar one, and Percy bit back a smile as he watched Rhea try to avoid accepting his sister's dinner invitation. If Rhea knew Patience as well as he did, she would have simply accepted without a word of protest. His sister seldom to no for an answer.

"I couldn't simply appear without the Countess's invitation."

"Nonsense. Whenever any of the family is in town, we

always make it a point to have dinner together at Melton House." Patience's smile faltered slightly, and he knew she was remembering why the family spent so much time together. It was a momentary hesitation on her part as her smile brightened. "Helen and Sebastian are accustomed to someone unexpected joining us for dinner."

"But I—"

"Surely you must eat supper, Miss Bennett. Meals at Melton House are very informal and early enough that even our elderly guests find it difficult to decline making appearance."

"It's quite kind of you—"

"Then you'll come," Patience exclaimed with satisfaction.

"But I—"

"No more protests, Miss Bennett," Patience said with a laugh. "You've agreed to come. Percy shall pick you up in plenty of time."

"But I—"

"You won't win, Rhea," Percy said quietly as he met her frustrated gaze. "Patience is far more stubborn than I am. I rarely bet against her."

"My brother is correct, Miss Bennett. I expect to see you this evening around five-thirty as dinner is at six," Patience said confidently. With a frustrated twist of her lips, Rhea accepted defeat and nodded.

"Very well." At her reluctant acceptance, triumph surged through Percy. The sensation died quickly the instant Rhea scowled at him, and he immediately questioned whether she would actually come to Melton House for dinner this evening. With a frown, he kissed his sister goodbye. When the two women had exchanged their farewells, Percy escorted Rhea out of the orphanage to their waiting carriage.

With Rhea situated inside the vehicle, he instructed the driver to take them to Hyde Park. Short of riding around the city in the carriage, the only way he could talk with her without too many interruptions was if they walked along the Serpentine. It was also his best option to prevent Rhea from escaping his company. And if he was to gain her trust, he needed time to convince her that he was trustworthy. She frowned as he climbed into the carriage and closed the door behind him.

"Why are we—"

"The boy—he recognized you." His interruption made the color drain from her cheeks. The minute she appeared on the verge of refuting his statement he shook his head. "Don't try to deny it Rhea. You've been on tenterhooks since you first saw the boy."

Stark fear made Rhea's violet eyes become a deep, dark purple. Percy frowned as he waited for her reply. Resignation twisted her lovely mouth as she shook her head.

"I don't deny knowing Edgar."

"I take that to mean the boy is a member of Ruckley's band of thieves," Percy said with confidence, but still seeking confirmation of his assumption.

"Yes, and he'll not hesitate to tell Ruckley he's seen me *and* where."

"Then you won't return to White Willow House until the man has been dealt with."

"Whether I return or not is irrelevant. Ruckley now has a way to find me," Rhea said with a world-weary resignation that startled him.

"And so you're simply going to give up?"

"I am *not* giving up," she snapped bitterly. "But thanks to you, my options have become severely limited. I told you not to interfere, but you refused to listen."

"Even if I'd heeded your warning, neither of us could have foreseen Edgar being at White Willow House today." The irony of his words caused Percy to grow tense. The suggestion that it was impossible to foresee things wasn't quite accurate. If Rhea were to learn of his ability. She might easily view his gift of sight as a way for him to peer into the dark recesses of her past—even her thoughts. The idea nipped at him like a dog worrying an old shoe. Rhea slowly turned her head to look at him.

"You'll need to hire several men to guard the children, Mrs. Hughes, and anyone else in the orphanage," she said softly.

"Bloody hell," Percy exclaimed under his breath.

He'd been so focused on Rhea and her situation that he'd failed to consider the ramifications to anyone else. With a hard knock on the carriage ceiling he ordered the driver to take them to Sherrington House. Her startled reaction to his order tugged a grim smile to Percy's lips.

"The Rockwoods might be known for their reckless behavior, but we're also known to act quickly when circumstances call for it," he said firmly. "I've no intention of giving Ruckley unfettered access to the children at White Willow House, and I refuse to let the man come anywhere near my family *or* you."

Rhea didn't respond. She simply turned her head to look out at the passing scenery. Percy studied her in silence as he debated how to gain her trust. The anguish and fear shadowing her features made him lean forward to take her hand in his.

"Let me help you, Rhea."

"You can't," she said without looking at him.

"I think what you really mean is that you won't let me," he said with frustration at her obstinate refusal. The sharp tenor of his words made her jerk her head toward him. In a vicious twist of her hand, she yanked free of his grasp.

"What makes you think you could *possibly* help me," she said bitterly. "Ruckley *will* find me, and he has the means to make me do what I've always refused to do where he was concerned."

"What will he make you do?" Percy shook his head in bewilderment.

"He wants to see me grovel," Rhea whispered as she closed her eyes. The anger in her voice had become one of defeat and disillusionment. "And I've never begged him for anything. I fought him. I defied him. I could make him see the advantage of doing one thing when he was about to do something else. But *not once* did I ever plead with him. All of that's changed now."

"How has it changed?" Percy asked quietly. She opened her eyes to look out of the window.

"Because I'll do just that. I'll beg," she choked out, and he was certain she was holding back tears. "If I don't, he'll…he'll do terrible things to the people I love."

"Then let me help you."

"I don't *need* any more of your help," Rhea said fiercely. She jerked her gaze back to his, the full force of her anger darkening her eyes until they were a dark, purplish hue of fury and fear. "After all, with me as bait, your goal of finding that bastard just became much easier."

The vicious accusation made Percy straighten up in his seat to stare at her in cold silence. Even though he knew her words were rooted in fear, they still stung. He would never use her as bait. The idea that she'd even considered the possibility made him realize why it was difficult for her to trust him. She'd been right in stating he'd not believed her where Ruckley was concerned. He'd believed she'd been giving the man too much credit. A sudden flush of color filled Rhea's pale cheeks, and she bent her head in obvious remorse.

"I'm sorry. You didn't deserve that. You could have handed me over to the magistrate the other night, and you didn't," she said softly. "As you said, neither of us had any idea Edgar would be at the orphanage."

"And perhaps I've been too hasty in dismissing your warning about Ruckley," he said quietly. "Tell me why Edgar would be at the orphanage to begin with. He's clearly old enough to be on his own.

"Edgar is working to fill Ruckley's rank-and-file."

"Explain," he bit out with concern.

"Edgar finds vulnerable children, gains their trust, and makes them believe life with Ruckley will be better than the life they currently lead." Rhea's gaze was cast downward to where her fingers picked at the silk of her dress. "But the minute Edgar tells Ruckley he saw me at White Willow House the man will do what he can to find out where I am. He's capable of anything when it comes to getting what he wants."

The air of hopelessness about her caused a knot of anger to form in his abdomen. Rhea was a fighter. She'd proven that to him in a relatively short time. But the defeat reflected in her demeanor troubled him. How could he make her understand she was no longer alone when it came to the threat Ruckley posed?

"Rhea, I promise I'll protect you."

"*Don't.*" Rhea jerked her head up. "*Don't* make promises you can't keep."

"My word is of great value to me. I do not give it lightly."

"Perhaps, but I think you're apt to find you've miscalculated the situation badly."

"A challenge," he said with a small smile. "As my sister and I have said, my family has more than a passing acquaintance with accepting challenges. We excel at beating the odds."

Rhea stared at him in the silence for a moment then shook her head and turned away from him once more. The desire to reassure her surged through him. Percy leaned forward and caught her hand in his again.

"Rhea, trust me." At his words, she shuddered. The vibration of her trembling passed its way into his hands, and he fought the urge to gather her into his arms. A closed, shuttered look on her face, she eyed him with something close to antipathy.

"Why?" she asked in a voice devoid of emotion. "Why should I trust you?"

It was a valid question, and he wasn't sure how to answer her. What possible reason could he offer her as to why she could trust him?

"There is no reason at all for you to do," he said with quiet patience. "Just call it a leap of faith."

As her gaze met his, he silently urged her to believe he only had her best interests at heart. Something flickered in her violet gaze, and he suddenly realized how important it was to him that she believe he was sincere in his desire to help her— to have her trust him. In the back of his head bells clanged a wild warning cry. He quickly silenced the alarm. His interest in Rhea was to help her and to right an injustice, nothing more. Instinctively he knew it was a lie, but he wasn't willing to examine his true motives. At this moment the only thing that mattered was seeing Ruckley destroyed and Rhea safe.

Chapter 6

The warmth of Percy's hands sent heat pulsing its way through Rhea's skin. She didn't understand why his touch invoked such a sensation. Nothing about him or their odd association made any sense at all. He was asking her to take a leap of faith where he was concerned. She'd already done that to some extent.

What he asked of her now was to go one step further. The brown eyes studying her reflected a warm sincerity Rhea found compelling. With each passing second, her ability to refuse his request became more difficult. She'd told Arianna she trusted Percy. So why was it so hard to take the last step and admit it to him as well?

"Is taking that leap so hard?" he asked quietly. The gentleness in his voice struck at the very core of her. It created a tiny fracture in the wall of ice she'd built around every part her heart and soul.

"Yes," she swallowed the unexpected knot forming in her throat. "When you are accustomed to the worst life offers, the idea of something good happening is an almost unbearable thought."

"Ruckley has a great deal to answer for," Percy said grimly.

"And you continue to overestimate your ability to make him pay for all the things he's done."

"You seem determined to challenge me to prove you wrong," he said with a slight twist of his sensual mouth.

"I am not encouraging you to do any such thing," she snapped. "I am simply pointing out the reality of the situation."

"Yet you insist on ignoring that fact yourself." The stern note in his voice made her stiffen. She was about to reply when he shook his head.

"Don't bother trying to deny it," he said with exasperation.

Percy released her hand and sank back into the black leather cushions of his seat. Rhea immediately experienced disappointment that he'd let go of her hand. Startled by her reaction, it took her several seconds to gather her wits and respond to Percy's allegation.

"It's rather difficult to deny something when I have no idea what you're referring to," Rhea said coolly as she fought to maintain her composure.

"Vincent explained what you've been doing."

Percy's words made her suck in a quick gasp of air. Their gazes locked, Rhea's heart pounded wildly in her chest. Was Percy bluffing? Vincent knew from his years with Ruckley not to give up information to people he didn't know. A sudden thought careened through her. Dear God, had Percy seen Lucy? In a split second, she understood her sister's reluctance to tell Blake the truth. She wasn't even in love with Percy, and the idea of him discovering her past and thinking the worst of her was not a pleasant thought. A chill danced across her skin despite the heat of the day.

"Whatever Vincent told you, I'm sure it's some flight of fancy on his part. He's just a child."

"The boy is far older than his years, and deeply afraid for your safety." Percy's face hardened into harsh, forbidding angles of anger. "He told me how you've been spiriting children in Ruckley's band of thieves out from under his nose and taking them to Green Hill House. Vincent also said you were planning to rescue another child this coming Friday night, which would explain your refusal to my dinner invitation."

Unable to think clearly, Rhea sat frozen in her seat. Vincent had shared far too much with Percy. Had he done so under duress? Had Percy threatened the boy? Without even thinking twice she ruled out that possibility. Even on such short acquaintance she knew Percy was incapable of threatening a child. Then why would Vincent tell Percy what her plans were? Almost as if he could read her churning thoughts, Percy released a low noise of aggravation.

"The boy overheard me asking your aunt how I could find you in London. He stopped me before I left and threatened me with bodily harm if I hurt you." His resentment made her smile.

"Vincent has always been protective of me," she said softly. "I looked after him from the first day Ruckley bought him from his parents. He was only five years old."

"*Five*," Percy exclaimed with a quiet outrage that emphasized his disgust.

"It's not unusual for young children to be sold into thievery. Some are born into the life."

The thought of Lucy made Rhea's stomach lurch. At least her niece would never know the pain, fear, and heartache her mother and aunt had endured.

"And what about you and your sister? How did you come to be in Ruckley's employ?"

"We were not in his employ," she said bitterly as the all-too-familiar numbness engulfed her. "Ruckley owned us."

"Owned you," Percy bit out in furious disbelief.

"Our father sold us to Ruckley to pay off his gambling debts."

"*Sweet Jesus.*" Percy's soft exclamation was little more than a hiss of air between clenched teeth. "How old were you?"

"I was eighteen, almost nineteen." Rhea heard the

mechanical sound of her reply. It allowed her to distance herself from the horror of the past. "Arianna was fourteen."

"*Bloody hell*." The anger and disgust in his voice didn't surprise her. But to her dismay his outrage at her plight pierced the thick layer of ice she'd encased her heart in long ago simply to survive.

"And your mother didn't object?" His words made her stiffen with anger.

"My mother had been dead more than a year when my father sold us to Ruckley. She would *never* have allowed my father to do what he did if she'd been alive." Rhea glared at him as a cold, brittle anger slashed its way through her. At her chilly reply, he offered her an abrupt nod of apology.

"It was wrong of me to suggest such a thing."

The quiet words echoed with sincere remorse. Rhea realized how difficult it must be for him to comprehend what her life had been like for the seven years she'd been under Ruckley's control. Rhea looked away from Percy to stare out at the neat row of houses that lined the street they were on. They were such a stark contrast to the horrible nature of the life she endured for seven years.

"I understand why you asked the question. If my father could do something so vile, perhaps my mother could have done so as well." Rhea drew in a breath of air and released it as an image of her mother's gentle features filled her head.

"And your aunt? Was she unable to do something?" This time there was no judgement in his voice.

"Father never liked Aunt Beatrice. He refused to let her in the house. I once overheard mama arguing with him about it. But he refused to listen. It's why Aunt Beatrice had no idea what had happened to us until the lawyer for father's estate finally located her. By then we'd been doing Ruckley's bidding for more than six years. It took almost another year for Aunt Beatrice to find us."

Her voice cracked slightly at the memory of when

Ashford had first taken them to Fremont house. Aunt Beatrice had looked so much like her mother that Arianna had immediately burst into tears. She'd allowed her sister to cry for the both of them.

"Only someone with great strength and courage could survive what you and your sister have, Rhea." The gentleness in his voice caused an unfamiliar emotion to swell inside her and form a knot in her throat. She jerked her gaze from the passing scenery to look at him. There was no condemnation in his brown eyes, only a gleam of admiration. Rhea shook her head in a dismissal of his words.

"I did what I had to do to survive. We both did." The memory of everything the statement included made her flinch and her stomach roil.

"Is that why you've decided to take it upon yourself to free these children? Vincent said you've managed to rescue three children already, including him. Exactly how have you managed that?"

"A private detective is assisting me." At her reply, Percy drew in a sharp hiss of air.

"His name." The harsh demand made her stiffen.

"Luke Ashford," she snapped. "He's been quite competent in helping me."

"Did you secure any character references for the man?"

"I didn't need—"

"*Good God, Rhea,* how do you know this man can be trusted?" The repressed anger in his voice made her glare at him.

"Mr. Ashford *is* trustworthy."

"And you know this how? What's to stop him from taking advantage of your purse?"

"*He won't,*" she said fiercely. "He's the one who found Arianna and me for my aunt. It's because of him that we escaped Ruckley."

"All right," he said with a bob of his head. "You've

secured the assistance of someone reputable. But how many children do you have to save before you stop this risky undertaking of yours? How many will it take for you to realize you can't save all of them?"

"Do you think I don't know that?" she cried out passionately. As she admitted the thought out loud, her heart ached as if someone had ripped it out of her chest. "But leaving the children I cared for while I was under Ruckley's thumb is something I refuse to do. I'll not leave them at the mercy of that monster."

Anger flooded Rhea's veins at the possibility Percy might think she shouldn't save the few children she could. He had no idea what it was like for the children she'd left behind. Heaven knew what perverse tortures Ruckley had already done without her being present to intervene. The thought of what had happed to Timothy sickened Rhea. The terrible memory of that night made her tremble as she focused her gaze on the man seated across from her. Percy's obvious empathy and compassion aroused unexpected emotions that confused and frightened her. Was it possible for someone who'd never known the harsh life she'd endured to understand her reasons for saving children she'd come to think of as her own? Percy cleared his throat.

"Let me help you." The strength and conviction in his voice urged her to agree to his request. It was a tempting offer. What would it be like to have someone like Percy to lean on when something went wrong? With a slight shake of her head she wrestled with the idea of accepting his help.

"Trust me, Rhea. Trust me to keep you and the children safe from harm."

"And what about your desire to bring Ruckley to justice?" she asked with renewed distrust. The question made Percy grimace.

"I'll wait until all the children you intend to rescue are safe before I do anything. But I'd wager that Ruckley has already realized you're the one behind the children disappearing from his band of thieves."

It was a thought she'd already considered, but she'd pushed it aside in the hope she could rescue all the children without Ruckley discovering her involvement. That Percy had spoken her thoughts out loud sent a bolt of fear crashing through her. The carriage rolled to a stop, and Percy leaned forward to block her exit with his arm. Startled, she met his determined gaze as the driver opened the vehicle's door.

"Give me your answer, Rhea." The quiet demand reverberated with understanding and an emphatic determination that she found impossible to ignore. She stared at him for a long moment and nodded.

"Very well," she whispered. Rhea didn't know if she was more surprised by his relief or by her own reluctant agreement. He captured her hand once more, but this time he raised it to his lips. The touch sent heat pulsing its way through her as if she were being consumed by a wildfire.

"Thank you," he said softly. "I'll make sure you don't regret doing so." Percy slowly released her hand. "I'll return for you at five."

"I don't—"

"Five o'clock, Rhea. I expect you to be ready."

His voice and the stubborn set of his jaw dared her to think twice about arguing with him, and she agreed to his command as he exited the vehicle. Rhea accepted his hand and descended from the vehicle. He saw her to the foot of the steps leading to the door of Sherrington House. As she made her way up the brick stairway, fire skimmed across the back of her neck. The sensation told her that Percy was watching her, but she refused to turn her head. She was feeling far too vulnerable at the moment. As she opened the door of Sherrington House, she heard the carriage rolled away.

The sound left her feeling relieved and bereft at the same time. She'd agreed to trust Percy and accept his help. She wasn't exactly sure what that entailed, but for the first time in years she didn't feel quite so alone in her efforts to protect those she loved. The front door closed behind her, Rhea removed her hat and laid it on the highly polished surface of the hall table. Marston emerged from the main salon and bowed slightly.

"Lady Sherrington and Mrs. Fremont are in the salon, miss. Her ladyship asked that you join them as soon as you returned."

Startled to hear her aunt had arrived in London, Rhea's chest tightened with fear. Had her aunt brought the children with her? If Ruckley were to find her—no, *when* he found her—the children would be in jeopardy.

"Thank you, Marston," she said with a nod then walked into the salon. Beatrice Fremont saw her first and extended her hand in a warm gesture of affection.

"There you are, dearest, we were wondering when you would return."

"I didn't think you'd planned on coming to London for another few weeks." Rhea bent and kissed Beatrice Fremont's cheek as she struggled to keep her fears at bay. "Did you bring the children with you?"

"No, I left the boys in the capable hands of Albert and Mrs. Turner." Beatrice's explanation made Rhea breathe a small sigh of relief. It was one thing for Ruckley to find her, but if he found the children—she crushed the thought as her aunt turned her head to smile at Arianna. "However, I did bring Lucy as I know how fond Arianna is of the child."

"I always love seeing Lucy," her sister said a happy smile that made her glow.

"She is a sweet little thing, isn't she? And I'm convinced she's going to be terribly spoiled when she's older. The boys adore her." Aunt Beatrice said with a laugh. "And with your happy news, dearest, it means Lucy will have a child close to her own age when you visit Green Hill House."

Rhea looked at her sister who was smiling, but the brief flicker of anguish in Arianna's eyes made Rhea's heart ache for her sister. An image of Ruckley flitted through her head, and Rhea bit down on her lower lip. Her sister was strong, but Arianna's pregnancy would make it difficult for her sister to manage her emotions as well as she usually could. Before she could share her bad news, Beatrice Fremont turned her attentions to Rhea again.

"Your sister tells me Percy Rockwood came calling this morning, and how he spirited you away to lunch with his sister."

Rhea's gaze jerked her head to look at her sister. Had Arianna told their aunt how they'd left Percy for dead in the museum? Arianna sent her a small smile as if she'd read Rhea's mind.

"I told Aunt Beatrice that Mr. Rockwood seemed quite smitten."

Arianna's apologetic look made Rhea wince. Clearly Arianna had maintained her silence about the museum, but in exchange, her sister had offered her up like a sacrificial lamb to their aunt's aspirations for Rhea's marital status. Beatrice Fremont smile was brilliant with satisfaction as she looked at her nieces.

"I'm not surprised. The man was quite disappointed yesterday afternoon when he paid us a visit," Beatrice Fremont said with a smile of delight. "And to arrive here this afternoon to learn you'd gone to have lunch with Mr. Rockwood and his sister gives me hope."

"Hope, Aunt Beatrice?" A puzzled frown furrowed Arianna's forehead as Rhea rolled her eyes and grimaced.

"Yes, hope, Arianna," Beatrice Fremont said with a happy smile. "Your sister has been adamant in her refusal to consider the possibility of marriage."

"I would hardly call lunch with Percy Rockwood and his sister reason for you to hope, Aunt Beatrice," Rhea said with annoyed exasperation.

"That's where you're wrong, dearest." Beatrice shook her head with a complacent smile. "The man took you to meet his sister. A man doesn't introduce a woman to his family unless his intentions are serious."

"He wanted to show me the orphanage his family sponsors. We hardly know one another," Rhea said between clenched teeth. God help her when the man arrived in a few hours to take her to dinner with the rest of his family.

"Perhaps, but it's still an excellent sign that the man finds you intriguing."

"Not nearly as intriguing as Lord Foxworth found you, aunt," Rhea said in a desperate effort to turn the conversation away from Percy.

How she was going to leave the house this evening without her aunt becoming even more gleeful was a problem she wasn't sure how to avoid. As she met her aunt's gaze, Rhea noticed how Beatrice Fremont's cheeks had flooded with a dark pink color. Rhea narrowed her eyes at the older woman.

She'd found her aunt's Achilles' heel. From now on, Rhea could counter Beatrice Fremont's matchmaker efforts with her own suggestions about Lord Foxworth. As she met her aunt's gaze, the older woman shook her head sternly.

"Marriage is for the young, and my history with Lord Foxworth does little to endear the man to me."

The moment her aunt spoke, Rhea knew she was lying. Whether it was to herself or to her nieces, it was difficult to discern. Her aunt was definitely not admitting the truth. She'd seen the older woman in Lord Foxworth's company. Despite her objections to the man's authoritative manner, Lord Foxworth clearly had a disturbing effect on her aunt. With a shake of her head, Rhea didn't bother to continue the argument. She could no longer put off her bad news. The fear spread its tight web around her. It made it difficult to breathe as she looked at Arianna.

"Something's happened," Arianna said and paled with trepidation as she slowly rose to her feet to stand stiff and unmoving in front of her chair. Rhea flinched at her sister's words and nodded.

"Ruckley has a way to find me—us." Silence greeted her words as her sister and aunt stared at her in horror. Beatrice was the first to recover.

"But how? Mr. Ashford has assured us repeatedly that his movements have gone undetected in his efforts to rescue the children," her aunt exclaimed with concern. "How could Ruckley possibly know where you are?"

"Unfortunately, one of Ruckley's boys was at the Rockwood orphanage. He saw me."

"Perhaps the child didn't recognize you, dearest." Her aunt's optimistic tone caused a look of hope to lighten Arianna's features. Rhea's gaze locked with her sister's, and when she slowly shook her head, Arianna paled.

"It was Edgar." The moment her words filled the air, Arianna clutched at her throat.

"Who is this Edgar?" Beatrice asked in a worried tone.

"He's one of Ruckley's trusted lieutenants," Arianna whispered as she focused her gaze on Rhea. "He had to have been at the orphanage to recruit younger children to fill Ruckley's needs."

"Dear Lord," Beatrice gasped in dismay before another look of optimism replaced her fear.

"Simply because he saw you at the orphanage doesn't mean he can find you."

"Edgar is very resourceful, especially if he believes Ruckley will reward him well for information," Rhea said softly as despair threatened to overwhelm her as it had when she'd left the orphanage. The memory of Percy's determination to help her eased some of that fear.

"I refuse to believe this man has any power over you now, my darlings," Beatrice said in a firm, defiant voice.

"His power is in what he knows, Aunt Beatrice," Arianna's terse reply made Rhea's heart skip a beat. Lucy. It wouldn't take long for Ruckley to discover Blake knew nothing about his wife's daughter. One word from Ruckley in Blake's ear could destroy Arianna's marriage. Beatrice didn't speak for a moment then released a breath of air that indicated she'd reached a decision.

"You'll simply have to tell Blake the truth."

At Beatrice's matter-of-fact statement, Rhea and Arianna stared at the woman in mute surprise. The older woman rose to her feet and brushed out the wrinkles in her coral silk skirts. She studied their startled expressions for a moment then sighed.

"Don't look so surprise, my darlings. Lucy has Arianna's complexion, blue eyes, blonde hair." Beatrice waved her hand as Rhea opened her mouth to protest. "I knew from the moment I saw her in Arianna's arms that the child wasn't the motherless waif you said she was. I can also see the pain in Arianna's eyes every time she says goodbye to Lucy. I know how hard it is—I'm sure it must have been terribly difficult for you, dearest."

"But we never said that we…that…" Arianna's voice died away, and Beatrice quickly closed the distance between them to embrace her niece in a warm hug. She pulled back and brushed a tear off Arianna's cheek.

"You didn't have to say anything, Arianna," their aunt said with a deep sadness that made Rhea's throat close with emotion. "I would have been a fool to believe either of you had only been pickpockets. I never asked because I knew you would tell me if you wanted to. I could never pass judgement on you for what you were forced to do, and it didn't make me love either of you less. If anything, it made me love you both of you that much more for being so strong and brave."

As her aunt finished her impassioned speech, Rhea blinked quickly to hold back the tears threatening to fall. She swallowed hard as she met her aunt's gaze then looked away.

"You are not alone anymore, my darling girls," Beatrice Fremont said in a strong, defiant voice. "We will find a way to defeat this Ruckley fellow once and for all, but that means you must tell Blake everything, Arianna. I have a strong suspicion you've told Blake something of your past, but that you have failed to mention Lucy."

"Yes, I didn't know how to tell him about her. I still don't know. I don't want to lose him."

"The man adores you, Arianna. You will not lose him, although I will not be surprised if he becomes angry that you failed to trust him with the full truth," Beatrice said as she patted Arianna's arm.

The sudden sound of Blake's muffled voice filtered its way into the salon from the entryway, and Arianna paled. Aunt Beatrice quickly caught her niece's hand and squeezed it as she whispered something in her ear. Rhea saw her sister nod as Blake entered the room followed by a short, stout man close behind. The smile curving Blake's mouth broadened as he looked at Beatrice Fremont.

"Aunt, you're the second surprise visitor in just two days," Blake said with a quiet chuckle as he moved forward to greet the older woman with a light kiss on the cheek. "In fact, I'm beginning to think my wife is preparing to do some great battle and has called for reinforcements."

At her husband's playful comment, Arianna made a small sound of dismay. Concern darkened Blake's brow, as he caught his wife's hand and kissed it with loving tenderness. Beatrice laughed and shook her head.

"I doubt Arianna has need of any reinforcements, Blake. She's stronger than she realizes." Beatrice eyed Arianna with an encouraging smile.

"I'll not argue that point with you." Blake laughed as he kissed his wife's hand again. "However, she's about to learn that there are some battles I will not allow her to win. Allow me to present Dr. Hopkins."

Blake turned to the man behind him who greeted them with a bow and a jovial smile. At her husband's introduction of the physician, Arianna drew in a sharp breath. It was a sound of fear that was reminiscent of the moments when Ruckley had threatened them or one of the children. Blake frowned again, but before he could speak, Dr. Hopkins stepped forward.

"Lord Sherrington informed me you were reluctant to have a physician attend to you, my lady," the doctor said with a jovial smile. "It is my experience that first-time fathers are far more in need of reassurance than their wives."

Arianna's mouth curved in a wan smile, while Blake shot a look of annoyance in the doctor's direction. Beatrice laughed.

"I can see my nephew by marriage is not happy with your observation Dr. Hopkins."

"Indeed," Blake said with a look of irritation. "My first concern is for Arianna's health."

"And I am not implying otherwise, my lord. I have no doubt your wife is your first and foremost concern," Dr. Hopkins said in a soothing voice. "But at first glance, it appears Lady Sherrington's health is excellent, although her complexion suggests she's a trifle anemic. However, I shall need to examine her before I can confirm my initial observation."

Blake still appeared annoyed by the doctor's amusement, but nodded his agreement. The viscount turned back to Arianna and kissed her hand again lovingly. He murmured something to his wife, and Rhea saw her sister flinched. Arianna's gaze left her husband's as she dragged in an audible breath and looked at the stocky physician.

"If I may, Dr. Hopkins, might I have a private word with my husband first, please."

"But of course, Lady Sherrington," the physician said

with a smile.

Startled by her sister's request, Rhea studied Arianna's pale features with concern. Was her sister going to argue with Blake about the doctor? She took a step toward her, but Aunt Beatrice caught her arm.

"Come, Rhea, let's leave these two alone for a few minutes. We'll entertain Dr. Hopkins in the morning room."

Still confused by Arianna's behavior, Rhea nodded but continued to watch her sister as her aunt ushered her out of the salon. The last thing she saw as Aunt Beatrice closed the door behind them was Arianna's expression of panic and fear.

Arianna watched the door close behind her aunt and sister with a rising panic. What in the name of heaven had she been thinking to choose this moment to tell Blake about Lucy? She shivered as she looked at her husband. A frown of concern creasing his brow, he took a step toward her. Startled she uttered an unintelligible cry and took a quick step backward. Blake's frown darkened as he eyed her with puzzlement.

"What's wrong, sweetheart?"

"I… I have to tell you…" Arianna drew in a deep breath of air as she fought back the tears threatening to overwhelm her. The concern on Blake's features changed to one of deepening alarm.

"*Christ Jesus, Arianna.* What's wrong?" The harshness of his voice scraped along her senses.

She should have asked Rhea to stay. The moment the thought fluttered through her head, she tossed it aside. Too often in the past she'd leaned on her sister for moral support. It was time she relied on her own inner strength. Arianna swallowed the fear threatening to paralyze her as she met her husband's worried gaze. He took a small step toward her, while still respecting her desire to keep distance between them.

"If this is about the doctor, my love—"

"No, it's not about the doctor." Arianna shook her head as with great effort she held back her tears.

"*Damn it to hell, Arianna.* Just tell me what's wrong," Blake demanded. A tremor shook through her as she pressed one hand to her throat.

"I've lied to you."

"Lied to me?" Puzzlement and confusion replaced Blake's frustrated concern.

"Yes," she choked out. "I told you... I said I told you everything."

"It's all right, sweetheart. I love you. Whatever is troubling you, we'll work through it. Simply tell me what's wrong." Blake took a step toward her, but she sprang backward.

"*Don't.* Don't touch me."

"What?" Blake's amazement evolved quickly into indignation. As he straightened to his full height, she winced at his offended expression.

"I can't tell you what I need to if you're holding me," she whispered.

"*Damn it, Arianna,* just tell me whatever it is you have to say." Blake shook his head angrily.

"Before we were married," she choked out as she struggled with the emotions clawing at her. "You asked me if I had any other secrets in my past, and I told you no."

"Is that what this is all about? Your past?" A thundercloud of fury darkened his features. "Has that bastard you refuse to name been here and threatened you with some piece of information?"

"*No.* No one has threatened me."

She shook her head as her tongue tripped over Ruckley's name, and she caught herself before speaking it out loud.

There was no doubt in her mind that Blake would go after Ruckley, and she refused to send her husband into the viper's nest.

"Then I don't understand what's wrong." Shoving his hand through his golden hair, Blake blew out a breath of exasperation as he studied her. As she watched frustration, worry, and confusion cross his handsome features, Arianna drew in a deep breath. Her trembling eased slightly as she imitated the calm composure Rhea always exhibited when facing a difficult situation.

"I have a daughter."

The words echoed in her ears like the sound of a gunshot. For a moment, Blake simply stared at her as if she'd lost her mind. When she didn't move, his shock ebbed away until his face was an unreadable mask, but she saw a dark fury glittering in his hazel eyes.

"What do you mean, you have a daughter?" His voice was devoid of emotion as he asked the question.

"I had a child...while I was..." she stammered beneath Blake's icy glare. "I tried...I wanted to tell you—"

"But you didn't," he said in a freezing tone. In a fraction of a second, his countenance had become a stony façade of unrelenting anger. There wasn't a trace of the man she'd married standing opposite her. This was a stranger, and her heart twisted painfully in her chest.

"How could I," she exclaimed as she took a step toward him. This time, he was the one who retreated. Arianna's mouth went dry as she stared at him in horror. She should never have listened to Aunt Beatrice or Rhea. Telling Blake the truth about Lucy had been a mistake. A terrible mistake.

"Blake, please. I wanted to tell you, I simply didn't have the courage to do so."

"And yet you found the courage to tell me you were soiled goods." The cold words made her head snap back in shock. He'd never referred to her in that way before.

"Do you have any idea how difficult it was to even *tell* you I was a whore?" she cried out in anguish. Blake didn't move, but a muscle twitched in his cheek as he studied her. For a moment, she thought she saw a softening of the cold, marble-like façade on his features. It vanished, and her heart sank.

"Why this sudden revelation, Lady Sherrington?" Blake's use of her formal title made her jerk as if he'd slapped her. His gaze narrowed at her. "Were you afraid I wouldn't marry you if I knew about the child?"

"Yes," she whispered.

The moment she answered his question, she realized her mistake. Her reply had made her lie sound even worse. It made it appear as if she'd married him for reasons other than love. Pain ricocheted through her as Blake eyed with contempt and fury.

Arianna hurried forward to close the gap between them and grasp his arm. Beneath her fingers, his arm was solid as hardwood. "Oh God, Blake, I didn't mean it like that. I love you. I was terrified you wouldn't love me anymore, and I couldn't bear the thought of losing you."

"Is the child mine?" The coldness in her husband's voice made Arianna shake her head in confusion.

"What? I don't understand."

"The child you're carrying now? Is it mine?"

The brutality of his question pulled a horrified gasp from her, and she swayed on her feet. As she met his gaze, she saw something flicker in his eyes, but it disappeared as an icy contempt took its place.

If she'd been struck with a whip, she could not have felt the sting any less than the pain Blake's look was inflicting on her now. Arianna released her grip on his arm as if it was on fire and took several steps backward. Stiffening her spine, she tilted her head at a defiant angle and eyed him with equal contempt.

"You're the only man I've ever welcomed into my bed willingly," she said firmly. "The child is yours, my lord."

The silence stretched out between them until Blake jerked his head in an abrupt nod.

"And are there any other revelations you feel compelled to share with me today, my lady?" There was a bitterness in his voice that frightened her.

"No," she whispered. "I have no other secrets."

"So you've said before."

The cold disbelief in Blake's voice sent a chill through Arianna. It seeped its way through her pores and down into her bones, which she was certain would snap at the first bit of pressure.

"I shall send Dr. Hopkins in. Make whatever arrangements necessary to ensure the babe...and you, come to no harm in the coming months."

His expression hard and inflexible, he strode toward the exit. Horrified he was leaving without having resolved the matter between them, Arianna rushed after him.

"Blake, please," she pleaded as tears formed in her eyes. "Try to understand."

"I understand all too well, my lady. You wanted a husband, and you were unwilling to jeopardize that ambition."

"Ambition?" she sputtered in horror. "I married you because I love you."

"I find that statement questionable at best, my lady."

"It's the truth," she exclaimed fervently.

"Is it? I wonder." His gaze was cold as he looked her up and down then sneered as if he'd found her wanting. "Do you even know what the truth is?"

"*Yes.* I love you. *That's the truth.* I have from the first moment we met." Her words made him arch his eyebrows in skepticism.

"A meeting that was no doubt contrived."

"No, our meeting was purely accidental. I would never

have done such a thing."

"I find that doubtful under the circumstances."

"*Dear God, Blake.* How can I make you understand how difficult it was for me to believe you could love me, let alone overlook my past? I couldn't risk losing you. I love you.

"Love requires trust, my lady. Something you clearly lacked in me, or you would have entrusted me with all your secrets before we were married."

Blake didn't wait for her reply, but strode out of the salon. The door crashed shut behind him with a violence that emphasized his rage. Arianna stumbled toward the nearest chair, sinking down onto the needlepoint seat cushion. A shudder rocked through her. What she'd feared the most had happened. She'd lost him.

Rhea and Aunt Beatrice had been wrong. Blake didn't love her enough to understand why she'd kept Lucy a secret from him. She'd gambled and lost. The realization drove a spike so deep into her she thought she would die from the pain. Tears pushed past her closed eyelids and she buried her face into her palms. Once more, Ruckley had destroyed her life.

Chapter 7

“B last it, Patience, it’s Sebastian’s birthday,” Percy bit out between clenched teeth as he glared at his younger sister.

“I attended the celebration at Melton Park this past weekend.” Patience tilted her chin upward in a mutinous manner. “It’s highly unlikely I’ll be missed at the party next week.”

“You know good and well that’s not true,” he snapped.

“In other words, you mean the Marlborough Set will be disappointed I’m not on display for their amusement,” Patience said with equal vehemence.

“Don’t be absurd,” he ground out. “I’m talking about the family. To hell with the Set.”

Frustration pummeled him as he tried to navigate the treacherous waters of his sister’s fragile emotions and fear. It had been a blunder of monumental proportions to take Rhea to the orphanage this afternoon. Patience had been extremely hesitant to attend Sebastian’s party in London to begin with. Now, in his eagerness to have a few private moments with Rhea, his lack of foresight had pushed Patience into a corner and an outright refusal to attend. Hell, she might even decide not to return to the orphanage. The family would drag him over the coals if that happened.

Patience glowered at him from her seat on the sofa in the main salon of Melton House. Frustrated not only by his sister’s obstinate refusal to attend the party, but by his own ineptitude, Percy scowled back. He might have erred this afternoon, but it was time Patience came out from the shadows. Although her reconciliation with Julian had restored a great deal of her confidence, she still had difficulty going out in public.

Aside from the two morning rides she'd accompanied Sebastian on last fall, Patience had refused all invitations to any public outings since the fire. Whenever she and Julian traveled from Crianlarich to London, it was either for a family gathering or when Julian had business in town. He glanced toward the fireplace where Julian stood. Percy knew his brother-in-law agreed with him, but the man never interfered in sibling quarrels.

The Highlander was all too familiar with Patience's headstrong nature. When his wife had refused to see him for months after the tragedy at Westbrook Farms, the tall Scotsman had been tormented by her rejection. The Rockwoods had always liked Julian, but the man's obvious distress at Patience's refusal to see him had only strengthened their affection for their brother-in-law. Percy studied his sister's rebellious expression for a moment before he narrowed his gaze at her.

"This is about this afternoon at the orphanage." The statement caused Patience to jerk slightly.

"I'll not deny your arrival with Miss Bennett in tow only emphasized it would be a mistake to attend the party."

Patience's soft confession made Percy grimace. The dark scowl on Julian's brow was an indicator of how his entire family would view his reckless behavior earlier in the day. Percy wasn't sure what irritated him the most, his misstep in unexpectedly forcing Rhea on his sister this afternoon or Patience's stubborn refusal to realize her scars were not as disfiguring as she believed. Percy contemplated the mutinous set of his sister's mouth for a long moment before his jaw tightened with determination. It was time to change tactics.

"What you really mean is that you wouldn't have been at the orphanage if you'd known Rhea was accompanying me." The clipped statement made color flood Patience's cheeks and her mouth thinned with anger.

"You betrayed me, Percy." The bitterness in his sister's voice made Percy's gut twist viciously.

"I never intended to do so, Patience. I hadn't planned to bring Rhea to the orphanage for lunch," he said with sincere regret. "It was a spur-of-the-moment invitation. Once the invitation was extended, it was impossible to retract. It's a mistake I deeply regret. I'm sorry."

"You should be," his sister said sharply. The glare she directed at him only deepened Percy's remorse. After a long moment of silence her features softened slightly before she looked away to stare at the royal blue carpet with its cream-colored floral design.

"In truth, I suppose I should be grateful."

"Grateful?" he murmured hopefully.

"Yes." Patience nodded as she continued to study the carpet. "Today illustrated how terribly difficult the party would be for me."

"Difficult how?" he snapped with self-frustration. "You appeared to enjoy yourself the other night at Melton Park."

"That was different. I knew almost everyone in attendance." She looked up at him with a look of irritation.

"And you'll know most everyone at the ball."

"Know perhaps, but not well enough to think they'll ignore..."

Her voice died away as she shook her head. There was a look of fear and horror in her brown eyes that made Percy want to scoop her up into his arms as he had when she was little and had been hurt or frightened. He'd always been able to help her overcome her fears as a child, that he couldn't do so now pained him deeply. If there was anything he hated, it was to see anyone in his family hurting.

"Except for your initial shock, I think you enjoyed Rhea's company at lunch," he said gently.

"Miss Bennett was kind. She ignored my…my scars."

"And people will be equally kind at the party," he said quietly. "I think you know that or you wouldn't have invited Rhea to dine with the family this evening."

Out of the corner of his eye, Percy saw his brother-in-law jerk in surprise. He saw his sister dart a quick glance at her husband who was eyeing her with amazement. Patience's mouth twisted slightly as if in pain.

"I won't deny I found Miss Bennett quite pleasant. But that's not why I asked her to dinner this evening."

"Then why did you?" Suddenly feeling as though he had fallen into a spider's web, Percy met his sister's steady gaze warily.

"Because she's important to you."

The simplicity of Patience's response was emphasized as she rolled her shoulders in a small shrug. Almost as if she were waiting for a reaction from him, her gaze narrowed with calculated assessment. Tension slid through him until his muscles were stiff and rigid. Slowly clasping his hands behind his back, Percy studied Patience's serene and confident expression. She knew her observation had hit its mark. While it was an accurate appraisal, it wasn't for the reason Patience believed. Derisive laughter filled his head, and he blocked out the sound.

"Perhaps you'd care to elaborate on that statement," he said in a voice devoid of emotion.

"It means I believe you care about Miss Bennett. I'm simply undecided as to whether she's just another stray waif you feel compelled to care for or if she's special in another way."

"I do *not* take in strays," he growled.

The instant Patience raised her eyebrows and nodded toward Hercules, sprawled out on the carpet, Percy grimaced.

The family was accustomed to him bringing home stray animals in need of shelter and a good home. Hercules had been no different. The old dog had been a treasured member of the family since the day Percy had brought the animal to Melton House more than ten years ago. Curled up in the pit of the dog's chest and front legs, was the newest member of the house, Andromeda. Percy had found the kitten wet and half-dead from starvation near the Thames shortly after the first of the year. Hercules had taken on the role of protector the moment Andromeda had entered the house.

"Hercules wasn't your first stray or your last," Patience observed softly. "There have been others."

Although his sister didn't mention her by name, he knew Patience was referring to Nellie. Percy's hand tightened its already painful grip on his wrist, as he continued to keep his hands clasped behind his back. With deliberation, he forced himself to appear nonchalant. As Patience studied him with a calculating look, he eyed her coldly.

"Rhea is not Nellie, and my interest in her is solely because her sister is married to my best friend."

Percy's jaw tightened further. His reply was a complete fabrication, and he knew it. But the last thing he wanted was Patience probing deeper into his connection with Rhea. If Patience discovered the circumstances of their first meeting, his sister would feel less than charitable toward Rhea. Actually, that was a mild turn of phrase for the outrage the entire family would heap on Rhea's head. His brush with death had followed close on the heels of Caleb's and Devin's tragic deaths. The fear, worry, and panic his siblings had suffered the night after the museum theft was still an open wound in their minds. Patience cocked her head to one side as she stared at him intensely.

"I think there's more to all this than meets the eye."

"Now, you're going to tell me you've had a vision," he said with a harsh sarcasm that covered a moment of panic.

Had the *an dara sealladh* shown his sister something about Rhea? No, she would have interrogated him the minute he'd enter the drawing room a short time ago. Ever since the fire, Patience had taken to asking questions whenever she'd had a vision that made no sense to her. Percy was certain that deep down Patience still blamed herself for Caleb's and Devin's deaths.

Everyone knew there was no blame to place on anyone. It had been a terrible accident, but he knew his sister well. They'd always been close, and he, more than anyone, understood how self-recrimination could cripple you. His stomach knotted as the horrifying image of Nellie's death spilled its way into his mind. Ruthlessly, he shoved the terrible memories back into the abyss from where they'd emerged. His own past allowed him to understand Patience better than she thought, and she needed to confront her fear. A voice in the back of his head snorted with disgust at his hypocrisy. As he met Patience's gaze, she shook her head in disagreement.

"No. I'm referring to the fact that you experienced the *an dara sealladh* at the orphanage." Patience raised her hand as he opened his mouth to refute her words. "Don't deny it. We both know you never have a migraine after the *an dara sealladh* unless your vision concerns someone who's important to you."

"How do you know the *an dara sealladh* didn't involve you?" he hedged trying to guide the conversation in a different direction than where Patience clearly was headed. She rolled her eyes and glared at him.

"You've never taken me for a fool, Percy Rockwood. Don't start now."

His sister's scorn made his jaw tighten as he fought to keep his expression devoid of emotion. He wasn't about to admit her astute observation had hit far closer to home than he'd been willing to acknowledge until this moment. It had been easier to ignore the fact that his interest in Rhea wasn't simply because of Ruckley. She was strong, resourceful, self-reliant, and courageous. They were admirable qualities in anyone, but it was the vulnerability hiding beneath those attributes that aroused a need to protect her by whatever means necessary.

Patience was correct. Rhea was important to him. He'd known their paths were destined to cross from the first time the *an dara sealladh* had shown him those beautiful violet eyes of hers. His vision had never been clear where Rhea was concerned, and it wasn't until that night in the museum when his gaze had locked with hers that he'd realized he was meant to help her. But deep inside he knew there was another purpose to their connection. A link he wasn't quite ready to consider.

"You're mistaken," he said in a flat and emotionless voice. But he realized his stiff posture belied his denial. Patience narrowed her eyes.

"Am I?" There was a note of sisterly rebuke in Patience's voice as she arched her eyebrows at him. "You don't sound all too certain of that."

"My interest, or lack thereof, in Rhea Bennett is not a topic of debate."

"I am *not* debating the issue with you, Percy," his sister said with a frown. "I'm simply making an observation."

"An observation—I see." Percy's voice echoed with suspicious disbelief as he saw the complacent smile on Patience's lips. With the skill of a politician, Patience had shifted the focus of the original discussion, and he had no intention of allowing the subject to fall to the wayside.

For weeks, the family had been gently coaxing Patience to attend Sebastian's birthday celebration here in town. The fact she'd attended the party at Melton Park had been almost as big a step forward as her decision to return working at the orphanage whenever she and Julian were in town. It wasn't the fear of being stared at that bothered Patience the most. It was the fear of being pitied.

What she didn't understand was that she'd met death head on and lived despite the horror of it. A few probing questions or piteous looks from insensitive members of the Set were nothing compared to what she'd endured. She had the heart of a lion, and he needed to drive that point home to her. To do so meant he had to be cruel, and the knowledge already tasted bitter and foul in his mouth.

"Perhaps I'm the one who should be making observations."

"About?" Patience eyed him cautiously.

"The fact that my sister isn't just being stubborn, she's acting like a coward."

"*A coward*," Patience exclaimed as she sprang to her feet. She whirled around to look at her husband. "Julian MacTavish, are you going to stand there and let him call your wife a coward?"

"I did nae hear Percy call you a coward, *mo ghràdh*. He said you are acting like one," Julian said soothingly. "He's saying you are allowing your fear tae control you. The mon is right, *mo leannan*. You can nae keep hiding from people."

"I am *not* a coward," Patience fumed as pain replaced her anger. Before Julian could go to her, Percy was at his sister's side. Gently, he took her hands in his.

"I told you once before you were the bravest person I've ever known," he said quietly as he stared down at his sister. "I still believe that."

"You just called me a coward," she said with humiliation and resentment. The brown eyes meeting his were dark with anger and hurt. He shook his head.

"No, as Julian said, I think you're *acting* like a coward," Percy said with a shake of his head. "I know you're afraid, and there's no need to be. There isn't a single member of the Rockwood family who would allow someone to say or do anything to hurt you. Julian and I will be at your side just as we were the other night. The minute someone is uncharitable or dares to make you uncomfortable, they'll be shown to the door, never to be acknowledged by a Rockwood again."

"Aye." His brother-in-law's response was short, and to the point.

The fiercely protective note in Julian's voice made Patience look at her husband. A silent message was exchanged between the two, and his sister drew in a deep breath as she looked back at Percy. It was obvious his sister was wavering in her decision, and Percy remained silent for fear of pushing her in the wrong direction. Patience's features darkened with reluctance.

"Very well, but—" Her response was cut short by Constance's laughter.

"I take it Lucien and I now owe you money, Percy." At the amused comment from the oldest of the three Rockwood sisters, Percy scowled at her. Immediately, Constance's amusement became that of contrition.

"Bad timing?"

"Quite," he growled. He'd forgotten all about the wager he'd made several weeks ago with Constance and her husband the Earl of Lyndham. He looked back at Patience and saw anger furrowing her brow. *Christ Jesus.* Just when she'd been on the verge of acquiescence.

"Am I to understand you made me the *subject of a wager?*" Patience's voice was tight with displeasure, and Percy suppressed a groan.

"He didn't initiate the wager, dearest," Constance said in a soothing voice as she leapt to Percy's defense. With a remorseful look, the oldest Rockwood sister crossed the floor to sit on the cream-colored stripe sofa next to Patience. "He was quite reluctant to agree to it, but I goaded him into accepting."

The fragrance of heather brushed against his nose as his aunt entered the salon and came to stand at his side. With a chuckle, Matilda Stewart eyed him with affectionate despair.

"Aye, yer sister made it impossible for him nae to accept the wager."

"If it helps, my winnings go to the orphanage fund," Percy said ruefully as he met Patience's angry gaze. She continued to glare at him for a moment before she shook her head in disgust. The small sign of forgiveness made Percy relax slightly.

"Well, dearest, is it true? Has Percy actually convinced you to attend the ball next week?"

Constance wrapped her arm around their sister and gave her an affectionate hug and waited for an answer with an expectant air. Patience glanced over her shoulder at her husband who had moved to stand behind the couch. One large hand rested on the mahogany scrolled edge of the plush sofa, while the other gently squeezed his wife's shoulder. A second later, Patience turned her gaze back to Percy and narrowed her gaze at him.

"Yes, I'll go, but on one condition." His sister's words indicated there was a provision being added to her agreement, and Percy frowned. As Patience eyed him shrewdly, he knew he would not like what his sister had to say.

"Condition?" he murmured suspiciously.

"You must escort Miss Bennett to Sebastian's birthday party."

The quiet, but firm, edict stunned Percy. Slack-jawed with amazement, he stared at his sister while Constance's gaze darted back and forth between him and Patience.

"Who is Miss Bennett?" she asked with a frown of puzzlement as Aunt Matilda laughed softly.

"I believe she's the lass Helen introduced ye brother tae at Melton Park the other night." Aunt Matilda said in her lilting Scottish burr. "Am I right, Percy?"

"Yes," he growled as he glanced at first Aunt Matilda then Constance who eyed him with growing curiosity. His gaze shifted back to Patience who returned his glare with smug satisfaction. With a shake of his head he gritted his teeth.

"Rhea told you this afternoon at the orphanage that she was returning to the country Saturday morning, Patience. She's given no indication of when she intends to return."

"I thought you were discussing a Miss Bennett. Who is Rhea?" Constance asked with a perplexed frown.

"Miss Bennett," Percy and Patience exclaimed at the same time.

"Such familiarity seems a bit odd under such short acquaintance, Percy," the eldest Rockwood sister said with a raised eyebrow. A second later a look of devilment enhanced Constance's lovely countenance. "You barely know the woman. You must be quite taken with her."

"For the love of God," Percy muttered in a dark voice as he saw the assessment on Constance's face matched Patience's.

"I thought the same thing too when he brought her to the orphanage today," Patience said serenely as she leaned into her sister. "I've simply not been able to decide whether she's Percy's pet project of the month or if she might be special."

"He brought her to the orphanage?" Constance gasped as she directed a glowering glance of disapproval in Percy's direction. "Did you tell Patience you were coming?"

"No, he didn't." The scars on Patience's cheek tightened slightly as her mouth thinned with the same disapproval Constance was displaying. "But I liked her, and I invited her to dine with us this evening."

"You invited...good heavens." Constance's eyes widened as she stared at Patience in astonishment while Aunt Matilda's mouth fell open in startled amazement. Percy suppressed a groan.

"I did," Patience said with a great deal of satisfaction as she eyed him with a small smile. "So what is your answer, Percy?

Feeling trapped, Percy glared at his sister as he tried to come up with a plausible reason not to do as Patience was demanding, while ensuring she attended the party next week. He failed miserably.

"*Damnation, Patience.* I just reminded you that Miss Bennett is returning to the country this weekend, and she told us she has no idea as to when she expects to return."

"Then you will need to convince her to return for the party, won't you?" The challenging note in his sister's voice was emphasized by the gleam in her brown eyes that dared him to refuse. It had been a long time since Patience, or any of his brothers or sisters had managed to back him into a corner such as the one he was in now.

The fact irritated him immensely. Particularly when it involved his personal affairs. It was one thing for him to confront Patience about her fears, but he'd never meddled in her relationship—he didn't complete the thought. It was disingenuous to state he'd not interfered in Patience's life where Julian was concerned.

The knowledge only increased his irritation. It was an outrageous condition. He wanted to throttle Patience for proposing it *and* Constance for needling him into accepting the wager that he could convince Patience to attend Sebastian's party. If it weren't for that damned wager, his sister would never have made such a ridiculous provision. The most galling thing was that Patience had seen through his nonchalance where Rhea was concerned.

It was an insight he'd have preferred to ignore for a little while longer, and not just by Patience. Over the next few days he would suffer interrogations by his siblings unlike any in recent memory. The thought did little to endear Patience to him at the moment.

Chapter 8

W ell, Percy?"

"It's an unreasonable request," he snapped.

Patience arched her eyebrows and studied her brother's handsome face carefully. She'd thrown an obstacle in his path, and he was far from happy with her.

She had no doubt he was working on a way to refuse her provision in exchange for her agreement to attend Sebastian's birthday party. It was also not too hard to imagine he was contemplating every way known to mankind when it came to seeking brotherly retaliation. The idea filled her with a small amount of satisfaction.

Most of her life, she was the one who always bowed to Percy's decree. Begrudgingly, she admitted he was rarely wrong in his assessment of any dilemma she encountered. But this time she was the one with insight. Rhea Bennett meant something to her brother, and Patience was certain it wasn't simply because he possessed a kind and generous heart.

Percy hadn't shared what he'd seen in his vision at the orphanage. But his expression and headache afterward made her certain the mental images had disturbed him deeply. He was worried about Miss Bennett, and not simply out of the goodness of his heart. This afternoon at lunch she'd seen the way Percy had looked at the woman when he thought no one was watching.

Then there had been Rhea Bennett's reaction the minute Edgar appeared in the dining room. The woman had been terrified—so much so that she'd thought the woman might faint. Patience knew her brother well, and he'd been ready to do battle the instant he saw the Miss Bennett's fear. His reaction had only strengthened her belief that Rhea Bennett was important to her brother, even if he was unwilling to admit it.

She was also certain Percy had been thinking about Nellie Owens in those few moments when Edgar had posed a threat. The woman's death still haunted him. He'd never discussed the tragedy with anyone in the family—not even her—but she knew he still blamed himself. After the inquest more than two years ago, Percy had left for the continent and remained there until he'd learned Caleb's wife had died in childbirth. Percy had returned home to mourn Georgina with the rest of the family. As Caleb's handsome features filled her head, phantom flames licked across her skin. Patience drew in a quick breath of dismay and forced herself to turn her attention back to the matter at hand.

"You've not agreed to my condition, Percy."

"As I've already said, it's an unreasonable one," he growled. His irritation almost made her smile. The stipulation she'd made was outright bribery, but if it meant him finding happiness, she was more than willing to resort to it.

"I disagree. No one in the family has mentioned it before, but we all think it's time you settled down and started a family." Her declaration caused her husband's hand to tighten over the curve of her shoulder. She ignored the silent warning.

"*Settle—bloody hell.* It's not for any of you to discuss my personal affairs," Percy snarled as his stony expression gave way to indignation and outrage. His gaze traveled across the faces of everyone in the salon. Constance and Aunt Matilda both winced in the face of his anger.

"So your family has no right to express a desire to see you happy? I find that ironic given the wager you made with Constance and Lucien."

"I've already apologized for that," he growled with a note of regret in his voice.

"Yes, you did. Just like you apologized for bringing Miss Bennett to the orphanage today," she said wryly. "It seems you have an unbalanced view of when you're entitled to interfere and when others are not."

"My personal affairs are my own."

"What so-called personal affairs?" Patience sniffed and rolled her eyes at him.

Percy had always been a popular guest at the Set's soirées, but ever since Nellie's untimely demise, he avoided any lasting relationships. There had been the occasional discreet liaison. But the only danger for him there was scandal, and heaven knew the Reckless Rockwoods were not unfamiliar with scandal. For the most part, Percy devoted the majority of his time to the museum's musty books or traversing the disreputable sections of the city rescuing strays. Animals and wayward souls such as Nellie. The man needed someone to rescue him, and something inside her said Rhea Bennett was her brother's salvation.

"Perhaps Patience is right, dearest," Constance said quietly. "We simply want you to be happy."

"I'm quite happy with things the way they are. Interfering in my *personal* affairs is unwarranted *and* unwelcomed."

"And why is that?" Patience met her brother's fierce glare with one of her own. "You've never hesitated to interfere in *our* personal affairs if you thought it was in our best interest. I see no reason why we shouldn't express our love and concern for you in equal fashion."

Percy had the decency to look chagrined at her angry reminder. With an abrupt nod, he frowned darkly.

"I have no doubt you believe you're acting in my best interests. However, I'll settle down when I'm ready, and not before."

"And when might *that* be? The next time you're shot?"

Patience snapped. The man was being completely unreasonable. She glared at him. "*Which*, I might point out is a very distinct possibility given your proclivity for spending time in some of the more deplorable parts of London. You seem to have forgotten we almost lost you last summer."

"The incident at the Museum was an unusual event," he said with cold anger. "There was no need for me to have concern for my safety that night."

"Perhaps, but it's a perfect example of what could happen if you continue frequenting places that are far less reputable. Can you blame us for worrying about you when you visit the docks and the East End looking for your latest stray?"

The memory of Percy's assault and subsequent hospitalization was still fresh in the minds of the entire family. The recklessness of his visits into the East End and down to the docks at all hours of the day and night frightened her. In some small way, she was certain his reckless behavior was because of Nellie's death. A misguided means of atonement for an event he bore no blame for.

"If you're suggesting I've easily forgotten what it's like to be shot, you're mistaken." Sharp, staccato beats, his words indicated his anger was on the verge of getting the best of his tongue.

"*Mo leannan*, this is nae—"

"It *is* the time and place," Patience snapped as she cut off her husband's protest. "If he insists on making me confront my fears, then it's high time he faced his own."

"And what fears might those be, Patience?" The sarcasm in Percy's voice made her wince. It was only when he was furious with her that Percy ever addressed her so coldly. It didn't matter. She'd already started down this path and refused to stop now.

"I'm referring to the fact that you blame yourself for Nellie's death."

The silence in the salon stretched out for a long moment,

and she struggled not to squirm in her seat as Percy's gaze pinned her to her chair. It wasn't just her brother who was upset with her. She could feel the weight of her family's censure weighing down on her shoulders.

While the family had discussed the matter out of earshot from Percy, no one had dared to express their concerns directly to her brother. But if anyone were to do so, it was logical to assume she should be the one to confront him. The two of them had always shared a special bond, and she knew he would listen to her more than anyone else in the family. Although she was certain Rhea Bennett would be a good influence on him, she was certain the woman's past was a troublesome one if she knew Edgar. That fact alone made it imperative he understand safety for both himself and Miss Bennett could not be discounted. Patience had no idea what connected Percy and Rhea, but she knew there was more to their relationship than a simple interest on Percy's part and Rhea's as well.

It was another reason she'd insisted Rhea Bennett come to dinner this evening. She wanted Constance and Aunt Matilda to witness Percy's interaction with the woman. Now, as she met Percy's hard gaze, Julian's other hand came to rest on her opposite shoulder and squeezed it tightly. This time there was no mistaking the unspoken message. Her husband was telling her to be quiet. But when a Rockwood was being reckless, they were rarely quiet, and never unwilling to accept a challenge or offer one.

"Have you nothing to say, Percy?" she asked quietly.

For a long moment her brother simply stared at her before he took a small step forward. His anger might have been frightening if she didn't know how much he loved her. But his reaction did make her wonder if she'd gone too far. Was it possible he might not forgive her for pushing him in this manner? The thought was like a worrisome bee buzzing around her head.

"You go too far, Patience." There was a menacing tone in his voice that made her hesitate before she shook her head.

"I've gone no further than you did every time you told me to return to Julian. I should have taken your advice long before I returned to Crianlarich, and I firmly believe I am offering the same type of wisdom you offered me." She stood up and moved to stand in front of her brother taking one of his hands in hers. "You're not responsible for Nellie's death. No matter how many times you try to tell yourself you are, it's not true. Until you accept that fact, true happiness will be outside your grasp. And none of us want that for you."

Percy slowly pulled his hand from hers, and Patience's heart sank at his unforgiving look. Her brother's reaction was far more chilling than she'd expected. Had she erred so badly that he might never forgive her? He stepped back from her and gave her a small bow.

"Since you saw fit to persuade Miss Bennett to come to dinner, I must fetch her. However, I'm warning each of you not to put her under the microscope or you'll have me to deal with," he said coldly as he turned to leave the room.

"And what of my condition?"

Behind her, Patience heard Julian release a low growl before he muttered something incoherent. Percy slowly turned his head to glare at her, but she saw the resignation in her brother's gaze.

"I'll find a way to convince Rhea to attend Sebastian's party, so I suggest you be prepared to make an appearance Saturday evening."

Without another word, Percy strode out of the salon. A moment later the front door slammed shut. Patience sagged slightly as the tension that had been holding her hostage ebbed from her body. Slowly, Patience turned to face her family. Disapproval was visible on each of their faces, and she sighed. With what she knew was great restraint, Julian circled the couch to stand in front of her. As she met her husband's fierce gaze, the Scotsman shook his head sternly.

"You are nae to meddle in your brother's affairs again, Patience MacTavish." The outrage in his voice made her touch his arm in a placating gesture. As he glared down at her, she smiled.

"I don't think any of us will need to meddle in Percy's affairs in the future," Patience said softly as she went up on tiptoe to kiss her husband's cheek. "I think Miss Bennett is going to occupy Percy's attention for some time to come. In fact, I think his life is about to change forever."

Julian scowled at her before he released a growl of disgusted resignation. It was clear he'd have more to say when they were alone. But for now he was willing to drop the matter.

"Have ye been touched by the *an dara sealladh* where Percy is concerned, lass?" Aunt Matilda asked. Curiosity mixed with concern running beneath the inquisitive burr of the Scotswoman's voice.

Beside her, Julian stiffened, and she touched his hand in a small gesture of reassurance. Since the fire, she'd experienced the *an dara sealladh* only a few times. Julian knew how her gift of the sight sometimes proved disturbing, but the visions she'd had were of minor incidents.

"I didn't need the *an dara sealladh* to tell me Percy's interest in Miss Bennett is far more complicated than he's willing to admit," Patience said with a shake of her head.

"So you think his interest is one of a romantic nature?" Constance asked with a smile of satisfaction as Patience nodded her head and returned her sister's smile with a conspiratorial one of her of own.

"Yes, it's why I persuaded Miss Bennett to come to dinner this evening. I wanted someone else to confirm my suspicions."

"Have you nae heard a word I've said, Patience MacTavish?" Julian bit out with exasperation. "You're nae to interfere in your brother's affairs."

"And I'm not," Patience said firmly. "I simply want to know if I'm right about Rhea Bennett being the woman who can make Percy happy."

Her words made Julian mumble an oath as he exhaled a deep breath of exasperation. When Patience smiled up at him, he glowered at her severely, which only made her laugh. Before he could chastise her again, the sound of feet pounding down the main stairs announced the arrival of the children. Braxton was the first one to barrel into the salon. The boy was the spitting image of his father when Caleb had been the same age. Her nephew raced straight for her.

"Aunt Patience, tell Alma to stop saying Papa died," the six-year-old demanded belligerently. "You said he's in heaven."

Patience opened her arms to the little boy who leapt up into her embrace. Hugging the child close, she sank down onto the couch with the boy and looked up at Julian with a sense of helplessness. Ever since the first anniversary of the fire at Westbrook Farms, Alma had been fixated on her father's death and had taken to tormenting her younger brother with the details of that terrible night.

She quickly turned her attention back to the little boy. Tenderly, she brushed the dark brown hair that was so much like Caleb's out of his eyes. His silky dark hair and brown eyes he'd inherited from his father, but his sweet manner had come from his mother, Georgina. The memory of her brother and his wife made Patience's heart ache for the little boy and his sisters.

"Well, Alma is partly correct. Your papa did die, but he died saving you because he loved you so much." She squeezed Braxton's hand. "He saved you and all your cousins, which is why he went to heaven. Your papa was a very brave man, and God wants all of us to be brave in our own way."

"Like you were brave?" Braxton reached out to touch the

scars on her cheek.

There was a look of awe on his face that made Patience's heart skip a beat. A strong hand gripped her shoulder in a silent message of love and reassurance. It wasn't the first time Braxton had expressed interest in her scars. He'd often asked her if she'd been on a pirate ship, which had in some odd way always struck her as funny. It had also reinforced Julian's and other family members' comments that her scars were not as bad as she had once believed them to be.

"Precisely, laddie," Julian's voice was gruff with emotion. "Your Aunt Patience is the bravest woman I've ever known."

A small chorus of agreement whispered through the room as Constance and Aunt Matilda softly echoed Julian's sentiments. Her gaze flitted upward to her husband's strong features. The emotion darkening his face made her heart ache. It was clear he was remembering not only the fire, but the pain they'd both endured in the months that followed.

"Does this mean you'll go to heaven?"

"*Sweet heavens, laddie,*" Aunt Matilda exclaimed in horror. "All this talk of death. Your Aunt Patience isn't going anywhere."

"Alma says we'll all be dead someday, but she says we don't have to be scared. She says we'll just be ghosts then," Braxton said with all the cockiness of a six-year-old. The words made Patience look at her sister and Aunt Matilda. The maternal figure of the Rockwood family shook her head and shrugged slightly.

"The child has nae mentioned having the ability, but I would nae be surprised if she does," the burr in her aunt's voice seemed to soften the blow of comprehension reeling through her.

Patience suddenly understood Constance better than she ever had. Her sister's acceptance of Jamie's gift could not have been easy, particularly when her nephew's abilities were extraordinarily powerful. Although her sister seemed to have come to terms with her son's ability as well as her own, Patience knew it still troubled her sister.

The raucous chatter of children floated into the salon, barely giving Patience a moment to contemplate the idea that Alma might have inherited the Rockwood gift of sight. A moment later, the girl walked through the salon doorway. Greer's hand was locked in hers, while Imogene followed her into the salon with Aiden balanced on her hip.

Involved in an animated discussion, Jamie and Theo walked into the room followed by the rest of the Rockwood offspring being herded forward by Louisa and Helen. What had been a fairly quiet room became rowdy with laughter. Most evening meals were like this when the Rockwood clan gathered at Melton House or Callendar, their aunt's Scottish estate.

In most households, it was unusual for children to eat dinner with the adults. But Patience and her siblings dispensed with society's customary practice when the fire had taken so much from them. They'd witnessed first-hand how quickly the future of the Rockwood clan could have been wrenched from them. The sound of deep voices in the foyer announced the arrival of the Rockwood clan's patriarch, Sebastian, and Lucien, the Earl of Lyndham, Constance's husband.

If not for Caleb and Devin, things would have been quite different tonight. In the back of her head, Patience heard Julian's voice reminding her that she'd been a part of saving the children that horrible night. But she knew her sacrifice wasn't of the same magnitude as her brother's or Devin's.

With Greer toddling slightly behind her, Alma stopped in front of Patience and leaned forward to kiss her scarred cheek. It had become a ritual with the girl. Even when Patience's scarred cheek was turned away from Alma, the child always made an effort to kiss the burnt flesh. Despite her age of seven years, the girl had always been a quiet child, but she seemed to have become even more solemn since the anniversary of the fire. Patience smiled at her as she caressed her niece's cheek.

"You look lovely tonight, Alma. We should have Nanny always pull your hair back. It makes you look very much like your mother." No sooner had she spoken than Braxton tugged on Patience's sleeve.

"Tell her, Aunt Patience. Tell her we're not orphans."

"You are *not* orphans," Patience said firmly as she directed a stern look in Alma's direction. "The word orphan is a way of saying you have no one to look after you. But you have me and Uncle Julian to look after you."

"But if you're not our mother, why does Greer call you mama?"

At the boy's question, the little girl clinging to Alma's skirts suddenly stretched out her arms to Patience and called out mama loudly and plaintively. With one arm still wrapped around Braxton, she took Greer onto her lap. The little one snuggled into Patience in a way that made her heart expand with happiness.

"Well, Greer doesn't remember your papa, and she never knew your mama," Patience said in a quiet voice.

"Why don't *you* have any children, Aunt Patience?"

Braxton's demanding question made her grow rigid where she sat. A knot formed in her throat as she fought to keep tears from forming in her eyes. The adult conversation died away, and Julian was at her side in a flash of movement. Before anyone could speak, Alma stepped forward and touched Patience's scars.

"Papa says it's so she can take care of us." The confidence in the girl's voice made Patience forget her pain as she stared at Alma in amazement. A sudden smile curved Alma's mouth as she chuckled. "Papa thinks you look just like a startled mouse surprised by the cat."

"Dear lord," Constance whispered next to her as the familiar saying their brother had always used echoed in the air.

With a quick move, her sister took Braxton out of Patience's arms, while Julian lifted Greer up. The child squealed her objection, but Julian easily silenced her by tickling her side until she was grinning happily. Patience's gaze hadn't left Alma's face who smiled at her.

"Papa says he's glad you and Uncle Julian are our parents now."

The girl's words made the tears Patience had been holding back spill down her cheeks. Consternation darkened Alma's brow, and she closed the small distance between them. One hand touching Patience's scarred cheek, the child shook her head.

"Please don't cry Aunt Patience, please don't cry. Papa says it wasn't your fault. He says you couldn't have known," Alma frowned. "What does he mean by that?"

The tears flowed harder now as she tried to suppress the sob ripping from her throat. In seconds, she was in Julian's arms as he lifted her up off the sofa and carried her out of the room. Behind her the sound of Alma's distress made Patience cry even harder. Desperately clinging to Julian, she sobbed into his shoulder. A slight jerk rippled through his body into hers as he closed the door of the morning room behind them.

Keeping her wrapped tightly in his arms, Julian sank down into a blue chintz, wing-backed chair. He pressed a kiss against her brow then allowed her to cry in his arms without saying a word. After several moments her sobs eased, and the moment she finished crying a white handkerchief was provided for her use. Patience dried her tears then looked up into her husband's eyes. His eyes, which were the color of Turkish-coffee, were dark with concern as he studied her. Strong fingers stroked her scarred cheek.

"The child did nae meant tae upset you, *mo ghràdh*."

"I know," she sniffled as she wiped a fresh tear drop off her cheek. "I simply wasn't prepared..."

"For Caleb to have his daughter tell you what the rest of

us have been telling you for so long?" There was a gentle note of chastisement in his voice that made Patience nod her head.

"I...it was so unexpected." She drew in a deep breath. "I had thought that if Caleb were to reach out to anyone, it would be to one of us—his siblings."

"And yet he chose his daughter," Julian whispered gently against her brow.

"She's never said anything that made me even think she had the gift like other members of the family." Patience shook her head as she grappled with what had just happened.

"I do nae think anyone expected Alma tae have the gift of the *an dara sealladh*, let alone as strong as it appears to be," Julian said quietly. "She will need your guidance, Patience."

She nodded at her husband's words, but she wasn't so sure Alma needed her as much as Julian might think. The child seemed quite comfortable with her gift, but it was possible Alma's only experience had been communicating with her father. Julian might be right in thinking her niece would need someone to confide in. A soft knock on the morning room door made Patience slide free of Julian's grasp, and he chuckled.

"It is nae like we are nae married, *mo leannan*."

His amusement made her glare at him as she invited the visitor to come in. The sight of Aunt Matilda sent a wave of reassurance through her. The Scotswoman was the only mother she'd ever really known as her own mother had died from a terrible fall when Patience was five. The older woman moved toward her with a gentle smile on her still young-looking features. As her aunt stopped in front of Patience, the older woman tenderly cupped Patience's cheeks with her hands.

"Are ye all right, me darling lass?" There was a shadow of deep concern in her aunt's eyes, and Patience nodded.

"Yes," she said with a nod. "As usual, Julian knew precisely what to say."

"Aye, I've nae doubt he did." Matilda Stewart beamed at the Highlander before returning her attention to Patience. "Do ye feel up tae returning to the salon? Alma is beside herself. The wee bairn thinks she's responsible for making you cry."

"But she didn't," Patience exclaimed softly with regret that she'd managed to upset her niece.

"Aye, but she's a true Rockwood. She's stubborn and somewhat blind tae the truth of things just like her aunt." The gentle chastisement made Patience wince, and her aunt smiled then leaned forward to kiss her brow. "Do nae take my teasing tae heart, lass. I would nae have ye any other way."

With that, her aunt turned and headed for the door. Patience remained immobile for a brief second as the door closed behind the Scotswoman. Julian pulled her back into his arms and brushed his mouth against her ear.

"We can nae replace their parents, *mo ghràdh*, but like Aiden, they are ours to love just as if they were our own," Julian whispered. "We might nae have our own bairns, but that means we have even more love to give them."

A wave of emotion swept through Patience as she looked up at her husband. The deep love she saw darkening his eyes made her heart soar. She had no idea what she'd done to deserve such a man, but she would love him now and beyond the veil. With a tender kiss, she wrapped her fingers through his and pulled him toward the door. As she did so, she glanced over his shoulder and could have sworn she saw the faded outline of Caleb watching them with a grin of satisfaction. His shadowy image was a bittersweet moment, but it filled her with hope.

Chapter 9

id you finalize arrangements this afternoon to secure additional footmen for the orphanage staff?" Percy asked as he stared into his glass of his port before taking a drink.

"Yes, I had Madison select three footmen to reside at the orphanage beginning tonight," Sebastian said with a nod. "I'm also making arrangements for permanent security to ensure the family is safe when they visit the orphanage."

"Have you had any success in discovering how Miss Bennett knows this Edgar fellow Patience mentioned earlier this afternoon?" Julian's voice echoed with a trace of concern as Percy met his brother-in-law's gaze.

"I believe she encountered him in her efforts to relocate several children to the country." His vague reply made Sebastian and Julian arch their eyebrows in surprise, and Percy winced at the skepticism reflected in their expressions.

"I think it's time we join the ladies," his brother murmured.

Grateful Sebastian hadn't pressed him on the matter, Percy followed Sebastian and his brothers-in-law out of the dining room. As he entered the salon, he saw Jamie seated next to Rhea on the settee across from his aunt and Patience. From the moment he'd ushered Rhea into the house this evening, she'd been the subject of a subtle, yet persistent, inquisition by his family. Outsiders would have simply put their questions down to his family being polite. Percy knew better.

Although his family's interest was genuine, it was far from superficial. The Rockwood clan was attempting to discern if Rhea was worthy of him. Not that his family's probing would bear fruit. The only thing binding him and Rhea together was their hatred of Ruckley.

Percy stopped himself from snorting with disgust as he reluctantly admitted his interest in Rhea bordered on the edge of something he'd never experienced before. A second later, he was forced once again to catch himself from expelling a noise of aggravation.

The younger children had been taken up to the nursery shortly after dinner leaving only his nephew Jamie and Lucien's niece Imogene to join the adults in the salon for post-dinner conversation. As he approached the settee, he saw Jamie lean into Rhea.

"Might I show you the garden, Miss Bennett? It's quite lovely at this time of evening, just as dusk is setting in." The boy's words made a small laugh break free from Rhea's mouth as she shook her head.

"It sounds delightful, Lord Westbury, but—"

"Miss Bennett has already promised me the pleasure of her company for a walk in the garden," he growled as an emotion he preferred not to name flooded his body with tension.

Not quite ten, Constance's son had already earned himself a reputation for his quick wit and charm. If the boy were older, Percy knew he would have had a battle on his hands to capture Rhea's attention. Pink color flared in Rhea's cheeks as Jamie jerked his head to glare in Percy's direction.

The look indicated that his nephew had formed a clear interest in Rhea. The sudden visceral sensation of his gut knotting again with the same unpleasant emotion he'd experienced just seconds before made him scowl at the boy. Clearly amused, Patience coughed to cover her laughter while Aunt Matilda shook her head and restrained her amusement behind a smile. Percy eyed both women and wondered if they'd put Jamie up to his small flirtation.

No, the boy was simply a born charmer, but he also accepted the fact it was doubtful the female contingent of the Rockwood family had discouraged his nephew's pursuit of Rhea's company. As his gaze met Rhea's he saw her purple-hued gaze darken with an undefinable emotion before it disappeared. She turned her attention back to his nephew.

"Perhaps you might care to join us, my lord," Rhea said as she smiled at Jamie. The boy brighten at the invitation, while Percy experienced disgruntlement at the idea he would have to share Rhea's company. The instant he acknowledged the fact, he tried to dismiss it, but failed.

"It would give me great pleasure to do so, Miss Bennett." Jamie exclaimed with a grin of delight, which only furthered Percy's exasperation at the sudden possessiveness he felt for Rhea. From across the room Constance expressed her disapproval.

"Not this evening, Jamie," his sister said as she refused Rhea's invitation on behalf of her son. "It's late, and you agreed to ride with Lucien and Uncle Sebastian in the morning."

"But Uncle Percy doesn't know the difference between a rose and a lily," Jamie said with scathing disdain.

"Your uncle's knowledge of gardening isn't relevant to the matter at hand, young man," Constance scolded, although her mouth twitch in a visible sign of amusement.

"Well, Miss Bennett deserves an escort who doesn't scowl at her."

"*Scowl,*" Percy exclaimed with surprise before he shook his head in denial. "I *do not* scowl."

"Yes, you do," Jamie declared with obvious annoyance. "You did nothing but scowl every time someone spoke to Miss Bennett during supper."

Laughter filled the room, as Constance hurried over to

the couch and pulled her son to his feet.

"That's quite enough, Lord Westbury," his sister said in a firm rebuke. "Your tongue is getting the best of you, which tells me you're more than ready to retire for the evening."

"Yes, mother," his nephew said with a look of disgust at being thwarted. When Constance narrowed her eyes at the boy, a cheeky smile curved his boyish mouth as he met his mother's look of reproach. "But, I'm right about Uncle Percy scowling at Miss Bennett. You said so yourself when you and Aunt Helen were coming into the salon."

His sister's embarrassment as her gaze locked with Percy's might have made him laugh at any other point in time, but the fact she'd been discussing him and Rhea annoyed him. Constance offered her apologies with a chagrined wince and a small shrug. Aware that his accusation had diverted attention away from himself for a brief moment, Jamie turned back to Rhea. The boy took her hand in his and lifted it to brush his mouth over the tip of her fingers in a courtly gesture.

"Good night, Miss Bennett. Please forgive Uncle Percy's ill temper. He means nothing by it. He's becoming quite irritable in his waning years."

The boy's words made Rhea laugh out loud while this time Percy was certain he was scowling as he glared at his nephew. Laughter erupted in the room once more as Constance gasped at his nephew's insult. Aware of the fact he might have gone too far, Jamie's nose wrinkled in regret.

"My apologies, Uncle Percy." Jamie nodded his head at Percy in a gesture of regret.

Prepared to chastise the boy, Patience's loud cough made him glanced at his sister. Eyebrows arched, she narrowed her gaze at him in a silent warning. He had no call to berate the boy given his own error this afternoon with Patience. With a resigned sigh he offered a placating gesture to Constance.

"Apology accepted," he said brusquely. As if aware he'd angered Percy , his nephew closed the distance between them.

His demeanor one of penitence, Jamie lowered his voice.

"I truly am sorry, Uncle Percy." The quiet apology was heartfelt, and a wry smile curved Percy's mouth as he tousled the boy's hair.

"You come by that reckless streak naturally, Jamie." He bobbed his head in Constance's direction. "I think maybe it's best if you make a dash for it or there will be the devil to pay."

With a relieved smile, Jamie nodded his head and walked toward the door under his mother's censorious look. Despite the look of disgust Imogene cast in her companion's direction for his bad behavior, it was obvious the girl intended to offer Jamie moral support. The two children had reached the doorway when Jamie came to an abrupt halt. Imogene touched his arm as a look of trepidation crossed her somewhat unremarkable features.

Jamie turned around and his gaze focused on Rhea. His nephew's expression was one he'd seen before, and as Jamie fixed his gaze on Rhea, Percy's heart sank. The last thing he wanted was for Rhea to be the recipient of a warning from the *an dara sealladh* without knowing the Rockwoods had the gift of sight.

"Miss Bennett, Timothy says you're not to blame yourself for what happened. He says you did everything you could."

"What?" Rhea's voice was a strangled sound of horror and panic. "How could you…"

Percy jerked his head in Rhea's direction as her voice trailed off into silence. The vibration of dismay and concern flooded the room as Constance stared at her son in stunned horror. Percy's gut twisted at the way shock had made Rhea's skin take on a deathly pallor. Instinct drove him forward, but Patience had already moved to join Rhea on the settee. As his sister took Rhea's hand in hers, Percy looked over his shoulder at Constance.

His oldest sister's helpless look reminded Percy how the

strength of Jamie's abilities had always made Constance fear for her son. Lucien quickly moved to where his wife was standing. The earl murmured something, and Constance nodded then placed her hand on Jamie's shoulder. By now, Jamie's expression was one of deep remorse and a hint of fear.

Percy caught his sister's gaze again and nodded toward his nephew then mouthed the words not to be angry with her son. She didn't respond as she and Lucien urged the children out of the salon. As the four of them disappeared through the doorway, Percy moved around the couch to study Rhea. Some of her color had returned, but her confusion was evident as she looked at Patience.

"I don't understand," she whispered in a dazed manner. "How could he...Timothy died more than two years ago."

"It's a bit difficult to explain," Patience said softly and squeezed Rhea's hand.

"I think the lass might feel better with a wee bit of fresh air, Percy." His aunt's words echoed with silent encouragement to explain the *an dara sealladh* to Rhea. The prospect wasn't one he'd been ready to address quite this soon. Unfortunately, his nephew had unwittingly forced his hand.

"I think my aunt's suggestion is an excellent one. Come," he said quietly and extended his hand to Rhea. The moment her fingers slid across his palm, his jaw clenched at the icy feel of her hand. Like a lamb meekly following a shepherd, she rose to her feet and allowed him to gently guide her toward the door that led into the garden.

"Percy." His sister-in-law, Helen, hurried to his side and offered him a plaid shawl. "It's warm out, but Miss Bennett might find it chilly."

With an abrupt nod he accepted the light-weight wrap and placed it over Rhea's shoulders. Linking her arm in the crevice of his, Percy ushered Rhea out into the night air. As he closed the door behind them, he heard the quiet whispers of curiosity reverberating in the salon.

With the exception of the soft sounds from the street in front of the house, the garden was quiet. Rhea stumbled slightly, and he paused to give her the opportunity to regain her balance. When she'd steadied herself, he led her across the grass to the small alcove that contained a wrought-iron bench. They sat in silence for several moments before she turned her head to him.

"How did you know about Timothy?" she asked hoarsely. "And why would you tell young Lord Westbury about him?"

"I didn't tell Jamie anything, because I don't know who Timothy is," he replied with a shake of his head. "I still don't. However, I can surmise he was important to you."

Rhea met his gaze for a long moment before she turned her head to stare out at the garden that had taken on a blackish purple hue in the early evening's light. There was a forlorn air about her. Whoever Timothy was, he'd obviously meant a great deal to her. The thought shot a bolt of emotion through him that he was forced to recognize as jealousy. First Jamie, and now someone who was dead. He didn't like the implications of the sensation.

"Who was he? Someone you loved?" The moment he asked the questions, Percy experienced a possessiveness for her that told him he was treading dangerous ground.

"No," she said with a shake of her head and eyed him with distrust. "If you didn't tell your nephew about Timothy, then who did?"

The immediate return to the original question said she wasn't about to explain who this person was. Her stiff, controlled manner reminded him of the demeanor Sebastian had often exhibited before his brother had married Helen. He wondered if she realized how strong she was. Percy clenched his jaw as he struggled to find the words that would explain the special ability his family had—he had. In a violent motion, he shoved his hand through his hair. How in the hell was he supposed to explain his family's clairvoyant abilities or his own for that matter? With a sigh he studied the shadows darkening the quiet garden.

"Well?" Her hand grasped his forearm until her fingers were biting down into his skin through his coat sleeve. The single word question and physical gesture were a challenge, a gauntlet thrown down in a demand that didn't surprise him. Percy turned his head toward her as he tried to explain the unexplainable.

"My family has more than one trait we share. Our tendency toward reckless behavior is legendry among the Set, but there's one talent several family members have that isn't as well known."

Percy paused for a moment as he remembered the family's reaction to Constance's discrete readings for members of the nobility. To say Sebastian had been unhappy with the knowledge was an understatement. The patriarch of the family didn't have the gift, and while he'd never dismissed the various predictions, his siblings had made over the years, it had always been his preference not to discuss the issue outside the family.

He glanced down at Rhea's hand pressing into his arm and drew in a deep breath then released it. Other than Jamie, he was the only male in the family to possess an intuitive nature. The Rockwood women were the ones who possessed the real ability in the family. His gift was a shadow of what his sisters and Aunt Matilda possessed. Percy gritted his teeth and steeled himself for what was to come.

"My family has the gift of sight."

"I don't understand." Rhea studied him with a confused frown.

"The Gaelic word for it is the *an dara sealladh*. It's run through the family for centuries. For those who possess the ability, they're able to see bits and pieces of the past and future." At his quiet explanation, Rhea jerked her hand away from him and shrank back into the opposite corner of the bench.

"Do you take me for a fool?" she snapped. "If this is your way to avoid telling me the truth about how you came to know about Timothy, I find it despicable."

"I would never take you for a fool, Rhea. In fact, I'd hoped never to tell you about my family's ability."

"I don't believe you."

Rhea sprang to her feet, and he quickly followed suit. As she turned to leave the alcove, he caught her arm. The electric current that streaked up his arm caught him by surprise, but he ignored it as he forced her to look at him.

"I am *not* a liar," he bit out harshly. "The first time I heard this Timothy's name was when Jamie mentioned him this evening."

"Are you trying to tell me that your nephew has this *gift* as well?" Rhea sneered with skepticism.

"That's *exactly* what I'm telling you," he said with frustration. Her skepticism wasn't unsurprising, but his need to ensure she believed him was. "Jamie's abilities surpass everyone else's in the family."

"And I suppose you're telling me that you have this gift as well."

The sarcasm in her voice scraped across his senses, and he jerked his hand away from her. It wasn't the first time he'd wished he was incapable of having visions. But the scorn in her voice stung more than he liked. When he didn't reply she narrowed her gaze at him. Suddenly her eyes widened in bewildered astonishment.

"That night in the museum," she whispered as she paled with fear and panic. "You knew. You knew who I was."

"*No, I didn't know who you were.*" Percy shook his head in denial. "I'd had a dream about you, but the only thing the *an dara sealladh* showed me was your eyes. A beautiful pair of violet eyes filled with fear and pain. I knew you were in trouble, but I didn't know how to find you, and when I did, I wasn't able to help you."

Rhea stared at him in silence. Confusion mixed with fear and distrust flitted across her face, and his body tensed as he waited for her to flee. When she remained immobile, he eyed her cautiously. After a long moment, she met his gaze steadily.

"Have you had any other…other visions about me?" The question tightened his muscles until they were rock hard. Percy jerked his head in an affirmative nod.

"Yes," he muttered.

"Today?"

"Yes." Short and abrupt was the best he could manage at the moment because his jaw ached as if he'd taken a jab from a sparring partner at the club.

"What did you see?" The question held the smallest hint of trepidation, which was almost buried beneath the strength he'd come to admire in her.

"You were surrounded by a group of children." Deliberately, he refrained from sharing the image of her fighting with Ruckley.

"The children," she murmured with a nod of her head. A second later, her gaze locked with his as if knowing he was holding something back. "What else."

"I saw you struggling with a man I assume was Ruckley," he said softly. She flinched and Percy stepped forward to rest his hands on her shoulders. "I won't let him hurt you anymore, Rhea. I give you my word."

For a moment, she appeared ready to argue before she dropped her head and nodded. Beneath his hands her tremor vibrated into him. Without thinking, he pulled her into his arms in a protective embrace. She didn't protest, but melted into him. It felt right holding her like this with her body burrowing into his and her cheek pressed into his shoulder. He tried to discard the thought, but it was impossible to do so. A soft sigh escaped her as she straightened and lifted her head to look at him.

"I'm beginning to think you should be called Sir Percy." The small smile curving her mouth made him smile in return.

"Why is that?" he chuckled.

"Because you seem to have the penchant for taking on the role of a knight in shining armor." Her observation made him arch his eyebrows before he laughed. When she eyed him with puzzlement, he laughed again.

"I own a white gelding I'm partial to riding every morning." The confession made her eyes widen in surprise before she laughed. It was a pleasant sound, and he enjoyed knowing he was responsible for it.

"Then I really will have to begin referring to you as Sir Percy."

"Somehow, I think you'll find a way to mock me with that title."

"Of course not," Rhea said with a distinct flash of mischief in her eyes.

She had the look of a woman free of any cares. It made her beautiful. Without thinking, Percy ran his thumb across her bottom lip. His touch made her draw in a sharp breath, and her violet eyes shimmered with something undefinable as her gaze locked with his. The tip of her tongue flicked out to wet her upper lip, and his entire body hardened in reaction to the innocent act.

"You're a complex woman, Rhea Bennett."

"Am I?" she said as a soft pink blush crested over her high cheekbones. It created a sudden, acute need to taste her sweetly shaped mouth.

"Yes, and I wonder if you have any idea how strong and courageous you are."

"I think you must have had too much port after dinner." She brushed the compliment aside, but he could tell she'd enjoyed the flattery.

"And if I were to say you're beautiful, would you blame

that on my imbibing port as well?"

"Don't mock me."

Although she rejected his compliment quickly, there was just a hint of pleasure flashing in her violet gaze. Percy suddenly realized he'd spoken the truth. She *was* beautiful at this precise point in time. He knew he'd disconcerted her, and her confusion had softened her eyes to a dark purple and her mouth was parted slightly in a silent, yet innocent, invitation.

"I would never mock you, Rhea," he said quietly.

Without thinking, Percy bent his head and lightly caressed her mouth with his. A small gasp of surprise escaped her, but she didn't retreat. Unable to stop himself, he slowly deepened the kiss as he tightened his arms around her. She came willingly, and a rush of pleasure coursed through his blood. With a gentle nip on her lower lip, he enticed her into parting her mouth beneath his. As he probed the honeyed sweetness of her warm mouth, he half-expected her to push herself free of his embrace.

She didn't. Instead, her tongue probed his mouth in one tantalizing stroke after another. Passion surged through his blood as she pressed her body deeper into his. There was a natural sensuality about her that ignited a fire inside him. Even the quiet scent of vanilla and citrus wafting off her skin was intoxicating.

Desire guided his hand across her waist and upward until his fingers stroked the rounded curves of her breasts just above the edge of her bodice. What would she feel like in his hand? Images of her naked in his bed heightened the desire pounding its way through his body. The pictures in his head made his cock stiffen.

With each thrust of his tongue against hers, he imitated the carnal act he wanted to experience with her. To his surprise and delight, she shifted her hips deeper into his and the moment the softness at the apex of her thighs pressed into his erection, he groaned. Eager to taste more of her, his lips left hers to caress the edge of her jawline and then the silky smooth curve of her neck.

A low moan escaped her as she arched her body into his, and he ached with the need to explore every inch of her with his mouth. He didn't know if her action was a deliberate or unconscious response to his caresses, but she rubbed her body against his like a sleek cat begging to be stroked.

His heart slammed into his chest as the hot and sweet taste of her made him realize how much he wanted to have her beneath him. The thought of pleasuring her body with his made him kiss her with a fierce urgency. The hunger driving him was more intense than anything he'd experienced with any woman. And he'd had more than his fair share of liaisons over the years.

He swallowed the soft mewl rolling out of her then jerked as her hand brushed across his cock. Instinctively his hips thrust forward as her thumb stroked the length of him. The erotic touch tugged a dark groan out of him as he deepened their kiss. Another moan escaped her, and he swallowed the sound with his mouth.

From the sweetness of her scent to the sugar-spun taste of her lips, everything about her made his body ache with a painful need that surprised him. Pleasurable tension tightened his erection as it shouted its demand for release. With each brush of her tongue against his, the desire barreling through him intensified.

Her response was passionate and unrestrained. It illustrated the fiery spirit running deep beneath her cool, serene countenance. The fire in her was equal to his own, and he struggled to control the arousal flooding his muscles as a voice deep in his mind shouted a warning. The moment her hand brushed against his cock once more, he realized he was completely lost.

Percy's scent drifted beneath her nose as the heat of his kisses singed her mouth. She'd never allowed the men who'd bought and used her body to kiss her. It had been her way of blotting out the horror. But this was different. Even though she recognized his arousal, his actions weren't those of a man concerned only with his satisfaction.

With each kiss he coaxed her to take part in the mutual pleasure of their embrace. It was a heady emotion. Fire streaked through her as she returned his kiss with a fervor that surprised her almost as much as it excited her. Her exhilaration was enhanced by the warm, spicy smell of him as she breathed him into her senses.

Palms braced against his chest, the beat of his heart pulsed through his clothing into the tips of her fingers. The rapid pounding of his heart gave her a sense of power. It signaled a control she'd never had over a man before.

The strength of his caress coaxed her surrender, but it didn't demand utter submission. It vibrated its way through her, and she clung to him as his mouth grazed its way across her cheek. Fire warmed her skin as his lips blazed a trail of kisses down the side of her neck. The sensations it aroused inside her were foreign, but intense and pleasurable. As his mouth brushed over the tops of her breasts, her entire body exploded with one sensation after another.

With every kiss, he ignited a firestorm that threatened to consume her. Between her thighs, the core of her sex throbbed with a demand for something she'd never experience before until she grew weak in the knees. The potency of the sensations spiraling through her drove a need to have him touch her intimately—to fill her—to satisfy the ache between her legs. Desire rose to a fine-tuned pitch inside her until she released a moan of pleasure, and her body throbbed with an unrestrained, wild passion.

Rhea didn't think. All she could do was react. Thrusting her hips forward, she pressed her body into his in a silent invitation. Her hand slid down across his chest down to his waist then over his hard length. The moment she ran her finger along his erection, a violent shudder pulsated out of his body and into hers. The intensity of his reaction startled her, but pleased her at the same time.

When she stroked him once more, a groan rumbled deep in his chest then escaped his lips in a quiet growl. His response to her touch encouraged her to stroke him again. Another primitive sound rolled out of him, and a second later, he captured her mouth in a hard kiss. The caress reflected the same raw desire flowing through her veins.

In the back of her mind, she tried to understand why his touch excited her so much. She'd never expected to ever feel anything for a man. But this man was different. His touch ignited feelings inside her that were as intense as they were alarming. She didn't question it. Instead, she reveled in the fiery pleasure sluicing through her veins. As her tongue mated with his in a passionate dance, it intensified the ache between her legs. She was blind to everything except him and the way he made her senses come alive.

Without warning, he thrust her away from him in an abrupt move. Bereft of his embrace, she stared at him in shock. He put several feet between them and turned away from her. Stark and visceral, her body cried out its protest at the loss of his heat. Confusion wrapped an icy blanket around her as she fought to steady her erratic breathing. With a sudden clarity of thought, she realized why he'd rejected her so suddenly. The manner in which she'd responded to his kisses—caressed him. He knew the truth. No well-bred lady would act as she just had. He'd realized she was a whore.

The knowledge chilled her as she acknowledged her failure to show restraint. She'd opened herself up to Percy in a way that betrayed what she was. The realization mortified her as the depth of her shame sliced into her the same way Ruckley's whip had left its mark on Timothy. Hot tears pressed against her eyelids as she fought to keep them from flowing down her cheeks.

Terrified she might fail in her efforts to maintain her composure, she turned and headed back toward the house. The best way to save herself from further humiliation was to put as much distance between her and the Rockwoods as she could. She'd only gone a few feet when Percy's muscular hand caught her arm and dragged her to an abrupt halt. Not about to reveal how deep his rejection had affected her, Rhea blinked back her tears. She had no intention of furthering her humiliation by becoming an object of pity.

"Rhea—"

"Let go of me," she said fiercely as she tried to pull free of his grasp.

"Not until you accept my apology."

"There's nothing to forgive, Mr. Rockwood," she said with a calm stoicism that sent relief dashing through her. The serene façade she'd perfected under Ruckley's control had returned.

"I think there is," he said firmly. "It was wrong of me to kiss you. You're a guest here. You should feel safe from unwanted advances."

"The idea that I'm afraid of you is not only ludicrous, it's the height of arrogance," Rhea snapped as she realized she *was* afraid. She was afraid of herself. The way she'd responded to his touch terrified her. She'd been engulfed in a blaze of passion that had consumed her to the point of being oblivious to anything resembling rational thought. She never believed it possible a man could make her feel desire so profoundly. Determined not to reveal her fear, she met his gaze with one of defiance. Although she was certain her emotions were confined behind a wall of serenity, the way his eyes narrowed with assessment alarmed her.

"If you're not afraid, then why are you running away?"

"I am *not* running away," she snapped. "I simply have no wish to be an object of pity."

"What in the name of hell would make you think I pity you?" The defensive note in his voice caught her off guard. Clearly incensed by her statement, his brown eyes were dark with indignation. Unwilling to expose her deepest fears, Rhea tilted her chin upward.

"I would think that obvious to anyone. The moment I responded to you in a manner that no...respectable woman would, you realized I was soiled goods. Your reaction is understandable. But I have no wish to be pitied for my past." Bitterness wove its way through her as she swore to make Ruckley pay for destroying her life. Percy shook her slightly, and her gaze met his.

"My reaction to your—my reaction had nothing to do with your past," Percy snarled. "I pushed you away because I was on the verge of losing control and making love to you on that damn bench. Pity is the *last* thing I feel for you."

His confession stunned Rhea, and she stared up at him in open-mouthed amazement. The powerful line of his jaw was rigid with tension, and the intensity of his gaze made her heart skip a beat as she saw the banked blaze of passion darkening his eyes. Slow to recover from her surprise, she swallowed hard beneath Percy's intent gaze. The desire ebbed from his expression, and he shook his head as he studied her with puzzlement.

"Is it so difficult to believe a man is capable of being a gentleman where you're concerned?" His question made her close her eyes for a brief moment as she struggled with her sense of worth.

"I expect only what any other woman in my position expects." She paused to draw in a deep breath before she continued. "Whores quickly learn their real value to men."

Silence greeted her declaration, and she forced herself to meet his gaze. His visibly raw fury made her take a quick step back of alarm. Percy uttered a harsh oath, but didn't move. Rhea watched his throat bob as if he were struggling to speak. His features stern and forbidding, he cleared his throat.

"You are *never* to refer to yourself in that manner again."

"I cannot deny who or what I am," she said stiffly.

"You do yourself a grave injustice, Rhea."

"*No*, I speak the truth. You know nothing about me *or* my past." Tension held her stiff and unmoving as she eyed him with scorn.

"I know enough to believe you sacrificed your honor to protect others." The gentle note in his voice sent a shudder streaking through her.

It was as if he were urging her to forgive herself for the past. She wavered on the brink of absolution before casting the notion aside. Forgiveness and acceptance could be dealt with when the children were safe. At the moment, Percy Rockwood was her biggest problem. She should have found a way to keep him out of her life. Rhea shook her head slightly as she stared up at him.

There was a stubborn tilt to his beautiful, firm mouth. Only moments ago, his lips had ignited a blaze that still smoldered in her belly. The thought made her tremble. She jumped as Percy stepped forward to capture her hands in his. Slowly, he caressed the tips of her fingers with his mouth. The gentle touch sent another tremor cascading through her, and she swallowed hard as she met his gaze.

"I told you this afternoon to trust me," he said quietly. "I failed you a moment ago. It won't happen again."

"The blame does not lie solely at your feet," she murmured as the memory of his touch caused a wave of heat to rise in her cheeks.

"Nonetheless, I'll not take advantage of you again," he said firmly. The resolve in his voice caused disappointment to spike through her. Rhea had enjoyed the way he'd kissed her. She'd relished the rush of pleasure his mouth had aroused in her.

"You didn't take advantage of me." The conviction in her voice surprised Rhea as she pulled her hands out of his and brushed her fingers over her lips. Bewilderment swept over her as she stared at him. "Other than you, no man has ever kissed me before, and I thought it quite pleasurable."

Rhea's heart slammed to a halt. What in God's name was she thinking to have made such an outrageous statement out loud—let alone think it? Slack jawed with dumbfoundment, Percy stared at her in amazement. Heat burned Rhea's cheeks again. Her rash confession had made a bad situation worse. Percy's astonishment quickly dissolved into a dark frown, which made her throat close with trepidation. Bowing her head, Rhea struggled to keep the humiliation out of her voice.

"I'm sorry. I should not have said that."

"What? That I'm the first man to kiss you, or that you enjoyed it?" The words were brusque, but the gentleness of his touch as he forced her to look at him softened his response.

"Both," she whispered. "I...I never thought I could—"

Rhea came to an abrupt halt with her explanation as she came close to revealing one of her darkest secrets. Her heart pounded frantically in her chest. She'd never told anyone, not even Arianna, how she'd endured the revolting touch of all the men Ruckley had sold her to. It wasn't a topic either of them had ever discussed.

She was certain it was because the subject was as disgusting, humiliating, and painful for Arianna as it was for her. Confusion held her in its grip as she saw the compassion and questions in Percy's brown-eyed gaze. He didn't say anything, he allowed her to decide whether to continue of not. Just as he'd done this afternoon, his understanding melted some of the ice encasing her heart.

"I…when…by not letting anyone kiss me, I was able…I could distance myself from the horror," she whispered.

Each of her words echoed with shame and disgust, and a shudder ripped through her as she remembered all the times she'd lain beneath the foul-smelling men who'd bought the use of her body from Ruckley. Despite the warmth of the summer evening, an icy chill sank through Rhea's skin and muscles down to the bone. First one shiver and then another gripped her, and a second later she was engulfed in the warmth of Percy's embrace and the comfort he offered was given in silence. Rhea didn't move for several moments, grateful for the strength flowing out of him and into her body. For the second time in just a few hours, she didn't feel alone.

"I promise you Rhea, I'll see to it the bastard pays for what he did to you."

The dark rage reflected in his voice made Rhea turn her face into his chest as she fought back tears. She knew he would do his best to make good on his promise, but he didn't know Ruckley as she did. Somehow, she would find a way to battle Ruckley on her own, if only to keep Percy safe.

Chapter 10

Behind the glass pane of Luke Ashford's office door, Rhea heard the quiet murmur of voices. For a moment, she hesitated knocking on the beveled glass that formed the top portion of the door bearing Luke Ashford's name and title in gold lettering. Had she recorded her appointment incorrectly on her calendar?

Certain she had the correct time, Rhea tapped the glass with her knuckles. Upon hearing the verbal command to enter, Rhea passed through the door into the small, almost barren office. The moment he saw her, Luke Ashford was on his feet. Another man sat in front of the investigator's desk, and Rhea's muscles tightened in dismay as she recognized Percy's broad shoulders.

Slowly rising to his feet Percy turned to her. With a jerky movement she rolled up the veil of black netting covering her face until it rested on the brim of her hat. Although she knew full well why he was here, Rhea swung her gaze back to the private investigator.

"Did I err in thinking we had an appointment today, Mr. Ashford?"

"Not at all, Miss Bennett," the investigator said with a shake of his head. His hand extended in a polite gesture, he pointed to the second chair in front of his desk. "Please, won't you be seated?"

When Rhea didn't move, Percy arched his eyebrows as he silently challenged her to either stay or run. Irritated by his arrogance, she glared at him before taking a seat in the other chair that faced Luke Ashford's desk. Deciding to confront Percy head on, she clasped her hands in her lap and turned slightly to look at him.

"Why are you here, Percy?"

"I came because I wanted to meet the man you selected to assist you in this dangerous venture you've taken upon yourself. I wanted to ensure your safety was in good hands."

"And now you have," she said in a dismissive tone. "So, if you don't mind, Mr. Ashford and I have plans to discuss."

"Plans that put you in harm's way." Percy's quiet words made Rhea jerk in surprise before she narrowed her gaze in his direction.

"My plans are *my* business, and I would appreciate you not interfering."

"If you'll recall, I have a vested interest in your efforts." The reference to his desire to make Ruckley pay for his transgressions made Rhea flinch. There was a determined glint in his eye that warned her not to challenge his presence. As silence filled the office, Ashford cleared his throat.

"Mr. Rockwood was expressing his concern for your safety tomorrow night." The private investigator eyed her intently, and Rhea's mouth tightened with anger. It was the same argument she had with Ashford every time they pulled one of the children out of Ruckley's grasp.

"While I appreciate your concern, we've had this discussion before," she said coolly. "We both know the children will be less than cooperative with you if I'm not there to ease their fears."

"Nonetheless it's still dangerous for you," Percy interjected quickly in a voice tight with frustration.

"Of course it's dangerous," Rhea snapped as she turned her head and glared at him. "However, I'll be well-hidden in a carriage with the driver to keep me safe from harm.

"And if Ruckley discovers where you are and has you

followed? What then?"

"I've always taken extra precautions for these rescues." Rhea eyed him with disgust. "I'm well-versed in how to deceive a potential mark. The only difference this time is that the mark is Ruckley, or rather the children Ruckley believes are his property."

"A man who is capable of murder and won't hesitate to express his fury where you're concerned."

Percy's oblique reference to that night in the museum made her wince. She knew he was right. What she was doing *was* dangerous. But her life under Ruckley's rule had been no less precarious. She tilted her chin upward as she studied the disapproval on Percy's strong features for a long moment. Before he could say anything else, Rhea jerked her gaze toward the man seated behind the desk.

"Mr. Ashford, am I the one paying your fee or is Mr. Rockwood?" The question made Ashford frown with a look of discomfort. The man clearly didn't like being caught in the middle of an argument between Rhea and Percy.

"You are, Miss Bennett," the investigator replied politely.

"I'll double your fee if you rescue the child *without* Miss Bennett's participation." Percy's words rang out clear and firm in the office.

Stunned by his offer, Rhea jumped in surprise then twisted in her chair to eye him balefully. Satisfaction crossed his features, and Percy met her gaze steadily. The man was determined to thwart her being present during the rescue operation. The anger spiraling through her at his interference made her fingers dig into the hard wood arms of her chair as she glared at him in silence. She wavered between haranguing him like a fisherman's wife or simply walking out of the room.

Even despite her anger, a small voice in the back of her head expressed delight that he would go to such lengths to protect her. But she didn't want Percy Rockwood's protection. What she wanted was to ensure the safety of the children

Ashford had agreed to help her extract from Ruckley's charge. Her gaze shifted back to the private investigator who appeared even more uncomfortable now.

The man had been placed in an untenable position. There was little she could do except find an alternative route to save the children. It meant taking a more dangerous, drastic approach, but Percy had left her little choice. Rhea pulled in a deep breath as she met the private investigator's gaze.

"I cannot match his offer, Mr. Ashford," she said in a cool, serene voice. "Therefore, I believe it necessary to terminate our business relationship."

Not waiting for a response, Rhea rose from her chair and walked toward the door. The instant Percy gripped her arm she quickly jerked free of his grasp and eyed him imperiously.

"If you don't mind, Mr. Rockwood, I have another appointment," she snapped in a low voice.

"*Damnit, Rhea*, I only want to ensure your safety."

The harsh anger in his soft words emphasized his concern was genuine. Inside her chest, her heart skipped a beat. His persistent efforts to protect her made Rhea consider the possibility of giving way. It would be so easy to let someone else take charge of the operation. Percy clearly wanted to help. Rhea halted her thoughts and the direction they were headed. The children were her responsibility. It had been difficult enough trusting Ashford to help her. She refused to shirk her duties completely.

"While I appreciate your desire to do so, your assistance is unnecessary. I've managed quite well without your assistance until now."

"Don't be a fool," he growled as he lowered his head until their foreheads were almost touching. "You warned me not to underestimate Ruckley, and yet you've done just that from the moment you started pulling these children out from underneath the man's nose."

"But that's the difference between you and me. I have

never underestimated Ruckley," she said with quiet resolve. "I know how he thinks, how to respond in certain situations. You do not."

"Just because you know the man, doesn't make him any less dangerous."

"I don't deny that, but let me ask you this. If Ruckley had a member of your family in his power would you allow someone else to take charge of their safety?" Her question made Percy frown darkly then answered her question with a sharp jerk of his head. Rhea nodded with resignation. "Then you can understand why I'll not surrender involvement when it comes to the children I care for. I didn't make my decision lightly. It is simply a matter of love and obligation."

With a barely audible growl, Percy shoved a hand through his hair. His frustration vibrated through Rhea as she watched his beautiful mouth thin with anger. With an explosive grunt of aggravation, he glanced over his shoulder at the private investigator who hadn't moved from behind his desk.

"Consider your fee doubled, Ashford, simply because Miss Bennett will be present tomorrow night. See to it that an additional man is hired to ensure her safety.

"Gladly, Mr. Rockwood." At the other man's response, frustration darkened Percy's features as he turned back to her. Grateful for his reluctant agreement, Rhea touched his arm in a conciliatory gesture.

"Thank you."

"I need my head examined," he muttered tersely.

"Perhaps we both do," Rhea said with a sigh. "But I see no other way to resolve the situation."

"Ashford, how many other children are there to retrieve out of Ruckley's hands?" Percy asked as he turned back toward the investigator.

"After tomorrow night, three."

"Isn't it possible to rescue the other children at the same

time?" Percy frowned in puzzled frustration.

"Only if they happen to be with the child in question. I monitor one child's behavior at a time. It's the best way to plan for their rescue. If we were to attempt rescuing all the children at once, we risk certain failure and the definite likelihood of Mr. Ruckley seeing to it there are no further opportunities to mount another effort in the future."

Ashford's response made Percy nod his head then fixed his gaze on Rhea again.

"You're not to leave the carriage at any point during the rescue. Is that clear?"

"Yes," Rhea said with a nod. Her brevity caused Percy's mouth to twist in a wry grimace.

"Why is it I'm sure you'll disobey that order if it suits you?"

"Actually, it's an agreement I've had with Mr. Ashford from the beginning."

At her response, Percy released a quiet noise of exasperation then turned back toward the private investigator.

"I'll be joining you in this venture tomorrow night, Ashford." At Percy's matter-of-fact statement the other man nodded.

"I recommend clothing that is of a…less fashionable kind. We need to be as inconspicuous as possible."

"Understood." Percy nodded and Ashford turned his gaze to Rhea.

"I take it I'm to use the standard phrase when approaching Rufus?"

"Yes," she whispered. "Never forget Timothy."

"Very well, we'll meet here at nine o'clock tomorrow night. I need to point out that on several different occasions the boy has been in the company of a girl. She matches the description you provided."

"Fanny?" Rhea exclaimed in a breathless voice. "You've not mentioned this before."

"I'm not sure I should have now," Ashford said with a sardonic note in his voice. "I don't want to get your hopes up. However, I wanted you to be aware if we're able to rescue the girl as well. I know there will be accommodations you'll need to make."

"Thank you," Rhea said with a nod as hope flared inside her.

If Ashford could help Rufus and Fanny escape Ruckley's control, that left only Harry and Peter to save. It meant she'd be done with London, and she'd be free. Free to live a quiet life in the country with the children. A life that would allow the children to grow up cared for and loved. A life they would never know in the East End. Her gaze darted to Percy's patrician profile as he nodded at something Ashford said. Despite her best efforts, her life was becoming more entangled with his hour by hour.

The fact that Percy had taken it upon himself to become her knight errant dismayed and pleased her at the same time. It also made her question why he was doing so. Last night when he'd explained how his nephew had known about Timothy, she'd initially thought him a liar. The concept of someone speaking with the dead wasn't something she found easy to grasp.

The small bit of trust she'd awarded Percy had immediately teetered on the brink of destruction when he'd explained he came from a family of psychics. The entire idea had struck her as an outrageous story one might use to explain away a lie. But it was his reluctant admittance that he had the same gift as his family that made her consider the possibility he was telling the truth. It had been quite clear he'd been uncomfortable telling her about his gift.

As the idea of his ability had begun to sink in, she remembered the night in the museum. Over the past year she'd tried to understand his words to her the night Ruckley had shot him. Then there had been the odd incident at the orphanage. Braced against the wall, he'd appeared ready to slide to the floor. He'd had the look of someone in a trance, and it had alarmed her. Then there was the reaction of Percy's family to Jamie's declaration.

None of them had exhibited any surprise at the boy's announcement, only dismay. Oddly enough, she knew their reaction wasn't because a secret had been revealed. Their behavior had been one of genuine concern for her and the distress Jamie's words had caused. Their empathy and caring nature for her anguish had been more than evident as Percy had led her out into the garden.

She liked Percy's family. They were a close, tight-knit group. She'd recognized the polite inquisition they'd put her through for what it was. They wanted to know whether she was good enough for him. Sadly, the answer to that question was a resounding no. The thought speared its way through her heart, and she barely managed to keep from gasping at the physical ache it caused.

Why should she care whether she was worthy of Percy Rockwood? She didn't like the reply whispering through her head. Her mouth suddenly dry, she jumped as Percy touched her elbow. The pulse of electricity that sped up her arm sent her heart racing. Alarmed by her response, Rhea quickly pulled away from him. Percy frowned slightly as he met her gaze.

"I'll see you home," he said quietly.

Still struggling with her reaction to him, and the emotional upheaval assaulting her, Rhea merely nodded. Hastily covering her features with the veil attached to her hat, she said goodbye to Ashford and walked out of the office with Percy on her heels. The moment they left the building, the fetid odors of the East End pushed past the veil and filled her nostrils. She almost gagged at the smell. How had she ever tolerated the stench to the point it hadn't sickened her on a daily basis? Bile rose in her throat, but she forced it back.

"Let me wager a guess you came in a hack and didn't ask

it to wait." The rebuke in his comment made her look up at him. Although he appeared stern, there was also a hint of amused resignation. When she didn't answer, he nodded in reply to his own question and gestured to a small hansom cab parked a few feet away.

"Fortunately for you, Miss Bennett, I came in my own carriage." The softly spoken admonishment tugged a small sound from her as she silently acknowledged her lack of forethought.

It was completely unlike her. Life here in the East End had taught her to always have a plan then a backup plan, and after then another plan that could be put to use as the last resort. But ever since Percy had reentered her life, she found herself forgetting things and not thinking clearly.

Percy assisted her into the vehicle, and once more a pulse of current spread its way through her. As he sank into the seat opposite her, Rhea averted her gaze to stare out at the squalid street. The confines of the small carriage pressed Percy's long legs into hers. The close proximity was unsettling. If she were to lean forward, she would be close enough to kiss him. Horrified at the direction of her thoughts she darted a look in his direction to see him studying her intently.

"The phrase Ashford is using to identify himself as someone the children can trust is quite unusual." Percy's comment caught her off guard, and she remained mute, uncertain what to say. Eyebrows arched quizzically, he frowned when she didn't reply. "Was Timothy one of the children you looked after while at Ruckley's beck and call?"

The question cleared her mind of everything but the image of Timothy's pale, terrified features. She stared in consternation at Percy through her veil. The man had an uncanny ability to know things about her. Was it his talent for seeing things others couldn't? The thought alarmed her. The idea of him seeing into her past wasn't something she wanted to contemplate.

His demeanor said he was awaiting an answer, but the horror of Timothy's death made her hesitate to share the story. Rhea closed her eyes for a brief moment then turned her head away from him. It was easier to tell her tale without watching his reaction. She drew in a deep breath and released it.

"Ruckley is a brutally vicious man."

"Of that I have little doubt." The hard edge to his words indicated he loathed the criminal almost as much as she did.

"In addition to my...to Ruckley selling my body..." She stumbled over her words and looked at him for a brief instant. Outrage had made Percy's mouth grow thin with repressed fury, and she quickly averted her gaze. Rhea swallowed hard. "I was also forced to pick pockets. Our thievery was directed by Ruckley from a distance. It allowed him to avoid criminal charges if one of us was caught."

Percy grunted and muttered an oath beneath his breath. She ignored the sound and distanced herself by looking down at her hands fiddling with the skirt of her dress. If she looked at him, she wasn't sure she would be able to continue with her story.

"One of the cardinal rules was to never take anything out of the purses we stole. If Ruckley caught you..." Her voice trailed off into silence, and Percy shook his head in disgust.

"If you did, then Ruckley punished the offender," he said quietly.

"Yes," Rhea nodded as she remembered Ruckley's expression the night Timothy had died. "Timothy's parents sold him to Ruckley when he was nine. He was willful and constantly at odds with Ruckley. One day, he pocketed a few coins he'd stolen. Unfortunately, Edgar saw him steal the coins and reported him to Ruckley."

As if it were yesterday Rhea was standing in the small shed behind the pub Ruckley operated his business from. If there was one thing Ruckley enjoyed it was tormenting his victims. Even now, she could hear the soft, menacing sound of Ruckley's voice.

"Come now, Master Timothy. We're all in this together, and you know you can trust your old friend Ruckley. What happened with that wealthy gent you bumped into this evening?"

Rhea glanced around at the small group witnessing the mental game Ruckley was playing with Timothy and the rest of them. Every child in the small band looked terrified, except for Edgar. One of Ruckley's lieutenants, the boy was actually enjoying the older man's treatment of Timothy. As if aware of her gaze, Edgar looked in her direction, and his smug complacency made her stomach churn. It told her Timothy was about to pay dearly for just a few pieces of silver. Ruckley had deliberately waited until their return to the tavern before interrogating the boy.

Ruckley ordered Edgar to tie the boy to one of the shed's support structures, and the boy looked over at Rhea his eyes glazed with terror. The boy clearly understood something terrible was about to happen, but he didn't know what. Ruckley found this to be one of the most pleasurable parts of his torture—keeping his victims guessing. Sometimes he would use a whip—at other times a riding crop. Rhea had even seen him brand a young girl for refusing to sleep with a paying customer.

Despite knowing what was to come, Rhea still stiffened in horror the moment Ruckley lifted the large whip off the far wall of the shed. In another split second a wave of nausea rolled over Rhea. Oh God, not the whip. The last time the man had used it his victim almost died. Beside her, she heard Arianna make a barely audible moan. Instinctively, Rhea grasped her younger sister's hand and squeezed it tight. If any of them attempted to leave, protest, or stop Ruckley in the pursuit of his pleasure, they would find themselves enduring the same punishment.

Bile rose in her throat, and to keep it at bay she kept her

gaze on Ruckley. With each beat of her heart, she allowed hate for the man to spread its way through her body. It was the only sane way she would be able to watch the horrifying spectacle to come. Timothy had no idea of the terror and pain Ruckley was about to inflict on him, and she prayed to a God she no longer believed in that the boy would survive Ruckley's torture.

Fear prevented her from trying to stop Ruckley, and she could only look away from Timothy's pale, frightened expression. Her heart lurched in her chest at her cowardice.

The sound of Timothy's shirt being ripped open made her stiffen with horror, and her gaze jerked back to the terrible scene in front of her. When the first lash of the whip struck the boy's skin, Arianna's hand gripped hers so hard Rhea winced with pain. Again, the whip snapped through the air to land on Timothy's back. Stubbornness one of his traits, the lad did not cry out at either lash of the whip. Infuriated by the boy's obstinance, Ruckley increased the pace of his whipping. Again and again, the black leather streaked through the air until Timothy's back was splayed open and drenched with blood. Still Ruckley repeatedly brought the whip down on his victim. Sickened by the torture, Rhea leaped forward and grabbed the enraged man's arm.

"Enough, Ruckley. You'll kill him."

Cruel laughter exploded through the shed as the crime lord met her gaze. Ruckley lowered his arm, and with his free hand, he grasped Rhea by the neck and pulled her close. The foulness of his breath pulled bile up into her throat. If Ruckley knew she was nauseated by him, he'd know she was afraid. With great effort, she swallowed hard and refused to try and free herself from Ruckley's grasp. She wouldn't give the bastard the satisfaction of showing fear.

"Dear, sweet, Rhea. Always looking out for the weak ones in this little tribe of mine. One of these days, you're going to have to pay me for all the latitude I give you."

Ruckley bent his head in an effort to set his lips on hers in a rancid and foul caress, but she quickly turned her head away. With a grunt of anger, the man lowered his head and licked across the tops of her breasts. Rhea didn't know how she kept from shuddering as she pushed him away from her. In an exaggerated gesture of disgust, Rhea dragged the sleeve of her dress across the exposed skin above her bodice then spat a portion of bile out of her mouth. Fury and hatred blazed through her as she faced the man laughing at her reaction.

"If you ever touch me like that again, I'll kill you."

"Come now, my poppet. We both know ye don't 'ave the killer instinct in you, or you would have already tried to do away with me," Ruckley said with obvious amusement. "Fact is, we both know you'll wind up in my bed sooner than later."

"I'll see you in hell first," she bit out in a vicious hiss of air.

Ruckley simply laughed once more and wrapping his arm around Edgar's shoulders walked out of the shed. When the man disappeared into the night, Rhea wheeled about and ordered several of the boys in their group to cut Timothy down. As they laid the boy on his stomach, no sound passed his lips. The small band huddled around the youngster as Rhea dropped to her knees and pressed her fingers to his throat. When she could find no pulse, she hastily grabbed the boy's wrist. Again, she could find no sign of life. A small cry broke past her lips as she buried her face in her hands and tears soaked her palm. Remorse and guilt swept through her. How could she have allowed her fear to paralyze her for so long? Not even when her father had sold her and Arianna to Ruckley had she felt so helpless.

One by one, the group slowly dispersed. A gentle hand pressed her shoulder through her dress.

"Come Rhea, there's nothing more you can do for him. He's in a better place now. Harry and the boys have gone to find a cart to take him to Tower Hamlets."

With a nod, she wiped the tears off her cheeks and rose to her feet. Her gaze fell on the horrible wounds on Timothy's back. Rhea clenched her jaw in fury and hate until it ached from the pressure. She looked at her sister then back at the child lying so deathly quiet on the floor. She would never forget tonight, and she would make sure the children never did either. It was the only way to ensure they stayed alive. Timothy's death would be a reminder never to cross Ruckley.

"*Christ Jesus,*" Percy exclaimed with a violence that startled her and the images of the past vanished. Before she could say anything, Percy leaned forward to pull her out of her seat and onto his lap. As he held her snuggly against him, he quickly pulled the shades over the windows. The abrupt action startled her, but she didn't protest as he held her close. As his fingers rolled up the veil attached to her hat, she suddenly realized her cheeks were wet. She was crying. She hadn't cried since the night Timothy had died.

"You're not to blame, Rhea." His voice tender and gruff with emotion, he gently wiped her tears away. At his words, she sniffed and shook her head. She desperately wanted to believe him, but the memory of Timothy's battered body made it difficult.

"I should've stopped him. If I'd had the courage to stand up to Ruckley–"

"No," Percy's voice was harsh and emphatic. "There was nothing you could have done. If it hadn't been Timothy, it would have been another child. He's a sadistic bastard, and I won't listen to you taking the blame for circumstances that were beyond your control."

Rhea wished she could believe what he was saying. But the memory of how she'd left Percy wounded and dying on the museum floor tortured her. She'd failed him *and* Timothy. Twice she'd had the opportunity to stand up to Ruckley, and she'd failed each time.

"You've said it as well," she whispered. "I was more

concerned with saving my own life instead of standing up to Ruckley and ensuring you and Timothy survived the man's brutality."

"*Bloody hell*, I said that without knowing the truth. I would never have blamed you if I'd known you and your sister were Ruckley's victims as well."

When she didn't answer him, Percy caught her chin with his strong fingers and lifted her chin upward. She closed her eyes beneath his intense gaze.

"Look at me," he rasped. When she didn't do as he instructed, he jostled her against his chest. "*Look at me, Rhea.*"

She opened her eyes to stare up at him. Admiration and something else darkened his brown eyes. Respect. His gaze was filled with deep respect.

"There's only one other person I know who matches your strength and courage. That's Patience." His fingers brushed across her wet cheeks again as he stared down at her. "Both of you think yourselves to blame for things completely out of your control, and yet in facing all the terrible odds both of you fought back. That is the very definition of courage. You were afraid and yet you took action in spite of that fear."

"But I failed him," Rhea whispered desperately wanting to believe Percy's words.

"No, Rhea, you didn't fail him. You can't fail someone when you're not in control of the situation."

In a tender gesture Percy's mouth brushed across her forehead. Biting back another bout of tears Rhea turned her head into his shoulder. There was something so overwhelmingly comforting in doing so. The strength and security she found in his arms warmed her. She'd never felt so safe in her entire life. Silence filled Percy's carriage as she allowed herself to nestle herself in his protective embrace.

As the rancid odors of the East End dissipated, she lifted her head to see they'd entered a more respectable part of the city. Rhea dragged in a deep breath of relief at the fresh air that flowed into the vehicle. As she did so, another smell brushed across her senses. The moment Rhea breathed in his warm and spicy scent a small tremor swept through her. He smelled wonderful. The knowledge made her body tense as she recognized the danger of being in his arms.

Instantly, Rhea tried pulling away from him. It was a futile effort as Percy's embrace tightened around her. Her gaze jerked upward to look at him. His brown eyes had darkened until they were almost black, and desire glittered in his gaze. A knot formed in her throat, and she quickly swallowed it to keep breathing. Percy's fingers lightly stroked her cheek as his thumb slid across her bottom lip pressed down on it.

"I said I wouldn't take advantage of you," he said hoarsely. "But God help me, I'm finding it damn difficult not to do so."

A small thrill sped down her spine at his confession. He desired her, and it filled her with a sense of joy. With a harsh growl, Percy moved to shift her off his lap, but before he could do so, Rhea wrapped her hand around his neck and pulled his head downward. As she kissed him, a groan rumbled in his chest. The sound reverberated against her lips as Percy took command of the kiss. With a gentle force he slid his tongue past her lips to explore the inside of her mouth.

Pleasure and excitement spiraled through her as her tongue danced with his. The heat of his kiss warmed her, and she answered the increasing intensity of his passionate caress. Every inch of her was alive with a wild, exhilarating sensation that spiraled through her at a blinding speed. There was nothing shameful, sordid, or repulsive about this moment. It felt right.

Delight threaded its way through every fiber of her being as her tongue swirled around his. He tasted of cinnamon and coffee. The scent of bergamot wafted beneath her nose. Never in her life had she ever thought a man could smell or taste so wonderful. Her hand cupped his cheek as his mouth left hers to blaze a trail to her ear. As he nibbled on her earlobe, she spiked her fingers through his dark brown hair and released a soft sigh of pleasure.

Heat singed her skin as his mouth blazed a trail of fire down the side of her neck. The moment his fingers pushed aside the silk scarf that covered her throat, she gasped in surprise. Immediately, his mouth captured hers again. A warm lethargy took hold of her body, and she responded to his heated kiss with passionate abandon. Hands pressed against his chest, his muscles were hard and solid beneath her palms.

The warm summer air brushed across her skin, and a moment later the tips of his fingers caressed the base of her throat. She quivered at the touch. It was arousing, and her reaction startled her. For years she'd only felt degradation and shame when a man touched her. But this was something completely different. It was heavenly. There was nothing degrading, repugnant, or revolting about this moment. It felt more than wonderful. It felt right.

Fire skimmed its way through her limbs as he lowered his head and traced the edge of her bodice with his mouth. One small caress after another whispered across her skin. The sweetness of it made her long for more. A second later she jerked with surprise as his tongue plunged into the valley between her breasts. The hedonistic caress sent a shudder through her, and she moaned as her nipples hardened. The soft linen of her chemise rubbed across the stiff peaks creating an exquisite tension that spread its way through her body like wildfire.

The intensity of it was pleasurable and painful at the same time. An unexpected wave of arousal pushed its way through her until the spot between her legs throbbed in a manner she'd never experienced before. Instinctively, she knew only his touch would ease the keen ache throbbing at her core.

"Touch me," she rasped. "Please."

The moment she made the plea, his body jerked, and he

lifted his head to stare down at her. Passion blazed in his eyes, and it heightened the need pulsing its way through her body. Without saying a word, his head swooped down and his mouth captured hers in a kiss that made her heart race. As if from a distance, she heard the soft rustle of silk and cotton before a warm breeze danced across her thighs. His fingers trailed lazily over her stocking then across her garter to reach the skin of her upper thigh.

A delicious anticipation of something unknown to her made her blood flow fast and furious. Beneath her fingers, his heart pounded at a rapid fire pace. As his tongue continued to dance with hers, his palm gently rubbed its way to the inside of her leg. Desire sped through her limbs, and she arched her hips upward in a silent plea for his touch. A brief second later, his fingers parted her slick heat. At his touch she bucked against his hand and bit back a cry of pleasure. It became a quiet moan as his thumb found a spot at the top of her sex that he rubbed gently, but firmly.

The intimate caress sent first one and then another ripple of pleasure sliding through her. The delight building inside her pulled a moan out of her, and she bucked once more against his hand as he slipped two fingers inside her. Instantly her body exploded with sensations. Clinging to him she writhed in his arms for several moments. The waves of pleasure slowly ebbed away until she grew still.

Embarrassment streaked through her as she pressed her face into his chest. Dear God, what he must think of her. She'd behaved in a manner one might expect of a whore. Rhea's stomach lurched at the thought. The skirt of her gown fell back over her legs as he adjusted her clothing. The warmth of his lips on her temple made her start, and she lifted her head to look at him. There was still a smoldering fire burning in his gaze.

Her shame intensified, and she quickly wiggled into an upright position. As she did so, she saw him wince. For the first time she felt the hardness of his erection pressing into her thigh. Not only had she behaved like a harlot, she'd failed to give him satisfaction. Rhea bit down on her lower lip as she glanced up at him then looked away.

"I... I'm sorry. I should have—"

"Don't," Percy said hoarsely.

He caught her chin in his fingers and held her head steady as he kissed her roughly. Just as quickly as he'd kissed her, he released her and set her back on the seat opposite him. Even in the dim light, she could see the desire holding him rigid against the seat cushions.

Shakily she adjusted her scarf around her neck. Percy's gaze was like a branding iron as she fumbled with the blue silk. Her heart skipped a beat as she looked up at him. Color warmed her cheeks as she reached out to raise the window blind. The awkwardness of the situation made her uncomfortable as she met his gaze then looked away again. The moment she leaned back in her seat, Percy reached out and caught her hand in his.

"There's no shame in enjoying pleasure, Rhea."

"I felt no shame," she replied softly. It was the truth. Nothing of what had just transpired between them had made her feel soiled or unclean. It only made her feel alive.

"Good, because I have enough guilt to bear," he said tersely. "I gave my word, and I broke it."

"If I recall correctly, I...I kissed you." At her words Percy shook his head as a wry grimace touched his mouth.

"It doesn't eliminate my culpability. I ignored my promise to you."

"I'm glad you did," she said as she met his gaze steadily. A muscle tugged in his cheek at her response.

"I won't let it happen again," he growled and looked away from her to stare out the window. Heart in her mouth, Rhea swallowed hard.

"Why?" The quiet query made him jerk his head back to

her. With a shake of his head he frowned.

"Because I'm beginning to realize I want something more than a stolen kiss or touch from you."

"Oh," she breathed as something warm cracked the layer of ice around her heart. "I see."

"Do you? I'm not so certain of that." His forbidding expression sent a tidal wave of disappointment rolling over her. Without hesitation, she shielded her thoughts and emotions to retreat behind a familiar wall of stone and ice she'd developed years ago. A wall that guarded her heart from pain and allowed her to survive the horrors of her existence.

"I cannot change my sordid reputation or offensive past."

"I don't give a damn about your past," he snarled. "I *do* care what you think of me."

"What I think of you?" Surprise made her cool composure slip.

"Yes, me," he growled. "If I were to make love to you, a *decidedly pleasurable thought*, I risk the possibility of you believing I am doing so simply because of your past. I am nothing like the men who used you."

Rhea stared at him for a moment in confusion. The man had just said he desired her, but refused to act on it because he thought she would compare him to the swine Ruckley had sold her to? Impossible. She would never believe such a thing of him. In the back of her head a voice question that belief. It was immediately trampled by the sudden realization that she had been hoping for something more tangible where Percy was concerned.

Alarm streaked through her. It was far too dangerous to expect Percy or any man to want her solely for herself in spite of her sordid past. The carriage rocked to a halt, and Percy quickly exited the vehicle then stretched out his hand to her. Rhea placed her hand in his and stepped down onto the sidewalk. The pulse of energy that glided up her arm filled her with a mixture of emotions. Feelings she didn't want to have. His fingers squeezed hers with a gentleness that warmed her heart. Their eyes met, and she shook her head in bemusement.

"You're nothing like the men in my past, Percy Rockwood," she said softly. "And if I were to offer myself to you, it would be because of that very reason."

Despite all the noise on the busy street, Rhea only heard her rapid breathing as her heart pounded fiercely in her breast. Percy carried her hand to his mouth, his lips brushing her fingertips in a manner that was almost reverent. Part of her wanted to reach out and run her fingers through his hair, but she suppressed the inclination. He straightened upright and retained his hold on her hand.

"Let me take you to Covent Garden this evening," he said with a small smile. "The Drury Lane Theatre has a production of *The Bride Effect* that is apparently quite good."

Rhea hesitated to accept his invitation. The desire to be in this company and in his arms was at war with the logic of staying away from him. He squeezed her fingers again, and she realized she'd known all along what her answer would be.

"Yes," she replied softly. At her simple answer he kissed her fingers again. This time his mouth lingered. Heat spread across her skin and into her cheeks. Percy's smile broadened. With a small tug, she pulled her hand free of his grasp and started up the steps to Sherrington House then paused to look at him.

"What time should I expect you?"

"I'll call on you at seven o'clock. We'll have dinner at a restaurant I know of in Covent Garden," Percy said as he stood at the foot of the house steps. The last thing she saw as she closed the door to the house was Percy standing on the sidewalk watching her.

Chapter 11

"**R**eally Percy, must you scowl so fiercely? Surely you didn't find the play that tedious." Percy met his sister's amused gaze as she tilted her head in an inquisitive manner. "I'm beginning to see what Jamie meant the other night."

"I am not scowling," he said through clenched teeth.

"Yes, you are." Rhea, seated next to Constance, contradicted him. Percy disagreed with a shake of his head, which made both women laugh. Seated beside him in the carriage, the Earl of Lyndham leaned into Percy.

"I've learned it's best not to argue with Constance," Lucien murmured. "I think she is the most stubborn of the Rockwoods."

"I heard that, my lord," Constance said with obvious disapproval. Her husband grinned unapologetically.

"You were meant to, my darling." At his teasing, the countess laughed.

"You are a wicked man, Lord Lyndham." Constance laughed then smiled adoringly at her husband.

Percy glanced at Rhea who was observing the affectionate exchange with a wistful envy. The moment his gaze met hers, the pensive look vanished from her features. He studied her for a long moment attempting to discern what she was thinking.

"You must forgive my brother, Miss Bennett. The entire family is baffled by this cross nature he's developed recently,"

Constance said in a pseudo-whisper.

For not the first time this evening, Percy deeply regretted telling Aunt Matilda he was taking Rhea to the theater this evening. The matriarchal figurehead of the family had immediately suggested Constance and Lucien join him and Rhea at the theater. Before he knew it, his plans had been commandeered to the point where his sister and husband had accompanied them not only to the theater but to dinner as well.

At every point possible during the evening, Constance had teased him with unmerciful, yet sisterly, affection. The fact was not lost on him that the evening would have been much more pleasant if he'd gone straight home from Sherrington House instead of stopping to see Sebastian this afternoon. His gaze met Rhea's, and when she smiled at him it stirred an emotion that had been growing in strength every time he was near her.

He'd refused to reflect on his feelings simply because he knew Rhea would resist any emotional involvement. She had no reason to trust any man. She'd been betrayed by her father and suffered at the hands of Ruckley. It was humbling to know she trusted him enough to let him help her with her rescue efforts. But he also knew that trust was a fragile one. And he'd jeopardized that trust with his behavior earlier this afternoon.

Rhea's reassurance that his touch had been welcomed and pleasurable had not eased his guilt. It didn't help matters either when he remembered the way she'd responded to his kiss and the intimacy of his touch. Hell, she'd pleaded for his touch. If he'd not been cognizant of where they were, he would have satisfied his own needs by burying himself inside the slick heat of her.

The memory of her velvety smooth passage made his cock stir in his trousers. Desperate to ease the sudden craving surging through him, Percy glared at his sister as he tried to remember what Constance had just said. As his sister's words came back to him, he frowned. She'd been scolding him for being cross. With great effort, he forced himself to smile.

"I'm as pleasant as I've always been." His response made Constance release a small noise of amused disbelief.

"It's quite possible I'm the reason your brother has been irritable of late, my lady," Rhea interjected as she directed a smile at him. "I also have a rather stubborn nature, which I believe is a source of great exasperation to Percy. However, in spite of his frustration with me, he's been nothing but solicitous since we met at Melton Park."

At her words, Percy gave a start. Had she just come to his defense? Constance's surprised, delight made him believe his sister was thinking the same thing.

"I see," the countess said with a smile.

Percy wanted to groan at the approval in his sister's voice. When Constance glanced in his direction, he scowled at her. His silent response made her smile widen, and an inaudible sigh of frustration escaped him. There was little doubt in his mind that Constance would relay this small exchange back to his family. Clearly the female contingent of the Rockwood family was planning a full frontal assault when it came to interfering in his life.

He didn't offer a response to Constance's observation, which she offered up like bait to a fish. The sudden expression of complacent, sisterly affection was a familiar one. It said she was setting a trap. Born solely out of sisterly love, no doubt, but a snare nonetheless.

"Tell me Miss Bennett, has my brother mentioned anything to you about Sebastian's birthday party next weekend?" The question made Percy's body become rock hard in a split second. This wasn't a trap, it was a bloody ambush.

"I've not had the time to speak with her about Patience's request," he said coldly. "Primarily because the women in my family seem hell bent on interfering in my personal affairs."

Constance had the decency to flush with embarrassment, while Rhea appeared puzzled. Beside him Lucien chuckled, which earned him a severe glare from his wife. His brother-in-law shrugged.

"Percy's correct, sweetheart." Lucien smiled at his wife whose appearance was one of regret. With a nod, Constance tipped her head toward Rhea.

"I apologize, Miss Bennett. The Rockwood women often find themselves treading where even angels fear to go." Constance looked at Lucien. "Darling, would you tell the driver to take us home first? That will give Percy time enough to explain his agreement with Patience." This time Percy didn't bother to silence his growl of disapproval.

"Blast it, Constance. Even when you try not to interfere, you still do." The anger in his voice made his sister frown in disgust.

"I was *not* trying to interfere, Percy. I simply thought—"

"You, and the rest of the family, have been doing too *much* thinking of late," he said tightly. Constance flinched and despite his anger, Percy released a sigh of regret. "But since you've raised the subject, I will address it after we've delivered you and Lucien to your doorstep."

Constance eyed him with remorse, and he closed his eyes for a moment. If there was one thing his sisters were good at, it was making him forgive them quickly. Especially since he knew they wanted to see him happy. Patience in particular was concerned that he was allowing Nellie's death to prevent him from finding a wife. Perhaps she was right. Guilt was a powerful emotion, and he still experienced regret whenever Nellie entered his thoughts. But he'd never thought of his regrets as the reason why he'd not made any effort to marry. Beside him Lucien opened the small window that allowed him to communicate with the coachman. As his brother-in-law gave new orders to the driver, Percy met his sister's gaze and shook his head. Satisfied that she was forgiven, Constance smiled happily. Rhea, in an obvious effort to change the subject to something less volatile, turned to Constance.

"Tell me, my lady. What did you think about Mr. Conway's performance this evening?"

"I confess I'm not a huge fan of Conway," Constance said with a wry grimace. "He tends to play all of his roles in the same wooden manner, no matter what part he's playing."

"I thought he was rather dry as well," Rhea said with obvious relief. "But I hesitated to say so for fear of revealing my complete ignorance regarding the man's work."

"Is this the first time you've seen Conway perform? He's been quite popular for the last several years. Do you not attend the theater regularly?" The surprise in Constance's voice made Rhea pale, and Percy immediately realized the danger of answering the question.

"Rhea rarely visits London."

"Then that explains your lack of familiarity with Conway's work." Constance nodded with understanding and smiled at Rhea.

"Where do you live when you're not in London, Miss Bennett? Percy's not been all that forthcoming when it comes to you."

"I live with my aunt. Beatrice Fremont."

"Fremont?" Constance frowned in contemplation. "The name sounds terribly familiar. Lucien, do you recall the name?"

"No, perhaps it was someone grandmama mentioned," the earl said with a shrug.

"Perhaps." A small frown furrowed Constance's brow until a triumphant look brightened her features. "I remember now, Lord Foxworth was making inquiries about Mrs. Fremont at the party last weekend. I overheard Mrs. Delamere and Mrs. Harrington discussing a scandal involving Lord Foxworth—"

Constance abruptly stopped speaking, and Rhea looked

at his sister in puzzlement before she glanced in his direction then back to Constance.

"A scandal?" Rhea asked with curiosity. "If it affects my aunt's happiness with regard to Lord Foxworth, I would like to know the truth of it."

"I should not have mentioned it," Constance sighed as she shook her head and lightly touched Rhea's arm. "There's rarely any truth to gossip, especially where those two women are concerned."

Rhea still appeared troubled, but she didn't attempt to pursue the matter. When it became apparent she wouldn't persist in her queries, Constance relaxed in her seat.

"I've enjoyed our time together this evening, Miss Bennett. I hope Percy will convince you to come to dinner again one night next week. This time my son will be put on notice with regard to any unexpected revelations." Constance bit down on her lip. "And as I said earlier this evening, I apologize for Jamie's comments the other night."

"I know he meant no harm." Rhea smiled reassuringly then glanced at Percy. "Your family's...unusual talent must make it difficult for someone of Lord Westbury's young age to hold his tongue. And his charm makes it quite easy to forgive him of any indiscretion."

Percy stiffened as he recalled his resentment at his nephew's attention to Rhea. The memory of Jamie's flirtation still had the ability to irritate him, which made him feel like a fool. To be jealous of a boy—jealous. He'd been jealous of Jamie. An emotion he'd never experienced where any woman was concerned—until now. Constance glanced in his direction and tension latched onto him as if a noose had been placed around his neck. The knowing gleam in his sister's eyes made his jaw flex and tighten. With great effort, he schooled his features into a blank mask.

"Yes, Jamie is most definitely a Rockwood," Constance said with a small laugh then looked at Rhea in a pleading manner. "But, please say you'll join us for dinner again next week."

"I'm…I'm returning to the country Saturday morning. I'm uncertain when I'll return," Rhea said with a shake of her head. While she tried to hide it, Percy saw the flush of pleasure that crested in her cheeks at his sister's persistent invitation.

"Then I'll rely on Percy's considerable charm to convince you to return quickly. Sebastian's birthday ball for the family's friends here in town is a week from Saturday. Hopefully Percy will be able to convince you to at least return for that event."

Constance's eyes were dark with an unspoken warning as she stared at him. The silent reminder of his bargain with Patience made him bite down on the inside of his cheek. The carriage suddenly rocked to a halt, and Percy experienced an overwhelming relief. Quickly exiting the vehicle, he extended his hand to his sister. Mischief curved Constance's lips as he glared at her.

"You're frowning again, Percy," she murmured. As she offered her cheek for him to kiss, he shook his head in disgust.

"You're as bad as Patience." He kissed her cheek and nodded at his brother-in-law as the earl climbed out of the carriage. "How the devil do you live with her meddlesome nature, Lucien?"

"I love her." The earl said with a grin as he met his wife's happy gaze. With a sympathetic pat on Percy's back, his brother-in-law tossed a nod in Constance's direction. "But I shall attempt to talk some sense into her as to interfering in your personal affairs."

Percy nodded his gratitude as Lucien escorted Constance up the steps to their front door. With a sense of doom, he climbed back into the carriage. Now he had to deal with the mess Constance had made. With a light tap on the window behind him, he signaled for the driver to take them to Sherrington House.

He had planned on gently easing his way into asking Rhea

to attend Sebastian's party. Unfortunately, his sister had made that rather difficult. Percy glanced at Rhea who was staring out the window. Silence hovered between them, broken only by the clip clop of horse hooves against the cobblestones. After a long moment, Percy leaned forward and cleared his throat. Amusement shimmered in her eyes as she turned her head to look at him.

"You don't like it when your sisters tease you, do you?" Her accurate observation made him grimace.

"No, but I tolerate it, because I am equally merciless at times. But the truth is, I was more concerned about you.

"Me? Why?" Confusion made her tip her head to one side.

"Because I don't like the idea of someone hurting you, unintentionally or not." Percy reached out to take her hands in his in an effort to convince her of his sincerity.

The instant he touched her, the *an dara sealladh* barreled into him with the force of a battering ram. The images flowed fast and furious like a raging river. Turbulent and chaotic they jumped from one scene to the next. One moment he was staring up at his family gathered around his bedside. In the next he was in a dark corridor watching Ruckley holding a door open for Rhea.

The bastard's smug, lascivious smile aroused a raw fury and hatred in Percy as he watched Rhea walk toward the man. Rhea glanced over her shoulder, and he saw the fear and horror in her violet gaze despite the resignation on her face. Suddenly, his friend Blake was at his side, offering him a pistol. He began to run. The doorway Rhea had passed through was now closed, and with each step he took toward it, the door seemed further away.

Behind him Blake shouted a warning. A gunshot cracked loudly in his ear, and he stumbled forward to see Rhea covered in blood. With a wild cry, he tried to reach her, but he was plunged into darkness. Desperately, he crawled up from the depths of his vision. Somewhere as if from a great distance, Rhea called to him. Percy turned toward her voice fighting through the dark, violent images still swirling in his head.

As he fought his way to her, Percy became aware of the fact he was partially lying down, his head pressing into soft silk. A gentle hand stroked his forehead in a soothing manner. It took him several long moments to realize where he was, and he groaned at the sharp pains ricocheting in his head.

"*Christ Jesus*," he rasped.

"Hush," she said softly. When he tried to nod, a jolt of pain sliced through his head. It tugged a groan from him, and he heard Rhea make a quiet noise of exasperation.

"For heaven's sake, Percy, lie still. The driver is taking you home right now so we can put you to bed.

He wanted to protest, but didn't have the strength to do so. He made an unintelligible reply then grunted as the carriage wheel hit an uneven portion of the road. Damn, it had been years since a vision had incapacitated him so badly. Although he knew he should see her home, Percy couldn't deny feeling a sense of relief that he would soon be in his own bed.

The ride to Knightsbridge seemed endless, but he knew his small house was only a ten-minute ride from Lyndham house. When the carriage finally rocked to a halt, Percy realized he didn't want to move. It meant his head would do much more than throb.

"Percy, would you like for the driver and your manservant to carry you to your room?"

"No," he mumbled.

The thought of appearing weak in her eyes appalled him. He heard the small sound of annoyance she made, but was unable to do anything more than make a slight grimace in reply. With Rhea's assistance, he slowly sat up, suppressing a groan of pain as he did so. The carriage door opened, and Rhea quickly exited the vehicle. Determined to make it to his bed without help, Percy stumbled out of the carriage and up the steps into the narrow entryway of his house.

Jenkins met him at the front door, worry creasing his brow. He waved the man aside then gripped the stairway banister to pull himself up the steps to the second floor. Through the haze of his pain, he heard the muted sound of Rhea's voice followed by the sound of Jenkins tread on the stairs behind him. His steps unsteady, Percy made his way down the upper hallway and into his bedroom where he collapsed onto the bed. A soft hand stroked his brow, but he didn't open his eyes to look at her. The sweetness of her touch pushed through the throbbing in his head. Somehow it made his pain easier to bear.

"Percy, you need to let Jenkins undress you. You'll rest better that way."

With a groan of protest, he pulled himself up into a sitting position with his valet's assistance. Rhea murmured something and Jenkins replied, but Percy was too focused on controlling his pain to listen to what was said. The soft thud of a door closing told him Rhea was gone. Instantly, he missed her. The touch of her hand on his forehead had soothed him, and he wanted her near him again. Jenkins remained silent as he helped Percy undress, a fact for which he was grateful. It seemed as if every small sound in the room echoed like a loud church bell in his head. Jenkins offered him his nightshirt, but Percy refused. He wanted nothing on his skin that would constrict him while he slept. By the time he was undressed, he wanted nothing more than to crawl beneath the covers and sleep. As he closed his eyes, he thought he heard the quiet sound of Rhea's voice, but quickly dismissed the notion. He'd heard Rhea leave several moments ago, but the softness of her voice was the last thing he echoing in his ears before he sank into a deep sleep.

Ruckley's smile mocked Percy as he struggled against the thick rope holding him immobile in a chair. Helpless, he watched Rhea walk through the doorway Ruckley held open for her. As the door began to close, Percy shot upright in bed. A small fire burned behind a sturdy fire screen, providing more than enough illumination to reassure him he was in his own bed.

He slowly fell back into his pillows and closed his eyes. The nightmare had been an extension of the *an dara sealladh*. Whatever it meant, he knew Ruckley intended to harm Rhea in some way. With Ruckley standing there, waiting on Rhea to enter an unknown room, Percy could only surmise it represented the potential for harm the man could do to her.

A soft mumble filtered its way through his thoughts. Startled, he jerked his head toward the sound. In the dim light of the fire he saw Rhea curled up on top of the bed covers. Stunned, he simply stared at her sweetly curved body. She'd discarded most of her clothes until the only thing she wore was her chemise. He'd never seen such an enticing sight in his entire life. Slowly he stretched out his hand to caress her cheek. Rhea stirred at his touch and Percy quickly pulled his hand away from her.

What the hell was she doing here? Didn't she realize her reputation would be in shreds if someone saw her leaving his house unescorted? In the back of his mind he reminded himself that he could always say it was one of his sisters nursing him while he was sick. That didn't change the fact that she was in his bed and far too close for comfort. Percy closed his eyes and tried to gather his cluttered thoughts. He failed the minute a soft hand stroked his upper torso. Jerking his head in her direction, Percy met a violet-hued gaze filled with worry.

"How are you feeling?"

The question made his entire body tense. How was he feeling? Did the woman have any idea how difficult it was not to pull her into his arms and kiss her? Make love to her? He sat up, prepared to get out of bed, and remembered he'd refused his nightshirt. He didn't have a stitch of clothing on. The small clock on the mantle chimed the hour of three, and he seized on the fact that at this time of the morning the likelihood of anyone seeing her leave was doubtful.

"I asked you a question, Percy."

She sat up and pressed her body into his shoulder. Instantly, the warmth of her barreled through him. Unlike her voice, which contained resolute determination, her body was silky soft against his shoulder. Unable to help himself his gaze drifted down to her neck then lower to where the thin lawn of her chemise covered her breasts. The material barely left anything to his imagination, and at the moment his mind was racing in a direction that was reckless beyond anything he'd ever done. Without warning his cock stirred against his leg and hardened, and he barely managed to keep from reaching out to cup her breast.

"I'm fine," he said through clenched teeth. "What the hell are you doing here?"

"I stayed to ensure you were all right."

"And how the devil did you explain your presence in my bedroom—half naked?"

"I told Jenkins I was your mistress."

"You did what?" Thunderstruck by her revelation, Percy stared at her in shock.

"I believe my words were distinctly audible."

"Oh, I heard you *quite* clearly," he snarled angrily. The woman was mad. "What I don't know is why."

"Because I wanted to stay with you. I wanted to be sure you were all right."

"*Damnit, Rhea*," he growled. "Have you lost your mind?"

"I thought the Rockwoods approved of reckless behavior." The fact that there was just a hint of amusement in her gaze made him grit his teeth.

"The situation is at a level of recklessness that even I wouldn't dare to achieve."

"Are you saying you're unhappy I'm here?"

"I didn't say that."

"Then you *are* glad."

Before he could reply to her softly spoken words, Rhea gently pushed him back into the pillows and straddled him. Even with every alarm going off in his brain, he didn't need any warning that the situation was out of hand. His body had gone rigid with need, and he was barely holding on to what little self-restraint he still possessed. If he didn't end this quickly, something would happen—something she would regret.

"Well, Percy?" she whispered as she lowered her head and brushed her lips across his jaw. "Am I right? Are you happy I'm here?"

"*Christ Jesus.*" His voice was thick and unsteady. "How am I supposed to answer that?"

"Honestly." She lifted her head to study him and the flash of trepidation in her eyes tugged at his heart. Did she think herself so sullied that no decent man could want her? Care for her? She was wrong to think such a thing. He could easily come up with a dozen reasons why any man of good breeding would be proud to call her his. He reached up to stroke her cheek with his fingers.

"Yes," he rasped. "Yes, I'm glad you're here."

It was the truth. Even though he knew it was foolhardy for her to be here. God help him, he shouldn't allow this to go any further. He should carry her downstairs, order a hack, and send her home. But he couldn't. He didn't want to let her go. A small smile touched her lips as she caught his hand and kissed his palm. The featherlight caress sent desire barreling through him. As she nuzzled her mouth against his palm, she looked at him.

"I want this, Percy. I want you."

Her words were a mere whisper of sound. It was an open display of vulnerability and trust. Percy swallowed the knot that formed in his throat. Damnation, he couldn't take advantage of her like this. As if she sensed his struggle with his sensibilities, she kissed the palm of his hand then reached for her chemise.

"If I wasn't sure about this I wouldn't be here," she whispered.

In a breathtaking, lethargic movement, she slowly pulled her chemise up over her thighs then up over her body. The moment her breasts came into view, he sucked in a harsh breath of air. She was exquisite. As if it had a mind of its own, his hand reached out to stroke the side of one round, full breast as she finished removing her chemise. The thin garment slipped from her fingers as she let it fall off the side of the bed to the floor.

Desire darkened her eyes to a deep purple hue. In one languid movement, she lowered her head to kiss him again. It was a velvety soft caress that teased and enticed at the same time. His hand curled around her neck, and he pulled her close then nipped at her bottom lip. The small gasp she made gave him access to the warmth of her mouth. Fresh honey on a hot summer day could not have been sweeter.

With each stroke of his tongue against hers, a growing need hammered at his body. The urgency of it surged through his body, through his blood, and into his already stiff cock. It stretched and hardened further. The ache it produced was a pleasurable one that demanded a release. Every inch of him shouted with a need to slide into the slick heat of her and make her his. Quickly twisting his body, he rolled her onto her back and hovered over her.

She murmured her disapproval, but he silenced her objection with a hard kiss. Her protest became a quiet mewl as his lips left hers to caress the side of her jaw and down to the side of her neck. As he explored the curve of her shoulder with his lips, she released a soft sigh of pleasure, and he smiled at the sound.

"I like the way you taste," he murmured as he continued his downward path to her breast.

A shudder rippled through her followed by a quiet sound of delight as he grazed the tip of her nipple with his teeth. The moment he pulled the stiff peak into his mouth, she gasped and arched her body upward. Satisfaction gripped him hard at her response. In a slow, deliberate motion, he scraped across the tip of her with his tongue.

"Oh God, Percy," she moaned. He paused and raised his head slightly.

"I take it, you enjoyed that."

"Yes," she whispered as she met his gaze. Violet eyes dark with passion, she caressed his temple with the tips of her fingers.

"Good," he said gruffly.

He brushed the side of her with his mouth then kissed her breastbone as he turned his attention to the other soft, rounded breast. The only response she made was a sharp inhalation of air as he flicked his tongue over the tip of her. Desire pounded its way through him, and he lifted his head to look at her. Eyes closed, her face was flushed with pleasure, and she cried out again as he gently tugged at her rigid nipple with his teeth.

Releasing the stiff peak, he swirled his tongue around the tip of her then sucked at the hard pebble again taking pleasure in the moans pouring out of her. The moment he lifted his head and blew a small puff of air against her flesh, she cried out his name. It was a gratifying sound that wrapped around him and pushed its way through his skin until it rushed through his veins driving with it a need to possess her completely.

Heart pounding with exhilaration, he lifted his head to look at her. The bliss reflected on her lovely face shot a bolt of something unexpected through him. He was responsible for that look of ecstasy. It made her beautiful beyond words. Silently he vowed no other man would ever see her this radiant and exquisite as long as he drew breath. From this moment on he would be the only man to touch her—pleasure her.

The depth of that commitment set off fire alarms in his head, but he silenced them. In a leisurely fashion he briefly explored the valley between her rounded flesh. A faint floral scent filled his nostrils. It was as if she had been lying in a field of wildflowers at Melton Park. The sudden erotic image of seeing her naked in a bed of flowers made his body flex with tension. The pictures in his head aroused an intense need to assuage his desire for her this instant, but he held back.

Instinctively, he knew everything about their relationship going forward hinged on him putting her needs first. The men who'd used her had done so for their own gratification and nothing more. He needed to make her understand her needs and pleasure were just as important as his own were. His cock protested with a violent jerk as he strengthened his resolve not to give way to his desire. It tightened and stretched in retribution for his self-denial.

His mouth captured her nipple and teased it as he had the other. With a whimper of need, she bucked against him. The instant her hands slid downward to reach for his erection, he caught her hand and held it up over her head. When she froze beneath him, he quickly released her and lifted his head to stare down into her eyes. Apprehension darkened the purple hue until the violet orbs were almost black. Keeping his touch gentle, he stroked her cheek.

"Don't be afraid, sweetheart," he soothed. "I just want to focus on pleasing you without any distractions. And I confess that every time you touch me I'm definitely distracted."

Surprise lightened her wary expression before she smiled slowly. It was a womanly smile that said she understood she possessed power over him at this moment in time. He was only grateful she didn't realize precisely how much power she wielded over him already. A delicate flush of pink crested in her cheeks as she shook her head slightly.

"It would please me if we…I want you inside me."

Her words pulled a groan out of him, and for a brief second he closed his eyes to battle the demons urging him to do as she asked. When he looked at her again, her puzzlement tugged a wry smile to his mouth.

"There's much more to pleasure than simply the act, my sweet." The statement made his cock protest viciously. He swallowed hard, then kissed her lightly. Her mouth tried to cling to his, but he quickly pulled away. The protest she murmured made him smile as he caressed the side of her jaw with his mouth then continued his way downward. His lips brushed across her breast and she drew in a sharp breath.

It was obvious she expected him to take her into his mouth. Instead he continued kissing his way downward to her waist then to her hip where he playfully nipped at her flesh. She yelped in surprise, and he chuckled at the sound before he soothed the area with this tongue. With each taste of her creamy skin, his desire strengthened exponentially. Silk couldn't be any softer than every inch of her body.

Each curve and dip of her made his body ache with a craving that had already begun to blind him to everything but the scent, taste, and feel of her. His body roared angrily at his persistent refusal to satisfy his desire, But he ignored the demands of his cock as he kissed the top of her thigh. The moment he kissed the inside of her leg she gasped. In a clear effort to prevent him from accessing the heart of her core, she tried to shift her body away from him. Ignoring her reaction to the intimate caress, his hand stroked its way up to the apex of her thighs where his fingers found the white heat of her.

"Dear Lord, Percy, surely you–"

Her protest died as a keening cry escaped her lips the

instant his mouth nibbled at her silky folds. Hot and tangy, the first taste of her cream swept across his tongue. A low moan echoed above his head. The throaty sound became a sob of pleasure as he flicked his tongue across the small nub of flesh at the edge of her sex. In response to the deeply intimate caresses of his mouth, her body writhed beneath him, while he devoted his attention to the delicious taste and feel of her. As much as his body urged him to bury himself in the slick buttery feel of her, he held back. This moment of pleasure was for her and only her.

Chapter 12

ire skimmed across her skin. With each flick and stroke of his tongue he aroused her body to a fevered pitch until the flames consumed her. It had only been in the darkest point of the night that she'd imagined what it would be like to be in his bed. None of her fantasies had prepared her for this.

It was as if he were worshiping her body with his hands and mouth. The sudden shock of his teeth lightly nipping at the small nub between her legs made her cry out in surprise and delight as he swirled his tongue around the sensitive flesh.

The acute pleasure of the hedonistic act forced her hips to arch upward in a wild response to his mouth stimulating her darkest of desires. An odd sensation unfurled in her belly. It built inside her with a speed that overwhelmed each of her senses. The power of it pulled her upward to a pinnacle of delight only to have his mouth send her plummeting over a delicious abyss of sensation that singed every inch of her. The strength of her reaction made her back arch as she screamed from the sheer joy of his intimate caresses.

Shudder after shudder rocked her body as his tongue continued to stroke her core. The mind-numbing pleasure reduced her to a primal state of being. The only thing she was aware of was him and the sensations he created inside her. Frisson after frisson raced through her body until her breathing was mere gasps. Time after time she was pulled upward to a peak of ecstasy before she crashed downward into a pool of fiery sensation. Certain she couldn't bear another moment of such intensity she cried out his name, pleading with him that she couldn't bear the pleasure he was giving her.

His response was to use his teeth to tug at the nub of flesh at her core before he sucked on it hard. Another wild cry of pleasure escaped her lips as she arched upward, her body frozen in place as pleasure held her hostage. A second later her body convulsed violently, and she fell apart in a wild, glorious moment of pure unadulterated rapture.

Ever so slowly, the waves of pleasure rolling across her skin eased until they were soft ripples of warmth. His mouth warmed the inside of her thigh as he leisurely worked his way up over her stomach to her breasts. The instant his tongue swirled around the sensitive flesh she released a soft cry.

"Oh, please, no," she gasped. "Not yet. I don't think I could bear another moment like that again so soon."

A low growl rumbled in his chest, and she suddenly realized the tip of him was pressing at the edge of her sex. With a grunt, he rolled off her to lie on his back. One arm flung over his eyes, his breathing was erratic while the corners of his mouth were white from facial muscles that were pulled taut from restraint. Self-recrimination sped through her. Even after satisfying her so completely he was willing to forgo his own physical release in order to please her. It warmed her and created another crack in the wall of ice surrounding her heart.

She glanced down to where his hard, thick erection jumped slightly against his stomach. Desire tugged at her body as she stared down at the beautiful maleness of him. She wanted him—wanted to give him the same pleasure he'd given her. The moment she straddled his thighs, he jerked with surprise. His dark brown eyes flew open to meet her gaze. The passion blazing in his eyes made her tremble. In a languid gesture she trailed her forefinger across his chest and downward. A white droplet clung to the tip of him, and she smeared it across the top of his erection in a slow teasing gesture. A dark groan escaped his lips, and he closed his eyes again.

"*Christ woman,*" he said in a strangled voice. "I'm trying to give you breathing room. Don't make it harder for me than it already is."

The words split off a large chunk of the ice encasing her heart. It stirred to life the banked fires inside her. She leaned over him to kiss him. The tangy flavor of her essence hovered on his lips and another groan rumbled in his chest. A sense of power flooded its way through her, and her tongue slipped past his lips to tangle with his. When she started to lift her head, a firm hand curled around her neck to hold her in place. She allowed him the small measure of control, but only for a moment.

Breaking free of his hold, she sat upright then slowly slid her body over his until he filled her completely. There was something so right about this moment. The feeling was so intense it heightened each of her senses. The friction of their joining caused her body to tremble against his. It was a physical connection that opened the door to an emotion that made her heart slam into her chest. She ignored the thought to devote all her attention to this moment with him. Strong fingers grasped her hips in a silent demand that she increase her pace. She smiled down at him and shook her head.

"Not yet," she whispered.

His reply was a growl of complaint, and his fingers dug into her thighs with a bit more force. Instantly she lifted her body until she was almost completely free of him.

"Behave," she said with a smile.

"For the love of God, woman. A man can only take—"

Before he could finish his sentence, she thrust her hips downward to bury him deep inside her. A shout of pleasure escaped him as she slowly lifted her hips and repeated the swift sharp motion. Another shout reverberated out of his throat. In a clear demand for her to increase the pace of her body against his, he gripped her hips even more firmly in an attempt to make her move faster. She resisted.

She wanted to extend the pleasure of this moment for as long as possible. Leaning over his chest, she swept her tongue over his nipple as he'd done to hers. The scent of pine and sandalwood drifted off his skin. It created a smell that was distinctly his. A growl rumbled in his chest and vibrated across her lips. With a powerful thrust he threw his hips upward to sheath himself inside her. In punishment for his impatience, she bit down on the hard pebble against her lips.

The soft roar escaping him made her smile, and she sat up again to slide her body upward until only the tip of him was inside her. Her gaze met his, and what she saw in his brown eyes stole her breath away. It would be so easy to drown herself in those eyes. Her heart skipped a beat at the mesmerizing intensity of his gaze. Passion blazed in his eyes and it held her breathless as she quickly thrust her hips downward once again.

The sharp thrust tugged a deep groan from him as she rocked her hips against his. Pleasure seeped its way into her blood until it flowed fast and furious through her body. A strong, powerful hand stretched out to caress her breasts before he gently pushed her backward slightly all the while her body rocked against his at an ever-increasing pace. The position increased the strength and depth of their mating.

A white-hot heat shot through her veins, and she was certain she would burst into flames from it. Hands braced against his thighs, tension tightened her body as pleasure curled tight in her belly ready to spiral out of control. The sensation made her tremble, and her breasts grew heavy and ached for his touch. Without thinking, she caught his hand and pressed it to one of her breasts. Instantly he came upright, pulling her tight against him to suckle her. The hedonistic caress made her sob with delight.

Fingers spiking through his hair, she continued to rock

her hips against his at a frantic pace. The rough edge of his tongue teased her nipple mercilessly as a vibration slowly built inside her. Stroke after stroke her body tightened and gripped the hard thickness of him. Every part of her was alive with sensation, and when he captured her lips in a hard kiss, she responded with an unrestrained abandon as their bodies pounded against one another.

Fire and ice raced across her skin, burning her as their bodies pulsated with the heat of blinding passion. The spicy scent of him invaded her senses even more potently than before. It enveloped her the same way his embrace was holding her hostage. The raging heat of his kiss whipped through her with the strength of an out-of-control blaze.

With each stroke of their bodies against one another desire spiraled through her. It drove her to the edge of a familiar abyss, the sensations inside her building to a feverish pitch until she convulsed violently around him. First one wave of pleasure and then another rolled over her in a rapid succession. As her body tightened, convulsed, and clenched around the fullness of his erection, her head fell backward and she cried out his name. With a speed that only intensified her own pleasure, he thrust his body into hers at a blistering pace.

A brief second later he released a guttural shout of fulfillment and throbbed inside her. They remained frozen together for a few seconds before Percy fell back onto the mattress pulling her with him. Harsh breaths echoed between them as they remained locked in each other's arms for several long moments. Still astride him, she nuzzled the side of his neck. The warmth of his skin, his scent, and the powerful strength of the arms holding her close made her sigh with happiness. At the sound, Percy forced her to look at him.

"You, Miss Bennett, go to my head in the best possible way."

The compliment sent heat rushing into her cheeks at the emotion in his gaze. It was a look of possession, and she kissed him gently. His hand curled around her neck as he pulled her closer and kissed her with an intensity that startled her. When he released her, she slid off him to lie beside him. Almost as if he were unwilling to part with her, he tugged her into his side his arm holding her in a snug embrace that was as tender as it was protective. She'd never felt so safe or cherished in her entire life. It was the last thought she had before she drifted off to sleep.

Rhea wasn't certain how long she'd been asleep, but when she awoke, her backside was curled up against Percy's chest. She didn't move for a long moment, instead she chose to savor these last brief seconds in his arms. Deep inside she'd known tonight would be all they'd ever have. The reality of her past made it impossible to hope for anything where he was concerned. Tears formed in her eyes.

Tonight he'd given her the most beautiful gift she'd ever received. But she'd already sacrificed a small piece of her heart to him. She couldn't risk losing all of her heart to him. If that were to happen, it meant surrendering not only control of her body, but her soul as well. She could never yield to any man in that way again—not even Percy Rockwood. As gently as possible she slid out from his embrace and off the bed.

The one candle in the room burned low, but it gave her enough light to make her way about in the darkened room. She moved with stealth as she gathered her clothes, and in a matter of minutes the only item of her appearance not completely repaired was her hair. Unable to find her hairpins, she quickly braided it as she'd learned to do while under Ruckley's command.

Her tread soft and barely detectable, Rhea moved to the side of the bed and leaned over Percy intent on brushing his brow with a kiss. She froze just before her lips caressed his skin. Her touch might wake him, and she knew she had no defenses left to say no to him if he awoke. It was best to leave now while he was asleep. With one last glance over her shoulder, she memorized his beautiful male figure sprawled across the bed. It was a memory she would carry for the rest of her life. The moment she experienced the desire to run back to his arms, she brutally crushed the urge, determined not to ignore common sense. Despite her resolve, a voice inside her head whispered that pragmatism was a cold bedfellow. She ignored the thought and left the bedroom.

It wasn't until she was standing on the front stoop of Percy's home that she realized she had no way back to Sherrington House other than her own two feet. Trepidation spiraled through her at the thought of walking home at such a late hour. The feeling lasted for only seconds before she remembered how she'd lived for the past seven years. It startled her that she'd forgotten her past if even for a few brief moments. Was it possible Percy had done that for her? The thought made her bite down on her lip. Percy had always treated her as a lady and had consistently indicated her past was of no consequence. But she knew better. She was who she was. It was laughable to think she could go back to being the girl she'd been before her father had sold her and Arianna to Ruckley. It was why she could make her way home without help. Despite Percy's misgivings, she was more than capable of taking care of herself. Her life under Ruckley's thumb had taught her how to survive. Fear was a means of defense. It sharpened the senses. It gave one the means to do what others would not. Fear no longer her enemy, she headed toward Sherrington House.

The muted sound of early morning street traffic filtered its way into Percy's bedroom. His bedroom was still fairly dark, and when he didn't feel the warmth of Rhea's sweet curves burrowed into his side, he sleepily reached out for her.

When his hand touched nothing but rumpled sheets, he jerked awake. Quickly sitting up, he stared at the empty spot where Rhea had slept last night. The sudden thought it might have been a dream made him close his eyes for a split second.

Certain he'd not imagined things, he stared at the spot where Rhea had slept and frowned. She'd left without saying goodbye, and his gut twisted. He'd compromised her in the worst possible way. Even if she *had* been eager to share his bed, he'd ignored the consequences to her reputation if someone saw her leaving his house in the middle of the night. He'd also broken his word again. He'd allowed desire to override his good judgement.

Memories of the night before filled Percy's head. The way she'd responded to his caresses convinced him that he was the only man who'd ever pleasured her the way he had. He closed his eyes for a brief moment as he relived the pleasure of her riding him with abandon. The passion he'd experienced with her had touched something deep inside him. Now all he had to do was persuade Rhea to marry him. The unexpected thought made him stiffen. When had he decided to take a wife? If he were honest with himself, he'd decided from that first kiss in the gazebo at Melton Park. Somewhere in the back of his mind, he'd known even then that she belonged with him—that they belonged together. In fact, the idea of waking up with her in his bed every morning filled him with anticipation.

Unfortunately, it would be difficult to make Rhea understand that marriage to him wouldn't make her a possession, but a partner. For years she'd been under Ruckley's control. Percy had no doubt her experience with that bastard would make her view marriage as a sort of prison. Then there was the matter of how Rhea viewed herself.

Percy remembered how she'd referred to herself as a whore. That moment had emphasized her vulnerability and the horrors of her past. Intuition told him she might easily view herself unworthy of him given her past. Percy had no idea how he'd be able to convince her a future with him would be a happy one. And he was certain it would be good between them.

It wasn't until now that he'd actually considered the attributes he wanted in a wife, but the word that came to mind now was partner. He wanted a wife he could share things with as one would a good friend. Someone he could turn to in times of difficulties—a lover to hold and caress. In a word, he wanted Rhea. They could be all that to one another. He had no illusions as to it being a love match.

Laughter reverberated in his head at how easily he dismissed the idea of love. The laughter was followed by a mocking voice murmuring he was a fool to think he didn't want Rhea's love. Percy ignored his inner voice as the memory of his vision came back to haunt him. While the images were still jumbled in his head, the core theme was the growing danger Ruckley posed to Rhea. It made him uneasy about the rescue Ashford had arranged this evening, particularly when he knew Rhea would never agree to stay away.

He could tell her about his vision, but he had no doubt she would dismiss the images as either him worrying needlessly or perhaps even a ruse to keep her from being there this evening. It all came down to the fact he had to be all the more vigilant where Rhea was concerned. Eager to see her, Percy rang for Jenkins. He wanted to visit Sherrington House as quickly as possible.

Almost two hours later, Percy entered his club feeling more irritable than he had in a long time. He'd arrived at Sherrington House ready to convince Rhea to marry him. Upon his arrival, he'd been informed she wasn't at home. From there he'd gone to her aunt's house only to be told Rhea wasn't there either. All the more frustrating was the fact that no one knew where she'd gone.

Intent on venting his anger in a sparring session, Percy

made his way to the boxing ring in the gymnasium. To his surprise, he saw his friend Blake boxing with a partner who was losing as if the man had never been in the ring before. Percy moved to the sidelines into his friend's line of sight, and the viscount ended his sparring match to join Percy on the edge of the boxing mat.

"Percy, it's good to see you," Blake said. Tension had tightened the viscount's mouth to a thin line giving him an austere look. "I don't know how we've managed to keep missing each other these last few months."

"I would imagine between your duties in Parliament, your new wife, and my own affairs in the country and here in town it's quite understandable why we've not seen each other." Percy smiled at him. "So I'd like to offer my congratulations on your recent nuptials. I regret I was unable to attend the wedding."

An odd look crossed the viscount's face as he acknowledged Percy's words with an abrupt nod. Almost as if he were eager to change the direction of their conversation, Blake jerked his head toward the mat.

"Would you care to go a few rounds?"

"If I recall correctly, the last time we sparred you indicated you wouldn't do so again anytime soon," Percy said with a chuckle.

"Circumstances change." Blake's voice was cold and distant, causing Percy to arch his eyebrows at his friend, but he refrained from asking the viscount about his mood.

Blake walked to the center of the ring and assumed a fighting stance. With a slight shrug of puzzlement, Percy joined his friend on the mat and barely managed to dodge the viscount's initial punch. As the two of them danced and parried with each other on the floor, Percy deflected a blow to the head and darted back a few feet. Blake followed him, forcing Percy to continue dodging and deflecting his friend's punches. The viscount's intense concentration made Percy think his friend had to be battling not only him, but an army of invisible demons as well. Another one of Blake's punches slammed into his shoulder, and Percy grunted. The exercise was beginning to hurt.

"What the hell is wrong with you?" Percy's disgusted tone sent a flicker of remorse sliding across the Blake's features before his expression hardened again.

"If you prefer, I can find someone else to spar with me."

The viscount's words made Percy expel a harsh breath of air as he shook his head. The moment he was back on his feet, Percy threw a hard punch that connected with his friend's jaw. Blake's head snapped backward from the jab, which sent him staggering backward. Immediately Percy grimaced with regret at the strength of his blow. The viscount came back at him a moment later with a blazing flurry of punches. It took every bit of skill Percy possessed to keep from losing ground.

They'd been sparring for almost five minutes when Blake held up his hands in a silent request to end their physical blows. Hands on his hips, Percy bent over at the waist and dragged in deep breaths of air into lungs that were burning from his exertions. Still bent over, Percy turned his head toward his friend. Blake was also bent over and breathing hard. Percy slowly straightened.

"If I didn't know better, I'd say you are having wife difficulties."

"Would you care to clarify that remark," Blake snarled. The air crackled as if the ground beneath Percy's feet was a thin layer of ice. The viscount's stony expression made Percy shake his head in disgust.

"It was just a bloody observation. Whenever my brother is irritated with home life, he spars like you do. Although, given your wife's pleasant company—"

It was as if a brick had slammed into Percy's jaw. He staggered backward then crashed to the hard mat. Dazed, he stared up at the viscount. As Blake bent over him, Percy couldn't remember the last time another man had glared at him so menacingly.

"How do you know Arianna?"

"I met her the other day when I called on your sister-in-law," he said irritably as he gently shifted his jaw and spit blood out from inside his mouth.

"Rhea?" Blake said hoarsely. "You know Rhea?"

"Yes. Did you think I would call on your wife without you being present?" he snapped as he rubbed his jaw and looked up at his friend. Blake's confusion and jealousy made Percy grunt with disgust. Regret wrinkled the viscount's brow before he stuck out his hand to assist Percy to his feet. Percy hesitated a second before accepting his friend's silent gesture of apology. When he was standing again, he scowled at Blake.

"You need to have a little more faith in your friends *and* your wife. You chose well."

"Did I? I wonder," Blake said in a voice dark with pain.

"I have no doubts about the woman I met being in love with you."

"I'm no longer sure of that."

"Then you clearly have a problem."

"One I don't think I can solve," Blake said in a tight voice.

"I don't recall you ever being at a loss for a solution, especially where women were concerned," Percy said with a touch of irony as he removed his sparring gloves.

"This is different," Blake muttered. "She's my wife."

"Do you love her?" His question made the viscount stiffen for a moment before he nodded.

"Yes," Blake said quietly. "But what stands between us is something I don't think I can easily dismiss."

"Perhaps it would help if you considered things from her point of view." Percy narrowed his gaze at his friend the moment cold anger darkened Blake's countenance.

"That sounds as if you know what's come between us,"

the viscount bit out with a look of restrained rage.

"I have no knowledge of why you and the viscountess are at odds, but if you love her, you'll work to overcome whatever stands between the two of you."

Blake didn't answer him. Instead he began to remove his leather sparring gloves. Percy did the same as silence filled the space between them. He'd removed his gloves completely when Blake jerked his head toward him. The man's scowl made Percy shake his head in disgust.

"What?"

"I'd like to know your intentions where Rhea is concerned."

"I intend to make her my wife," Percy said without hesitation.

"Do you love her?" At the question, he hesitated, unable to answer. He simply wasn't willing to step out onto that limb at the moment. When he didn't reply, Blake eyed him with contempt. "If you can't answer the question, Percy, it means you've decided to marry her for other reasons, and she deserves better than that."

The contemptuous note in his friend's voice stung, and Percy clenched his jaw as anger surged through him. It wasn't his place for his friend to judge him.

"My intentions where Rhea are concerned is none of your affair."

"You're wrong. As my sister-in-law, I have every reason to care about her happiness," Blake said in an icy voice. "So help me God, Rockwood. If you hurt her, you'll answer to me."

For a long moment, Percy stared stoically at his friend. Then with a breath of disgust passing viciously past his lips, he turned and walked away from the viscount. Blake was right. Rhea did deserve to be happy. He just wasn't sure love was part of the bargain, for either of them.

Chapter 13

"I s there nothing I can say that will make you change your mind, my darling?"

"No." It was a short, abrupt response that made Beatrice flinch as she eyed Arianna with concern.

Her niece had arrived on her doorstep only hours after Blake had left Sherrington House. When he'd sent word he intended to stay at his club overnight, Arianna had come to Beatrice. Her niece shook her head in reply to Beatrice's question as she rocked Lucy in her arms. The child was sound asleep, and Beatrice understood Arianna's need to keep Lucy close, particularly when the viscount seemed to have rejected her.

"Arianna, I should not—"

"You are not to blame, Aunt Beatrice. Rhea warned me to tell Blake everything before the wedding." Arianna shook her head in despair. "I made the wrong choice, and I have no one to blame except myself."

"Blake loves you, Arianna. I'm certain of it." Beatrice hesitated, reluctant to suggest the obvious. "He will come around."

If there was one thing Beatrice was certain of, it was the viscount's love for Arianna. Only a man deeply in love was capable of marrying a woman with her niece's background. An image of Alfred's kind features filled her head. She understood better than most how love could make someone do things others couldn't. Her late husband had married her despite knowing she wasn't in love with him and had borne another man's child out of wedlock. Although she'd tried to make Alfred understand she could never love another man, her dead husband had persisted in his marriage proposals. He'd made it clear that his happiness was based on caring for her and making her happy. Over the years he'd become very dear to her, and when he'd died, she'd mourned him as she would have a beloved friend.

"Even if Blake loved me enough to marry me, he might not have loved me enough to accept Lucy. I should have trusted him—had more faith in his love for me," Arianna replied softly. "Especially now when I realize I can never let Lucy go again. If Blake cannot accept her then I will have no choice but to leave him."

Arianna's words made Beatrice draw in a sharp breath. If her niece's marriage ended because of her insistence that Blake be told the truth about her great-niece, she would never forgive herself. The despondency in Arianna's voice made her shake her head.

"I cannot leave you like this. I'll send word to Melton House that we're both unwell."

"No. You *will* go," Arianna said with a firmness reminiscent of Rhea. "It will be insulting enough to Lord and Lady Melton that I've declined their invitation at the last minute. I'll not have that compounded by you feeling obligated to remain here with me."

"You cannot possibly expect—"

"Yes, I can. I'd prefer to remain alone here with Lucy. Now go or you'll be late."

"I don't—"

"*Go.*"

It was a sharp command that emphasize Arianna's desire to be alone with her daughter. Beatrice nodded and reluctantly left the nursery with the door closing softly behind her. For a long moment, she stood motionless in the narrow second-floor hallway. Like Arianna, she'd made far too many wrong choices in her own life. One of the worst was not trying hard enough to discover why Olivia had stopped answering her letters.

When she'd finally realized something was terribly wrong, it was too late. Her sister had been dead for several months. The memory of Thomas Bennett's coldly worded letter informing her of her sister's death made Beatrice's heart ache with grief. There had been a distinct note of smug satisfaction in her brother-in-law's communication. Beatrice had no doubt Thomas had taken pleasure in writing the letter. A cruel man, she'd never understood why Olivia had married him. Beatrice could only assume her sister had loved her husband.

Almost as terrible as the cruelty in the wording of his letter, Thomas had refused to let her see her nieces. He'd even gone so far as to inform Arianna and Rhea she was dead. Even if she'd tried to see the girls, Thomas would never have let her set one foot in his house. She had no doubt that a large part of his behavior was retaliatory in nature. The man had loathed her for refusing his advances.

When her brother-in-law had propositioned her not long after he'd married Olivia, she'd been horrified and sickened by his revolting attempt to seduce her. She'd found his desire for a liaison when he was already married despicable. But that he would attempt to do so with his wife's sister was beyond contemptible. Even if she'd been inclined to take another lover after Lionel, she would never have betrayed her sister. The memory of Thomas's insulting proposal still had the power to make her shudder. It was one of the reasons she'd not fought harder to see her sister or the girls.

As much as she hated admitting it, she'd been afraid of Thomas. The man had been capable of great cruelty, and she'd instinctively known he would have found a way to divide her and Olivia in the cruelest way possible. But her failure to stand up to the man had prevented her from seeing her sister one last time. Worse, her inaction had done nothing to save her nieces from a terrible fate.

The fact that she'd failed to pursue her attempts to see the girls still haunted her. He'd already sold Rhea and Arianna into bondage by the time he'd replied to her insistent queries. By then he'd become a profligate drunkard. It had taken more than a year after his death for his solicitor to locate her about his estate, which had delayed her efforts in finding Arianna and Rhea.

The quiet sound of a man's voice echoed up the stairs and into the hallway to break through her thoughts. One hand pressing into the base of her throat, a flame of hope flared to life inside her. Had Blake come for his wife? Optimism flooding through her, Beatrice hurried downstairs. Biggs was just emerging from the salon as she reached the foot of the steps.

"You've a guest, madame. A Lord Foxworth," the butler said quietly. Panic held her rigid for a moment as she took in Biggs's announcement, before she quickly turned to retreat upstairs.

"Tell his lordship that I've dinner—"

"I'm well aware of your plans for the evening, Beatrice. Melton told me you were dining with his family this evening, and I offered to escort you to dinner," Lionel's voice echoed quietly in her ears as he appeared in the salon doorway.

Beatrice swallowed hard as she slowly turned around. Framed in the doorway, he seemed even more powerful and dangerous than he had the other night. His bearing one of purposeful nonchalance, he eyed her as if she were a morsel he was contemplating eating.

Something old and familiar stirred inside her. Despite her efforts to control her reaction to him, she failed. She'd thought her response to him at the Melton affair had simply been a remembrance of the past. But she knew differently now.

Lionel had always been able to set her heart racing, and nothing had changed. Dismayed at the way her heart was pounding, she forced herself to assume an expression of indifference. With a polite gesture, she directed him to return to the salon.

"May I offer you some refreshment?" she asked as she moved toward the doorway.

For a moment, she thought he might not allow her to pass, but he stepped out of her way just enough that she was forced to brush against him as she entered the salon. As she slid past him it was impossible not to breathe in the warm male scent of him. It assaulted her senses in the same way it had done all those years before.

Eager to put physical distance between them, she quickly moved deeper into the room and jumped at the sound of the salon door closing. Whirling around, the determined look she saw hardening his features caused consternation to send tension spiraling through her. It was obvious he was a man on a mission. But what terrified her was not knowing what tactics he would employ to achieve his goal. Suddenly in need of something to fortify her, Beatrice turned away from him and went to the side cart that held cognac and Madeira. Hands trembling, some of the wine she poured spilled out onto the top of the small sideboard. She drew in a deep breath in an attempt to steady her nerves.

"Shall I pour you some cognac?"

"Not at the moment."

The quiet response only made her all the more nervous. Lionel had always been at his most resolute when he was quiet. It meant his plan of action would be either verbal or something far more dangerous. God help her if he decided to use seduction as a means of achieving his objective. She reached for her glass of wine only to find her body engulfed with heat as he reached around her and forestalled her. Dear Lord, he'd chosen seduction.

"In fact, I think I'd prefer something a bit more flavorful."

The husky sound of his voice filled her ear and reminded her of other times he'd used persuasion to secure her agreement to do as he commanded. Although his body wasn't touching hers, it still felt as though she was pressed into his chest. The sudden desire to lean back into him made her heart skip a beat. No sooner had the thought entered her head than his mouth was caressing the side of her neck.

It was the only part of him that touched her, yet it was as if he'd bound her to him with an invisible rope. Alarmed by her growing desire to simply lean backward into him, she drew in a sharp breath. Beatrice knew she was in great peril, and she quickly darted away from him. The fact that she was able to do so without him stopping her made her realize he'd allowed her to do so. Facing him, Beatrice eyed him warily.

"Why are you here, Lionel?"

"I think you know why." Steel could not have been more inflexible than his voice as he studied her from across the space separating them. His assessing gaze sent a tremor through her. As quickly as she could, she hid her trepidation behind a feigned puzzlement.

"No, I don't. I thought we'd settled things between us the other night." She arched an eyebrow at him, and he muttered something unintelligible.

"I'm here because you owe me an explanation."

"*An explanation,*" she gasped in disbelief. The arrogance he projected as he scowled at her emphasized his height and strength. Despite the years that had passed, he still reminded her of a sleek, dangerous tiger. Even the smallest of gestures he made reflected power. The fact that he could still affect her so easily caused a long-buried anger to slowly rise to the surface. "I owe you *nothing.*"

"Don't you?" he snarled as he took a step toward her.

"*No.*" Beatrice tilted her chin upward in outrage refusing

to retreat or cower from his anger. After all this time, *he* believed he was owed an explanation. She was the one who'd been left waiting at the chapel hoping he had only been delayed and not abandoned her. She was the one who'd suffered the agony of losing not only him, but their child as well.

"I think you should go, my lord. As I said the other night, we cannot resurrect the past."

"I'm not trying to resurrect the past, Beatrice," he said in a voice tight with anger. "But I do want the truth."

"*Truth*? What truth?" she exclaimed with a bitterness that sliced open wounds she'd thought were long healed.

"The truth about our child."

"Our child?" she choked out.

At his words, the past rushed up to meet her. It filled the space between them like an unexpected deluge that threatened to drown her. How could Lionel have uncovered the truth? Other than the doctor and midwife, her sister had been the only soul who'd known she was carrying Lionel's child. It was her sister's hand she clung to throughout her labor, and her sister who had comforted her through the three horrible days that followed. Even if he had uncovered the truth, he'd given up the right to question her the day he'd deserted her. She owed him nothing.

"Are you going to deny that Rhea is my daughter?" Lionel ground out the words as anger slashed across his autocratic profile. "*Our* child?"

"Rhea—*yes, I deny it*," she snapped. "Rhea is my niece."

"A niece who looks remarkably like you."

"Olivia and I were sisters. We were often mistaken for one another." She shook her head fiercely. "It is not surprising she looks like me, but Rhea is *not* your daughter."

"I've found a midwife who says differently."

"And where did you find this midwife?" she demanded with antipathy as her heart twisted in her chest.

"In Breaton Village."

The simple reply pulled the air out of Beatrice's lungs, and she fought to keep from swaying on her feet. He'd visited the quiet place she'd retreated to during her confinement. As she met his gaze, Lionel's mouth was a thin line of determination and anger. When she didn't speak, he released a violent noise of disgust.

"*Damn it, Beatrice*, tell me the truth. Is Rhea my daughter?"

"*No*," she cried out with an anguish that etched its way into the depths of her soul. "Our child is dead."

Horror etched fine lines of pain and despair into Lionel's features, and his reaction made her heart slam into her chest with regret as she realized she'd erred in thinking it wouldn't matter to him that he'd lost a child. Regret spiraled through her at the way she'd revealed the truth in such a brutally shocking manner. Dismayed by her lapse in good judgement, she stared at him uncertain of what to say. The stillness in the room was cold and unmoving. It settled between them like a heavy weight as Lionel stared at her in disbelief. After several moments, he shook his head as if by doing so he could dismiss what he'd heard.

"Dead?" he rasped.

Like a violent thunderstorm, anger swirled through her. Years ago, his expression would have incited her to go to him and offer comfort, but today it simply filled her with a deep bitterness. Why should she feel the need to console him when he'd left her? He'd left her alone to deal with the responsibility and the pain.

"Yes," she said in a harsh, brittle voice. "The midwife was correct. I did have a child, but not a daughter. I had a son who only lived three days before he was taken from me."

"*Sweet Jesus, Beatrice*," Lionel's voice was restrained and rough with emotion. "If I'd known—"

"What? You wouldn't have deserted me?" she sneered with contempt.

"I did *not* abandon you." Anger slashed across his features as he took a step toward her. "*You* made the choice not to marry me the day you didn't come to the chapel."

"Didn't come—you're the one who didn't come as promised," Beatrice exclaimed with cold resentment. "You walked away, and I was left to pick up the pieces."

"*Walked away?*" His voice was a rumble of thunder in the salon as fury darkened his visage. It emphasized the rising storm surrounding them. "I *never* walked away. I sent my brother to the chapel to escort you to the ship. There were problems with the ship's cargo manifest that Terrence didn't know how to fix. He offered to bring you to the docks so we wouldn't miss the evening tide."

"Do you honestly expect me to believe your lies?" she gasped in horror at the blatant falsehood. "*No one* came. Not you—and certainly not your brother."

"*Christ almighty, Beatrice,* I'm telling you the truth," he growled. "When Terrence returned without you, he said you'd sent word to the reverend you'd reconsidered. I couldn't believe it and was determined to go after you, but Terrence said he'd already visited your house. He said your butler wouldn't tell him where—"

Lionel came to an abrupt halt in his explanation as with stunned incredulity he stared at her in bleak disbelief. His gaze reflected a desolate look of pain, and it triggered feelings deep inside her. Was it possible he was telling her the truth? She quickly discounted the thought. The idea of subjecting herself to more lies was too unbearable.

"I don't know what you thought to gain with this fanciful tale, my lord, but this conversation is at an end," she said hoarsely.

His only response to her icy words was a nod of his head. It was obvious he'd barely registered her remark. Startled that he'd not protested her decree, she studied with suspicion. Doubt, incredulity, and anger hardened his facial expression as he rubbed the back of his neck and studied the floor in obvious contemplation.

"He lied. Your family didn't have a butler," Lionel muttered. As if trying to comprehend something unfathomable, he shook his head in puzzled uncertainty while he continued to have a quiet discussion with himself. "He lied to me. If he'd actually gone to your house, he would have known you didn't have a butler. He lied and like a fool…like a fool I believed him. Why would he lie when he knew I loved you?"

The confession that he'd been in love with her made Beatrice's heart slam into her chest and stop for a long moment before it resumed its beat. Once more the possibility that Lionel was telling the truth unfurled inside her? Was it possible his brother, not Lionel, had been the one to destroy her happiness so cruelly? Confusion slowly wove its way through her as she watched Lionel begin to prowl the floor continuing to mutter to himself. Was it possible he hadn't deserted her after all? If that was the case they'd both suffered. A knot formed in her throat as she watched him pace like a caged predator ready to pounce at the first opportunity. When he abruptly came to a halt, Beatrice stiffened with uncertainty at what to expect from him next.

"He lied to me, Beatrice. I'm a fool for having believed him. I should have seen through his lies. I have no excuse for believing him other than I was out of my mind with despair at the thought of having lost you. I should not have allowed him to stop me from going after you," he rasped. Anger and grief darkened his gaze as he met hers. "I would never have left England without you if Terrence hadn't been so damn convincing. Until this moment, I truly believed you had changed your mind."

The confession caused her to waver, and she struggled with the idea of accepting that he was telling her the truth. In the end, it didn't matter anymore. The past was gone and could never be regained. Beatrice closed her eyes for a brief moment then shook her head.

"I want you to leave, Lionel." She saw him take a step forward, and she quickly retreated. "*Now.*"

"I *didn't* walk away from you, Beatrice," he said in a rough voice that echoed with a pain that made her want to believe him. "I loved you. I have *never* stopped loving you. It's why I never married."

The declaration made her gasp, and she swayed slightly as she tried to comprehend what he was saying to her. A chill skimmed its way across her skin in the same way the first layer of winter ice formed on the pond at Green Hill House. An invisible, icy finger scraped down her back as she shook her head. She didn't have the courage to risk her heart again.

"The past can't be undone." Beatrice looked away from him as pain clawed away at her heart. "We cannot go back."

"You're right. We can't go back, but we *can* go forward. I love you, and I refuse to let you go a second time."

Beatrice drew in a sharp breath at the quiet, resolute sincerity in his voice. It made her waver in her belief that he'd betrayed her. It was the final blow that shattered her belief he'd betrayed her all those years ago. But she was no longer the woman she'd once been. When Alfred had died, she'd learned how to be alone. She'd become self-sufficient, and she enjoyed being independent. Deep inside she questioned whether she was making a mistake, but she ignored the possibility. She was too old to start over. She drew in another breath that was as painful as the last.

"It's impossible," she said with a shake of her head as she met his resolute gaze then looked away.

"Why?" he demanded.

"Because I like my life as it is now. I have no need of a husband."

"What about love, Beatrice? Have you no need of love?"

His question made her heart skip a beat as she met his

penetrating gaze then looked away. Panic swept through her as she frantically dismissed the hope that had already taken root inside her.

"I'm no longer that starry-eyed young girl."

"No, but you're as pig-headed as ever," he bit out through clenched teeth. With a speed that took her by surprise, Lionel closed the distance between them and grasped her upper arms to keep her from retreating. "Look me in the eye and tell me you don't love me."

The moment he touched her she shuddered. As hard as she tried it was impossible not to breathe in the scent of pine and leather she remembered all too well. Fire skimmed across her skin until the years melted away to leave her heart pounding wildly. Overwhelmed by the mere proximity of him, a tremor streaked through her.

Palms splayed against his chest, his heart pounded out a fierce rhythm against her fingertips. She looked into his intense gaze, struggling not to flinch for fear he would see the truth. With great difficulty she swallowed the knot in her throat then looked away from him. A soft growl echoed in her ears as he shook her slightly.

"You can't do it, can you Beatrice?" The authoritative note in his voice was one she remembered well. "You can't look me in the eye and say you don't love me."

"And you ask too much after all this time," she whispered as another tremor swept through her.

"No, Beatrice, I'm not asking too much. I'm asking you to believe me when I say that I love you. I want—need you to believe that if nothing else," Lionel said softly and fervently.

"Please don't." She closed her eyes as his persuasive plea coaxed her into admitting she loved him. The gentle touch of his finger on her check made her realize tears had slipped past her eyelids. A shudder wracked her as he kissed her damp cheeks.

"I never stopped loving you, Beatrice." The gentleness in

his voice equaled the tenderness of his touch. She shuddered as he pulled her into his warm embrace. "I was a blind fool to believe Terrence. I should have said to hell with the damn cargo and gone to find you—to hear you tell me you no longer loved me."

"And I should have gone to the docks," she whispered. "I should have had the courage to know for certain that you didn't want me."

"God help me, Beatrice, I've *never* stopped wanting you with me. I've spent far too many nights longing to hold you in my arms again." Lionel brushed his mouth against her brow before tilting her chin up to stare into her eyes. "I didn't return to England until I realized that for my own peace of mind, I had to confront you. But when I returned more than a year later you'd already married Fremont—I wavered between despair and fury. Afterward, I left England to try and forget you. I still wouldn't have returned if not for the fact that with Terrence dead, my father's title passed to me."

The pain in his eyes made Beatrice's heart ache, and she shook her head in sorrow for all the time they lost.

"Alfred married me knowing I didn't love him. He became very dear to me, but he knew I'd never stopped loving you."

In a loving gesture, she cupped his cheek with her hand. Lionel immediately turned his head to kiss her palm as his hand came to rest on top of hers. After a brief moment, he turned his head to kiss her. It was a sweet caress filled with love and a restrained passion. Powerful arms pulled her deeper into his embrace, and she eagerly pressed her body into his. The past fell away as his mouth teased and cajoled her into parting her lips. Heat spread its way through her with blinding speed. No sooner had the kiss begun than he quickly drew back.

"Not like this. Not here. I want more than one moment of pleasure with you, and this is not the place for a leisurely night of lovemaking," he said hoarsely. "But believe me, Beatrice I fully intend to make you mine again. At the first moment possible I'll secure a marriage license."

"Marriage," she gasped then shook her head. "You move too fast. I need time—"

"Time for what?" he demanded with the same confident arrogance she'd learned to love so many years ago. But time had changed her. She was no longer a young woman who made rash decisions.

"I happen to like the freedom I have now. I have no desire to give it up."

"I am happy to indulge your every wish or demand. But you will marry me." The confidence in his voice made her glare at him. A split second later he'd pulled her into his arms and kissed her.

Rhea emerged from the hack as it stopped in front of her aunt's house. Handing the driver the fare, she slowly turned to climb the steps sighing wearily. It had been a long day, and it would be an even longer night. Although it had proven exhausting, she had taken the early morning train to the country. After spending the night in Percy's arms, she'd needed time to think.

Instinctively, she'd known Percy would seek her out, but she felt far too vulnerable to see him so soon. So she'd spent the better part of the day at Green Hill. Despite the two-hour train ride there and back, the visit to the country had helped clear her head. Seducing Percy last night had been as impetuous as it had been foolhardy, but she had no regrets.

If she'd not been so worried about him as she'd helped him into his house, she would have returned home. Instead, she'd chosen to spend the night, despite knowing the scandal it would cause if she were discovered. Her own reputation was of no consequence, but she knew a scandal could hurt her aunt. It was something she'd not considered until she was leaving Percy's house early this morning.

Even her audacious claim to be Percy's mistress had caught her by surprise. Her impulsive words had poured out of her without thinking. His valet hadn't batted an eyelid at her announcement and had left her alone with Percy who had fallen into a deep sleep. Everything that followed had seemed natural and right.

The thought of being intimate with any man after being sold so often by Ruckley had always been a repulsive thought until she'd met Percy. Not once had she ever experienced revulsion when Percy had touched her. With every kiss and caress, he'd aroused feelings inside her that were not only incendiary, but dangerous as well. When she'd left him early this morning she'd done so with far greater reluctance than she expected.

It made Rhea realize her feelings for Percy were more serious than she'd believed. Where Percy was concerned, she was on the edge of a cliff that could well be her undoing if she were to take one more step forward. Going to Green Hill House had allowed her to adjust her bearings and regain her realistic perspective of her relationship with him.

Last night had been a wonderful experience, but she couldn't allow it to happen again. It wasn't simply about who or what she was that mattered. It was the possibility of Percy trying to do the honorable thing that troubled her. She had vowed that never again would she place herself at the mercy of any man, even a man as good as Percy. Rhea closed the door behind her as she entered Fremont Place. Intent on changing for the rescue of Peter, she headed toward the stairs. She'd barely placed a foot on the first step when she heard her aunt's voice raised in indignation followed by a man's voice. Fear and horror slithered through her. Ruckley. The bastard had found her and was threatening her aunt.

Frightened for her aunt's safety, Rhea rushed to the older woman's aid. The salon door made a loud crack as it slammed against the wall, as she charged into the salon intent on doing battle. The sight that greeted her drew her up short. Eyes wide with amazement, she watched her aunt break free of Lord Foxworth's embrace. Beatrice Fremont's skin was a rosy hue, although whether from excitement or embarrassment, Rhea wasn't certain. Embarrassed at having interrupted what had been an intimate moment, Rhea met her aunt's gaze in what was clearly an awkward moment.

Her chagrin quickly faded to be replaced by affectionate amusement, and she struggled not to smile too broadly. Her aunt, for all her efforts to secure a match for Rhea, had fallen for Lord Foxworth. She should have suspected something like this would happen from the moment the couple had appeared at the gazebo the night of the party at Melton Park.

"Forgive me, Aunt Beatrice, I thought…obviously I was mistaken." Rhea started to back out of the room when Lord Foxworth took a step toward her.

"Please, stay, Miss Bennett, or Rhea if I may be so bold, since we shall soon be related." Despite her suspicions, the man's words still took Rhea by surprise and caused her aunt to gasp.

"I have not agreed to marry you, my lord," Beatrice snapped.

"Do you intend to reject me?" Lord Foxworth narrowed his gaze at Beatrice as she opened her mouth to respond. "I suggest you think twice before answering that question, my love."

For a moment Rhea's aunt stared at Foxworth before she shook her head and a reluctant smile curved her mouth.

"No, I'll not refuse you."

Her soft response made Foxworth catch Beatrice's hand and carry it to his mouth to kiss it with restrained passion. The display of adoration made Rhea envious. If Percy were to openly demonstrate such a deep affection for her—she quickly dismissed the thought. Cheeks flushed with a mixture of embarrassment and happiness, Beatrice looked at her niece. Rhea's heart swelled at the joy reflected in her aunt's expression and she hurried forward to kiss her aunt's cheek.

"I cannot be happier for ycu, Aunt Beatrice," she exclaimed then turned to the man at her aunt's side.

"My congratulations, my lord."

"It would please me greatly if you called me uncle, my dear." The distinguished gentleman sent her a charming smile. "You and your sister are both dear to Beatrice's heart. Whatever Beatrice treasures, so do I."

The sincerity in Lord Foxworth's voice made Rhea smile at him warmly.

"I should be pleased to do so, my—" Rhea stopped as Lord Foxworth raised his eyebrows, and she laughed. "Uncle Lionel."

The man immediately stepped forward to kiss Rhea's cheek. Caught off guard, Rhea flinched. Although she knew the gentleman's gesture was merely congenial, it still made her uncomfortable. She retreated a small distance from the couple, and her gaze met her aunt's. Concern marred Beatrice's look of happiness, but Rhea forestalled any questioning as she smiled at the couple.

"If you'll forgive me, I must change as I have an evening engagement."

Beatrice Fremont's concern became a worried frown, and Rhea directed a warning look at the older woman. Beatrice was well aware of Rhea's destination this evening. While her aunt expressed a deep concern about her niece's actions, she'd not made any attempt to stop her. Lord Foxworth on the other hand might provide the support Beatrice needed to persuade Rhea to remain at home. With obvious reluctance, her aunt gave way to Rhea's silent warning not to say anything.

Her resignation was quickly replaced with dismay and guilt as she pressed her hand to her throat.

"Perhaps you might look in on Arianna, dearest," Beatrice said. "I'm quite worried about her."

"Of course," Rhea said as she kissed her aunt's cheek once again. With another smile at the couple she left the salon. Delighted at her aunt's happy news, Rhea's weariness ebbed away. She'd come to love her aunt dearly in the short time since Beatrice had found her and Arianna. When Rhea reached the top of the stairs, she moved along the corridor toward the nursery. As she walked into the small room, she saw Arianna playfully blowing against Lucy's hand as the child reached up to touch her mother's hair. Giggling, Lucy laughed harder every time Arianna blew against the child's hand. A smile curving her mouth, Rhea walk toward the two, and her sister looked up at Rhea then smiled at Lucy.

"Look who's here, my darling. Auntie Rhea has come to visit." At her sister's remark, Rhea planted a quick kiss on the child's cheek then touched Arianna's shoulder.

"Have you received any word from Blake?" The question made her sister pale, and Rhea immediately regretted asking about her brother-in-law. "He'll come, Arianna. He loves you."

"So Aunt Beatrice says as well."

"It's the truth," Rhea said firmly. Silently she vowed to go to Sherrington House herself if her brother-in-law didn't visit his wife soon. The man needed to understand how wonderful and generous his wife truly was. "He won't be able to stay away."

Arianna's expression illustrated she wasn't as confident as her aunt or sister. She turned her attention back to her daughter and smiled as the child beamed up at her. Without looking at Rhea, her sister sighed softly.

"Do you still plan to bring Peter and Fanny home with you this evening?"

"Yes. Although Mr. Ashford said there is no guarantee Fanny will be with Peter, but I'm hopeful."

"Please promise me you'll be careful Rhea," Arianna said quietly as she looked up at her.

"If Ruckley were to–"

"I promise you, I'll not do anything rash. I have no desire to see Ruckley again." The response seemed to reassure her sister, and with a small tickle of her niece's chin, Rhea left the nursery.

Chapter 14

hea entered the foyer outside of Ashford's office. The small entryway was dark, but light shimmered through the frosted glass of the private investigator's office door. She knocked quietly to announce her arrival then entered the small office. Ashford was loading a pistol, while another one lay on the desktop. As he loaded bullets into the rotating chamber, he looked up to greet her with a nod.

It always unnerved her seeing the man load his weapon. Although he'd never had to use it, the thought of the man being hurt while helping her was a troubling one. Almost as if he could read her thoughts, he met her gaze and a small smile twisted his lips.

"It's merely a precaution," he said in a matter-of-fact voice. Rhea nodded her understanding. Before she could reply the office door opened, and Percy strode into the dimly lit room with a grim look.

"Ashford, have you seen, Miss Bennett?" Percy's voice held a sharp edge that covered a distinct note of concern.

"I'm right here," she said as she realized the low light made it difficult for Percy to easily recognize her in her wig and male attire. At her quiet reply, he jerked his head in her direction. Eyes widening with surprise, he stared at her for a brief moment before his mouth thinned in disapproval.

"What the devil are you wearing?" he bit out.

"What I always wear when I go with Mr. Ashford." She looked down at her coarsely made clothing then back up into the condemnation in Percy's gaze. "If I were to dress as I do during the day, I'd draw attention to myself and others."

Percy appeared ready to argue when Ashford cleared his throat.

"Miss Bennett is correct, Rockwood. It's for her own safety."

After a short hesitation, Percy nodded his head then was at her side in two quick steps. Her fingers gripping her elbow, he threw a quick glance toward the private investigator.

"I need to speak with Miss Bennett for a moment," he bit out in clipped tones. "We'll wait for you in the entryway."

Ashford raised his eyebrows but didn't reply as Percy pulled her out of the office into the small foyer. Startled by his actions, Rhea had no time to protest as he shepherded her out of Ashford's office. The door closed behind them, Rhea recovered from her surprise and pulled free of his grasp. Irritated by his behavior she scowled at him, but he didn't give her the chance to say a word.

"You left in the middle of the night and according to Jenkins you left on foot without an escort," he growled. "Not to mention the fact that you didn't even say goodbye."

Caught off guard by his fierce rebuke, she bit down on her lip. Although she'd expected him to be put out with her for not waking him, it was apparent he'd been worried about her. Guilt bit into her as she met his angry gaze.

"My past has taught me how to take care of myself, but I'm sorry that I worried you."

"*Worried?*" he snarled. "*Christ Jesus*, when I couldn't find you today, I expected the worst. What if something had happened to you walking home like that?"

"But it didn't." Her calm demeanor seemed to anger him even more as he glared at her.

"And your failure to say goodbye?" The question was issued with a silent demand for a reply.

"You were sleeping soundly," she said quietly. "But this

is neither the time nor place for this discussion."

"I think it is," he snarled. "I spent the entire morning trying to find you then repeated my efforts this afternoon."

"I went to Green Hill."

"*What*? Why?" he demanded.

The fierce, possessive note in his voice filled her with conflicting emotions. Resentment rose in her at his domineering manner, while another part of her experienced a rush of pleasure that he'd been worried enough to still be angry with her. It meant that he cared what happened to her. The thought sent an immediate jolt of apprehension through her. As he arched his eyebrows in a silent command for her to answer him, she sighed.

"I needed time to think. Last night... Last night was..." Words failed her as she remembered the pleasure she'd experienced in his arms.

"Incredible," he said softly.

His anger vanished as he closed the distance between them. Rhea caught the scent of spice, and her heart skipped a beat as her gaze met his. Fire flared to life in his brown eyes as he bent his head toward her. Certain he was about to kiss her, she drew in a sharp breath at the anticipation streaking through her. Desire warmed her blood in a split second. The sudden sound of a door opening made Percy jerk upright and turn toward Ashford as the man emerged from his office. If the private investigator had witnessed anything, his expression didn't reveal it.

"Ready?" Ashford said quietly.

Rhea nodded as did Percy. In silence, the three of them filed out of the office building and into the waiting carriage. Tension began to grow inside her as it always did at this stage of the rescue. Traffic was light as they headed toward the docks in the East End, and they reached the outer edge of their destination in less than thirty minutes. As the carriage came to a halt in an unfamiliar spot, Rhea frowned.

"This isn't Southampton Street," she observed as she looked out first one window and then the other.

"This is where I first saw the boy, and my informant says he's here three times a week, and always the same days, including Fridays at approximately the same time."

"Then that means Ruckley has expanded his holdings. This used to be Bilkin's territory."

"Bilkin's body was found in an alleyway not too far from here about a week ago." Ashford's response echoed with a note of frustration.

Although she didn't know any of the investigator's clients, she knew he did a great deal of work for solicitors and barristers in the courts. Ruckley's expansion meant the investigator would find it more difficult to secure information. Informants always faced the prospect of retaliation by the man in control of a territory. And Ruckley was renowned for his vicious and sometimes fatal methods.

Ashford exited the carriage followed by Percy. Aware of her role in the rescue operation, Rhea remained where she was. The private investigator murmured something to Percy before moving to speak with the driver. Percy leaned back into the carriage to study her for a moment. There was a look in his dark eyes that made her realize how deeply worried he was.

"Ashford says he placed a man at the end of the street in the event of trouble. But you're to stay in the carriage," he said sternly.

A sudden urge to stop him from leaving swept through her, and Rhea quickly reached out to grab his forearm. Almost as rapidly as she'd reached for him, she drew back. Before she was out of reach, Percy caught her hand and tugged her toward him.

"After the way you left this morning, I was beginning to think you didn't care." The husky sound of his voice caressed her like velvet. Fire burned her cheeks, and she hoped the dim light hid the pleasure his words gave her. She shook her head as she tried to free herself from his grasp.

"I have no desire to see you or Mr. Ashford injured."

"Of that I have no doubt," he said softly as he bent his head to kiss the inside of her wrist. "But somehow I think the concern you feel for me is quite different from what you feel for your friend, Mr. Ashford."

The way his mouth lingered on her skin sent a tremor through her, and she suppressed the desire to lean forward and kiss him. With a shake of her head, she tried to dismiss his observation. But Ashford reappeared and tapped Percy on the shoulder. With one last kiss to the inside of her wrist, Percy stepped back and closed the carriage door. Left alone in the darkness of the vehicle, Rhea tried to quell a sense of dread that wrapped around her like a heavy cloak. She reminded herself that she always felt this way every time she returned to the East End. Rhea leaned back into the leather squabs of the carriage's seat and closed her eyes.

"Breathe, Rhea. Just breathe," she murmured.

Deliberately she forced her thoughts to focus on the good things that had happened to her since her aunt had pulled her out from under Ruckley's control. One image after another flowed through her head. Arianna's marriage, the children playing with carefree abandon at Green Hill House, even the simple fact that her belly was full was a blessing. And then there was last night.

As much as she tried to deny it, she wanted to be in Percy's arms again. When he'd kissed her wrist moments ago, she'd been terrified something might happen to him. She still felt that way. The strong feelings she developed for him in such a short time frightened her almost as much as the idea of him being hurt.

The sound of voices outside the carriage sent tension streaking throughout her. She was accustomed to Ashford taking much longer than this to spirit a child away. Rhea leaned forward to peer out to the window and saw a young girl trying to fight off a man who was clearly intent on having his way with her. The girl could not have been any older than Arianna had been when their father had sold them to Ruckley. Without thought or hesitation, Rhea quickly exited the vehicle and crossed the street to where the girl was struggling with the man.

"Hear mate, get on with you," Rhea said in a rough, but passable male voice. "The girl don't want nothing to do with you."

The man spun around with a grunt of irritation. A nearby lamp post cast off a shadowy light and highlighted the man's face. The moment she recognized him, Rhea experienced the sensation of being pushed into the Thames in the dead of winter. Edgar. The self-preservation instincts she'd honed well while living in the East End automatically rose to the surface. It was possible Ruckley's lieutenant might not recognize her if she maintained a cool head.

"Who the devil are you telling me to leave this tart alone." Edgar turned his head only to see his prey had disappeared. With his back turned, Rhea deliberately shifted her position to ensure she remained in the shadows. The young man whirled around to challenge Rhea once more Despite her natural reaction to retreat, she held her ground. The one thing she remembered clearly about Edgar was how he exhibited the same type of propensity for cruelty Ruckley did.

"What the fuck do ye think you're doing pushing your nose in me business," he snarled. "That whore was simply bilking me out of more coin than she were worth."

"Then I've saved you a few quid," Rhea said quietly.

"But I didn't ask ye to help save me money," Edgar said with furious outrage.

When Rhea didn't respond, the young man uttered an oath, and with the speed of a striking snake, his fist connected with Rhea's jaw. The blow caused her to stagger backward several steps to avoid falling into the slick, fetid street. The world shifted beneath her feet again as Edgar grabbed her by her wig and tugged hard. The pins holding the wig in place scraped across her scalp as the hairpiece came off in Edgar's hand. She heard a low shout and footsteps pounding the cobblestones in the distance, but she ignored the sounds.

The boy stood still staring at the wig in amazement before his gaze swerved to Rhea. Eyes widening with amazement, Edgar stared at her for a moment before his expression grew malevolent. He tossed the wig aside and pulled something from his pocket. The sudden glint of silver in the dim light made Rhea's limbs grow taut. Danger was something she was well acquainted with, and this was no different than any other time. Rhea's gaze swept over Edgar looking for any sign of weakness she could exploit. Nothing revealed itself, but she knew he would underestimate her and make a mistake soon enough.

"Well now, lookee here. If it ain't the high and mighty Miss Rhea," the young man sneered. "Come to kidnap more of Ruckley's family? He ain't gonna like that none. But he sure will like it when I bring you home as a present?"

"Family?" Rhea ignored the threat of Edgar handing her over to Ruckley and eyed the young man with cold contempt. "Ruckley's sense of family died the day he was born. In fact, I think the two of you are the closest thing to family each of you has. It's almost buggery the way you do his bidding."

Shock registered on Edgar's face before, with a vicious rage, he slashed out at her with his knife. Rhea easily darted out of reach as she recalled all the times she'd been forced to watch others fight Edgar. A wave of hatred crested over her as she dodged him a second time. The thief growled with fury and lunged forward to grab her arm. Despite being caught off guard by his attack, Rhea quickly twisted away. To break free of his hold, she swiftly bent her head and bit down on Edgar's filthy hand.

It was a defensive move she'd learned a long time ago in

these rat-infested streets. Like a repulsive vermin scurrying in retreat, the young man cried out in pain then jerked his hand away from her. Rhea wiped her mouth on the sleeve of her jacket in an attempt to erase the taste of the boy's unwashed body. Edgar stood a few feet away nursing his hand, and Rhea took advantage of his distraction. In two quick steps she was in striking distance, and she planted her foot viciously into the thief's side.

With a grunt Edgar stumbled backward before he quickly recovered and flipped his blade to his good hand. Despite the tension threatening to hinder her mobility, Rhea centered her thoughts on the threat at hand. As she watched him advance, she saw him shift to the left, and she smiled grimly. She had him. Whenever Edgar feinted to the left, it meant he intended to feint to the left a second time and then go right. It gave her the opening she was hoping for.

Prepared for his move, Rhea tensed as his knife flashed in the light of the gas light as the blade moved in her direction. She'd already twisted her body and was preparing to deliver a vicious blow to Edgar's kneecap when a hard body came between her and Edgar. She heard Percy make a hoarse sound of pain and immediately knew Edward's blade had connected with Percy shoulder.

"Damn it, Percy," she snapped as she ducked under his arm and planted a hard kick between Edgar's legs.

The boy howled with pain as he clutched his crotch and sank to his knees. Rhea didn't hesitate as she kicked outward again. This time her boot connected with the side of Edgar's head, and the boy fell backward into the street with a grunt and remained still. Rhea whirled around to see Percy hold his injured arm as he stood watching her with a mixture of anger, amazement, and what she thought might be admiration. Rhea glanced away from him to see Peter staring out the carriage window while Ashford and another man stood next to the carriage. Tension reflected in their stance both men were clearly poised to do battle.

Rhea turned back to Percy. The dark disapproval in his gaze angered her, and she glared back at him. Percy didn't say a word. He simply nodded in the direction of the carriage. Rhea didn't fail to understand the silent command and blowing out a harsh breath of exasperation, she whirled around to stride toward the carriage. Peter's eyes were wide in his small face as he stared at her from the vehicle. But his smile was bright and cheery. When Ashford opened the carriage door, the child flung himself forward to wrap his arms around Rhea's neck. A small crowd was beginning to grow around Edgar's unconscious body and Ashford touched Rhea's arm.

"I suggest we leave now," he said quietly. With a quick glance over her shoulder at the gathering crowd, she hopped into the carriage followed by Percy and Ashford. As the vehicle rolled forward, Rhea's heart sank as her gaze scanned the vehicle's interior.

"Fanny?"

"Harry could have come with us Miss Rhea, but he said he'd stay and bring Fanny with him when these gents come next week. Peter leaned into Rhea's side as she wrapped her arm around him and hugged him close.

"I'm sorry it took me so long to keep my word to you Peter," she said softly.

"It's okay, Miss Rhea I knew you'd come for me, just like you always said you would if you ever escaped Ruckley," the child said with a confident smile that made a knot rise in her throat. "When Vincent and Rufus went missing after you and Miss Arianna disappeared, I knew you were trying to get us away from Ruckley, so I just waited real patient like."

The boy sighed with obvious relief and Rhea looked at the two men seated opposite her.

"Did you have any trouble?"

"No, we had no problems at all." Ashford's statement was both an explanation and rebuke. Percy uttered a quiet oath as the carriage hit a rough patch of street, and he was thrown into the sidewall of the carriage. Rhea pulled away from Peter and scooted forward in her seat.

"Let me see how badly Edgar cut you."

"I'm fine," Percy bit out in a tight voice.

"Oh for heaven sakes, Percy. Stop being an ass and let me see your arm," she snapped. Clearly surprised by her chastisement, Percy didn't protest as she gently pushed his coat off his arm then tore the bloodstained shirt apart to examine his injury.

"You need stitches," she said with a frown as she looked up to meet his unreadable expression. Unwilling to try and determine what he was thinking, Rhea turned to Ashford.

"Where shall we drop you off Mr. Ashford?"

"I instructed the driver to take you home first."

"All right," she said with a nod and looked back at Percy. "I'll see to your shoulder as soon as I turn Peter over to Arianna."

"I can—"

"No, you can't. I'm well skilled in sewing up cuts." Before Percy could respond the child seated at her side leaned forward.

"You should let Miss Rhea fix you up, sir. She does a right good job. She even gives you a kiss on the cheek if you don't cry once."

"Indeed," Percy murmured as heat suffused Rhea's cheeks. As her gaze met Percy's, her heart skipped a beat at the fire she saw burning in his eyes. Rhea quickly retreated from him and sank back into the cushions of her seat. Silence filled the carriage for a moment before Ashford cleared his throat.

"Do you mind explaining why you left the carriage, Miss Bennett when you were specifically instructed not to?" The investigator eyed her carefully. "We made an agreement when I first took on this assignment."

"I know, and I apologize. But Edgar was troubling a young girl. I couldn't let him do that. I didn't even know it was Edgar until he turned around."

"You took an unnecessary risk, Miss Bennett," the private investigator said quietly. "If you wish for me to complete our task, then you'll have to remain at home next week."

"You can't possibly—"

"I'm afraid I can, and must, Miss Bennett. If something happened to you, I would not be able to forgive myself, and I've no doubt your aunt would lay the blame at my feet."

Ashford's harsh, unyielding expression assured her that nothing she might say would change the man's mind. Her gaze flitted to Percy who was clearly pleased with Ashford's decision. Defeated, Rhea sank deeper into the seat cushions. Silence descended on the interior of the vehicle, and she wrapped her arm around Peter once more.

The ride home seemed interminable, and Rhea avoided looking at either of the men across from her. While she knew she'd taken a risk leaving the carriage, it had been the right decision. Edgar had been forcing himself on the girl, and the sight had opened up old wounds, which had compelled her to interfere.

Accustomed to taking care of herself, she'd never doubted her ability to handle Edgar. It had been unnecessary for Percy to interfere. Although she had to admit his efforts warmed her heart. It made her feel that she was valued for something other than bringing in coin.

The carriage halted at the front door of her aunt's house, and Rhea ushered Peter out of the carriage then looked at Percy. There was a stubborn set to his mouth indicating he intended to argue with her. Rhea narrowed her gaze at him then smiled.

"If you're afraid, I'm sure Peter can hold your hand for such a…" She paused for effect. "Major surgery of this nature."

Without waiting for his answer, she exited the carriage and heard his vicious oath filling the air behind her. She didn't bother to turn her head to confirm whether he was following her or not. The heat of his gaze burned the back of her neck confirming he was only a few steps behind her despite his reluctance. She bit back a smile of satisfaction. For once he was on the receiving end of his own medicine. The front door opened and at the sight of Arianna, the boy uttered a soft cry of happiness and raced the last few steps into her sister's arms.

Gently, Rhea pushed Peter deeper into the house as Arianna kept her arm wrapped around the boy. Percy followed and closed the front door behind them. Arianna quietly greeted Percy before she raised her eyebrows at Rhea.

"Arianna would you mind looking after Peter while I tend to Percy's arm."

As Rhea moved out of the shadows into the middle of the entryway Arianna's eyes widened with horror as a gasp of alarm escaped her. Startled, Rhea met her sister's shocked gaze and arched her eyebrows.

"What?"

"Your jaw." Arianna stared at her in dismay, and Rhea reached up to touch the spot where she remembered Edgar had hit her. It was still tender, and she winced then shrugged slightly.

"It's nothing." At her careless reply, Percy quickly stepped forward and forced her to turn around. His eyes narrowed before raw fury hardened his handsome features.

"Did Edgar do this?" The dark fury in his quiet question told her that her jaw had to be bruised far worse than it felt. At Percy's question, Arianna released another soft cry of dismay.

"Do you mean Ruckley's Edgar?"

"He was troubling a young girl." Rhea's voice held no emotion as she met her sister's gaze.

Pain and humiliation flickered across her sister's face as she nodded her understanding of Rhea's reason for interfering. Deliberately changing the subject, Rhea motioned for her sister to take Peter upstairs. Arianna gently pulled Peter away from Rhea and Percy. With a tender gesture, she brushed the hair out of Peter's eyes as she guided the boy upstairs with the promise of a soft bed, a hot meal, and a warm bath.

The child responded positively until the mention of a bath. He protested, but Arianna made it quite clear that a bath would be unavoidable. A quiet chuckle made Rhea glance over her shoulder to see amusement twisting Percy's mouth in a grin as he watched Peter climbing the stairs. Their eyes met, and Percy's amusement disappeared as he frowned at her once more. Before he could say a word, she nodded toward the salon.

"Wait for me in the parlor. I need to find needle and thread for that cut."

She didn't wait to see if he would comply, but hurried to the kitchen to secure the items she needed to tend to Percy's injury. When she returned to the salon several minutes later, Rhea halted just inside the doorway at the sight of Percy sitting on the couch bared to the waist. His head tipped to one side, he was examining the wound on his shoulder. He took her breath away.

The pounding of her heart echoed so loudly in her ears, she was surprised he couldn't hear it. Swallowing hard, she used her hip to close the door behind her. At the sound, Percy looked up and watched her approach. She set down the bandages and lavender cream along with the bowl of hot water. Avoiding his gaze, she turned to examine his shoulder. A sigh of relief broke from her lips as she finished her examination and shook her head slightly.

"It's not too deep and once it's stitched up it will heal nicely," she murmured. In response he grunted something incoherent.

Unwilling to engage in conversation, Rhea quickly set about tending to the gash. Carefully cleaning the wound, she removed the dried blood then reached for the lavender cream. As gently as she could, she applied the natural analgesic to the skin around the long cut. When she'd threaded the needle that looked like a fishhook, she met his gaze.

"This is going to be uncomfortable. The lavender poultice only numbs the area so much."

"I'll survive," he muttered.

Rhea nodded and pinched the gash closed with her fingers. The first stitch caused Percy to suck in a sharp breath. She glanced up at him then back down at her task.

"Breathe through your mouth," she said quietly. "For some reason it makes it easier."

"I'm fine," he growled softly.

"Of course you are," she said with blatant sarcasm and pushed the needle through his skin again.

"Hell fire and damnation," he bit out between clenched teeth.

"I'm sorry." At her contrite apology, a strong hand gently brushed across her cheek. A tremor rippled through her, and she didn't move for a moment concerned her trembling could cause him unnecessary discomfort.

"You know what this means, don't you?" he said in a voice that wrapped around her like a sinfully warm blanket.

"Yes," she choked out as his fingers tucked a stray lock of hair behind her ear. The gentle touch made her feel treasured somehow. "It means you're going to be sore for a couple of days."

"No, it means I have to ensure you're always with me anytime I get cut." His remark made her stiffen, and she raised her head to look at him. He quirked an eyebrow at her, and the warmth in his gaze made her swallow hard. She quickly ducked her head and continued sewing up his wound.

"Rhea—"

"What exactly did Ruckley do in your vision?" she asked. She heard the breathless note in voice, and she knew it was because she was afraid he'd been about to broach a subject she didn't want to discuss. Percy frowned.

"I didn't say Ruckley did anything," he said in a tight voice.

"You didn't have to, Percy," she said softly as she pulled thread through his flesh and he grunted. "But don't you think it would help if you told me what you saw?"

"No." The harsh rejection made her flinch, and she looked up at him. His handsome features could have been carved in stone, and his mouth was thin with tension.

"Whatever you saw must have been disturbing or you wouldn't look so formidable." She pulled the last suture through his skin, knotted it and snapped off the remaining thread with her teeth. She dropped the needle onto the table and reached for the bandages.

"Leave it be, Rhea."

"When it comes to Ruckley, I can no more let it be, any more than you can."

"Why do you have to be so damn obstinate?" Percy tugged her into his side with his good arm. The unexpected movement caused the bandages to fall out of her hand, and before she could speak, he kissed her hard. Instantly she melted into him. Hands pressed against the hard muscles of his chest, she sighed as his mouth left hers to lightly brush across her tender jaw.

"Marry me," he said gruffly in her ear.

Despite the expectation that he would offer for her, his proposal still caught her by surprise. She immediately tried to retreat, but he kissed her again. This time his mouth lingered and teased hers into an eager submission. The warm male scent of him filled her senses until all she wanted was for him to hold her like this forever.

It was a dangerous thought, and as he lifted his head to

look into her eyes, panic spiraled through her. Although she'd anticipated his proposal, Rhea hadn't been prepared for her reaction. Never had she dreamed it would take every bit of will power she possessed not to fling her arms around his neck and say yes. Her heart beating frantically in her chest, she realized she was on a precipice about to fall into the abyss.

Fear washing over her, she pushed herself away from the edge of the cliff. She couldn't afford to give way to her emotions. She needed to rely on cold reason to save herself from doing the unthinkable. She'd already given up a piece of her heart to Percy. The prospect of giving up everything to him was terrifying.

Chapter 15

R hea trembled against him, and he stared into her violet eyes trying to discern what was going on in her beautiful head. With a quick twist of her soft body, Rhea pushed her way out of his arms.

"You'll need to have Jenkins clean and bandage the wound for a couple of days," she said in a breathless voice. "You want to avoid infection."

"Don't change the subject," he said with impatience as he watched her hands fumble with the bandages on the table. "I just proposed to you, and I think I deserve a response."

"I'll give you my answer if you tell me what you saw in your vision." The provisional demand reminded him of Patience and the bargain he'd made with his sister. Nothing was going right in his life at the moment, and he gritted his teeth.

"Damn it, Rhea, don't play games with me."

"I'm not," she said as she pulled in a deep breath then released it. "But if you want my answer, then you'll have to tell me what you saw."

"What I saw made no sense." Unwilling to share the graphic nature of his vision for fear of frightening her, he tried to catch her hand in his, but she easily evaded him.

"Perhaps not, but it had to trouble you deeply, otherwise you wouldn't be so stubborn about telling me what you saw." There was a confidence in her voice that declared she knew the *an dara sealladh* had shown him something more than he was revealing. He shook his head.

"As I said, it didn't make sense. There was no rhyme or reason to what the *an dara sealladh* showed me."

"Then why not tell me? My experience as to how dangerous Ruckley is exceeds your experience tenfold." She eyed him with skepticism. "If you're trying to protect me, don't, and until you tell me what you saw, I'll not answer your question."

"*Bloody hell*," he growled at the mutinous tilt of her lips. Her expression made him realize she refused to give way. Exhaling a loud whoosh of air, he glared at her. "I saw you entering a room with Ruckley, alone. There was a gunshot and blood—a great deal of blood."

Percy didn't try to soften the description. If she was so hell bent on knowing what he'd seen, then he'd make damn sure she understood why he believed she was in danger. Rhea paled at his harsh words, and he immediately regretted the manner in which he'd chosen to depict the images he'd seen. As she met his gaze, a sense of foreboding swept over him. It only increased the unease he'd been experiencing since they'd left Ashford's office earlier this evening. Rhea shook her head and bit down on her lip.

"How many of your visions actually come to pass?" Her question made him hesitate before he grimaced and steadily met her gaze.

"Most of them, but not necessarily in the way I see it. But what I saw concerns me because it makes me believe you're in danger." At his harsh response, she reached for the bandages once more. Percy saw her hands tremble as she did so.

"Will it make you feel better if I promise not to take any unnecessary risks until Ruckley has been dealt with?" She lifted her head to meet his gaze steadily.

"Yes, that will make me feel better," he said quietly. Percy caught her chin in his fingers and forced her to look at him. "I agreed to your terms, now it's time to honor mine. Will you marry me?"

"What happened last night was my choice, Percy. I had no expectations," she said in a quiet voice.

"That's not an answer." The terseness of his reply made her wince.

"Then let me be more concise. I won't marry you."

"That's the wrong answer," he bit out as he forced himself not to reach for her.

"Nevertheless, it's the one I'm giving you."

She'd refused him. Frustration ricocheted through him. He didn't know why the fact surprised him. He'd known it would be difficult to convince her to accept his marriage proposal. He grunted with exasperation.

"You're as stubborn as a mule," he said as he reached for his shirt. It cracked in the air as he shook it out angrily before pulling it on. Percy saw her flinch, but at the moment he was too irritated to care.

"I know you're trying to do the honorable thing—"

"Honor be damned," he snarled as he hastily buttoned his shirt. "This is about wanting to wake up with you in my arms every morning."

Eyes wide with astonishment, Rhea grew pale as she met his gaze, while something undefinable flickered in the violet depths of her eyes. Her expression softened as she stepped forward to touch his arm. It was an electric shock that sent a jolt through him.

"I think that's something I would like very much," she whispered. "If you made me your mistress, it would solve our mutual dilemma."

Stunned by her proposition, Percy stared at her with a sense of impending doom. Did she really think he cared so little for her that he would agree to such an arrangement? With unexpected clarity, he realized she did. Ruckley had convinced her she was undeserving of any man's respect or the chance for lasting happiness. The bastard had done his work well, and it would be an uphill battle convincing her that Ruckley was wrong.

"I don't want a mistress," he said quietly. "I want a wife, and I want that wife to be you."

Rhea quickly stepped back from him as if he'd hit her. A haunted look flitted across her pale features before she closed herself off to him, and her expression was as unreadable as a marble statue.

"I'll never marry," she said in a voice so soft he could barely hear her. "I'll never give *any* man control over me again."

"I don't want to control you, Rhea," he snarled as he grabbed his coat and shrugged into it, ignoring the sharp twinge in his shoulder as he did so.

"But marriage is about control," she replied with quiet conviction.

"Not if you love someone it isn't."

The moment he spoke, he experienced the sensation of having walked into an invisible wall. He loved her. It amazed him how he'd spent the entire day in denial of that very fact. Percy took in Rhea's panic and his gut twisted. He debated whether to say anything further, but for once self-control crushed his propensity for reckless behavior. If he had any hope of winning her, it was important to move slowly. He would need to restrain his natural tendency to rush forward without a plan.

"*Fuck*," he breathed so low she couldn't hear him.

Without looking at her, Percy stood up and strode quickly toward the exit. At the salon door he looked over his shoulder at her. Her dazed confusion gave him hope. It was almost as if she was struggling not to rush forward to stop him from leaving. Instinctively, he hesitated, silently urging her to stop him from going. When she didn't move, he clenched his jaw as he tried to find the right words to make her understand he wouldn't give up so easily. His gaze locked with hers, and he swallowed the urge to stride back to her, pull her into his arms, and kiss her until she understood how much he loved her.

"You underestimate yourself, Rhea," he said quietly. "You are far more worthy of any man than you realize, and I'm going to do my damnedest to make you see that."

As his words floated between them, Rhea stared at him in surprise. He knew not to push his luck, and Percy retreated from the salon, closing the door on his way out of the house. When he reached the front steps of Fremont Place a dark premonition touched the edge of his senses. He grew still as he waited for the *an dara sealladh* to roll over him.

When the warning slithered into the darkness without showing him anything, Percy grew even more uneasy. Something was on the horizon, and for once he wished his gift had made an appearance to give him any insight or warning about Ruckley's intentions. The bastard was a clear and present danger where Rhea was concerned, and even Ashford had admitted concern for her safety if Ruckley were to find her.

Vigilance was required to ensure no harm came to her, but at the moment he was lost in the middle of an ocean without any idea what direction to sail in. The fact didn't just frustrate him. It worried the hell out of him. How could he protect Rhea if he didn't know where the danger was coming from? Percy descended the steps and hailed a passing hack. At the moment, he needed someone's counsel where Rhea was concerned.

Patience was the one person who would understand Rhea. Patience understood what it was like to believe you were unworthy of being loved. It was a feeling he believed his sister still experienced to a small degree. If anyone could help him find a way to reach the heart of the woman he loved, it was his sister. He'd go to Melton House first thing in the morning. His arm was beginning to ache more noticeably now, and at the moment, all he wanted was a good stiff brandy and some sleep. As he sank back into the seat cushions of the hack, a sense of purpose descended over him. He finally had a plan of action, which lead to another plan. In the end, he would win Rhea's heart. Anything else was unacceptable.

Percy prowled the floor of Melton House's morning room as his sister read the note Rhea had sent him early this morning. The letter had arrived only moments before he'd left home to visit the family's London seat. Patience looked up from the stationary in her hand to scowl at him.

"Would you please sit down and let me read this? You're beginning to make me nervous."

The exasperation in Patience's voice made him grimace. With an impatient grunt, he threw himself into a nearby chair. Moments later he was on his feet again unable to remain still. Percy crossed the floor to the window, and with one arm raised slightly, he gripped the window frame as he stared out at the morning traffic, which was still light. The Set had yet to swell the streets with their daily round of social calls.

Tension held him rigid, and in an attempt to alleviate his tight muscles, he shrugged. The action pulled painfully at his wound, but it was inconsequential compared to the sense of despondency he was enduring at the moment. Behind him Patience gasped loudly, and he grimaced as he recalled his own reaction to the note. Percy turned his head to see his sister staring at him in amazement.

"You proposed to her?"

"You say that as if I made a mistake in doing so," he said irritably as he turned and narrowed his gaze at her. "I love her."

Patience shook her head again in apparent dismay then

returned her attention to the note. He'd read it several times on his way to his brother's house and had memorized the brief wording. The note reflected a resolve on Rhea's part that worried him greatly. The possibility that he might be unable to change her mind filled him with dread.

Dear Mr. Rockwood,

Last night you honored me with your proposal. I believe any woman would count herself fortunate to have such an honor bestowed on them. I know my reply was not the one you wished to hear. However, I must reiterate my refusal. I know you believe it within your power to change my mind, but I urge you to believe otherwise.

We both know my reasons for refusing your noble gesture, and it was noble of you, Percy. It is a trait few men have, and it is one of many attributes you possess that only deepens my feelings of admiration and affection for you.

Since you are unwilling to consider the alternative arrangement I proposed, we are at an impasse. When our partnership concerning our mutual adversary is concluded, there will be no further reason to continue our acquaintance. I trust you will respect my wishes and not pursue this matter to its inevitable, and only, conclusion.

Rhea Bennett

Once again Patience gasped loudly, and he turned away from the window to see his sister's appalled expression.

"Dear lord, she offered to be your mistress?"

Patience's scorn exacerbated his growing anger at her disdainful reaction. If he'd even thought for one moment that his sister would act with such disdain toward Rhea, he would never have shown Patience the letter. He'd expected better from his sister.

"Rhea believes herself unworthy of me."

"And rightfully so," his sister muttered with obvious

distaste.

"What the hell is that supposed to mean?"

"It means you know very little about the woman and what she's done."

"The *an dara sealladh* showed you something," he bit out with a growing sense of concern. Dismayed sympathy caused Patience to shake her head in sorrow.

"The *an dara sealladh* showed me she's wronged you Percy, and you don't even know it."

"We both know our gift never gives us a clear understanding of anything we see."

"I saw enough to know she shot you and left you for dead in the museum last year."

"She did not shoot me," he bit out in an icy voice. "A man by the name of Ruckley is the one who shot me."

"Even if that is true, she left you for dead," Patience protested angrily and sprang to her feet.

"She had no choice. She thought I was already dead."

"Don't be a fool. Has your infatuation with the woman blinded you to the fact that everyone has a choice, Percy? How can you defend her when she left you to die on that cold floor?"

"Even if she'd realized I was still alive, she couldn't have done anything. If she'd tried to save me, she would have been killed."

"I don't understand how you can defend the woman." Patience eyed him with disbelief. "You're asking a great deal of us to believe that Miss Bennett had no other choice but to leave you dying on that museum floor."

"Us?" The realization that his sister had told someone else about her vision increased his outrage. Percy pinned his gaze on her, and a color flushed her cheeks as she looked away from him. "Out with it, Patience. With whom have you discussed your vision?"

"Everyone," she whispered with a rebellious note in her

voice.

"Everyone? Since when do you speak to others about visions that involve me?"

"Since you seem to have lost your sense of perspective where this woman is concerned. I love you dearly, Percy, and I'm worried for your safety." His sister drew herself up to her full height as she met his gaze with a look of frustration. "Surely you can understand how upsetting it was to see Miss Bennett hovering over you as you lay dying."

Despite the anger flowing through him, Percy tried to empathize with his sister's explanation. He stared at Patience for a long moment then turned away from her and returned to the window. His hand brushed the translucent lawn curtain to one side as he struggled with what his sister had done.

While he didn't doubt Patience's fears for his safety, it was impossible to ignore the fact that she'd shared a vision involving him with the entire family. Simply based on Patience's own demeanor, he had no doubt the family now viewed Rhea in less than favorable terms. He now had only one of two choices. He could betray Rhea's confidence by sharing her secrets or continue to let his family think the worst of her.

"Percy, thank goodness you've come to visit." The sound of Louisa's voice made him turn, and his heart sank as she crossed the carpet to his side. The youngest sibling in the Rockwood clan turned her head toward Patience. "Did you tell him what you saw, Patience?"

"Yes," the abrupt note in their sister's voice made Louisa frown as she turned to look at him again.

"Are you all right?" Louisa said with a note of concern in her voice. "We're all quite worried about you."

"There is no need to be," he bit out between clenched teeth. Percy stiffened as Constance entered the morning room. The oldest of his three sisters halted a few feet away from him, and her gaze swept across all of their faces.

"Well, it's obvious Patience has told you the news," Constance said quietly. "I am sorry, Percy. This must be a terrible shock."

"What? Shocked to learn my sister betrayed me?"

"Percy," Louisa exclaimed with astonished dismay. "Patience didn't betray you."

"No? She shared her impressions about a matter that concerns me with the family. Worse she did so without speaking to me first." Percy glared at each of his sisters in turn, and Louisa stepped back in surprise at the fury he made no effort to contain. "Patience's images were incomplete, and each of you has reached a conclusion about Rhea that is undeserved. You've tried and convicted her of misdeeds that were out of her control."

"If that's the case, perhaps you should enlighten us as to what would prompt the woman to leave you dying on that museum floor," Patience snapped fiercely.

"I'm not at liberty to comment on Rhea's action that night. Suffice it to say that you must—"

"*For God's sake, Percy.* The woman left you to die," Patience exclaimed with a fierce cry of outrage and indignation.

"No, she chose to let others live. The man who shot me threatened to harm Rhea's sister and several children in her care," Percy snarled. "She believed I was dead already. Was she to abandon others to the same fate? She had no choice but to obey a man who owned her like one owns an animal."

His vicious outburst caused his sisters to gasp, and Percy immediately realized his misstep. In his anger, he'd betrayed one of Rhea's secrets. Furious with himself at having done so, he ignored the remorse and shame on his sisters' faces. He narrowed his gaze on Patience, whose demeanor had changed to deep regret and contrition.

"I would have thought *you*, of all people, *Patience*, would know better than to accept the *an dara sealladh* at face value."

"That's enough, Percy," Constance commanded quietly as their sister paled until her skin was almost the color of chalk. "Patience was only concerned for your safety."

"Do not patronize me, Constance." His gaze quickly swung from Patience to his oldest sister. "Are you going to claim you didn't think the worst of Rhea when Patience shared her vision with you? Did you, Louisa?"

The two women slowly shook their heads in a contrite manner. All three women in the morning room showed a significant amount of regret, but it didn't alleviate Percy's rage. They'd judged Rhea, and it would take time for him to forgive them for having done so. He looked at each of them with deep disappointment.

"Each of you have done yourself a disservice and injured a woman who rivals everyone in this family in courage and fortitude," he said coldly. "If I'm able to find a way to convince Rhea to marry me, I shall consider myself a fortunate man. However, at the moment, I cannot say the same where my family is concerned."

Percy barely took in the looks of devastation, consternation, and compunction on his sisters' faces. His anger and disappointment in their behavior was too deep. Without another word, he brushed past Louisa, tugging free of her grasp as she tried to prevent him from leaving and strode from the morning room. As he opened the front door, he heard his aunt call his name, and he glanced over his shoulder.

His aunt's visible dismay made him blow out a snort of anger before he viciously slammed the door of Melton House closed behind him. For the first time in his life, Percy realized just how reckless his family could be. He was no less guilty than any other Rockwood when it came to rash behavior. But this incident illustrated why his brother, Sebastian, made every effort to control the Rockwood trait of recklessness.

Unfortunately for him, Patience's impulsive decision to

share her vision with the family had cost him the counsel of someone he'd trusted—someone he'd hoped could help him find a way to convince Rhea to marry him. The worst of it was for the first time in his life there wasn't a Rockwood in sight to support or encourage him in his quest. It was an unsettling feeling, but he refused to let anything stand in his way when it came to making Rhea his wife. If there was anything the Rockwoods were known for it was their obstinance.

Chapter 16

*A*rianna sighed softly as she sealed the envelope of her short note refusing the Viscountess Starling's dinner invitation. More than four days had passed since she'd bared her soul to Blake. When it became clear he intended to stay at his club, she'd retreated to her aunt's home.

It had been too painful to remain at Sherrington House. Now with each passing day her hope of him seeking her out had diminished to the point of resigned despair. She closed her eyes to keep tears from streaming down her cheeks. The desolation she'd experienced while being enslaved by Ruckley had been horrible enough.

But this was as if her heart had been ripped from her chest. The hole it left behind was one she knew could never be filled by anything other than Blake's love. Not even her love for Lucy and the rest of her family could compensate for the loss of Blake's affections.

Quickly wiping the tear off her cheek that had escaped her closed eyelids, Arianna returned her attention to the stack of correspondence on the secretaire. The invitations had increased over the past two days, and she was certain it was because people knew she and Blake were estranged. The Marlborough Set was eager to uncover the reason, but she had no intention of satisfying the gossips. Letter opener in hand, she opened another invitation and quickly penned a note declining her attendance. When she'd finished, she laid her pen down, her gaze flitting toward the stack still to be dealt with. She wanted to simply throw them onto the fire and be done with the lot.

The thought made her frown. Perhaps she should do what Rhea had done and return to Green Hill House. Impulsively, Arianna swept up the stack of correspondence and sprang to her feet. Without hesitating, she crossed the room and threw the envelopes onto the fire. Flames immediately curled around the formal communications until they burned brightly in the fireplace. Relief swept through her at the cathartic exercise.

It wasn't until now that she realized she'd already made up her mind to join Rhea in the country. Although her chest ached at her decision, she felt better for having settled on a plan of action. The sound of her aunt's laughter in the foyer tugged a sad smile to her lips. Beatrice Fremont's recent news of her plans to marry Lord Foxworth made Arianna happy despite her own miserable situation. But the affection she'd witnessed between her aunt and Lord Foxworth had only served as a reminder of how her own marriage had failed.

The door to the salon opened, and Arianna turned to greet her aunt. Shock rippled through her at the sight of Blake filling the doorway with his tall frame. Behind her husband, Arianna saw her aunt looking at her with an expression of encouragement as she nodded toward Blake. A plethora of feelings crashed over Arianna like the waves in a tumultuous storm as she watched her husband close the salon door. Buffeted by the emotions engulfing her, Arianna pressed her hand into her stomach as her early morning sickness threatened to return.

"Good morning, Arianna."

Blake's voice was a deep, sensual sound that caused a frisson to streak across her skin. From the first moment they'd met, his voice had always had that effect on her. Arianna nodded a silent greeting as she studied him in silence. He looked exhausted. Had he missed her? A small flame of hope flared to life in her chest before she doused it. She was a fool to think he had arrived for any other purpose except to inform her he was seeking a divorce. The thought increased her nausea as she gestured toward the sofa.

"Let me ring for some tea," she murmured.

"Thank you, no," he replied.

The awkwardness between them made Arianna wince as she nodded. Blake took a step toward her, and she immediately retreated. It was a reaction born of self-preservation. A dark frown settled on Blake's brow, and she bit down nervously on her lip at his apparent anger. Anxious to keep some form of barrier between them, Arianna moved to stand behind a chair a short distance away. She wrapped her fingers around the wood trim on the back of the chair and looked at her husband. It was impossible to discern what he was thinking. Uncertainty gripped her and her nails dug into the wood trim of the chair as she clung to the furniture as if it were a life raft in a violent sea.

"Since you have no wish to partake of any refreshment, I can only presume you've come to inform me that intend to seek a divorce." Arianna was relieved to hear her voice didn't waver as she spoke.

The last thing she wanted to reveal was how devastating his rejection was. She'd lied to him not because she didn't love him, but because she'd been terrified of losing him. Blake uttered an oath beneath his breath. His indecision startled her. Blake had never shown anything but confidence in everything he did. Resolve replaced his hesitation as he clasped his hands behind his back.

"No, that's not why I'm here. I've come to take you home."

Arianna's heart skipped a beat at his words. He'd come for her. In the next instant her heart sank. He'd not uttered one word of love or forgiveness. Simply that he'd come to take her home. The realization made the hole in her chest expand.

She could never go back to Sherrington House without his love, his forgiveness—or Lucy. She shook her head.

"I'm quite happy here in my aunt's house."

Despite the soft, evenly spoken reply she knew it was a lie. She was miserable except for the time she spent with Lucy. Even then, her time with her daughter was bittersweet. Blake's frustration became a scowl of anger.

"I don't give a damn if you're happy or not," he bit out fiercely. "You'll pack your things and come home with me today."

"I beg your pardon," she stared at him with a growing sense of alarm as memories the past filled her head.

For years she had been forced to obey Ruckley's orders to do one vile thing after another. Blake had never commanded her to do anything except when they were intimate. Those commands had been given solely to enhance her pleasure. Not once since they'd met had her husband ever done anything to make her feel as if she was a possession. Until now.

A small flutter touched her stomach and a terrible fear swept through her. He'd come for her because she might be carrying his son. Blake was within his rights to take their child away from her, and a tremor rocked through her at the seriousness of her predicament. The horror of losing the baby made it almost impossible to breathe. Just as she had with Ruckley she was trapped with no means of escape.

"*Damn it*, I didn't mean it like that."

"Then what did you mean?" At her cold reply, he grimaced.

"I meant that Sherrington House is empty without you."

"I'm curious as to how you have reached that conclusion since you no longer reside there, but at your club." It was impossible to suppress the bitterness in her voice and Blake jerked at her icy reply then stiffened.

"I deserved that," he muttered.

There was almost a boyish, forlorn quality to his demeanor as he met her gaze. The impulse to run to him tugged at her, but she resisted. It would be a mistake to do so. Without forgiveness, whatever love he still felt for her would eventually become tainted. It would be far easier to lose him now, than to watch him grow to despise her. Silence stretched out between them like an invisible chasm. It was a divide so wide she doubted it could ever be bridged. When she didn't reply to his remark, Blake shoved his fingers through his hair creating a disheveled look that only increased her desire to fling herself forward and into his arms.

"I'm asking you to come home, Arianna."

Still no words of love or forgiveness, but it was impossible to keep hope from streaking through her blood. Would he have asked her to come home if he didn't care? She pressed one hand against her stomach as the new life growing inside her fluttered again. She experienced another bout of nausea as she realized his only concern might be her child. It would explain why he'd not said he loved her.

"I'm sorry, Blake. I cannot do–"

"Why the hell not?" he snarled. "Are you saying you lied to me when you proclaimed your love for me?"

"No. I do love you," she cried out. "I cannot possibly expect you to understand how—"

"Understand that you have a daughter?" He glared at her. "There's nothing to understand. You lied to me."

"A lie you seem unwilling to forgive." The quiet reply made him grow still as he met her gaze.

"It's not the lie I find difficult to forgive, Arianna. It's your lack of faith and trust in me." An emotion she could only label as pain flickered in his moss green eyes.

"I lied because I thought you would cast me aside as my father did," she said with an anguished cry. "You cannot possibly imagine what a betrayal such as that does to a person."

At Blake's astonishment, Arianna turned her head away from him. She refused to accept his pity. All she wanted was for him to understand her reason for lying to him. Arianna glanced at him, hoping to see some sign of his understanding, but it was impossible to tell what he was thinking.

Bleak dismay tightened its vise around her heart. It was possible she might never be able to make him understand how terrified she was of losing him—his love. Was she asking too much to think she could make him understand what had driven her not tell him everything? Perhaps it wasn't the why he needed to understand. All she truly needed him to know and believe was that it had been her fear of losing his love that had driven her to hide the truth. She released a small sound of despair as her gaze met his, and she straightened upright.

"Can you deny you would not have had second thoughts if you'd known about Lucy before we were married? Would you have even offered for me if you'd known?" She indicated her belief he would not have done so with a shake of her head. "It is one thing to accept the fact that your wife is a whore. You can hide such a fact from people, but you cannot hide or explain away my daughter's presence."

With a blinding speed that startled Arianna, Blake moved forward and shoved aside the chair between them. His hands gripped her arms as he shook her with a restrained force.

"You are not a whore. What that bastard did to you was abominable, but it does not make you a whore. As for your father, if he were alive, I'd thrash him and leave him for dead," he said harshly. He released her and took a step backward. "I'll not deny I might have had second thoughts if you had told me about your daughter. But in the end my decision to marry you would still have been the same. I don't care about your past. I never have because I love you. Nothing will ever change that."

There was a raw, powerful force in his voice that made Arianna stare at him in astonishment. The fierce intensity of his words was reflected in his harsh expression. As she met his gaze, she thought she saw fear flashed in his eyes.

"*Christ Jesus*, Arianna. Say something."

"I'm sorry. I'm so sorry, Blake," she whispered as she burst into tears. In less than a second, his arms were wrapped around her in a tight embrace. The familiar warmth of him engulfed her as she buried her face in his shoulder and sobbed. Blake murmured words of love, reassurance, and forgiveness as he held her close. After several moments, her sobs quieted and Blake tipped her head up with his forefinger.

"I was a brute, my love. I should have realized you would have good reason to hide the truth from me."

"I'm truly sorry, Blake," she whispered as she gulped back a fresh round of tears. "You never gave me any reason to doubt your love. I should have trusted you."

"Enough apologies, Arianna," he said huskily. "All I want to hear is that you love me, and that you believe me when I say I'll never betray you."

"I love you, Blake. I love you more than you will ever know."

"And do you trust me not to betray you?" The soft question made Arianna stiffen. As she looked into his green eyes, she struggled to say the words she knew he wanted to hear. Her mouth moved as she tried to answer, but the words failed to roll off her tongue. He winced before he bent his head and pressed his lips to her brow.

"It's all right, my darling. I'll simply have to work harder to make you believe I'd never do anything to harm you."

He kissed her forehead again and pulled her close. As her cheek pressed into his shoulder, she experienced a new sense of security. He'd forgiven her and he loved her. There was only one thing more she could ask of him. It was the one thing that would test their newfound understanding. She pushed away from him slightly and met his gaze. Before she could even speak, his fingers pressed against her lips.

"It seems we now have a dilemma on our hands," he said

with a wry smile. "What to say when we bring our daughter home with us."

Arianna stared at him in open wonder. Without any pleading from her, he was giving her the ultimate gift. He was willing to take in a child that wasn't his into his home simply because he loved her. The gesture illustrated the depth of love for her. She continued to stare at him in open-mouthed wonder. Blake shook his head and kissed her gently.

"Clearly I have my work cut out for me when it comes to proving how much I love you, my lady."

"You would do this for me? You would take Lucy into your home knowing the truth?"

"Our home, my love. How could I not take the child in? I love you," Blake said softly. "The child is innocent, and I'll do my best to be a good father to her."

The unbelievably generous declaration caused another round of tears to stream down Arianna's cheeks. Concern darkened Blake's brow, and he wiped away her tears.

"Why are you crying, sweetheart?"

"Because I love you, and I can go home now. I've missed you so much."

"Then let's go home, Arianna. Let's take our daughter and go home."

The words whispered across her senses as Blake kissed her. Gentle and tender, the caress healed a small piece of her heart. In Blake's arms she was safe. She was loved. She was finally home.

"Miss Rhea, Miss Rhea."

The excitement in Ginny's voice made Rhea look up from the sock she was darning. Nine years of age, the girl was already showing signs she'd be a great beauty. Dark auburn hair and soft green eyes, Ginny had always reminded Rhea of a woodland fairy. The child raced to Rhea's side and grabbed her by the arm.

"There's a lady come to call, Miss Rhea. She has the prettiest hat with a veil and everything." Ginny's excited description of the unexpected guest made Rhea laugh.

"I think you'll be a milliner one day with your love of hats."

Rhea set aside Vincent's sock making a note to buy him more on her next trip to the village. The boy's feet were growing so fast she hardly had time to repair one hole before his toes pushed through the wool socks to create another one. With Ginny's hand in hers, she allowed the child to lead her out of the dining room where she'd been working. As they entered the Hall, cook appeared just a few feet outside the kitchen.

"Vincent and Rufus came charging into the kitchen with news of a guest, miss. Should I put a kettle of tea on?"

"That would be lovely, Mrs. Turner. Even if our guest refuses tea, I would love a cup."

With a nod of understanding, the cook disappeared into the kitchen as Ginny tugged on her hand. A small laugh escaped Rhea as she allowed the girl to guide her to Green Hill House's generously sized parlor. Their female visitor was studying the portrait of Alfred Fremont that hung over the fireplace mantle. There was something familiar about the woman, and Rhea stiffened as her guest turned around.

Even through the thick black netting that covered her face, Rhea recognized Lady Patience. The first thought that flitted through her mind was that something had happened to Percy. She immediately dismissed the thought. Lady Patience's clothing was a bright shade of brilliant yellow, definitely not a mourning dress. Gently touching Ginny's shoulder, Rhea bent her head to catch the child's attention.

"Sweetheart, would you please go help Mrs. Turner? You

may ask her to put the sugar cookies you like on the tray."

"Yes, Miss Rhea." Ginny's disappointment at not being allowed to stay was obvious, but the child obeyed Rhea's dictates and left the room. When the girl had left the parlor, Rhea turned back to her visitor. Lady Patience rolled up her veil to eye Rhea with a look of assessment.

"Forgive my unexpected visit, Miss Bennett, since Melton Park was so close to you I thought I would pay you a brief call."

"That's very kind of you," Rhea said quietly then gestured to one of the room's Queen Anne armchairs her aunt was so fond of. "Won't you sit down? I've instructed our cook to bring us tea."

"Unfortunately, I must refuse the offer as I didn't exaggerate when I said my visit must be brief. I must not miss the last train to London for dinner with my family." Lady Patience sank down into the chair and perched on the edge of her seat. "As I'm certain you know by now, none of the Rockwoods miss a family gathering unless there are extraordinary circumstances. We've learned in the most painful way possible not to pass up our time together."

"I understand completely. Per—Mr. Rockwood mentioned the loss of your brother, and brother-in-law, as the reason your family always dines with the children."

"Their death still haunts all of us." The woman reached up to touch her scarred cheek. As if realizing she'd revealed something she'd not meant to, Lady Patience straightened in her chair. Her gaze pinned on Rhea, the other woman eyed her carefully.

"I have always been direct with people, Miss Bennett, so forgive me for being blunt. Are you in love with my brother?"

Stunned by the question, Rhea felt her skin grow cold as the color drained from her cheeks. Had the Rockwoods discovered her past? Dear God, had Percy revealed something to his family? The moment the question flitted through her head she dismissed it. She stared at the other woman for a moment before she shook her head.

"The state of my affections is my own, Lady Patience."

"I see. Again I must be blunt, Miss Bennett. Percy has told me he proposed marriage and that you refused him. Might I ask why?"

The question made Rhea stare at the woman in astonishment. To the woman's credit, pink color flushed her cheeks. With a shake of her head Rhea pushed aside her surprise.

"You may ask," she said quietly. "However, I shall keep my own counsel in that matter as well."

"Would it change things if I told you that I believe Percy has feelings for you?"

Rhea stiffened as she remembered Percy's words the other night. The indirect manner in which he'd mentioned love made Rhea's heart skip a beat. She swallowed hard as she contemplated the woman's question. Reality closed in on her a moment later. It didn't matter whether Percy might care for her. She refused to give up control of her body, mind, or soul no matter how much she loved him. A chill splashed over her like a bucket of cold water. She loved him. How had she allowed herself to fall in love with him?

"You haven't answered me, Miss Bennett. If you knew my brother loved you, would your answer to my brother's proposal be different?"

"No," Rhea exclaimed vehemently and leapt to her feet. "If Percy sent you here on his behalf, I confess you have made a terrible misstep."

"Please forgive me, Miss Bennett," Lady Patience exclaimed with obvious distress. "Percy doesn't know I'm here. If he did, I have no doubt he would be furious with me for interfering. But I adore Percy. We have always been close, and I'm convinced his heart is either lost to you or on the verge of doing so. It's why I took the chance to visit with you.

I only wish to see my brother happy."

"As I said, I keep my own counsel," Rhea whispered as panic began to set in. If the woman didn't leave, she might confess she was in love with Percy. The notion made her suck in a sharp breath. Percy would be relentless if he knew her heart. "I really must ask you to leave, Lady Patience. This conversation has taken a decidedly personal turn which is unwelcome."

Percy's sister eyed her in a manner reminiscent of her brother. It was such an intense assessment that Rhea feared the woman might actually be able to see through all the barriers she'd erected over the years. The thought was a terrifying one even though she was certain Lady Patience knew nothing about her past. Percy would never betray her in that regard. She was certain of it.

Her conviction as to his integrity emphasized how much she'd come to trust him, but the fact didn't change her position with regard to his marriage proposal. Lady Patience slowly rose from her seat without her gaze leaving Rhea's. With a nod, Percy's sister sighed with obvious sadness.

"You're as stubborn as I am, and it is apt to cost you dearly. Not so long ago, I almost lost my husband because of that trait." The woman flinched from what was clearly a painful memory. Lady Patience headed for the door and paused at Rhea's side to touch her arm. "Do not make the mistake of letting any real or imagined obstacles stand in the way of your happiness, Rhea. Love can conquer and forgive anything, if you allow it too."

With those parting words, Percy's sister left Rhea standing alone in the parlor. Frozen in place, she struggled with the warning Lady Patience had given her. Was it possible she was allowing her past to stand between her and Percy? The answer to that question wasn't as troubling as her desire to follow Lady Patience's advice and trust Percy completely with her happiness.

"Where has the lady gone, Miss Rhea?" At Ginny's soft cry of dismay, Rhea turned to look at the girl.

"Lady Patience had to return to London for an appointment."

"Oh, I was hoping she might let me see her hat up close." The stark disappointment in Ginny's voice made Rhea move forward to give the girl a small hug.

"I'm sure she would have if she'd had time to stay."

The moment she said the words, Rhea realized it was true. Lady Patience had appeared to have had an epiphany, for the other woman had left the house without covering her scarred cheek. Rhea's scars were of a different nature, and she didn't think she could put them aside to obtain the life Percy had offered her.

The front door to Beatrice Fremont's house closed behind Rhea as she paused in the foyer to remove her hat. She pushed the hat pin into the crown of the accessory then removed her gloves and dropped both items on the hall table. Critically studying her reflection in the foyer's mirror, she saw a woman who looked pale and drawn. She pushed aside the thought she might be feeling melancholy, but she couldn't deny she was tired.

She'd returned to London late yesterday in anticipation of Ashford securing Fanny's and Harry's freedom two nights hence. Unfortunately, she had not slept well last night as she wondered whether Percy would seek her out today. Early this morning, she'd visited Ashford's office to try and convince him to let her accompany him Friday night. The private investigator's refusal wasn't unexpected, but it was disappointing.

While she'd not asked, Ashford had indicated Percy had

visited the investigator's office the day before. It didn't surprise her to learn Percy intended to be present for the rescue, but she wasn't certain how she would react when she saw him again. Like a coward, she'd spent the rest of the morning until lunch in the National Gallery to avoid any possibility of seeing him.

She was still feeling far too vulnerable with the revelation that she loved him. The longer she could put off seeing him, the easier it would be to leave London for good. In the back of her head, she heard mocking laughter, but she ignored it. The soft murmur of voices penetrated her thoughts for the first time.

She heard the rumblings of a male voice, and immediately stiffened. Was Percy here? A woman's voice echoed loudly in apparent response to the man speaking. Rhea had barely taken a step toward the salon door, when the front door opened behind her. She immediately turned around and stared in surprise at the sight of Arianna entering the house.

"Arianna, I'm so happy to see you. Aunt Beatrice told me last night that you and Blake have reconciled. I had intended to come see you later today." Rhea hugged her sister warmly then pulled back to look at her sister. "What is it? What's wrong?"

"I'm uncertain. I received a note from Aunt Beatrice to come quickly as she needed to speak with me urgently." Arianna's puzzlement matched Rhea's, and an ominous sensation crested over her.

"Did she elaborate in her message as to what might be wrong?"

"No, and that's what concerns me."

Rhea didn't have a chance to reply to Arianna's comment before the salon door opened. Beatrice Fremont's was pale and drawn, and Rhea's stomach lurched. Had something happened to Lord Foxworth? She stepped forward to ask her aunt the question, but Beatrice Fremont simply stepped back to let her and Arianna enter the room. Rhea's heart began to race. Something was wrong—terribly wrong. As she crossed the room's threshold, Rhea heard her sister's gasp as a man at the fireplace turned toward them.

"Hello, my poppet."

At the sound of Ruckley's voice, Rhea swayed slightly as the room faded in and out. Struggling to control her panic, she clasped her hands in front of her and focused on regaining control of her senses. As she met Ruckley's gaze, she buried her fear beneath layers of hate. One of the lessons she'd learned from him was to never let your enemy see your fear.

Determined to adhere to the lessons the despicable man had taught her, she deliberately assumed a nonchalant demeanor. Rhea didn't take her eyes off Ruckley as she let all the hate and anger she'd buried so deep burn its way through her blood. It was easy to welcome the red wave of violent emotions as she stared at his coarse, pock-marked face. Hate was the strongest emotion that spiraled through her, and she drew strength from it as she eyed Ruckley in silence for a moment.

"Let me guess how you found me, Ruckley. Edgar succeeded where you failed." Her taunt made the man glare at her. A moment later he was smiling with smug amusement.

"Don't matter none how I found you, Rhea—"

"My name is Miss Bennett."

Her voice lashed out across the room with a white-hot fury. The quiet menace in the statement caused the stocky man's body to jerk in surprise before he narrowed his malevolent gaze at her. "So that's how it is, is it?"

"Arianna and I paid our father's debt to you, Ruckley. We paid it seven times over. You have no business here."

The criminal eyed her with malicious amusement and with a gnarled hand, he stroked at his grimy beard. "You've gotten all high and mighty since we last saw each other. Quite the lady now, isn't you?"

"What do you want?"

Rhea's fingernails dug into the back of her hands, and she forced herself not to look away from the beady eyes shrewdly assessing her. He was trying to determine how frightened she was, but she refused to let the bastard see her fear. He'd use it against her.

"That's what I always liked about you, Rh—Miss Bennett. Straight to the point. I've come with a business proposition." The absurdity of his statement made her laugh. He appeared surprised by her reaction, as did her sister and aunt.

"You have a business proposition for me." Each word a sharply pointed icicle, Rhea tightened her lips as she glared at the man who had destroyed her life and that of her sister's.

"Aye, are you willing to hear me out?"

"No. I'm not," she said with a quiet bitterness that she could see surprised him again. "I suggest you leave now, or I'll summon the police."

"Fancy words, Miss Bennett." The unkempt man picked up a miserable substitute for a hat and started slowly toward the door. "Perhaps I'll have to tell the police my own story."

"Your story?" She met his gaze steadily. "You have so many lies to tell, Ruckley, I doubt anything you say will hold any weight with the police. In fact, you're quite likely to implicate yourself."

"You don't say," Ruckley said with a nasty grin that exposed his rotting teeth and the gaping hole where one of his upper teeth was missing. "Perhaps you forgot about that little job you and Arianna did at the museum and that gent you killed."

"I didn't kill anyone," she bit out as she glared at the man. "You shot the man in the back."

"Ahh, but they won't know that. I mean Edgar was there with you and little Arianna. The boy will be quite willing to say you were the one to pull the trigger."

The veiled threat made Rhea freeze. The fact that Ruckley didn't realize Percy was still alive was a gift she refused to give up. She had no intention of the bastard going after Percy simply to tie up loose ends.

"Edgar's word against mine? Against the Viscountess Sherrington? Do you seriously think the police will take your word, a known reprobate, over our denials?"

"Don't get cocky on me now, Rhea. There are other stories I can tell," Ruckley's head turned toward Arianna. "What about that brat you had a year ago. I reckon your husband don't know nothing about her."

"Actually my husband knows everything about my past," Arianna said in a cold voice, but she flinched and Ruckley narrowed his gaze at her.

"Are you sure of that Miss Arianna?"

"Oh, I'm quite sure, you bastard. The only thing I haven't told him is how to find you, and I've not done so to save you, but to save him. He'd kill you, and I won't allow him to hang for the likes of you." The loathing in Arianna's voice made Ruckley arch his eyebrows.

"Well now, little Miss Arianna has developed claws since she left me high and dry."

"Get out, Ruckley. Your threats are pointless here. You cannot harm us anymore," Rhea said in a cold, icy voice. At her command, he scratched his chin through his beard.

"All right, it seems I came for nothing, after all."

The man shrugged and started for the door. The way he gave up so easily made Rhea stiffen. Ruckley was far too nonchalant to not have another trick up his sleeve. She didn't move as he walked toward her. The stench of the man swept over her as he brushed past her, and she tried not to gag. As she turned to watch him leave, he paused at the door.

"Oh, and don't go getting any more ideas about stealing my boys and girls out from under my nose."

"I don't know what you're talking about." At her reply,

Ruckley narrowed his gaze at her with a calculating look, and her heart sank.

"Now don't go playing games with me, Rhea," he chuckled with vindictiveness. "Did you think I wouldn't figure out who stole Vincent and Rufus away from me?"

"You're losing your touch, Ruckley. If any children are no longer a part of your band of thieves, I'm glad. But I had nothing to do with their disappearance," she lied with cold contempt.

"I see," Ruckley said with a slow nod of his head. "Well you can't blame a bloke for trying to find the truth of it. Of course, I'm going to be needing someone to replace them. They was some of me best dippers, they were."

"If you're expecting sympathy, you'll be waiting until hell freezes over."

"Oh no, Miss Bennett. I don't need no sympathy," Ruckley said with a familiar swagger. "I already know where I'm getting my next dippers."

Something in his voice made her eye him carefully, and she saw the malice in his eyes. With the White Willow orphanage off limits, the bastard had found another source of children to exploit. She shook her head.

"Take care with what you tell me, Ruckley. I won't hesitate to go to the police if I have too."

"No, I don't think you will, my poppet," he drawled with a venomous smile. "You see, you're the one who's going to get me my new dippers."

"I'm not about to help you do anything," she said with a derisive laugh.

"Oh, I think you will. After all, I know how much you love Fanny. I'd hate to see anything happen to her. Such a pretty little thing. Why she's just about the right age for the gents to have a go at her." Ruckley's threat drew every bit of air from her lungs.

"She's not even ten yet, you bastard."

"But that's how a lot of me clients like them, Miss Bennett," he gloated as he swung his glance to Arianna and back to Rhea. "All the men who fucked you and Miss Arianna over there didn't complain none when you first opened your legs."

At Ruckley's crude language, Aunt Beatrice gasped loudly behind her. Ruckley's malicious grin widened at the sound. The man craned his neck to look around Rhea and wink at her aunt. Immediately, Rhea shifted her body to block his view.

"If I do whatever it is you want, you'll give Fanny to me."

"Hmm, I don't know that I can do that. She'll eventually fetch me some pretty coins with that pretty blonde hair of hers," Ruckley said with a sneer as he bobbed his head in her sister's direction. "Just like her ladyship did."

The cruel words made Rhea move forward until she was inches away from the man. The rancid odor of his rotting teeth made bile rise in her throat, but she swallowed it as she made certain to hold his gaze without blinking.

"I will do what you want, but in exchange you will give Fanny to me or I will kill you. It's as simple as that, Ruckley. Do you understand me?"

The icy sound of her softly spoken words chilled the space between them and some of the triumph disappeared from the crime lord's cocky posture. For a long moment, he appraised her intently as if judging whether she was capable of carrying out her threat. The man's shifty eyes glinted with a trace of uneasiness, as she gazed at him with cold hatred. How she wished she had a gun now. With a slow nod of his head, Ruckley grunted.

"Yes, I believe you would. I never thought you had a killer instinct, but then you always did surprise me, Rhea."

"I'm glad we understand each other."

"You know, one of the things I always admired about you, Rhea, was you being so quick-witted. It's one of the things I missed the most when you and little Arianna flew the coop." Ruckley scratched the back of his neck as he arched his eyebrows at her. "That hurt me bad, it did. Lost my two best protégés. So, here's what I want. You're going to give me access to two or three of the boys in that orphanage where Edgar saw you."

"You're mad," she exclaimed as her cool composure slipped.

"I don't see that you have much choice, girl. Either you supply me with stock from that orphanage, or my sweet Fanny is going to start making me money sooner than I expected."

"You bastard." Arianna sprang to her feet and crossed the room to stand at Rhea's side. "You can't possibly expect her to condemn two children in exchange for Fanny. There must be something else you want. If it's money, we'll find it."

"Hmm…perhaps you're right," Ruckley said as a calculating look made his thin lips curve in a cruel smile. "But I can think of other ways I'd be willing to give you Fanny free and clear."

"What would that entail?" Rhea asked with a sense of doom. She knew what the man was about to say, and the idea horrified her.

"I think you know I've always had a soft spot for you, Rhea. You left before I ever got to taste your wares."

"Oh, dear God," Arianna gasped and swayed on her feet beside her. With one hand, Rhea steadied her sister as she heard Aunt Beatrice utter a cry of horror. Ruckley smiled.

"I reckon you know what I'm asking."

"You're not asking," Rhea said quietly, surprised at how calm she was. "You're blackmailing me."

"Blackmail is a nasty accusation Rhea. After all, it's not as if you've not enjoyed a bit of fun of late." The sly words made Rhea's heart skip a beat with fear.

"I don't know what you're talking about."

"Oh, I think you catch me drift real good. Edgar told me about a fancy-looking gent he saw with you at that orphanage." Ruckley's smug look made Rhea's stomach lurch. "Seems this gent likes his museums almost as much as his late night visitors."

"You're not making much sense," Rhea snapped as fear chilled her skin.

"Do you really think I've only just discovered your whereabouts, my poppet?" Ruckley chuckled with malevolence. "Edgar has been following you ever since the day you reappeared. I know everything, even how you're parting your legs for that gent you left to die in the museum a year ago. In fact, Edgar seems to think you're sweet on the gent."

The gasps of her aunt and sister barely registered with Rhea as she struggled to stem the tide of terror racing through her.

"Percy means nothing to me," her quick, vehement denial made her heart skip a frantic beat as Ruckley's gaze narrowed at her. Horror swept through her. For all his depraved manners, Ruckley was extremely intelligent. As she met his gaze, she realized her hastily spoken denial and use of Percy's first name had given her away.

"So you've gone an' given your heart to the man. Does he know?"

"Your imagination always was overly exaggerated," she sneered as she tried to find a way to redirect Ruckley's focus away from Percy.

"I'm beginning to think I'll pay this Rockwood fellow a visit and finish the job I failed to do last time."

"What is it you want, Ruckley?"

"You know what I want. I want to saddle and ride you, my poppet, and you're going to do it with a smile unless you want to see that gent of yours or little Fanny hurt."

"And when is this exchange to take place?"

Arianna and her aunt gasped loudly at her words, and her sister clutched Rhea's arm in a deathlike grip. Absently, she ignored her aunt's and sister's protests keeping her gaze focused on the man standing in front of her. She arched her eyebrows as Ruckley frowned slightly. With a shrug, a cocky look settled on his dirty face, and he laughed unpleasantly.

"I should wait so you can anticipate all the things I intend to do to you," Ruckley said with another broken tooth smile. "But I've waited too fucking long, my poppet. You remember The Bull and Hare tavern, don't you, Rhea? Tonight at nine."

Rhea's stomach roiled as the past rushed out to wrap its slimy tentacles around her. The Bull and Hare was where Ruckley sold her over and over again. Ice sluiced through her as she met Ruckley's gaze. The thought of his hands on her horrified her one. In that split second, she realized she would never let him touch her. Resigned to a fate that would most likely see her hung, Rhea allowed a small confident smile to curve her lips. He immediately narrowed his gaze at her.

"Very well, I'll be at the tavern at nine this evening. When I arrive, Fanny and Harry are to be handed over to my driver."

"Here now, I never agreed to give up Harry, only Fanny."

"Then you'll not have me, will you?" she said softly with a taunting note in her voice. Ruckley eyed her for a moment, clearly debating his options. With an abrupt nod, he agreed to Rhea's demands.

"You drive a hard bargain, my poppet, but don't you go getting any ideas of tricking me out of my pleasure."

"I have never had any need to trick you, Ruckley, but do not presume you will be able to control me simply because, how did you say it? I part my legs for you." Confidence warmed her as she met his surly gaze. "You will never control me. My father stole my future from me. You destroyed it for me. There's little more you can do to me that hasn't already been done. After tonight I'll be free of you once and for all."

"You always were a headstrong girl," he snarled, his features ugly with anger.

"Get out, Ruckley, and if you ever come back here after

tonight, I'll send for the local magistrate. I have nothing to fear from you anymore."

"We'll see about that, my girl. I'm not finished with you yet, Rhea Bennett."

Wheeling about, Ruckley stormed out of the salon. The sound of the front door slamming shut made Rhea sag with relief. Nauseated, she shrugged off Arianna's hand and slowly made her way to the fireplace in an attempt to warm her ice cold skin. She stretched out her hands toward the small flames, but she couldn't feel any warmth at all. Swaying slightly at the reality of what she planned to do, her fingers gripped the cool wood mantel, and she rested her forehead on her hands. She would never let Ruckley touch her. She'd kill him before he laid a hand on her. The fact that a few moments ago she'd calmly decided to kill the man caused her stomach to lurch.

"You cannot go through with this, Rhea" her aunt said with a fervent note of horror in her voice as she crossed the room to touch Rhea's arm.

"I have no choice. I cannot allow what happened to Arianna and me happen to Fanny."

"There has to be another way," Beatrice snapped. "We need to tell Lionel and Blake. Surely Mr. Rockwood should be told?"

"No," Rhea said sharply. "There's nothing they can do. If they interfere, Ruckley will only hurt Fanny. I'm the only one who can save her."

"But surely——"

"Rhea's right, Aunt Beatrice. If we allowed Blake, Lord Foxworth, or Mr. Rockwood to interfere, Ruckley would never give Fanny up. He'd kill her rather than give her up."

"Dear Lord." Beatrice looked at her nieces in abject horror. "There must be a way out of this. You cannot possibly suggest Rhea go through with this."

"I'm not suggesting anything," Arianna said softly. "But

I trust Rhea's instincts to do what's right, and she'll not be alone. I intend to go with her."

"*No*," Rhea and Beatrice objected at the precise same moment. Arianna met their horrified gazes with a steely resolve that startled Rhea.

"I intend to bring two of Blake's footmen with us. One of them will see Fanny and Harry to safety once Ruckley turns them over to you. I will wait with the second footman until your business with Ruckley is finished. We will be armed as well."

Arianna's voice was strong, steady, and resolved as she met Rhea's gaze. Suddenly, she realized her sister had guessed what her intentions were where Ruckley was concerned. The support and love in her sister's eyes made Rhea hug Arianna tightly.

"Do what you must. I'll bear witness that it was self-defense," her sister's whisper was soft enough that Rhea knew their aunt couldn't hear the reassurance Arianna offered. She pulled back from her sister and nodded. Tonight, she would ensure their freedom forever, or the worst would happen. Either way, at least Arianna and the children would be free. As for her, fate would decide her destiny.

Chapter 17

R hea opened her eyes and sat up in bed. Arianna had left shortly after Ruckley's departure to make arrangements for tonight. Her aunt had been ready to put off a visit to an ill friend, but there was little to be done before the evening, and Rhea had urged her aunt to go. In truth, she'd simply wanted to be alone. After her verbal duel with Ruckley and the lack of sleep last night, her exhaustion had driven her to lie down in an attempt to rest.

Although she'd thought it would be impossible to sleep it had not. A glance at the brooch watch lying on the table beside her bed declared there were only three more hours until her final battle with Ruckley. She stared listlessly at the black gown she'd laid out for the evening. The garment was a fitting choice. Not only did it have a pocket for the pistol Arianna would have for her, it also symbolized Ruckley's impending demise, as well as her own, whether by Ruckley's hand or the courts.

Arianna's display of support earlier had been given without realizing what tonight's outcome would likely be. If Arianna had even thought Rhea would fail to emerge unscathed from her battle with Ruckley, her sister would have objected vehemently. Even though she was certain the bastard would be dead by the end of the night, she had no doubt Ruckley would take her to hell with him. Her stomach churned at the thought. The entire time she'd been under Ruckley's control, she'd fought to survive—fought to see the day when she'd be free of him. Now her fate was tied to the man forever. A knock on the door made Rhea turn her head to see Bessie, the downstairs maid, peek into the room.

"There's a gentleman caller downstairs, miss. He asked for Mrs. Fremont, but she hasn't returned, and he asked to speak with you instead."

"Did he give his name?" she asked with puzzlement.

"I'm sorry, miss, Mr. Bartlett was in the midst of dealing with a small mishap and didn't say. He simply said he'd seen the gentleman into the parlor and ordered me to come fetch you."

Rhea frowned. It couldn't be Percy, he would have asked for her outright. Ruckley? Fear slammed into her chest. The idea of seeing the man again before tonight sickened her. She shook her head. No, Ruckley would never think to reiterate a threat twice. He'd simply act swiftly and brutally if he was crossed. She focused her gaze on the maid.

"Very well, I'll be down shortly," Rhea said with a nod.

The girl nodded then disappeared, leaving Rhea to quickly repair her appearance. The image in the mirror showed she looked more haggard than before she'd left the house this morning. It wasn't all that surprising given everything that had transpired this afternoon. The emotional resolution she faced tonight had only added to her pale countenance. With a sigh, she made her way down to the salon.

If she'd been thinking clearly she would've told Bessie to send the man away. As the thought filtered its way through her head, it further emphasized how draining the events of the last few days had been for her. Percy's marriage proposal, his sister's visit to Green Hill House, her realization that she loved Percy, and then there was Ruckley. It had all taken its toll, and she had little reserves left for polite behaviors. As she entered the salon, Rhea's heart skipped a beat as her gaze met Percy's. She quickly gulped down the flood of emotions rising inside her.

"I was told someone wanted to speak with my aunt," she said in what she could only hope was a voice devoid of all the emotions assaulting her at the moment.

"I asked to see Mrs. Fremont," he said quietly. "I was fairly certain you would refuse to see me, and I thought your aunt would petition my cause with you."

"Why are you here, Percy?" She looked away from him. The determined expression on his strong, handsome features made her realize she might not have the strength to refuse him anything if he were to ask it of her.

"I think you know why. Did you really think I would let your letter go unanswered?"

"I had hoped you would understand and accept the reasons I gave you," she said softly, unable to deny that his persistence warmed her heart.

The memory of how difficult it had been for her to write her note filled her head. Although she'd already made plans to take Peter to Green Hill House, she'd been grateful for any excuse to leave London. She now realized the real reason she'd been grateful to put distance between her and Percy was because she wanted nothing more than to give way to him. If she'd seen him prior to Ruckley's visit today, she knew she would have agreed to his marriage proposal. But the threat Ruckley presented to all those she loved, including Percy, made that impossible now. Almost as if he could read her mind, he walked toward her. With less than a foot between them, he lightly touched her cheek.

"We could be happy together, Rhea."

The quiet entreaty in his voice twisted her heart in a way that made her chest physically ache. Everything would change in a few short hours. At that point marriage would be out of the question. Percy could never marry a murderer. She would never embroil him in the scandal unfolding around her now. Loving him as she did made it impossible for her to do anything that might harm him in any way. Rhea averted her gaze.

"You ask too much of me, Percy," she said as a tremor rocked her body.

"No, you simply believe you're unworthy of being anything other than my mistress," he bit out angrily.

She stared at him in shock. Was that the truth? Had she offered her own arrangement because she thought herself unworthy of him? No, that wasn't why. She'd simply been terrified of being trapped in a prison of her own making. She shook her head.

"I don't feel unworthy of you, Percy. You've demonstrated time and again that I'm not what Ruckley tried to turn me in to. With you, there have been times when I've been able to forget my past for an hour or more. I'm grateful to you for that."

"I don't want your goddamn gratitude. I want you to marry me."

"Did it ever occur to you that I might view marriage as another kind of prison?" she snapped.

"*Fuck*. I'm *not* Ruckley. Do not *ever* judge me by that bastard's behavior." The explosive response made her flinch.

As she met his harsh, censorious gaze she realized how badly she'd insulted him. Remorse swept through her. He could *never* be anything remotely like Ruckley, and for her to make him think she believe such a thing pained her.

"I could never judge you like that," she exclaimed in a soft, apologetic tone as she caught his hand and pressed her lips into the heart of his palm. The familiar scent of him swept over her senses as he pulled her into his arms. Gently, he tipped her head so he could look into her eyes.

"Then how can you doubt me when I say I'll never treat you like a possession? I don't want to own you, Rhea. I want to keep you safe, make you happy, be there when you need someone to lean on and when you don't." Indecision flashed in his beautiful eyes, and she saw his throat bob. "I want to marry you because I love you."

The declaration made her heart slam into her chest. He loved her. The knowledge wrapped itself around her like a warm cloak. Rhea closed her eyes as joy spiraled through her. The sound of him clearing his throat made focus her gaze on him again. His questioning look made her stiffen with fear. If she confessed her heart, it would change everything.

"I'm a reckless Rockwood, sweetheart, and I'm usually quite good at weighing the outcome of my actions," he said with a trace of misgiving. "Was I wrong in my calculations that you care for me, if even just a little?"

On the verge of telling him the truth, Rhea was about to answer him when an image of Ruckley flashed through her head. The memory of the crime lord standing in the salon earlier today threatening Percy made her stomach lurch. How could she admit she loved him knowing they could never be together? The hopelessness of the situation made her release a soft cry, and she burrowed her body into his, one cheek pressed against the soft wool of his jacket. She wanted the world to fall away and simply stay in his arms forever.

It was a pointless wish. Ruckley had to be dealt with, and if Percy knew the truth, he'd insist on dealing with Ruckley himself, but that would be a terrible mistake. She knew exactly what Ruckley would do if she didn't present herself at the tavern tonight. Fanny would be sacrificed because of her. She could never allow that to happen.

If anything, Percy's words of love only strengthened her resolve to deal with Ruckley on her own terms. She'd made her deal with the devil, and all that mattered was keeping Percy safe. Clinging to him, she shuddered as Percy's embrace tightened around her. He pressed his mouth against the top of her head in a tender gesture.

"I know you're afraid, sweetheart, but I know you have the strength and courage to overcome your fear. Don't let fear keep you—us—from having the happiness we both deserve."

The conviction in his voice made her heart ache painfully. If only things had been different. Rhea lifted her head to look at him. She studied him closely, memorizing every facet of his handsome face in the event the worst happened tonight. If Ruckley killed her, she wanted the last thing she saw to be Percy's strong, patrician features in her head. The instant a tear slid down her cheek, Percy muttered something beneath his breath and wiped the salty drop off her skin. The futility of it all made her draw in a deep breath.

"Why are you crying, my darling?"

"I don't know," she lied forcing a watery smile to her lips. His mouth curved slightly.

"I'll assume it's because you're happy."

With a nod, Rhea pulled his head down and kissed him gently. The strength of him was as comforting as it was enticing. His mouth moved against hers as he deepened their kiss. Visceral and powerful, an abrupt escalation of need tightened her body with wild sensations until it created a pleasurable ache throughout her.

Percy's mouth left hers to blaze a trail of white-hot heat across her cheek and down the side of her throat. Passion pulsed its way through her and increased the fiery sensations taking control of her. She spiked her fingers through his hair, and nipped at his ear with her lips.

"Make love to me, Percy. Make love to me right here— right now. I need you." At her request, Percy stiffened and jerked his head up to stare down at her.

"*Christ Jesus,*" he rasped. "I'm beginning to think you truly are more reckless than any Rockwood. It's madness. If someone were to come—"

The sound of the front door opening made Rhea's heart sink. Her aunt had returned. If Percy were to say he'd proposed, Aunt Beatrice would insist on Rhea telling him everything. A groan escaped him followed by a low chuckle.

"Your aunt has impeccable timing, especially since

you've not answered my proposal."

"Tomorrow," she whispered. "It's all so new. I don't want to share our happiness with anyone just yet."

It was a lie. There would be no announcement, and certainly not any happiness. The knowledge sliced into her painfully like a blade. Percy eyed her with puzzlement for a brief second then with a nod, he smiled and kissed her quickly.

"Why do I think I'm going to have a difficult time saying no to you for the rest of our lives?"

The wry comment made her smile slightly while her heart split in two. As if sensing something was wrong, he frowned. Fearing he might question her again about her answer to his proposal, Rhea tugged his head down to kiss him. He murmured something against her lips before he quickly set her away from him as Beatrice Fremont's footsteps announced her approach. Relief rushed through Rhea as she turned to greet her aunt. The older woman smiled with pleasure as she entered the salon.

"Mr. Rockwood, what an unexpected, but delightful surprise."

"Mrs. Fremont," Percy said with a bow in the woman's direction as Rhea crossed the floor to kiss the woman's cheek.

The moment her aunt met her gaze, Rhea's body tensed with fear. There was a look in the older woman's eyes that said Beatrice was debating whether or not to mention Ruckley. The thought of putting Percy in harm's way frightened her more than the thought of what she intended to do tonight. With a forced smile, she touched her aunt's arm.

"Percy came to invite me to a small party Viscount and Viscountess Compton are hosting this evening." Not waiting for her aunt to reply, Rhea turned to Percy. "I'll be ready at a quarter before nine."

Percy smiled at her and as he moved to stand in front of her, he carried her hand to his mouth. His lips lingered, and the look in his eyes made her want to cling to him once more.

The thought she might never see him again filled her with an anguish that tore at every fiber of her being.

On impulse, she kissed his cheek, and Percy arched his eyebrows at her in a perplexed look. He paused for a brief moment as if to say something then released her hand, bowed in her aunt's direction and was gone. At the sound of the front door closing, Rhea went limp with relief.

"You didn't tell him," Beatrice Fremont said with a sigh.

"No there was little point," Rhea shook her head in resignation. "I'm doing what's necessary to protect him and others. I know Ruckley better than anyone else. If I give him what he wants, he'll honor his word, something I find ironic in someone so vile."

"But—"

"Please, Aunt Beatrice, don't argue with me on this. I know what I'm doing." The emphatic note in her words made Beatrice nodded with obvious displeasure, but her aunt didn't argue any further. "It will be all right, Aunt Beatrice. I promise."

Rhea gave her aunt a hug then left the salon to make her way upstairs to change. It would be all right. She was certain of it. Everything would be different tomorrow. Everyone she loved would be far beyond Ruckley's reach because the man would be dead. She would see to it that Ruckley would never hurt anyone she loved again. It was all that mattered to her. It would be her redemption.

Sebastian took a sip of cognac, his gaze never leaving Percy's face. The intensity of his brother's look made Percy feel as if he was a boy again having been caught in the act of some misdeed. Sebastian cocked his head slightly.

"I understand from Patience you've asked Miss Bennett

to marry you."

"Yes. It's why I asked to speak with you," Percy met his brother's gaze steadily. "I would like to present Rhea with one of the family rings on the occasion of our engagement."

"I see." Sebastian's detached tone of voice made Percy frown.

"It sounds as though Patience has told you about Rhea's involvement in my assault last year."

"Yes," Sebastian said quietly.

"Clearly you disapprove." He glared at his older brother, disappointed Sebastian appeared to have been so easily swayed in his judgment of Rhea. His brother generally questioned every vision anyone in the family had. In this case, it appeared Sebastian had decided to believe Patience. His older brother gently moved his hand to make the cognac in his glass swirl lazily against the glass surface inside the snifter.

"Actually, I'm not sure what to think." The reply startled Percy, and his anger ebbed somewhat.

"And why is that?" he asked quietly. One of the things Percy admired about his brother was Sebastian's analytical skills. The earl had the mind of a military strategist.

"Because your Miss Bennett reminds me of Helen."

Sebastian's word made Percy grow rigid. The family knew everything about how the countess had been abused by her uncle and how Sebastian had rescued his wife from a brothel before they were married. Unwilling to confirm his brother's suspicions as to Rhea's past, Percy remained silent. When he didn't speak, Sebastian nodded and a small smile touched his lips.

"Restraint, Percy? I noticed it throughout dinner. You never rose to take the bait whenever one of our sisters attempted to hook you. If Miss Bennett is responsible for this new discretionary behavior, I approve." Sebastian's smile broadened a bit more. "Would mother's sapphire ring be satisfactory?"

"It would," Percy said as relief swept through him. He'd always looked up to his brother, and Sebastian's approval was important to him. "Thank you."

"I propose a toast to your Miss Bennett. And your engagement." Sebastian nodded as he raised his globe-shaped glass of cognac in a toast. At his brother's words, Percy grinned and reached for his untouched drink and raised it into the air.

"To Miss Bennett," Sebastian said with a smile.

"To my bride-to-be."

As the slight hint of vanilla mixed with the nuance of aging ripened fruit crossed his tongue, Percy heard the grandfather clock in the main hall chime the half-hour. Rhea would be waiting for him. He set his unfinished brandy down and grinned at his brother.

"I should be going. I'm to call for Rhea shortly." At his statement, Sebastian nodded.

"I'll make arrangements in the morning for the ring to be delivered here."

"Thank you," Percy said with gratitude.

He'd just turned to leave Sebastian's study when the door flew open to reveal Jamie standing in the doorway. Startled Percy stared at his nephew in amazement while voices filled with surprise and astonishment floated out of the salon into the foyer. Percy glanced over his shoulder at Sebastian who looked as bewildered as Percy felt.

"Jamie, what in heaven's name is wrong," Constance exclaimed with a touch of frustration as she emerged from the salon and crossed the foyer to the doorway of the study. Percy met his sister's puzzled gaze then looked back down at his nephew. One hand on the boy's shoulder, he frowned at how badly the child was trembling.

"What is it, lad?"

"It's Miss Bennett, Uncle Percy. She's in trouble."

Jamie's words sent an icy breeze across the back of his

neck. The *an dara sealladh* had shown Jamie something about Rhea, and from his nephew's expression it was bad. Percy knelt, so he was eye level with his nephew. He squeezed the boy's shoulder once again in a reassuring manner.

"It will be all right, Jamie," he said with a growing unease. "Take your time and tell me what the *an dara sealladh* showed you."

"Yes, sir." Jamie nodded and inhaled a deep breath. "Miss Bennett was with another woman who had a pistol. There was a large bull near them. It was pawing the ground, and Miss Bennett didn't show any fear. But I know she was afraid, Uncle Percy. She was terrified."

Jamie's description caused Percy to stiffen in horror. Ruckley. The bull in Jamie's vision had to symbolize Ruckley. The front bell chimed wildly in the foyer, but Percy ignored the sound as he continued to focus his attention on his nephew.

"What else did you see, Jamie?" The boy paled and shook his head in a silent plea not to be asked to continue. "It's all right, lad. I just need to know how I can help, Rhea. I know you want to help as well."

"Yes," Jamie said in a strained voice. He drew in another deep breath. "I saw Miss Bennett, she was…she was…"

"She was what?" Percy said with as much patience as he could muster.

"She was in her petticoats." Jamie whispered as embarrassed color filled his cheeks before horrified dismay made him pale. "There was blood everywhere. Miss Bennett fell to the floor…and… I think she might be dead, Uncle Percy."

"*Christ Jesus.*" Percy sucked in a harsh breath as his gut twisted violently. In the foyer a familiar male voice penetrated the air. Percy looked over his nephew's head to see Viscount Sherrington pushing his way past Madison at the front door to head in his direction.

"They've gone to confront that bastard," Blake said in a low voice as he reached the door of the study.

"Ruckley," Percy stated grimly.

"Yes. I never knew his name until tonight. Arianna would never tell me his name for fear I'd do something to the man. She was right to think that." Blake's features were stony with the same cold rage Percy was experiencing along with another even more powerful emotion. Dread. Percy glanced at the small crowd of family members pouring into the foyer to see what was happening. Unwilling to elaborate any more than necessary, he looked back at his friend.

"How do you know they've gone to confront the man?" Percy asked as his body hardened with a growing disquiet.

"I arrived home later than usual this evening. Arianna wasn't at home, and I was told she'd gone to her aunt's. Normally I would not have thought twice about it, but when I learned she'd taken one of the footmen with her, I became worried." A muscle in Blake's cheek twitched. "When I reached Fremont Place, I learned Arianna and Rhea had already left to meet the bastard. Mrs. Fremont indicated this Ruckley fellow had blackmailed Rhea. Something about a young girl being harmed unless Rhea…" Blake's voice died off as his icy façade gave way to a dark rage, and Percy remembered Jamie's description of Rhea in her petticoats.

"*Sweet Jesus,*" he rasped.

Ruckley intended to have his way with Rhea. Galvanized into action Percy turned back to Sebastian only to see his brother had left the study by the side door. Percy whirled back around and saw Sebastian emerge from the back hall.

"Percy, I've ordered the carriage to be made ready. Come with me," his brother said with a deeply troubled look. In the back of his mind, Percy said a prayer of gratitude for his brother's ability to think strategically. Percy circled Jamie intent on following Sebastian, but the boy grabbed his arm and held him back.

"Will she be all right, Uncle Percy?" At the boy's question, he placed his hands on Jamie's shoulders.

"I'm going to do my best to see that she is, Jamie, my very best." Percy patted the child's shoulder and moved quickly to follow Sebastian into the library. As he entered the room, he saw his brother had thrown open the gun cabinet and had distributed weapons to Lucien, Julian, and Blake. A pistol in his hand, Sebastian finished loading it then handed it to Percy.

"I don't think I need to say I understand what you're both feeling right now," Sebastian said quietly as he glanced at Sherrington and then back to Percy. "I've had Madison send for Scotland Yard. Did Mrs. Fremont say where your wife and Miss Bennett were going, Sherrington?"

"The Bull and Hare."

"I know that pub," Percy exclaimed with a grimace. "It's near the Saint Katherine docks. It's a viper's nest of the worst rabble one might expect to find in the East End."

"I've never been happy with all your nightly excursions into the East End," Sebastian said with a shake of his head as he met Percy's gaze. "But this is one instance when I can say I'm grateful for it. Julian, Lucien, and I will follow as soon as the inspector arrives."

"Thank you," Percy said quietly as he clutched his brother's arm in gratitude and affection.

"Watch your back, little brother," the Rockwood patriarch said in a gruff voice. "Come home to us safely, and bring your bride with you."

Percy's gut twisted at his brother's words as he nodded then gestured to Blake to follow him. As he strode out into the foyer, the Rockwood women were gathered in a small circle. Their faces were strained with worry, and Patience hurried toward him to clutch his arm tightly.

"You mustn't forget Edgar. He's just as dangerous to you as he is to Rhea." At her words Percy squeezed his sister's hand and kissed her forehead.

"I'll remember."

He pulled free of her grasp and hurried to the back of the house with Blake on his heels. When they reached the stable yard, they were forced to wait while the grooms finished hitching the horses. Impatient to be gone, Percy paced the stable yard until the coachman was in the driver seat. Percy gave directions to their destination then joined Blake in the carriage.

With a glance in his friend's direction, he saw the fear beneath the viscount's stony expression. It was pointless to offer his friend any reassurance when he was feeling the same way. Blake cleared his throat as he stared out the window.

"Arianna is carrying our child." His friend's announcement made Percy draw in a sharp breath as Blake turned his head toward him. "And God forgive me, I'd rather mourn our unborn child than lose my wife."

The tortured note in his friend's voice made Percy nod then look away. Silence fell between them and Percy closed his eyes as he remembered Rhea's behavior earlier this evening. She'd known she wouldn't be at Fremont Place when he called for her. She'd asked him to make love to her because she'd been saying goodbye. If a sledgehammer had hit his chest, it couldn't have hurt more. She was going to submit to Ruckley's blackmail terms. She was sacrificing herself once more, and his gut knotted with raw fury at the idea of the man touching her. If the bastard laid one finger on her, he'd kill the man where he stood.

Chapter 18

Seated beside Arianna in the viscountess's carriage, Rhea accepted the small Derringer her sister handed her. She slid it into the pocket of her dress before her fingers wrapped around the small reticule in her lap. The weapon's cold metal sent a chill through the layers of her clothing until it seeped into her thigh. The icy sensation spread its way across her skin until it engulfed her.

"You don't have to do this Rhea," her sister said as she touched Rhea's arm. "We can send for Blake and Percy."

"They would still need me as bait, and you know they'd never agree to that. And you know I cannot ignore Ruckley's threat where Fanny is concerned. We both know he'll do precisely what he said he would if I don't show myself."

Even in the dim light of the carriage, Rhea saw the way her sister paled. With a resigned nod Arianna looked out the window. They'd entered the East End several moments ago. It hadn't taken long for the stench of the squalid living conditions to permeate the carriage. Rhea wondered if Newgate Prison smelled this bad. Bile rose in her throat, and she quickly swallowed the bitter-tasting matter. Outside her window she recognized a building she'd seen hundreds of times. It emphasized she was in familiar territory. She pushed aside the horrific memories of her life in the East End. They were a distraction. She needed to focus her energy on the matter at hand. Tension threaded its way through her until her heart was beating as fast as a wild bird trapped in a cage. It was an appropriate description. There was nowhere for her to run or hide. She reached out and touched her sister's arm.

"The Bull and Hare is up ahead. Does your footman know what to do?"

"Yes," Arianna's voice was soft as she nodded. "He's to accompany you into the pub and not leave until he has Fanny and Harry."

"When the children are safe with you in the carriage, you're to leave," Rhea said sternly. "Take the children to Fremont Place."

"I am not leaving you here alone, Rhea Bennett. I've already instructed Fairlie to summon a hack. He'll take the children to Aunt Beatrice while I wait for you."

"Don't be ridiculous," Rhea snapped. "You can't be here when the police arrived, and they will come."

"I'm not leaving you," Arianna said in a calm, firm voice.

"So you're willing to risk the safety of the child you're carrying?" Rhea's harsh words made Arianna flinch. Slowly the viscountess straightened her shoulders and met Rhea's gaze steadily.

"I'm armed, and I'll not let anyone do anything that might hurt my baby. Stedman will be here with me."

"Don't be a fool." Rhea grabbed her sister's arm and squeezed hard. As her fingers dug into Arianna's skin, her sister released a small gasp of discomfort. Her gaze dared Arianna to object further. "You're to leave here the moment Fanny and Harry are with you. Do you understand?"

For a moment it looked as though her sister intended to argue. Rhea narrowed her gaze at the viscountess before Arianna nodded sharply and jerked free of Rhea's grasp.

"Thank you," Rhea said softly in relief, but her sister ignored her.

The carriage suddenly rolled to a stop, and Rhea's heart raced even faster. Dear God, did she have the strength to do what was required of her tonight? The air left her lungs as the footman opened the carriage door. Rhea accepted his hand and stepped out of the vehicle. As the door closed behind her, Arianna softly called out to her.

"Rhea, be careful. You know Ruckley is always at his most dangerous when someone tries to cheat him out of something." Her sister's words echoed with fear, and Rhea reached out to squeeze the hand the viscountess extended to her.

"I've not forgotten." The simple words made Arianna flinch.

"No, I suppose we never will," her sister whispered. Arianna's air of hopelessness made Rhea's hand tighten on her sister's.

"We might never forget, but after tonight we'll be free of the man." Rhea turned away then stopped as she remembered one last detail. "I left a note for Percy in my room. Please see he receives it."

"You can give it to him—"

Arianna's eyes widened with horror as she suddenly realized Rhea was prepared not to return. Before her sister could say another word of protest, Rhea headed toward The Bull and Hare's door. She was only a few feet away when it swung open abruptly. A man stumbled into the street his arm slung over the shoulders of the woman at his side. He was clearly drunk, and the woman was encouraging him to join her in a dark corner.

The woman's suggestive words caused Rhea's stomach to roil as the scene in front of her stirred memories she'd fought to bury over the course of the past few months. Desperately, she pushed the past into the dark recesses of her mind and forced herself to focus on the matter at hand. Panic lashed out at her, but she pushed it aside. Fear could be a friend or an enemy. She chose to make it a friend she held close to her breast like a shield. She glanced over her shoulder at the footman.

"The moment you have the children, you're to see them to safety along with the viscountess. Do not let her remain here." Rhea frowned as the man shook his head in obvious disapproval. Not about to argue with him, she glared fiercely at him until he nodded his agreement. "Thank you. I'm entrusting the lives of three people I love dearly into your safekeeping."

"Yes, miss," the man said.

Rhea opened the tavern door and stepped inside. The first smell to assault her senses was that of sweaty, unwashed bodies. In the next breath, the scent of stale ale and tobacco smoke filled her nostrils. It nauseated her. From the farthest end of the bar, she heard Ruckley call her name. The sound forced Rhea to choke back another wave of panic that threatened to debilitate her.

As she watched Ruckley approach, she realized he'd been drinking. For the first time, a glimmer of hope pushed through her fear. Perhaps if he drank enough—she didn't finish the thought as he stopped in front of her. The rank stench of his breath made her breathe through her mouth in an effort to keep the horrid smell of him out of her nose.

"Well, my poppet, you're here at long last," he said with a smug satisfaction. "I thought you might back out of our little arrangement."

"Where are Harry and Fanny?"

"They'll be along, shortly," the crime lord said as he sidled up beside her to wrap his arm around her waist. "Why don't you and I find a quiet place to enjoy ourselves."

Without any effort, Rhea slipped free of his grasp and eyed him coldly.

"Our bargain was that Fanny and Harry would be delivered before any business was conducted between the two of us."

Behind her, Fairlie coughed in obvious dismay. She glanced over her shoulder at the man and glared. The footman was clearly concerned, but he remained silent beneath her stern look. Rhea turned back to Ruckley.

"The children, per our agreement, please."

"Please is it, now? That's right pretty speech, Rhea," Ruckley said with a chuckle before he turned and waved his hand.

From the back of the tavern, Rhea saw Harry guiding Fanny toward the front door. The moment Fanny saw her, the girl race forward to throw her arms around Rhea. Relieved and happy to see the excited child, Rhea hugged her close.

"I'm so sorry it took me so long to come for you, sweetheart," she whispered as she bent and kissed the girl's cheek. Her arm still wrapped around Fanny, she reached out to brush her hand over Harry's curly locks.

"Have you come for us, Miss Rhea?" the boy asked with a confused expression.

"Yes, I made arrangements with Ruckley. You're going to go with this gentleman here." Rhea gestured to Fairlie. "He's going to take you to Miss Arianna."

"Are you coming with us Miss Rhea?" Fanny's voice quavered as she clung to Rhea's skirts.

"I have a few things to discuss with Ruckley first, sweetheart."

Rhea shuddered as she gently pushed the child away from her. One hand on Fanny's back she urged the child to go to the man behind her. Fanny reluctantly did so, her eyes wide in her pretty face. Rhea forced a reassuring smile to her lips as she encouraged the girl forward. No matter what happened tonight, Fanny would be safe. She turned back to Harry who was studying her with suspicion.

"Go on, Harry, Miss Arianna is waiting for you."

"What sort of business do you have to discuss with the likes of him?" Harry bobbed his head in Ruckley's direction. With the speed of a snake, the crime lord lashed out and struck the back of Harry's head viciously.

"Get on with you. You got no business asking any questions."

Rhea jerked at Ruckley's violent actions, but knew better than to protest. Harry's freedom was too precious to risk insulting Ruckley.

"Please go with Fairlie, Harry," she commanded in the stern, but gentle, voice she'd always used when watching over the children.

"But, Miss Rhea—"

"Now, Harry," she said sharply. The boy jumped in surprise at her harsh order, but reluctantly moved toward the door. As Fairlie opened the tavern door, Rhea saw one of Ruckley's men beginning to move forward.

"Fairlie, please show Mr. Ruckley why he's not going to let any of his men interfere."

Rhea kept her gaze focused on Ruckley who scowled at her with annoyance. With a grunt, he angrily waved his men to stand down. The moment he did so, she knew Fairlie had displayed his weapon. Without taking her eyes off Ruckley, she ordered the footman to go. Both Harry and Fanny murmured protests, but she didn't look away from Ruckley. The soft thud of the door behind her caused Rhea to flinch. Immediately a cruel smile curved his mouth.

"Well now, why don't you give that pistol you're hiding in that pretty little bag of yours to me."

"I don't have a weapon."

She shrugged at Ruckley's expression of suspicion and disbelief then offered up the reticule. As he tugged at the bag's drawstrings, Rhea watched in silence. Just as she'd hoped, with his attention focused on the small purse, it was unlikely he would think to search her. As he pulled the bag open, Rhea released a scoffing laugh.

"They're simply tools of my trade," she bit out as a familiar sense of humiliation crashed over her. Amusement made Ruckley grin broadly as he pulled a French Letter out of the bag and held it up for examination.

"I don't think we'll be needing this," he chuckled.

"As you wish."

"You answered that a might too quick, my poppet." Ruckley's eyes narrowed with distrust as he studied her carefully.

"Perhaps I have a small, but unpleasant gift to share with you." Rhea smiled slowly, enjoying his sudden look of indecision.

When she'd been under Ruckley's control, she'd insisted the men who bought her use the French letters she'd provided. The protective sheath had protected her from disease and bearing a child. Her sister had also demanded the sheaths be worn by the men who bought her.

But on frequent occasions Arianna's demands were ignored or met with physical blows before she was forcibly taken by the men who'd paid for her. It had been one of those occasions that Lucy had been conceived.

The letters had been just one of many tricks she'd used to protect herself when she'd been sold to men by Ruckley. Now she used the French letter to her advantage once more. It was the suggestion that she might have something disagreeable to pass on that made the man hesitate.

"Why do I think you're lying to me, Rhea?" His distrust made her laugh.

"You seem to forget I've always spoken my mind, and I've never lied to you," Rhea said with a careless shrug as she offered him a complacent smile. "Believe me or don't believe me. The choice is yours."

With a grunt Ruckley shoved the French letter back into the small bag and tossed it back to her. The man's irritation quickly evaporated as he took a step back and gestured toward the stairs. When Rhea hesitated, a sly smile curved Ruckley's lips as he leaned forward.

"Come now, Rhea, surely you're not afraid of me." The

man's voice held too much complacency, and it aroused Rhea's anger. She arched her eyebrows and stared at him in disgust.

"Fear you?" she sneered. "I hate you too much to fear you."

"Excellent," he chuckled as his eyes glittered with lust. "That's the fire I want to see in my bed. It'll make things exciting. Shall we?"

With a sense of doom, Rhea moved forward to silently climb the stairs. As she reached the second floor, she saw the door to Ruckley's rooms at the end of the corridor. On each side of the wall were doors to rooms she knew far too well. Rooms where she'd given up a small piece of herself to every man who'd used her body. Bile rose in her throat to flood her mouth, and she gagged then swallowed hard in her effort not to throw up.

Behind her Ruckley laughed. He knew she was afraid, but he didn't know why. She wasn't afraid of him. What terrified her was that deep down inside she'd been imagining how good it would feel when she killed him. The idea of watching Ruckley's stunned expression as his life slipped away actually filled her with pleasure. She'd been thinking it would be hard to pull the trigger. If anything it would be difficult not to enjoy it. Ruckley brushed past her, the foul stench of him making her stomach roil. He opened the door leading into his rooms and leaned back against the doorframe as he invited her to enter with a sneering smile.

Compared to the dimly lit corridor the room was bright, and God help her, almost cheery. A fire burned in the hearth while a low-burning oil lamp, sitting on a roughly hewn table, illuminated one small corner of the room. As her gaze swept toward the bed, she grew rigid at the sight of Edgar, hands behind his neck, reclined against some dirty-looking pillows. Disgusted by the boy's depraved grin, she whirled around to see Ruckley closing the door behind him.

"Our agreement did not include anyone else," Rhea said in an icy voice. She was now certain the moment she pulled the trigger she wouldn't just enjoy watching Ruckley take his last breath. She'd revel in it.

"What I said was that I want to saddle and ride you, poppet, and I intend to do just that," Ruckley said with a smug smile before he grinned at Edgar. "The boy is here to watch how it's done."

"To watch or give you pointers on what to do?"

The moment she spoke she realized her mistake. An instant later, the back of Ruckley's hand slammed into her cheek. The blow connected with the bruised area of her jaw where Edgar had struck her days before. Rhea staggered backward until her back was pressed into a chest of drawers. Pain shot its way through her head, and each breath she took seemed to exacerbate the throbbing in her jaw. Her hand fell down to the pocket of her dress as she tried to focus on where both men stood in the room.

"Enough lollygagging. Get out of your clothes, Rhea, before I cut them off." All amusement was gone from Ruckley's voice as he flipped open a switchblade. The long narrow blade flashed in the firelight. Stomach churning with fear and pain, Rhea realized her hands were clammy and cold. Slowly she set her purse on the table. With her back to Ruckley, she began to undo the buttons of her dress.

"Turn around, poppet. I want to watch you." At Ruckley's command, she heard Edgar snicker.

Humiliation slashed through Rhea as she turned to face them both. She pushed the top portion of her dress off her shoulders. Ruckley's lascivious look filled her with horror as for the first time she realized how difficult it would be to avoid letting the bastard touch her. No, she'd die before she'd let that happen. The dress pooled at Rhea's feet, and she picked it up, folded it, and turned to lay it on the table. As she pretended to smooth out the wrinkles in the gown, she carefully pulled the pistol out of the dress pocket and gripped it firmly.

"Leave the dress be, Rhea. Turn around and show me that cunny of yours, because I plan on fucking you more than once tonight, me girl."

Rhea drew in a deep breath, cocked the pistol, and turned around. The moment the two men saw her weapon their eyes widened. Edgar's reaction was typical of someone staring down the barrel of a gun. Ruckley's reaction was different. The man stared at her for a long moment before he laughed boisterously. Oddly enough his laughter didn't surprise her. Somehow she'd expected it. Ruckley chuckled as he played with the switchblade in his hand.

"Now exactly what do you think is going to happen here, my poppet?" Ruckley shook his head in amusement. "Even if I let you go, do you really expect to simply walk out of here, dressed in nothing but your drawers?"

The question threw her for a moment as she stared at the crime lord. He was right she wouldn't be able to leave wearing nothing but her petticoats. A cold smile touched her lips as she met his gaze steadily. She shook her head.

"I won't have to," she said quietly. Ruckley raised an eyebrow at her response, his lips curling back over his teeth like a cadaver.

"Now exactly what does that mean, dearie?"

"It means you'll be dead and unable to stop me from dressing." Her cold reply made Ruckley snort.

"You never cease to surprise me, Rhea."

The man shifted his position, and Rhea knew her unusual behavior unsettled him. She allowed a small smile to touch her lips. Out of the corner of her eye, she saw Edgar slide off the bed.

"Don't, boy," she said softly. "One more step and I'll kill him. Then where will you be?"

"I'll tell the police you killed him."

"And I'll tell them you're lying." Rhea didn't take her gaze off of Ruckley who was now looking distinctively nervous. "Who will they believe, Edgar?"

Without a word, Edgar slowly sank back down onto the bed. Ruckley's eyes narrowed as he studied her carefully. She didn't flinch beneath his harsh gaze, and she saw a strange emotion wrinkle his brow. It wasn't so much a look of fear, but bewilderment. The man was uncertain as to how to react to her behavior. She could read it in his eyes.

"Now then, Rhea, you've had your fun at my expense. Give up the gun to old Ruckley," he wheedled.

"No. I don't think so," she said as she took pleasure in seeing the man beginning to sweat.

"Don't be a fool, woman. Everyone downstairs saw you come up here willingly." There was a growing note of anxiety in Ruckley's voice, and it made her smile.

"What you don't seem to understand, Ruckley, is that I don't care," she said with a quiet calm that surprised her. "I came here tonight knowing that I might be hung for killing you, but I decided it didn't matter."

"Surely we can come to some arrangement, Rhea. It doesn't have to be like this between us." Fear invaded his voice as he pleaded with her.

"No," she said as she leveled her pistol at him. "It's too late for—"

Rhea didn't get to finish as Ruckley flung his blade at her and it sliced into her arm, just above the elbow. She cried out in pain as Ruckley lunged toward her. Acting simply on sheer self-preservation, she supported her injured arm with her free hand and pulled the trigger.

The gunshot ricocheted off the walls of the room as Rhea stared at the man in front of her. Ruckley's mouth moved, but no words came out as blood spurted out of the hole in the side of his neck. The pleasure she'd been experiencing at Ruckley's fear had vanished. Where was it? Where was the pleasure, the satisfaction, the enjoyment she thought she'd feel right now? It was missing. Helplessly, she watched Ruckley slowly fall to the floor.

Sinking to her knees beside the dead man, the gun slipped from Rhea's fingers as she stared at the life pouring out of Ruckley. Why didn't she feel gratified? She'd killed the man who'd tormented her and others she loved. A loud cry roared out of Edgar and she fell backward as the boy threw himself on top of her. Pinned beneath the boy, she jabbed at his face with her fingers trying to make him release her.

"You sorry bitch. You killed him."

There was a look of madness about Edgar that terrified her. With a twist of her body she tried to knock him off balance and escape his hold. She gained a small amount of leverage only to have it disappear as Edgar pulled a thick piece of string from his coat pocket and wrapped it around her neck. In seconds, her supply of air disappeared. Instinct forced her to claw at the rope, but she knew it wouldn't help. Somewhere in the back of her brain, she heard Ruckley cackling.

The bastard would have enjoyed this, just as he would have enjoyed carving her up with his switchblade. The knife. Rhea flung out her hand, her fingers scrabbling for the knife Ruckley had thrown at her. Pain stabbed at her throat as Edgar tightened the cord around her neck. Fingertips scraping with desperation across the rough wood floor, she jerked as the blade sliced into one of her fingers. The pain was a welcome sensation because it said she'd found what she needed to survive. Rhea struggled to remain conscious as her fingers blindly searched for the switchblade's handle.

Lungs on fire from lack of air, she fought to grasp the weapon that would ensure she could breathe again. The cold metal handle of the blade in her hand, she threw her arm in a wide arc upward and slashed at the boy strangling her. Almost immediately, the pressure on her neck vanished. As she gasped for air, she slashed at the boy again. Edgar made a gurgling sound, and he fell forward on top of her. A metallic, coppery smell filled her nostrils as she continued to struggle to fill her burning lungs with air.

Choking from a lack of oxygen, Rhea frantically pulled at the cord wrapped around her neck, and allowed a huge rush of air to fill her body. With a strength born of desperation, she pushed Edgar off her body. Terrified he might throttle her again, she scrambled backward like a spider until she reached the wall. Her hands felt wet, and as she raised them to the light, she shuddered with revulsion at the blood covering her hands.

In blind panic, she looked down at the front of her petticoats and the large, dark stains on her corset. Frantic to rid herself of the blood, she tried to reach the lacing on her back. The cut on her arm made it too painful to undo the lacings. With a sob, she curled up against the wall. Every part of her seemed to ache, as her eyes remained fixed on the bodies of the two men she'd just killed.

Somehow, she was certain they were merely toying with her. They weren't really dead. They were simply waiting for her guard to slip, and then they would lunge out at her to inflict more pain and suffering. Dry, rasping coughs continued to rip through her body as she drank in deep breaths.

A gentle hand touched her arm, causing Rhea to scream and violently strike out at the touch. She scooted away in sheer terror. Again the touch came, and through the misty blur of blood and mayhem, Rhea saw Percy's face. She raised her hand toward him then saw the blood on her fingers. Horrified, she jerked away from him.

"Don't touch me."

"Christ Jesus, Rhea. It's me, Percy."

"Get away from me," she cried out again.

Percy stared down at Rhea in horror. She was covered in blood just as Jamie had described. He could see she was bleeding from a wound on her arm, but the blood on her corset prevented him from seeing whether she bore any other wounds. He reached out to her again, but this time he didn't touch her. Instead, he extended his hand to her.

"Rhea, look at me. It's over, sweetheart. They can't hurt you anymore."

At his words, she looked up at him, and the glazed look of terror in her eyes made him want to scoop her up in his arms. Percy could tell she was in a state of shock, and she had begun to tremble with a violence that scared him the hell out of him. He stretched out his hand to her once more, but she retreated from him. Harry, the boy he'd met the other night, appeared at his side and touched Percy's arm.

"Let me try, sir. Perhaps, she'll come with me." At the boy's suggestion, Percy stepped away from her and watched as Harry squatted down in front of Rhea.

"It's all right, Miss Rhea. We won. Fanny, Vincent, all the others, and me—we're all safe, just like you wanted. You saved us."

Rhea stared at the boy, and her expression was one of confusion. Her eyes shifted to where Ruckley and Edgar lay still on the floor, and she shuddered. Rhea's gaze swung back to Percy. It was obvious she was trying to discern if Harry was telling her the truth. As if reading her mind, Harry scrambled over to one of the bodies and prodded the corpse.

"See, Miss Rhea. They're dead. They can't 'urt you anymore. You did it. You saved us, just like you always said you would." Harry scrambled back to her side, and stretched out his hand to her. "Come on now, we need to get you home. Mr. Rockwood has a carriage all ready for you."

Hesitantly, Rhea stretched out her hand to Harry. When he took her hand in his, Harry helped her rise to her feet. "Now then, Miss Rhea. Mr. Rockwood and me, we're gonna take you to the carriage. Can you walk?"

Rhea nodded at the question. Harry stood on one side of her, as Percy gently wrapped his arm about her waist, his fingers cupping her elbow. She moaned and, he bent his head toward her.

"Will you let me carry you, sweetheart?" At his question, she looked up at him, her eyes glazing over again with pain and sadness.

"I can't marry you now," she whispered. "I can't even be your mistress."

For the first time in his life, Percy felt utterly helpless. She'd always been so strong, but whatever strength she'd possessed had disappeared until all he could see was her vulnerability. She was exposed completely, and it terrified him that she might never come back to him.

"It's all right, Rhea. Everything is going to be all right, sweetheart," he murmured as she sagged against him.

She didn't protest as he gently lifted her up into his arms. When she curled up into his chest, he pressed a kiss on her temple and carried her out of the room that held enough terror to last both of them a lifetime.

Chapter 19

"Why did you choose to address this yourself, Miss Bennett instead of calling on Scotland Yard to investigate the matter?" The inspector's voice held a note of censure as he wrote something down on the small note card he held. Rhea eyed him coldly, and the man frowned slightly as he looked up to meet her gaze.

"Exactly how many complaints a month on matters such as this do you receive, Inspector Graves, and how many are followed up on quickly?" At her question, the man had the good grace to flush beneath his swarthy complexion.

"I can assure you Miss Bennett, every request Scotland Yard receives for assistance is acted upon," the man replied with a touch of umbrage.

"I don't doubt that, inspector, but it wouldn't have helped Fanny, would it? By the time Scotland Yard investigated the matter, Fanny would have been forced into prostitution. A child not yet ten."

Rhea glared at the man seated across from her. The inspector's affronted expression had collapsed into chagrin. The man cleared his throat and nodded.

"You're right, Miss Bennett, it would have been too late for the child, but you cannot deny you put yourself in harm's way."

"Inspector Graves, I was sold to Ruckley by my father shortly before my nineteenth birthday. I knew what Fanny would endure, and I refused to let that happen to a child."

Rhea closed her eyes for a brief moment as she realized she wasn't being completely honest. She'd gone to the Bull and Hare intending to murder Ruckley. In the end it had been self-defense, but her motives were not completely pure. She'd plotted to kill a man, another human being.

No matter how vile, debauched, and evil Ruckley had been, planning his death had been wrong. It made her no less callous than the man himself. But she wasn't sorry for it. She refused to feel guilty for an act she performed in self-defense. She opened her eyes again to meet the inspector's chagrined and sympathetic gaze.

"I apologize, Miss Bennett, I'd not been made aware of this aspect to the case," Graves said quietly. "I understand why you felt the need to go to the child's aid. Nonetheless, the end result could have been far more calamitous than it was. But as it is, two criminals are dead, and you're safe."

"Thank you, is there anything else you need to know?"

"Just a couple more questions," Graves said as his gaze skimmed his notes. "I was informed by several witnesses at the tavern that you went willingly with Mr. Ruckley to his rooms. Is that correct?"

"Yes." Rhea didn't expand on her answer as she tried to breathe, frightened as to where the inspector's questioning was headed.

"Why would you do that, Miss Bennett? According to the witnesses, the children were escorted out of the tavern before you went to Mr. Ruckley's rooms," the inspector said in a curious tone that held just the hint of foreboding. Rhea met his probing gaze and her mouth went dry.

"Because…because Ruckley…"

"Because the bastard didn't ask for money. He demanded something of Miss Bennett that no gentleman would ever ask of a lady."

Rhea jumped as Percy answered the inspector's question in a freezing tone that made the man scramble to his feet in a manner that illustrated his discomfort. As the man met Percy's gaze, the inspector bowed slightly.

"Mr. Rockwood."

"I thought I told you not to interview Miss Bennett until after her physician gave his approval to do so." Percy's expression was harsh with anger, and the inspector cleared his throat as his discomfort grew.

"I summoned Inspector Graves," she said quietly as she met Percy's gaze. "He was attempting to understand why I would go willingly with Ruckley," she said as she looked at the inspector. "Is there anything else you wish to ask?"

"Actually....well...there is the matter of the Derringer we found at the scene," Inspector Graves said as he cleared his throat again. "We...ah...that is to say...was the weapon yours, miss?"

"Yes," she said with a nod.

"Rhea—" The warning note in Percy's voice made her wave him into silence.

"I lived under Ruckley's control for more than seven years, Inspector Graves. I knew what kind of man he was, and that he might attempt to renege on our arrangement, which he in fact did," Rhea flinched as she remembered seeing Edgar when she entered Ruckley's room. "Edgar's presence was never a part of our bargain."

"That's quite enough," Percy bit out in a low, menacing voice. "I think you have more than enough information to close this case, Inspector Graves. Miss Bennett is the injured party here, not Ruckley who attacked her with a switchblade, or the boy who tried to strangle her."

Rhea's hand went to her throat where the markings of Edgar's attempt to kill her were still clearly visible. At Percy's icy words, the inspector turned his head and grimaced as he looked at Rhea's neck. With a bob of his head, Graves bowed in her direction.

"Mr. Rockwood is correct, Miss Bennett. I apologize for

my curiosity." The man's words sent a bolt of relief skimming through her veins.

"Your line of questioning is understandable," she murmured. "But I assure you most emphatically that my actions were solely in self-defense. A position I believe is emphasized by my state of dishabille when Mr. Rockwood found me."

"A quite valid point," Inspector Graves said as if he'd not considered that fact before. Rhea pushed the thin shawl she wore off her shoulders and rose to her feet.

"Then if you have nothing further…" As her voice trailed off, the inspector shook his head.

"No, I have more than enough to recommend the case be closed," Inspector Graves said. "I appreciate your assistance in concluding my investigation."

The man bowed in her direction then quickly skirted Percy and darted out of the room. As Rhea watched the man leave, she experienced amusement as well as relief at the inspector's departure. In the next instant, a wave of trepidation washed over her as she looked at Percy. The last time she'd seen him had been three days ago when he'd found her in Ruckley's rooms. Her memories of the moments after Ruckley's and Edgar's deaths were a jumble of images and fear. The fear was what she remembered more than anything. But she also remembered what she'd said to him. Nothing had changed that.

"You should be resting," Percy said quietly.

There was a strained note in his voice, and she turned away from to pick up the shawl she'd dropped on the chair and began to fold it in to a neat square. Aunt Beatrice had said he'd come by at least twice a day since the night at the Bull and Hare. Was the man blind to scandal surrounding her involvement with Ruckley? Aunt Beatrice had tried to hide the papers from her, but she'd insisted Bessie bring them to her. The reports of what happened at Ruckley's had started out as a small article buried deep in the paper, but then someone had made a connection, and it had reached the scandal sheets.

"Aunt Beatrice tells me you've been a constant visitor."

"You sound surprised," he said with a hint of irritation. Rhea looked over her shoulder to see him scowling at her.

"I am under the circumstances." A sudden chill skated over her, and she moved to stand in front of the fire. Hands extended toward the flames, she tried to warm her hands.

"And what circumstances are you referring to?" he said with a notable amount of frustration. With a shake of her head, Rhea sighed exasperation and turned around. Eyebrows arched in scornful impatience, she narrowed her gaze at him.

"Do you expect me to believe you've not seen the papers?"

"I read the paper every day," he said in a silky tone of voice. "Is there anything particular I should be taking note of? A new bill in Parliament? The price of wheat falling?"

"Don't be absurd," she snapped. "You know good and well what I'm talking about."

"If anyone is being absurd, it's you."

"You are a blind man, Percy Rockwood."

"When it comes to a certain Miss Rhea Bennett, I would agree whole heartedly," he replied.

"Then you're a fool."

She worked hard to keep her voice as cold and brutal as she could. His gaze narrowed, and he took a step toward her. Instantly, she recoiled, certain that if he were to embrace her, it would be impossible not to cling to him as if he were a life raft in a choppy sea.

"No, I'm simply a man who doesn't care what the rest of the world thinks."

"And I'm a woman who does."

"Why?" The single word question made her jerk, and she stared at him in confusion. When she didn't answer, he shook his head. "I asked you why, Rhea."

"Because I have no desire to drag more names through the mud," she bit out in desperation. Surely the man could see that she was trying to save him and his family from being associated with a woman who was a known killer.

"I wasn't aware the streets were muddy as we've not had any rain in several weeks."

"Now, you're being deliberately obnoxious."

"Actually, I think I'm being quite patient."

"For a Rockwood, I imagine that must be quite difficult," she snapped.

"Indeed," he said. "Particularly when the woman I love is allowing people who are unimportant dictate her happiness—our happiness."

"This isn't about my happiness," she exclaimed as her heart skipped a beat.

"If not yours, then whose?"

The gentleness in his voice made her heart twist in her chest. The resolute set of his jaw said he was determined to convince her otherwise. Worse, she wasn't sure she had the strength to keep fighting him. She shook her head and turned back to the fire. Staring into the flames, she blinked fast to prevent tears from falling. If he were to realize how difficult it was for her not to run to him, he would press the issue. She couldn't let him do that. The man needed saving from himself.

Any association with her would damage him far more than he realized. As his mistress it would be difficult enough for him. But if he married her, it would be impossible for him to go anywhere without people whispering. The scandal wouldn't affect just Percy. It would impact the entire Rockwood family. She'd killed two men, and the circumstances weren't just tawdry, they were deplorable.

Everyone would believe the worst, and even then what people thought would never compare to the reality of who she was. Why couldn't she make him understand that? Couldn't he see that the redemption she'd thought Ruckley's death would give her was a façade? She'd saved those she loved, but she'd not erased what she was.

"You didn't answer my question, Rhea." The quiet resolve in his voice made her straighten her shoulders, and she slowly turned to look at him.

"I don't intend to, since it's pointless to do so," she said as she averted her gaze from his penetrating one. "I'll be leaving for Green Hill House in a few days. I want to put as much distance between me and the past as I possibly can."

"It's not like you to run away."

"I am not running away," she snapped as she glared at him. "It has always been my plan to return to Green Hill House to tend to the health and welfare of the children."

"Then I'll come with you," he said as if he'd just had an epiphany. "I'm good with children, and they'll need a father figure to ensure you don't mollycoddle them."

"I beg your pardon," she gasped as she stared at him with a mixture of disbelief and anger.

"Naturally, you'll have to marry me. As my mistress you'd be setting a poor example for the children, and I know you wouldn't want to do that."

"You're mad."

"Madly in love with you, I'm afraid," he said.

Percy's smile of satisfaction made her heart skip a beat. He wore the look of a man who'd just solved a difficult problem, and a small bud of hope began to flower inside her. Once again she struggled with the possibility he would be giving up far more than he realized if he were to continue along this path of insanity. She shook her head in dismay as he slowly closed the distance between them.

"I know your family is renowned for being reckless, but I'm certain this path you're proposing exceeds anything others in your family have done."

"Perhaps," he said as he pulled her close. "Although, I'm certain my brother would disagree with you."

Unable to avoid it, she breathed in the familiar male scent of him. With each breath she drew in, her body and heart cried out with a need to accept the happiness he offered. She knew she should fight him, but what he was proposing was laying waste to any of her objections. Gossip might reach the ears of people in the countryside, but she knew it wouldn't be of any real consequence. Still, a small part of her resisted. She was frightened for him and his family. By taking her into the fold, they would be subjected to a great deal of scorn and scandal.

"You mustn't do this, Percy,"

"What? Love you? How could I not?" he said as he bent his head and nibbled at her ear. "However, I would appreciate it if you would put me out of my misery and tell me what I already know."

"Please, Percy," she gasped as warmth spread through her.

"Tell me what I want to hear, my love."

His whisper blew across her skin like a hot breeze. Percy lifted his head and stared down at her. His determination was countered by the flash of concern she stared into his gaze.

"I...love you, but it's impossible. You can't—"

She didn't have a chance to offer up any other objections as his mouth captured hers. The warmth of him and his kiss invaded every cell in her body, and she melted into him. Here, in his arms, was happiness—the chance to be greater than she was because he believed in her. His kiss was tender and filled with adoration. Its warmth healed her spirit and pulled her into a place where nothing could hurt her as long as he was at her side.

His tongue laced her lips until she opened her mouth to allow his tongue to tangle with hers in a dance of fire and seduction. Passion spiraled through her, and the depth of her love for him made her long to be with him completely and utterly. With a quick twist of her body she pulled free of his embrace and hurried to the salon door. The soft thud it made as she closed it and turned the key sent her heart racing as she realized where he was concerned she would always be unredeemable.

Slowly, Rhea turned to see him staring at her with surprise and the beginning of comprehension as to her intentions. Her steps measured and unhurried, she closed the distance between them all the while her fingers were opening the buttons on her shirt-waist. Disapproval and desire crossed his face as she moved toward him.

The fact that he stood stiffly in front of her, clearly riveted by her approach filled her with a sense of power. The force of it flooded through her as she realized she was in complete command of this moment. Happiness skimmed through her as she saw the desire in his gaze deepen. He shook his head with dismay.

"Christ Jesus, marrying me doesn't mean you have to live up to the Rockwood tendency for recklessness."

"Do you want me to say yes?"

She pulled her shirt-waist free of her skirt and quickly undid the hooks on the front of her corset. With each word, movement, breath, and beat of her heart, she realized being with him would set her free. There would be no more fear—only happiness and joy.

"God help me, Rhea, you're not playing fair."

His throat bobbed furiously as he clasped his hands behind his back in a clear effort to keep from reaching out for her as she came to a halt in front of him. A tortured groan escaped him as she dropped her corset onto the floor and ran her hands upward from the waistband of her skirt to caress her breasts.

"Bloody hell," he choked out in a tight voice. "This isn't just reckless, it's madness. If someone were to—"

"Take off your jacket, Percy. Now." Although it was a command, she kept her voice quiet and seductive.

"What the hell are you going to do when someone

knocks on the door," he choked out as she pushed his coat off of him then pulled his tie off his neck.

"I'll say I seduced you," she whispered. "Seduced you so that you must redeem an unredeemable woman."

"You've been redeemed a thousand times over, my love. But clearly I'll have to remind you of that for the rest of our lives."

"Then start now. Prove that you intend to redeem me with love."

A dark groan rumbled in his chest as he roughly pulled her into his arms and kissed her. It was a hot, passionate, and demanding caress. Something about the way his mouth singed hers allowed one wave of pleasure after another to rise and swirl around her. Hands splayed across his chest, she reveled in the hard, solid muscles beneath the tips of her fingers. She opened her mouth to him once more, and his tongue coaxed then demanded a response. The hedonistic caress aroused her more. Eager to touch him, she tugged at the buttons of his pants.

The moment Rhea's hand brushed across his cock, he released a groan of need and protest. What they were doing wasn't just ill-advised. It was reckless, dangerous, worse, exceedingly intoxicating. His tongue still dancing with hers, he caught her hands and pinned them behind her back. It would take him a lifetime to ensure she knew just how wonderful and courageous she was. Everything she'd done for him—her family—ensured her the redemption she thought she needed as surely as every breath he took belonged to her.

In a swift move, he half dragged, half carried her to the sofa. His mouth teased hers into a passionate response. Eager to please her, he grasped the silk of her skirt and tugged it upward. A quiet moan whispered against his mouth as his hand skimmed upward over her stocking to the garter holding it in place. She trembled at the touch, and his fingers stroked her thigh before seeking the heart of her.

With a growing hunger, he trailed his mouth across her cheek, downward to where he could suck on the hard nipple pressing into her white lawn chemise. She whimpered at the caress and arched upward in a silent plea for more, and he gently nipped at the hard pebble. The sob of pleasure she released increased his desire, but pleasing her was more important. He slid downward until he was on his knees and he pushed her skirts higher. The moment his mouth caressed the rim of her sex, she dragged in a deep breath. It was followed by a small cry as his tongue swept into her folds.

She bucked against his mouth and her cream flowed warm and silky across his tongue. He reveled in the delicious taste of her. The sound of her soft cries caused his own arousal to intensify. With a small nip at the swollen nub of her sex, he quickly returned to the sofa and lifted her to straddle him. In one brief second, he sheathed himself in her white-hot heat. The way her body tightened around him wasn't just pleasurable, it was mind-numbing. He would never grow tired of loving her like this.

Suddenly, she began to ride him hard and fast. The movement blinded him to everything except her, and the raw sensation of her body joined with his. Heat engulfed his cock as the friction of her skin against his made his erection tighten and stretch in a manner that was at turns painful and erotic. It was a sign that he was on the verge of completely losing his control, and his hands brushed aside the silk of her skirts and petticoats to grasp her thighs.

Desire barreled through him as he urged her to ride him harder and faster. Like a beautiful instrument she bended to his will. Their rhythm was a force of nature that echoed with a passion and love he knew would never be lost. His body tensed as her core flexed violently around him. The tight spasms clutched at him, until with a restrained cry he made one last, hard thrust into her and spilled his seed in an explosion of raw, visceral sensation.

She fell forward into him, and he breathed in ragged breaths of air as his body continued to throb inside her. The stillness between them was filled only with the sound of their labored breathing, which slowly eased until she lifted her head to stare down at him.

"I suppose I have no other option now, but to marry you, Mr. Rockwood," she whispered with a sultry smile. "You've ruined me completely."

"If that's the only way I could convince you to do so, I'm not sorry for it," he chuckled then frowned as her smile faded to reveal her fear and vulnerability.

"Are you certain you want to marry me—to come to Green Hill House?"

"I'm afraid you leave me little choice since you insist on burying yourself in domestic bliss in the countryside," he said with a smile as he brushed his hand across her flushed cheek. She looked radiant despite the uncertainty in her beautiful eyes. "Although you'll have to agree to visit Callendar Abbey whenever the Rockwood clan gathers there."

Percy caught her face in his hands and kissed her quickly before setting her off of him so he could dress. As beautiful as she looked half-dressed, they'd already tempted the fates far too much. In a few brief moments, he'd dressed, and raised his head to watch as Rhea buttoned her shirt-waist. When she'd finished adjusting the upper portion of her clothing, she shook out the skirts of her dress making a fuss over smoothing out the wrinkles. With an intuition that was growing by leaps and bounds where she was concerned, he released a grunt of exasperation.

"Why are you doing your best to avoid looking at me?" At his question, Rhea's head jerked up, and he frowned. "Out with it, Rhea."

"Your brother's party is tonight."

"Yes," said quietly. "But we're not going."

"I don't understand," she said as she shook her head. "You have to go. The Rockwoods never miss any important family occasion.

"True," he said with a nod. "But I have no intention of feeding you to the wolves after what you've been through."

"But you need—"

"No, my family knows you come first. I spoke to Sebastian earlier this morning, and he agreed with my decision whole heartedly," he said quietly as he pulled her into his arms.

"You would do that for me?" she whispered with disbelief and wonder.

"It's a small sacrifice compared to the one you were willing to make the other night," he said somberly.

What she'd done the other night humbled him. She'd been willing to sacrifice herself to protect him and the children. The memory of how she'd clung to him when he'd carried her out of the Bull and Hare made his gut twist. It wasn't a moment he ever wanted to relive again. Her fingers brushed against his cheek, and he focused his gaze on her.

"I love you, Percy."

Tears shimmered in her eyes as she looked up at him. From that first moment in the museum when he'd looked into violet eyes filled with anguish, he'd known his destiny was tied to hers. His heart full, he kissed her again, sealing his devotion to her for the rest of his life.

Epilogue

April 1900

Rhea looked out the bedroom window at the gardens below. They'd arrived at Callendar Abby late yesterday, and she'd been too tired to wake at her usual time. Percy must have known to let her sleep as she'd been alone when she'd awoken.

Below, she saw Julian and Patience strolling through the gardens with more than a dozen children walking and running around the couple. Alma and Fanny were walking together their heads together as if they were plotting something. By his exaggerated hand gestures, Vincent was amusing Jamie and Theo with some wild story of his.

Greer, her little legs making her gait awkward raced toward the couple. Julian swept her up in his arms and Patience turned toward the pair. Her belly had expanded in recent weeks, and Aunt Matilda was certain the baby would arrive any day now. The couple was ecstatic about the upcoming arrival. Percy had said Julian and Patience had believed she couldn't have children, which made her understand her sister-in-law's happy glow and excitement.

It meant the family would have to wait for her news. She refused to take any attention away from Patience's moment of happiness. Rhea smiled at the thought and pressed her hand to her stomach. As she stood watching the happy scene, a warm hand slid around her waist, pulling her back into a solid wall of muscle. Rhea sighed with happiness at the strong touch.

"So you finally decided to rejoin the living," he teased with a nip to the curve of her shoulder.

"It's not that late," she said with amusement.

"For you, my love, it's practically unheard of for you to sleep past nine." It seemed the perfect moment to share her news, but he muttered something as he pointed toward Peter. "Do you want to know what that young scoundrel did? Alma dared him to climb the old oak down at the pond—"

"And he climbed it." At her laugh, Percy growled with irritation.

"It wasn't just that he climbed the damn thing, but he jumped into the pond. The water is icy cold, and he wasn't prepared for the shock of it. If Sebastian and I hadn't been out riding, and heard the children shouting, God knows what might have happened."

"Did you have to go in after him?"

Rhea gasped at the thought of something happening to the boy. Life with Percy had swept away every bad memory of her old existence into the darkest corners of her mind, where they had remained for the most part. There was the occasional nightmare, but Percy was always there to hold and soothe her afterward.

She'd left the past far behind, but it was not so distant that she didn't fear for the safety of the children she'd taken in to raise as her own. Percy's arm tightened around her, and he kissed her cheek.

"No, the scamp was coming out of the water when we reached him, but I've never heard someone's teeth chatter so loudly. I brought him back to the Abbey for dry clothes."

"And a sound lecture I hope," she murmured with relief.

"Although I doubt it was as severe as one of your reprimands, I don't think he'll be jumping into any ponds in the near future, although I cannot guarantee he'll resist climbing trees." Percy's chuckle became a sigh of resignation.

Satisfied that all was well in her small, but joyous world, Rhea released as soft sigh.

"Now that sounds like a happy sigh," he murmured as his arms tightened around her waist.

"It was," she said with a smile as she reached up over her shoulder to brush her fingertips against his strong jaw. Her gaze focused on Peter, Harry, and Ginny darting back and forth in an impromptu game of tag. "Look at them, Percy. I never ever thought to see them so happy. I never thought *I* could be so happy."

"We are more fortunate than most," he said quietly. "And our children could not ask for a better mother."

Percy's words expanded her heart until she was forced to blink back a sudden flood of tears.

"Say that again?"

"What? Our children are lucky to have you for a mother?"

"No, you said our children," she whispered as she turned and wrapped her arms around him then pressed her body into him as far as she could.

"Of course, they are, my darling."

Percy pushed her away from him slightly to eye her with an arched look that said she'd been foolish to doubt how much he'd grown to love all the children they'd rescued. Their lives at Green Hill House over the past several months been almost too idyllic. Percy had honored his words to her and had adopted the children with his whole heart.

The boys worshiped him, while Ginny and Fanny had him wrapped around their fingers. He was every bit the father he'd told her he would be. He had become Sebastian's estate manager when the old manager had retired, and it was obvious he enjoyed his work. He often took the boys with him. Their life together was richer and fuller than anything she could have ever hoped for. She sucked in a sharp breath as the past darted out to jab at her. It vanished the moment Percy tightened his arms around her.

"What is it, Rhea? You've been moody for the past few weeks," he said with something resembling alarm.

"Yes, I suppose I have," she said with a smile as she raised her head to look up at him. "I don't suppose you'd be willing to take in another child."

"Another child," he said as he arched his eyebrows in amused exasperation. "Six isn't enough for you?"

"Well, this particular child is quite needy. They'll require a great deal of care. It will mean late nights and early mornings."

"Why do I think you've found a baby in need of—" Percy stopped speaking as his jaw sagged, and he stared at her in disbelief. His befuddled expression made her laugh, and she pulled his head down to kiss him.

"Yes, a new Rockwood will join the fold in a few months."

"A baby," he murmured with a look of happiness and amazement. Percy pressed his forehead against hers.

"Then I take it you're pleased," Rhea asked with just a hint of worry.

"Pleased? I'm overjoyed, my love."

"Now, you're not to say a word to anyone, not even the children."

"Why the devil not?"

"Because Patience and Julian have waited so long to have a child, and I don't want to take away from their happiness. We can tell the family the news after their baby arrives."

"Knowing my sister, I doubt it would trouble her if we were to make the announcement," he paused as she narrowed her gaze at him.

"Percy."

"Very well, I'll let you have your way as you always do."

"You know good and well that's not true," she huffed.

"If anyone is indulged,—"

"It's the children," he said with a chuckle, and her heart skipped a beat.

"Oh Percy, do you really think I put the children before you," she gasped in dismay.

"What? No," he said with a shake of his head. "I was teasing you, my love. I have never been happier in my life. You and the children have given me more than a man could hope to have."

As he kissed her, Rhea experienced a rush of happiness unlike anything she'd ever known. She'd been redeemed time and again by a man who loved her with all his heart. She'd been adopted into a family who had accepted her for who she was, not what she had been, and in a few months she would have one more heart to cherish and love. Redemption had come at a price, but not the one she'd expected. It had been the price of happiness, and she accepted it gladly with all her heart.

Thank you for reading Rhea's and Percy's story. I hope you enjoyed it as much as I loved writing the book. If you could spare a moment, please help other readers find this book by writing a review on BookBub and Amazon about *Redemption*. Be sure to keep turning the page for a special preview of the award-winning *Forever Mine*.

Special Preview
Forever Mine

Chapter 1

Present Day

"I don't believe it."

"Which is *precisely* why you owe me fifty pounds, oh, ye of little faith." From her seat on the brown leather couch behind him, Nora snorted with laughter.

Nick Barrows ignored his sister's gloating comment as he stared in amazement at the two paintings set up on easels beneath the Barrows Art and Antiquities logo. Once authenticated, the landscapes by Constable would be the biggest pieces the shop had ever acquired.

"And you found these in *Nebraska*?"

"I told you unclaimed property auctions were worth the travel expense."

"Are you telling me there weren't any other art dealers there? "

"A few. Like other states, Nebraska puts ads in the papers about their yearly sale, but most of the time the items are jewelry, coins, electronics, and other collectibles. I don't think anyone realized what these were."

"I suppose you're going to want to go back," Nick Barrows looked over his shoulder and grinned before looking back at the paintings.

"Of course, and you know, I think this brilliant acquisition of mine deserves a raise."

"Uncle Charles gave you a raise a year ago," Nick chuckled at his sister's teasing jab. A second later, he realized his mistake and closed his eyes. He was an idiot. Filled with regret, he turned to face his sister. "Damn, I wasn't thinking, Nora."

"It's okay. He would have said the same thing." She shrugged her shoulders then laughed softly. "Then the next minute he'd be waltzing me around this tiny office of yours."

Nora was right. Uncle Charles would have been overjoyed by her find and its impact on the shop. The old man had loved this place as if it were his child. He'd always said the shop possessed a soul. Nick had never understood his uncle as well as Nora had. The two of them had often talked ghosts, past lives, and supernatural theories well into the night. It was one of the reasons Nora had taken his death so hard. She'd lost the one companion who 'got her' as she was fond of saying.

"Somehow I think he'd be more proud than excited," Nick said. "We've come a long way from those two angry American teenagers he brought to England and took into his home."

"I don't know how he managed it. Confirmed bachelors aren't poster children for parenthood." Nora shook her head in disbelief. "And we weren't exactly easy to live with."

"He understood. We were grieving for mom and dad, just like he was." Nick stared down at his shoes for a second before he looked up at his sister. "It always amazed me how he seemed to know exactly what we needed and when."

"I miss him, Nick." Sadness filled his sister's voice.

"I do too."

His gaze swung to the portrait of the Countess of Guildford on the wall across from his desk. His uncle had taken him to the Brentwood Park estate sale years ago and the moment Nick had seen Lady Guildford's portrait he'd stopped dead in his tracks. Uncle Charles had simply squeezed his shoulder then bought the portrait and gave it to Nick with nothing more than a simple statement that the portrait was his to do with as he wished.

How the elderly Englishman had sensed how much he'd wanted the countess' portrait, he would never know. But he'd worked hard to show his uncle how grateful he was for the extraordinary gift. Emotion pushed its way to the surface, and he swiftly buried it. Determined to lighten the atmosphere, he folded his arms across his chest and pinned his gaze on Nora.

"I imagine you're going to be impossible to live with for the next month or two."

"Oh, you can count on that." His sister's forced laughter revealed how close she'd been to tears. "Especially since a certain someone said my trip would be a waste of money."

Nora eyed him with a scowl, and he released a rueful sigh. She was going to make him pay dearly for having questioned her unusual gift at finding extraordinary pieces.

"Truce." He held his hands up in a gesture of surrender. "From now on, your word is law when it comes to acquisitions. Satisfied?"

"It's a start." This time her laughter wasn't filled with tears, and she waved a hand at the portrait hanging on the wall behind the couch. "What about her, are you going to start listening to me about the countess as well?"

A familiar tension slid through his muscles, tightening his chest. His amusement disappeared in an instant. His gaze flitted back to the portrait of Victoria Thornhill, Countess of Guildford before he frowned at Nora.

"That implies I need advice, and I don't. The woman's been dead for more than a hundred years."

"But you have to admit your attachment to her portrait is a little extreme."

"It's not unusual for an antiquities dealer to have art work hanging in their office." His comment made Nora snort.

"Artwork yes, but not a portrait you've drooled over ever since we were teenagers."

"You're exaggerating again."

"Am I?" She eyed him intently for a long moment. "Then prove me wrong. Sell it."

"No." Tension charged the air with electricity as he glared at his sister.

"That's what I thought." Her matter-of-fact tone rubbed him the wrong way.

"What the *hell* is that supposed to mean?"

"If I tell you, you're just going to tell me to fuck off."

She was right. He knew what Nora believed, but he just wasn't buying it. The notion that he'd known the Countess of Guildford in a past life was just as crazy an idea now as it was every time Nora broached the subject with him. Nick saw her sly look, and he clenched his jaw as he refused to take her bait.

Without a word, he turned away from her and picked up several invoices off the top of his desk. The figures were a blur as the image of Lady Guildford filled his head. What if his sister was right? What if he was—Christ, if Nora could read his mind right now, she'd hound him until the day he died. Who was he kidding, she'd do that anyway. He blew out a harsh breath of annoyance. At the sound, Nora scrambled to her feet.

"Oh for *Pete's sake*, Nick. Isn't it time you took a really hard look at yourself and that portrait?"

"Is there a point to this line of conversation?" he asked as nonchalantly as possible, while continuing his pretense of studying the invoices.

"Yes. The point is—you're in love with a ghost." Nora had never confronted him so bluntly before. He scowled at her over his shoulder then returned to his feigned review of the paperwork in his hand.

"Don't look at me like that, Nicholas Barrows. That bloody portrait is what keeps you from leading a normal life. When was the last time you had a date? Even a one-night stand?"

"My sex life isn't any of your *damn* business," he said through clenched teeth. The invoices in his hand crackled in his tight grip.

"Right. Sorry." The tense atmosphere hung between them for several seconds, before he released a noise of frustration. Dropping the papers onto his desk, Nick turned around to face her. Leaning back, he rested his hips against his desk then folded his arms across his chest.

"Look, you and Uncle Charles have always believed that old family legend. I never have." He didn't flinch as his sister glared at him. "That damn necklace is a myth. Even if the earl gave his wife those sapphires, they were either sold or stolen a long time ago. My money's on the sold theory. And I sure as hell don't believe Lady Guildford is coming back from the dead to reclaim the damn thing. It's a story. Nothing more."

"All right, if you don't believe the legend, why do you keep the woman's portrait on the wall?

"*For Christ's sake.* I like the painting. It gives me pleasure, how is that an issue?"

"It's an issue because you're pining after a dead woman."

"God damn it, Nora. It's *just a portrait.*"

"All right, then answer me this. Why is it you only date women with auburn hair and blue eyes like the countess?" The accusation in his sister's voice made Nick rolled his eyes, while scrambling for an excuse that would stop her inquisition.

"I don't only date women with auburn hair."

"Oh please," Nora snorted. "Shall I list them by name? Vivian, Viola, Veronica, Virginia, and my personal favorite, Vickie. Notice a pattern here? And isn't it ironic their names all start with the same first letter as Lady Guildford's name? Victoria."

"Coincidence," he snapped, glaring at his sister.

"The landscape painting? What about that?" Nora eyed him with that unnerving shrewdness that always made him think she could see through him or anyone else she talked too.

"What of it?"

"It's taken you almost twelve years to agree that we put it up for sale. Why don't you ask yourself why you've not been able to part with it or, for that matter, the portrait of the countess?"

"*Fuck*," he snarled. "You're blowing this out of proportion.

"And the third painting?" Nora narrowed her gaze at him. "The one Uncle Charles kept stored away? The moment you discovered it in his things after the funeral, you took it home."

"*Christ almighty*, Nora. I deal in art and antiques. What's wrong with me admiring the work of a man who painted two different portraits of the same woman as well as a landscape?"

Nick strode toward the window that overlooked the showroom. The second portrait of the countess had been far more intimate than the one he kept in his office. Although discreetly covered with a sheet, it was still a seductive, enticing portrait, one he'd not been willing to share with anyone. Even allowing the framer to see the portrait had filled him with a possessiveness he found confusing. Hands braced against the waist high window sill, he stared down into the gallery. There were a few customers studying various items, but they were nothing but blurred images in his head.

"Fine." Nora's voice echoed with irritation at her failed attempt to persuade him that he was obsessed with the Countess of Thornhill. Deep inside, he knew it was a true assessment on his sister's part, but admitting that to Nora would open up doors he wasn't willing to go through.

Nick fought to focus his gaze on the people in the gallery, but instead, the lovely features of Victoria Brentwood Thornhill, Countess of Guildford filled his mind as clearly as if she were alive and in front of him. Dark auburn hair framed around an oval face. Full lips curved in an inviting, sensual smile. Brilliant sapphire eyes sparkling with mischief.

Nick tightened his grip on the window ledge. Nora was right. He was in love with a ghost, or at least the image of one. A shrink would tell him he was avoiding personal relationships because of some trauma in his past, but it went deeper than that. There was a knowing that filled him every time he looked at the countess' portrait. He couldn't explain it, and he sure as hell wasn't going to tell his sister about it either.

About to turn away from the window overlooking the gallery, Nick's gaze caught sight of a woman standing in front of their collection of English pastoral scenes. When she tilted her head to study one of the canvases, the muted light from the ceiling's track lighting set her auburn hair on fire. In the next moment the woman turned to face one of the sales clerks, and he inhaled a sharp breath.

Almost immediately, his chest constricted and his heart slammed into his ribs. Only twice before had he ever experienced this sensation, and each of those times it had been when he'd found a portrait of the countess. Transfixed, he stared down at the woman.

"God, Nick, are *you okay*? You look like you're ready to pass out." Nora joined him at the window. The moment his sister's gaze landed on the woman, she gasped loudly. "*Holy fuck.*"

Without a word, Nick brushed past Nora. As he headed toward the door, her hand caught his arm. He paused to meet her gaze and shook his head in a silent order not to stop him. Reluctance visible on her face, his sister released his arm. Nick wanted to run down the steps to the showroom, but he forced himself to descend the stairs at a slow pace. He was insane to think this was anything more than a coincidence. As he approached the woman, her distinct American accent floated through the air as she spoke to the salesclerk.

"I don't know—thirty-five hundred pounds is a little more than I can really afford."

"Think of it as an investment, miss."

"An investment in the exchange rate you mean."

The dry note in her voice forced Nick to cough as he stifled a chuckle. She turned at the sound, an impish smile curving her full mouth. But it was her eyes that made him stare at her. They were the same sapphire blue as the countess's. Again, he marveled at the resemblance. Without warning, she queried his opinion.

"What do you think?" she asked.

Nick met the brilliant blue gaze twinkling up at him. If he didn't know better, he would have sworn Lady Guildford had stepped out of the portrait hanging in his office. The woman tipped her head back as she returned his stare with equal intensity. In an absent-minded gesture, her long fingers brushed a stray strand of auburn hair off her cheek. A quickening surged deep inside him like the sudden stirring of a long lost memory. The sensation swelled.

Stunned by the force of the emotion, he realized somewhere in his past he'd experienced a moment similar to this one before. The sensation grew in strength. The smile curving her full mouth faded as confusion furrowed her brow. Mentally shaking his head, Nick forced himself to answer her question.

"Like Robert says, art is an investment, but I like to think of it more as an investment of the heart. Ask yourself if you can live without it."

"No, I don't think I can." She turned back to the painting. Under the track lighting her auburn hair shone like lustrous silk. She sighed. "There's something so familiar about it."

For the first time, he looked at the canvas she was interested in purchasing and went rigid. He'd been so focused on her, he'd not even bothered to look at the painting she was standing in front of. It was Lockwood's oil painting of Goodman Cottage at Brentwood Park. The landscape depicted a pond glistening in the afternoon sun as it played host to a pair of swans. Not far from the water's edge, the thatched roof cottage sat nestled in the warm embrace of a small grove of trees. The sparsely covered trees with red, gold, and purple leaves indicated it had been close to the end of fall when the artist had painted his picture.

Nick had found the landscape in his uncle's bedroom

after the man's heart attack. A little known artist, John Lockwood had painted both portraits of the countess as well as the landscape. The barely legible inscription on the back of the Goodman Cottage canvas, *for my wife, Victoria. Nicholas – Christmas 1897*, indicated the landscape had been a gift from Lord Guildford to his wife.

"Have you ever been to Brentwood Park?" He clenched his teeth. Why the hell had he asked her that?

"Brentwood Park?" She shook her head in puzzlement.

"It's an estate a little southeast of the city. The cottage in the painting still sits on the grounds." He nodded toward the canvas on the wall, but kept his eyes on her.

"I've never heard of it. If I have time next week, I might be able to check it out," she murmured as she turned back to the painting and reached out to touch the frame. Uttering a small noise of decision, she turned her head toward the sales clerk. "Well, I guess I can't leave without it."

"Very good, madam. If you will come this way, I shall be happy to arrange the sale."

"Robert, I'll take care of the sale," Nick said quietly as he reached out to grasp her arm and hold her in place.

He never heard the sales clerk's response as electricity shot up his arm. The strength of the sensation barreling through him made him feel like someone was pummeling his entire body until he had no breath left in his lungs. Images flashed through his head like a carousel of pictures careening out of control.

Of all the faces dancing through his brain, she was always there. She was like the North Star, guiding him to a place he didn't know existed. He couldn't explain it, but it was as if this moment had happened before. As he stared down into her blue eyes, she shook her head slightly, and he was certain she was experiencing the same sensation.

"What's your name?" His voice was hoarse as he struggled not to say something bizarre that would frighten her or worse make her dart out of the shop.

"Victoria Ashton," she breathed as she reached up to

brush a lock of hair off his forehead. In the next instant, she jerked her hand away, clearly horrified by her action.

"Oh Lord, I'm sorry...that was incredibly rude of me."

"No. It felt right." He didn't have the slightest idea why her touch seemed so natural and perfect, but then nothing about the last couple of minutes made any sense to him.

"I...have we met somewhere before?"

"That's my pickup line, I think," he said with a grin.

"Yeah, I suppose it was."

Her laugh was as full-bodied as he remembered. Remembered? Nick pushed the absurd notion aside as he watched a flush of pink rise in her cheeks. Without thinking, he brushed his fingertips across her face. The moment he touched her, her hand came up to cup his, and she turned her mouth into his palm. The visceral emotion the action stirred in him made him pull in a sharp, deep breath.

"I don't know what the hell is happening," he rasped. "But you better tell me to stop now if you don't want me to kiss you."

Her sapphire eyes widened, before she closed the distance between them and there was only a hair's breadth of space between. Her hand reached up to touch his brow and she smiled.

"I won't stop you," she whispered.

Locked in the grip of something he didn't understand, Nick bent his head toward her. God, all he wanted was to taste her again. He needed to know if she tasted as sweet as he remembered. His mouth never touched hers as the explosion roared through the shop like a freight train.

The force of the blast threw him backward, and he fought to stay on his feet. A screech of metal tugged his gaze upward. Before he could react, the ceiling's track lighting crashed downward then slammed into Victoria's head and chest. He heard her grunt with pain as the blow sent her staggering backwards. In an involuntary effort to remain standing, she flung her arm outward to grab hold of something to save herself from falling.

Before he could leap forward or shout a warning, she grasped the black wire dangling from the ceiling. Agony contorted her features as electricity flowed through her then sent her flying backward to hit the wall like a rag doll. The unframed landscape of the cottage fell from the wall to the floor and landed beside her limp hand, the painting brushing against her fingers. Screams of pain and fear from inside and outside of the shop filled the air.

Leaping past the live wire, he crouched down beside Victoria's still form. His hands shook as he gently rolled her onto her back sliding the painting away from her. She wasn't breathing, and he couldn't find a pulse in her neck or on her wrist. A wave of helplessness rolled over him. It had been like this the last time. He'd not been able to do anything to save her.

A growl of rage erupted from his throat. No. Not this time. He'd lost her in the past, and he refused to lose her now. Without thinking, he began to administer CPR. He didn't know if he was doing it right, but he couldn't just stand by and do nothing. He'd failed the last time. He couldn't let it end like that again. Quick chest compressions then two strong puffs of air into her mouth. Repeat.

Somewhere in the distance he heard the sound of an ambulance. Panic set in as his efforts to revive her received no response. In a voice he didn't recognize as his own, he called out her name then blew two hard breaths into her before increasing the strength of his compressions against her chest.

"Fight, Victoria, fight," he commanded in a savage tone. "Do you hear me? I said fight."

His command was harsh and inflexible, and he sensed a stranger slipping into his head. Relentlessly, he alternated between breathing into her mouth and returning to the sharp cadence of chest compressions. Deep within his memory, he recalled the pain and agony of a similar experience long ago. The indefinable connection to her that he'd experienced moments ago had become something even more tangible. A gentle hand touched his shoulder.

"Nick, she's gone." His sister's words ripped a roar from him throat.

"No. You're wrong," he snarled as he knocked his sister's hand aside.

With renewed force he pounded on Victoria's chest then breathed air into her lungs. Logic disappeared to become raw, agonizing desperation. Unfamiliar images from a distant past merged with the present to fill him with dread. The savageness of his anguish choked him and threatened to push him over the edge as he worked to breathe and pound life back into her.

"God damn it, Victoria. Fight, damn you. Come back to me."

The savage command went unanswered, and his anguish was an unbearable vise engulfing his body. A wounded howl of grief ripped out of his throat. She was gone. He'd lost her again. Life had lost its meaning.

Chapter 2

October 1897

The darkness of the dream enveloped Victoria as she spiraled downward to land on her bed with a jerk as pain rippled through her. Thousands of razor sharp needles stabbed at every inch of her. God, it was as if someone had doused her in gasoline then set her on fire.

The dream had become a nightmare of agony, and she ordered herself to wake up. She forced her eyes open to see nothing but a white mist filled with gray shadows. Oh God, she was blind. Panic flooded her veins as she tried to reassure herself it was a nightmare. Her eyes fluttered closed for a fleeting second. When she opened her eyes again, there was nothing except the fog cluttered with dark shapes. Voices echoed nearby, but a loud ringing in her ears made it difficult to make out what they were saying. Yet out of all the indistinguishable voices there was one she recognized. It was demanding. Arrogant. But she couldn't remember where she'd heard it before.

Victoria tried to turn her head toward the voice, but the movement sent a stabbing pain through her temple. She cried out. A dark shape suddenly blotted out the cloudy landscape of her vision. A warm hand touched her forehead before the shape abruptly disappeared. Slowly, the voices and ringing in her ears ebbed away. Victoria blinked several times in an attempt to clear her vision then sat up.

The instant she moved, she uttered a cry of misery at the explosion of pain in her head. The heel of her palm pressed against her forehead, she bit back the bile threatening to rise in her throat. After several long moments of anguish, the pain and nausea eased.

This had to be the worst fricking hangover she'd ever had. Not that she'd had that many. She winced. Had she gone to a bar last night? She didn't remember going to one. Hell, she didn't remember much of anything over the last several weeks. The one thing she did remember was her argument with her father a year ago and what had happened a few hours later. She pushed back the tears. Images whirled and flitted through her brain. She was on vacation. She remembered that much at least. But there was one thing she was certain of. This was not her hotel room. Her gaze swept over the simplicity of the stark room. Despite the brilliant stream of sunlight flooding through the window it was cold. She shivered. Someone had set the AC way too low.

If it weren't for the fire in the hearth, the room would be even colder. It didn't make any sense why someone would have a fire with the AC going. Her gaze swept across the room's meager furnishings. Planks of rough-hewn wood served as the floor, while a white plaster covered the walls. It looked like something out of a Jane Austen movie. Oh God, had she decided to do one of those reality vacations? No, she couldn't afford something like that, even if she'd wanted too. What was the last thing she'd been doing? She breathed in a quiet breath as she tried to ignore the hot needles that assaulted the back of her head. Where was she, and exactly how had she gotten to wherever here was? She groaned as the headache spread to her temples.

Victoria tossed her blanket off to one side and swung her legs out of bed. Fire streaked across her skin once more, while her chest hurt like someone had kicked her repeatedly. Had she been mugged? Even though she was in pain, self-preservation had her on her feet the minute a woman scurried into the room.

"Good heavens, my lady. You shouldn't be out of bed just yet."

"Who are you?"

Her words sounded hoarse, stiff, and stilted. Laryngitis. Could you get that from a hangover? If you were shouting over loud music all night long? Maybe she'd been mugged and choked in the process. It would explain her voice, the pounding in her head, and the way her body ached. It would also account for not knowing where the hell she was.

"I'm Bessie, my lady. Thomas Goodman's wife. He found you near the pond this morning. You were like death warmed over when my Thomas brought you in."

"Pond?" The hoarseness in her voice had disappeared, but it still sounded funny to her.

"Yes, my lady. Soaked through and through. If my Thomas hadn't found you I fear the worst might have happened."

Victoria shook her head in denial and winced as she pressed her hand against her forehead. She hadn't been anywhere near a pond. She'd been in an art gallery. The sudden sliver of a memory tantalized her before it evaporated and pain took its place.

"Where am I?"

"Why Brentwood Park, my lady." Bessie patted Victoria's arm in a comforting manner.

"Brentwood Park," she murmured. Where had she heard that name before? Another stab of pain erupted in her head, and she groaned softly. God, jackhammers were going off inside her head. She looked down at the white cotton gown she wore. She never wore nightgowns. Normally, she chose to sleep in the nude, although she would occasionally sleep in a pair of pajamas. Nightgowns? Never. They were little more than straight-jackets, and she never got a good night's sleep with one on. Beside the bed, her hostess poured water from a beige earthen pitcher into a matching bowl. Wringing out a cloth in the basin, the woman turned her head to Victoria and smiled.

"Now then, my lady, let me see if I can clean that cut of yours."

"Cut?" Victoria blinked with confusion.

"I don't believe it will need stitching." Bessie's weathered features wrinkled up into a reassuring look as she dabbed gently at Victoria's forehead. "Lucky is what you were. Another inch lower and you could have lost an eye."

Baffled, Victoria gasped as cold water stung a tender spot just above her right eye. She lightly touched the wound and drew in a breath of surprise as Bessie gently pulled her hand away. When had she cut her head? Questions. Every time she answered one, half a dozen more sprang to life. She pulled away from the woman who was clucking over her like a worrisome mother hen.

"You said I'm at Brentwood Park. Is this a hospital of some kind?"

"Heavens, no, my lady. This is Goodman Cottage. Thomas and I are tenants of his lordship."

"His lordship?"

"Lord Guildford, my lady. Don't you remember?" The woman stared at her with a worried frown.

"I don't know any Lord Guildford." Victoria wanted to shake her head, but was afraid to for fear of pain.

"Oh dear…you must have hit your head much harder than we thought." Bessie clucked her tongue in sympathy. "Now don't you fret, I've seen this happen before. Your memory will come back right enough when you're ready."

"I haven't lost my memory," Victoria muttered stubbornly.

She remembered her name, her childhood, the night her father had died. She shoved that particular memory into a separate compartment. Right now she had to focus on figuring out where the hell she was. England. She was in England on vacation, by herself. It was impossible to know how long she'd been out, and right now all she wanted was to get back to her hotel. She frowned. Why didn't she hear traffic outside? The quiet reminded her of the woods near Kerrigan Stables where she rode twice a week. A chill ran down her spine. If it were quiet outside, it meant she was in the country. She'd been in the city. How in the hell had she gotten from London to wherever this was?

"If you don't mind, I'd like my clothes back so I can return to my hotel."

"But, my lady, you just can't—"

"Can't what?" she snapped, more out of fear than anger. "Please bring me my clothes. I want—"

The door swung open with a loud screech. Instantly, she turned toward the sound and inhaled a sharp breath. Everything receded into the background as she met the hard, green-eyed gaze of the man entering the room. Before his arrival, the room had been comfortable in size, but now it closed in on her.

Power. Sheer power was the first thing that came to mind as her gaze ran over him. He was dressed for riding, but he wasn't wearing jeans as one might expect. His apparel seemed more appropriate for a horse show. Fawn-colored breeches hugged sleek, muscular thighs. The snug fitting pants were tucked into a pair of shiny black boots with a dark brown cuff at the top. A starched collar jutted upward to part slightly at his throat, while a narrow, black tie encircled his neck. Dark wavy hair and those piercing green eyes of his completed the image of a man born to command. She swallowed hard. The man didn't just ooze sex appeal, he defined it.

Deliberate and unhurried, he removed his black riding gloves and slapped them into his hand with a vicious crack. She jumped. Like an animal fascinated with its predator, she met his narrowed eyes warily. His barely restrained anger saturated the room with its raw heat.

Okay, now she was worried. Had she wrecked her rental car and damaged his property? Wait, did she even have a rental car? Damn it, how could she remember things from months ago, while the past couple of days and weeks were hazy at best?

"That will be all for now, Bessie. You may bring the countess her clothes shortly." Despite her apprehension, the deep timbre of his voice turned her inside out. The man could easily give a woman an orgasm with that voice. Wait.

Countess? What countess?

"Yes, my lord."

Bessie quickly left the room as the stranger's gaze remained locked with hers. The door closed behind the older woman, and something flashed in the man's eyes as he moved forward. Victoria instinctively jumped backward as he brushed past her. He walked with a distinct limp as he crossed the room to the small window beneath an eave. Had he been in an accident or was the handicap from birth? The vague whisper of a memory teased her as she studied the back of his dark head. She tried to catch the thought, but it winked out of her grasp. Frustrated, she grimaced then started as the man turned and directed a harsh look in her direction.

"Do you want to tell me where the devil you've been for the last three weeks, Vickie?"

"I'm sorry?" She scowled at him. She'd never liked people calling her by that nickname. For some unknown reason, it had always had a negative connotation to it, and she hated the way it made her feel when someone called her by the name.

"Three weeks, Vickie." The sharp words cracked through the air and made her flinch. "I've had private investigators looking for you for the past three weeks."

"Look, you've obviously got me confused with someone else." Bewildered, she shrugged her shoulders. "I don't know you. My name is Victoria Ashton, and I don't know this Vickie person."

"Memory loss? Your creativity astounds me, my dear." The condescension in his voice made the hair on the back of neck stand upright. Sex appeal or not, the man was an arrogant bastard. Victoria narrowed her eyes at him.

"I didn't say I'd lost my memory. I said I don't know you." She silently dismissed her inability to remember the past couple of days or weeks. That didn't count. She knew who she was.

His eyes were shards of green ice as he stared at her for a long moment. Then with an indifferent air he took a seat in the room's only chair. Sitting sideways, he draped an arm over the wooden chair's spindled back and crossed his bad leg over one knee. His relaxed posture only enhanced his commanding presence. Sexy or not, she was certain he'd be a dangerous man to cross.

"So you think I've confused you with someone else." He surveyed her from head to toe with an insolent gleam before looking at the ring on his finger. "An odd statement considering I'd be hard pressed not to recognize my wife."

The soft words sent her reeling back two steps. Frantically, she tried to recall what she'd been doing before she woke up in this nightmare. There was no way in hell she could be married. Was there?

She squeezed her eyes shut as if that would help her remember. The image of a large room with paintings flitted through her head. An art gallery. She'd been debating whether to buy a landscape. Hadn't she? Images flew through her head so fast she couldn't recognize most of them. An explosion. Had there been an explosion? It would explain the cut on her head if she'd been near glass.

Desperately, she tried to remember more. She'd been with someone. Who? Acute pain pulsed viciously in her head. Victoria tried to ignore it, but the harder she tried to pull answers from the shadows, the more intense the vicious pounding in her head. She released a soft sound of misery and gave up trying to recall the last couple of days. The moment she did so, the pain eased to a minor throb.

She was barely aware the stranger had moved until his sudden proximity enveloped her in a white hot heat. Firm fingers grasped her chin, and he tilted her face toward the sunshine streaming into the room. The pads of his fingers seared her skin, and she drew in a sharp breath. Hell, this man wasn't just hot to look at. With one simple touch, he'd managed to make her legs wobbly as Jell-O. She dragged in another quick breath.

He smelled of horse, leather, and something spicy. He was raw male and the potency of him made her ache for something she hadn't had in a long time. All the man had to do was kiss her, and she'd be melting in his arms. The thought made her lick her lips nervously. His gaze narrowed and his eyes darkened to a shade of evergreen before he jerked away from her and put several feet between them.

"I grow weary of this game you're playing, Vickie."

"I'm not your wife," she snapped.

"Then tell me who you are, my dear." The cold contempt in his voice could have frozen the air between them, and for the first time she realized she might be in real trouble.

"I told you, already. My name is Victoria Ashton," she said as calmly as possible. "I don't know you or how I got here. I just want my clothes back so I can get a ride back to London."

For the briefest of moments, she could have sworn she saw doubt in his green eyes before a shutter fell into place, revealing nothing but amused cynicism. The insolence of his smile made her draw in a breath of irritation.

"A convincing tale, madam, but it lacks a certain, shall we say, finesse," he drawled.

"Are you calling me a liar?" She wanted to kick herself. Of course he was.

"I'm simply stating the obvious. Your acting abilities have improved considerably, but this is a bit much, even for you."

"Look, this is crazy. I was in an art gallery in London. I think there was some kind of explosion. The next thing I knew, I woke up here." Her words instantly made her head hurt, and she winced.

"I'm a patient man, Vickie, but this charade is growing tiresome." Anger tightened his sensual mouth. The fact that she was even thinking about his mouth annoyed her as much as his refusal to call her Victoria.

"So help me God, if you call me Vickie one more time…" She gritted her teeth and suppressed her anger. It wasn't going to help things if she lost her temper. "I'm not your wife. My name is Victoria Ashton. I don't know how I got here, and at the moment I don't really care. If you'll just give me my clothes back, I'll get out of your hair."

"Enough." The barely controlled fury in the command made her flinch. "If you continue with this farce, I'll be forced to have you examined by a physician from the county asylum."

"Don't you dare threaten me," she said fiercely as she returned his glare.

"It's not a threat, Vickie. You're clearly unwell."

There was something about his icy demeanor that sent a shiver down her spine. He was dead serious. Fear slithered through Victoria. The man was clearly off his rocker, her clothes were missing, and no one knew where she was. Hell, she didn't even know where she was. Out of the corner of her eye, she saw the door and lunged toward it.

**Buy Forever Mine At Any Online Retail Vendor
Audio Book Coming 2022**

Verified Purchase Reader Reviews

"I am so touched by this delicious, beautiful sexy love story, I am reading it back to back for a 2nd time. The first time I read it in one day. Now while reading it, I am taking my time to make sure I didn't miss anything the first time. Edited ****I didn't think I could handle it, but I just read it for the 3rd time this weekend." — **Amazon Reader**

"LOVED THIS STORY! The characters were well written. The story was engaging. I couldn't put it down! Step aside Jude Deveraux, Monica Burns is an author not to be missed!" — **Amazon Reader**

"Time-travel, Romance & a dash of the paranormal....But the end result was pure brilliance. Ms. Burns is a master (or mistress) of her craft. I don't have the words to do this justice....Just that you MUST read this." — **Amazon Reader**

Monica Burns Books

THE RECKLESS ROCKWOODS SERIES
Obsession #1
Dangerous #2
The Highlander's Woman #3
Redemption #4
The Beastly Earl #5

THE RECKLESS ROCKWOODS NOVELS
The Rogue's Offer
The Rogue's Countess

SELF-MADE MEN SERIES
His To Command #1 (Novella)
His Mistress #2

STAND ALONE TITLES
Forever Mine
Kismet
Mirage
Pleasure Me
A Bluestocking Christmas
Love's Portrait
Love's Revenge

THE ORDER OF THE SICARI SERIES
Assassin's Honor #1
Assassin's Heart #2
Inferno's Kiss #3

About The Author

Monica Burns is a bestselling author of spicy historical and paranormal romance. She penned her first romance at the age of nine when she selected the pseudonym she uses today. Her historical book awards include the 2011 RT BookReviews Reviewers Choice Award and the 2012 Gayle Wilson Heart of Excellence Award for Pleasure Me.

She is also the recipient of the prestigious paranormal romance award, the 2011 PRISM Best of the Best award for Assassin's Heart. From the days when she hid her stories from her sisters to her first completed full-length manuscript, she always believed in her dream despite rejections and setbacks. A workaholic wife and mother, Monica is a survivor who believes every hero and heroine deserves a HEA (Happily Ever After), especially if she's writing the story.

www.ingramcontent.com/pod-product-compliance
Lightning Source LLC
Chambersburg PA
CBHW072013110726
47910CB00005B/1740